W9-DBH-851

B96

That Year of Our War

Also by Gloria Goldreich

Leah's Journey
Four Days
This Promised Land
This Burning Harvest
Leah's Children
West to Eden
A Treasury of Jewish Literature
Mothers
Years of Dreams

That Year
of Our War

Gloria Goldreich

Little, Brown and Company
Boston New York Toronto London

COPYRIGHT © 1994 BY GLORIA GOLDREICH

ALL RIGHTS RESERVED. NO PART OF THIS BOOK MAY BE REPRODUCED IN
ANY FORM OR BY ANY ELECTRONIC OR MECHANICAL MEANS, INCLUDING
INFORMATION STORAGE AND RETRIEVAL SYSTEMS, EXCEPT BY A REVIEWER
WHO MAY QUOTE BRIEF PASSAGES IN A REVIEW.

FIRST EDITION

The characters and events in this book are fictitious. Any similarity
to real persons, living or dead, is coincidental and not intended
by the author.

Excerpt from "Reluctance" from *The Poetry of Robert Frost*, edited
by Edward Connery Lathem. Copyright 1916, 1934, © 1969
by Henry Holt and Company. © 1962 by Robert Frost.
Reprinted by permission of Henry Holt and Company, Inc.

Library of Congress Cataloging-in-Publication Data

Goldreich, Gloria.
    That year of our war / Gloria Goldreich. — 1st ed.
        p.   cm.
    ISBN 0-316-31943-0
    1. World War, 1939–1945 — United States — Fiction.
    2. Girls — United States — Fiction.   I. Title.
    PS3557.03845T43   1994
    813' .54 — dc20   93-20561

10 9 8 7 6 5 4 3 2 1
MV-NY
*Published simultaneously in Canada by Little, Brown & Company
(Canada) Limited*

PRINTED IN THE UNITED STATES OF AMERICA

To the memory of Gussie Goldreich, David Kirsch, Goldie
Pomerantz, Dorothy Dworkin, Rose Lemberg, and Nettie Tosher

and that of their parents, my grandparents
Leah and Harris Kirsch

That Year
of Our War

Prologue

My mother died on D Day. The last sound she made, the harsh whistle called *stridor,* a result of inhalation when swelling narrows the larynx (I know about such things now because I am a physician), came precisely at noon. At that hour, every working day of the war, a siren shrilled, signaling the lunch break at the defense plant on Surf Avenue. I, like my aunts who stood at my mother's bedside, heard the siren as it screamed its way through the open windows — I was in the auditorium of Abraham Lincoln High School, where I sat on the stage, one of a group of fifty students who had family on active duty.

An assembly, hastily convened when news of the invasion became official, was in progress. The principal solemnly announced that Allied forces had landed on Normandy. He wanted to offer special comfort and support to those with loved ones in the armed forces — hence our presence on the stage. A photographer for the *Brooklyn Eagle* took the picture which appeared in that afternoon's edition with the caption "Lincoln Students Pray for Loved Ones in Combat." In that picture, now yellowed with age, I look pensive and preoccupied. My dark hair falls to my shoulders and I wear a plaid skirt, a white blouse with elasticized sleeves, saddle oxfords, and white anklets. I was neatly dressed on the day of my mother's death.

I sat between Judy Bergman, whose brother was in the air force, and Joseph Guerera, whose father was in the infantry. We stood when Miss Glenn, the blue-haired music teacher, played "God Bless America." Judy began to cry and I clutched her hand. Joseph Guerera crossed himself, and the twin black girls, Leatrice and Letitia, linked arms. Their beautiful contraltos soared above our voices. They sang as though their hearts might break.

The principal, red-faced and white-haired, spoke very slowly. Tears glinted in his eyes as he explained what D Day meant to the free world. Later we learned that his son had been killed on Normandy, but surely he could not have known that as he stood before us.

"Our fighting men," he said, "are engaged in a battle to the death so that the world may be liberated from evil."

He passed a pointer across the large drop map of Europe, resting it on a yellow patch. Here, we were told, on this beach near Portsmouth, an armada had set sail, despite a severe storm on the previous day. The waves had risen to great heights, and clouds had darkened the skies over England.

We shivered. In Brooklyn the air was fragrant with the scent of new-cut grass, and rhomboids of sunlight danced across our school's sloping lawn. The principal moved the pointer to the narrow strip of blue that marked the English Channel. In its waters, many would drown. There had already been casualties, and many other brave Americans would die as they fought to crush terror and tyranny. His voice was stern.

I trembled. My father might be killed. Perhaps he had already been killed. Tears burned my eyes as Judy Bergman stepped forward to read from Isaiah. " 'Nation shall not lift up sword against nation, neither shall they learn war any more.' "

Learn war? Hilarity penetrated my grief. How was war learned? Were there theorems and conjugations — courses in Intermediate War, Advanced War? I suppressed a nervous giggle just as the door to the auditorium opened and my uncles, Robert and Leon, entered.

My heart stopped. The principal had been prescient. My father was dead, his body sprawled across a French beach, and my uncles had taken the extraordinary step of invading an assembly to inform me of it. I grew dizzy and would have fallen to the floor if Joseph Guerera had not reached out to steady me. He was a tall and husky boy but he supported me with great tenderness as he led me from the stage.

It was not my father who died on the sixth of June in 1944. It was my mother, whose death had been anticipated for so many months that its actual occurrence was almost anticlimactic. Her illness, diagnosed after my father had been shipped overseas, had been dramatic, involving as it did a change of scene from one city to another and a cast of characters that included all the members of her large family — her brother and sisters and their husbands and children and her parents, the bent and sad-eyed white-haired man and woman whom I called Buba and Zeidey and to whom I spoke in monosyllables. My mother had leukemia. She had learned of her illness when she went to the doctor in Brookline, where we lived then, to complain of her chronic fatigue, loss of weight, and loss of appetite. The doctor was a colleague of my father's and she had relied on him to scorn her symptoms.

"I think it's because I'm worried about your father," she had told me apologetically.

"Maybe. Probably."

I was fifteen years old and uninterested in her weariness and her lassitude, uninterested in everything but the long-awaited changes that were taking place in my body, the mysterious aches, the new tenderness of my breasts, the monthly flow of menstrual blood which I anticipated with terror and awe. My mother had placed a copy of "What Every Girl Should Know," delivered in a plain brown wrapper, on my bed and there was always a box of Kotex in my closet. She was loyal to Kotex because they published that important pamphlet and spared her the embarrassment of awkward explanations.

I was grateful for the information. "Your body is wonderful and beautiful," the writer advised and those words were printed in bright blue ink so that they would stand out on the page.

I repeated them as I stood before the long mirror that hung on the door of my bedroom. In the early morning, sunlight danced across it and I would stand before it naked and stare at my reflection. My skin was gold-spangled and my breasts were a tender rise, blue-veined and rosy-nippled. Sometimes I brushed my hair as I stood there and wondered when my beauty would begin. My mother, after all, was beautiful, and I was dark-haired as she was and I too had large blue-gray eyes. But her features were delicate, her face heart-shaped, while I had a long chin and thought my mouth too large, my nose too narrow.

"You will fill out," my mother had promised me. "Your father won't recognize you when he comes home."

She said this in a voice so enervated that I had to strain to hear her but still I was not concerned. I was too absorbed in myself then to worry about her pallor, her sleeplessness, the bruises that speckled her arms and legs like small lapis scarabs. I forgive myself now for the self-indulgence, for the egocentricity, which, my therapist explained, is typical of early adolescence. Still, it shamed me then and for many years afterward.

My mother's eyes were red-rimmed when she returned from her visit to the doctor. He had not, after all, scorned her symptoms. She was to be admitted to the hospital for tests. My aunt Edna, her sister, would come to stay with me.

She returned from the hospital even paler and weaker, and after Edna had helped her into bed, the telephone calls began. I was in my room, ostensibly studying and listening to my soap operas on the small Philco box radio my father had given me the night he left. "Our Gal Sunday" was preparing tea for visitors from England as Edna spoke to her sister Lottie.

"Leukemia," she said softly into the phone.

Leukemia. A character on "Portia Faces Life" had had leukemia. Had she lived or died?

"What should we do? What would be best?" Edna's voice was faint.

Lottie would know. It was Lottie to whom they all turned first. She was the eldest and that seniority vested her with strength and authority. Julius, her husband, was a wealthy furrier who had, at various times, lent or given money to everyone in the family, and I understood, even then, that this increased her power. My father had borrowed money from Julius to finish medical school and he had, ever afterward, deferred to both him and Lottie. My grandparents lived with Lottie and Julius, occupying the street-level apartment of their two-family red brick home. The presence of the elderly couple made that house the seat of the family, the unofficial headquarters where the sisters and Samuel, their brother, received their marching orders.

I switched stations until I found Frank Sinatra singing "Accentuate the Positive." I turned the volume down. Edna was talking even more softly.

"The doctors here say six months. Maybe a year."

I switched the radio off. My face was contorted and a wave of nausea washed over me, but although biliousness already soured my throat, I could not open my door and rush to the bathroom because Edna would surely stop talking and it was important that I hear everything she had to say.

"Julius should talk to Dr. Epstein. At Mount Sinai, maybe they could do something." My mother's family always spoke of Mount Sinai Hospital as though it were the biblical mountain itself and each doctor was a minor Moses, each medical chart imprinted with revealed truth.

Now my aunts discussed my father in the tone of mingled affection and toleration they used whenever they spoke of the men in the family.

"He doesn't know anything. How could he know? Miriam never even wrote him that she wasn't feeling well. And when he came home on leave, she put on rouge and made believe. You know her." My aunt was at once admiring and annoyed. *You know her.*

Miriam, my mother, was considered vulnerable and overly sensitive in that family of articulate and powerful women. Her voice was too soft, her attitudes too altruistic, her feelings too delicate.

"The doctor said he'd call the Red Cross. Maybe they could arrange for compassionate leave. But he didn't think so. They need doctors over there," my aunt said glumly.

My nausea had subsided and now I was trembling as I sternly willed myself to calm. I had the only-child's talent for interior monologue. *It will be all right,* I assured myself. *Everything will be all right.*

"I think the best thing to do is to close up this apartment. To bring Miriam and Sharon home."

Home, of course, was Lottie's house, where my grandparents lived and where there were extra bedrooms. Lottie's son, Aaron, was in the army and her daughter, Beth, had achieved the dream of every Brooklyn girl: she had gone "out of town" to college. She was a student at Arizona State University in Tempe, a location chosen because of her asthma. It was difficult for her to breathe in Brooklyn, Lottie had explained with some pride. Asthma, she implied, was an aristocratic illness.

"I imagine it would be hard for anyone to breathe in that house," my father had observed wryly and my mother had cast him one of her rare stares of disapproval. She tolerated no mocking of her family.

"We can leave in about a week," Edna continued. "I can manage everything by then. I'll start getting things organized." Edna was the organizer and manager of the family, a talent which had served her well professionally. She was one of those women who knew at once whom to call to get a household moved, office machinery repaired, an inventory processed.

No, I thought wildly. *I don't want to leave Boston.* I didn't want my mother to die. I didn't want my father to be called home on compassionate leave before I had filled out and graduated into beauty.

"No!" I shouted aloud, and Edna fell silent.

"I have to see to Sharon," she whispered to Lottie. "Of course she's upset. I mean, I haven't told her anything but she knows there's something wrong."

"Listen, Sharon," Edna said to me in her kind and competent administrator's voice when she came into my bedroom. "I know it's hard but we'll decide everything together. Okay?" She hugged me then. She was a kind woman but displays of affection were alien to her. She demonstrated her love with action.

But there were really no decisions to be made. Everything had been decided in that initial conversation, and within a week Leon, Edna's husband, had driven to Boston in his station wagon, using ration stamps for gas given to him by special dispensation of the Red Cross. That, too, Edna had arranged, sending certified letters from Boston to New York. No one else would have thought of it, Leon said proudly, and he was probably right.

He had helped my mother down the stairs because she would not allow him to carry her. She wore her tweed coat with the fur collar, and her dark hair was thicker and more lustrous than the pelt at her neck. Still, she had lost so much weight that the coat hung loosely on her, and although she had rouged her cheeks and applied Max Factor Pan-Cake makeup, beneath the coloring her skin was blanched. I thought she looked tragic and beautiful and I held her hand and tilted my head bravely upward so that we might look tragic and beautiful together to the neighbors who assembled on the landings to see us off.

Our furniture had been put in storage although there had been some talk of selling it.

"But *he'll* want it. If he comes back," Edna insisted and I noticed, not for the first time, that my mother's family seldom referred to my father by name.

Richard. Call him Richard, I directed silently. *And he will come back.*

I never asserted, even to myself, that my mother would not die. I took that as a given from the first and prepared myself for the day it would happen. I would be strong. Very strong. Everyone would be proud of me. But my father would survive the war. I refused, in those early days, to believe that there was even a possibility that he would be killed. He was, after all, a doctor, and this, I thought, endowed him with special status.

We were installed in Aunt Lottie's house amid a great deal of hugging and kissing, much forced laughter, and many hidden tears. My grandmother kissed me and wept but there were no tears

when she went into my mother's room. My grandfather took me
out to the backyard and showed me how he had begun to uproot
hedges in preparation for the victory garden he would plant when
the weather grew warmer. He was an old man and he wore
a heavy black overcoat and a pale gray fedora as he worked. A
bramble caught in his white beard and I picked it out very carefully.

My mother was admitted to Mount Sinai Hospital for more
tests. She was taken there by ambulance, and two days later Edna,
Lottie, and Dina traveled uptown to consult the doctor, the specialist recommended by Dr. Epstein. A big man, they assured each
other.

I imagine the three of them sitting on the straight-backed
wicker seats of the Brighton Express as it thundered its way from
one borough to another. Lottie wore her long mink coat with its
matching turban. Beneath the turban, her hair was silver, dusted
with blue that was deftly applied with a rinse at the beauty parlor
each Friday morning. Her hands, when she removed her leather
gloves, were red and rough because Lottie worked very hard and
always had. Wealth had not altered her domestic habits, her daily
routine.

Lottie's hands were always plunged in water. She was forever
washing vegetables, dishes, clothing, her mother's thick-lensed
glasses, even her father's teeth, which she handled with great tenderness, brushing them with Arm and Hammer baking soda and
carrying them back to him in a wide-mouthed glass that had once
held a memorial candle. At home she wore plaid housedresses and
dark brown oxfords with her stockings rolled to the knees, but for
an excursion to the city she encased her small feet in pumps, wore
a dark suit, a white silk blouse. She understood good clothing and
loved it. More surprisingly, she also understood good poetry and
loved it.

Perhaps she had carried a book of poetry with her on the trip
to the city, a leather-bound Modern Library edition of English poetry. She burst into poetry as others burst into song, her voice
rising above the rush of the kitchen faucet.

" 'My heart leaps up when I behold / A rainbow in the sky,' " she would call out to me as I sat at the kitchen table doing my homework.

But on that day, Lottie's heart would have been too heavy to leap. Her sister, my mother, was dying. Surely she had known that even as they made the appointment with the doctor.

I suppose Edna, her deputy, sat beside Lottie. Tall and thin, with dark hair cut into a head-hugging pixie style that was both fashionable and required little care, Edna moved with a swiftness and economy that startled others and allowed her to live several lives simultaneously. She had two children, Heidi and Bernie, but Bernie, who was only eleven, had already revealed himself to be a child who was and always would be self-sufficient. Stocky and thick-haired, he got all A's, polished his own shoes, and was junior air-raid warden. He hurried up and down the hills of their Midwood neighborhood with a wagon he had constructed out of a large crate and discarded roller-skate wheels collecting the tied-up bundles of newspapers, which were necessary, he told us gravely, "for the war effort."

"I will never have to worry about Bernie," Edna said, and that was both true and fortunate because Heidi, a year older than me, required all her efforts.

Heidi was the girl leader of Arista at the High School of Music and Art. She excelled in all subjects but she was a brilliant linguist and a brilliant pianist. She had the shy arrogance peculiar to the truly gifted, and her head was always tilted back, as though weighed down by the thickness of her long dark ponytail. Her face was long, her features equine, and when I stood before my first Modigliani portrait at the Museum of Modern Art, I thought that I was staring at my cousin.

Edna was Heidi's trainer. She listened to her daughter practice the piano, carefully setting the timer and the metronome. Because Heidi's skin had a yellowish cast and Dr. Epstein of Mount Sinai omnipotence had once announced her "borderline anemic," Edna cooked her broiled liver, bartering ration stamps with other family members, and fed her tablespoons of cod liver oil from a large brown bottle. She read all of Heidi's compositions and sent the one entitled "The Terror of Fascism" to the *PM*, where it was printed as "a guest editorial from a brilliant young reader."

Edna worked in the Long Island City office of Emanuel Weiner, a rotund, bold German Jew who owned a large baked-goods company but whose efforts for more than a decade had concentrated on the rescue of Jewish artists and intellectuals from Germany. Edna was an expert on affidavits and eclectic bits of immigration law. She was a tenacious wheedler of secretaries, mindful of the birthdays of congressmen and senators. She also knew how to call flour mills in Vermont and complain about the quality of their shipments, and dairy farmers on Long Island to complain of shortages in their egg count.

Once I had visited her office and watched as she spoke into two phones at once, sweetly into the instrument in her right hand ("But we must arrange a visa for this writer — he's on the shortlist for the Nobel and Mr. Weiner will surely not forget it if the congressman intercedes") and harshly into the receiver in her left hand ("I know there's a war on but if you can't supply us, Mr. Weiner will find someone who can"). I had marveled at her power, and Mr. Weiner had glanced at me and winked conspiratorially.

Edna was devoted to her husband, Leon, who owned a small record store but who spent more time practicing the violin in the stockroom than pleasing the occasional customer who wandered in to sort through the albums of seventy-eights. He was an omnivorous reader, a freethinker. Edna spoke of him with the bemused wonder of a woman who is still astonished that she had managed to attract and marry a man of rare talent.

The record store had been Julius's idea and it had been Julius who had lent Leon the money for the initial rental and stock.

"I let Julius back me," Leon said magnanimously.

Dina, the youngest of the sisters, had been pregnant, and she must have been given the window seat on that trip to Mount Sinai to consult the doctor. Enveloped in her black high-collared woolen cape, trailing a colorful paisley scarf, her bright hair tucked into a black beret, she had probably stared sadly through the grime-streaked window as the express train lumbered through the Midwood section with its oppressive look-alike red brick houses, on to Prospect Park with its mud-colored apartment houses, and then into the darkness of the tunnel which shielded the passengers from the slums of downtown Brooklyn.

Ugliness distressed Dina, and poverty pained her. She herself was beautiful, her hair red-gold, her skin creamy, her long lashes like fine strands of copper brushing her high cheekbones. She was aware of her beauty and nurtured it, applying thick white creams to her face and small damp pads to her eyelids. She smiled at herself as she brushed her hair and applied honey-colored lipstick, pursing her lips together and licking them very slowly. Her clothing was marvelous.

"Dina has style," her sisters said, but she had more than style; she had an eye, a gift. She could drape a plain black shift with a shawl shot through with golden threads, add a necklace of chunky, glittering gemstones, slide heavy bracelets across her wrists, and stand before us like a mysterious nocturnal monarch. She plucked lengths of fabric from pushcarts at Orchard Street, a bolt of peacock blue silk, another of jade green wool, and carried them back to Woodstock, where a dressmaker, following her instructions, fashioned them into wide-sleeved dresses, trim suits.

She wore the suits to make her rounds. She was a social worker and it was her job to visit impoverished families, to intervene in emergencies, and to write up evaluations. The poverty she confronted appalled her and confirmed her political convictions. She and her husband, Robert, were Communists.

Robert was a painter whose work depicted social realism. His portraits were of sad-eyed miners and granite-chinned welders. His cityscapes captured the stark silhouettes of tenements, the exteriors of factories. He was a tall man; his sand-colored hair fell about his head in silken sheaths, and his pale gold eyes were oddly narrow, metallic slits in his angular face. He spoke with an ease of phrase and a fluency of expression that confounded his listeners and his adversaries. He was unique in our family — the American-born son of American-born parents. He had graduated from Yale and had studied painting in Paris. The American-born parents were also wealthy. They had paid for the house in Woodstock and for the yellow Nash convertible which caused my heart to stop when I saw it.

Once, Robert and Dina had driven the Nash to Boston and I sat on my stoop with my friend Nicole and watched as they emerged from the car. They had been horseback riding in Connecticut earlier and they both wore jodhpurs. Dina's white silk shirt was wide-sleeved so that when she extended her arms to embrace me she seemed a winged angel. Robert stood beside her in his suede vest and polished boots like a movie star briefly fallen from the Hollywood firmament.

"My aunt and uncle." I introduced them to Nicole reverently, as though they were royalty and the yellow Nash was their golden coach.

Always they were on their way to a play or a concert, already late for an appointment with friends whose very names excited my interest. Franchesca and Randy. Misha and Sonya. Sarah and Teddy. Franchesca was a ceramicist. Misha and Sonya were sculptors. I assumed the others to be writers and editors who, like Dina and Robert, belonged to a variety of committees — Writers and Artists for World Peace, the League for Social Justice, Friends of the People. They too subscribed to the magazines that Dina left carelessly lying about Lottie's house — *New Masses, Partisan Review, The People's Voice.*

"They're rich enough. They can afford to be Communists," Julius said once and I glared at him, not understanding his comment but recognizing the truth behind it. His perception angered me because it was correct. Communism was a luxury. It took time to attend committee meetings and discussion groups, fund-raisers and musical benefits.

Julius, who left for work at six in the morning and did not return home until nine-thirty or ten at night, could not afford that time. He held his own meetings on Saturday nights after the *havdala* candle had been lit and he had swiftly intoned the blessings that separate the sabbath from the workweek. It was then that Lottie arranged apples and oranges and pears in a pyramid in her golden glass fruit bowl, set out miniature Danish and teacups for the members of Julius's *landsmannschaft,* the men and women who came from his town in Poland. The men who sat around the table spread out documents, lists. They needed affidavits for a family stranded in Guatemala, for a yeshiva student in Shanghai. They needed money for bribes and money for tickets and money to send to Palestine. They did not speak of organizing art shows or benefit concerts. They wrote checks, clutching their fountain pens tightly, forming the letters with great care as names fluttered around the table. *What of the Kleins? Vanished. The rabbi's oldest son, Eliezer, the one who wanted to go to medical school? Him we got to Palestine, you don't remember? A year ago.* They stroked the stubble on their chins. They had not shaved because of the sabbath. Their eyes were rheumy because they never had enough sleep and were consumed by worry. Business, even when it was good, was bad, and the needs of their families and their community were great.

The sisters returned from their consultation with the Mount Sinai specialist saddened and resigned. I understood from their silence that my mother would die. When Dina returned to Woodstock, it was clear to me that she had recognized defeat and abdicated, acknowledging that her presence would not help her sister. She sat beside my mother's bed before she left and my mother placed her hand on the swell of her sister's pregnancy.

"I can feel your baby," she said and Dina gently took her hand and pressed it to her lips.

We settled in then for the long vigil. I was enrolled at Lincoln High School and urged to join clubs, to try out for the cheerleading squad, to make friends. I did all these things to avoid going home to Lottie's house, where each day my mother became more wraithlike and the smells of ethyl alcohol and antiseptic wafted through every room. My grandparents, white-haired and stooped by age and sorrow, sat mutely in their living room and when they could bear it no longer they slowly ascended the stairway between the two apartments and hovered in the doorway of my mother's room.

"Miriam, *meine* Miriam." My grandmother's voice quivered. It angered me that she should visit her tremulous grief on my mother, who was exhausted enough by the energy required for dying.

I, on the other hand, became an entertainment committee. Before visiting my mother I brushed my hair and tied it into a ponytail because that was the way she liked it. I applied lipstick, Pond's Honey, a gift from Dina, who had said that it was just subtle enough to complement my olive skin. I feasted on the word and studied my complexion with new interest. I had thought my skin color dour, even dangerously dark, but Dina had endowed it with Mediterranean mystery and I took new pleasure in tilting my head toward the sunlight when I studied myself in the mirror.

I sat beside my mother's bed and held her hand, closing my eyes against the blue half-moons that formed beneath her fingernails and the cruel purple bruises that mapped her withered arms. I made up stories about my life at Lincoln High School. I told her that I had been selected as a cheerleader although the truth was that I had been eliminated in the cruel competition that required each girl to enter a classroom, turn about, and shout her name aloud.

"Sharon Grossberg!" I had practiced shouting with a smile but I did not survive even the first tryout. Cheerleaders had large busts, tiny waists, perfect skin, and lustrous hair. Their saddle oxfords were covered with affectionate messages, and their bobby socks were snowy white.

Still, I felt no guilt in lying to my mother. It comforted me to sit there in her dimly lit room and talk with her about the sweater I would have to buy, the short pleated navy blue skirt that would have to be ordered. I also told her that I had made friends, which was only a partial lie.

In my eagerness to escape the scene of her dying, I had signed up for library mending squad, the math team, the current events club. Two afternoons a week I worked in the dean's office, filing. This job was considered tedious, but I loved it because it gave me an opportunity to read personal records. It soothed me to learn of misery, death, and illness in the families of other students. I played a game as I read of divorces, welfare situations, retarded siblings, alcoholic fathers — worse than my situation or better than my situation. Like the cheerleaders, I graded on a continuum of 1 to 10 and sometimes I won and sometimes I lost.

I occasionally went to Judy Bergman's house to do my homework and there was always someone with whom I could sit in the cafeteria. I was not happy but I was not miserable.

When there was a letter from my father I read it to my mother, holding the tissue-paper-thin V-mail tenderly, as though it might crumble in my fingers. My father had been denied a compassionate leave. Doctors were urgently needed where he was. He advised my mother, who could swallow only soup and soft foods, to eat a great deal of liver. He wrote tenderly of his love for her, and I read his words with shy embarrassment. " 'My beautiful Mimi. I touch you. I kiss you. I dream of you.' " My mother smiled as I read, and touched her breasts, diminished now and pancake-flat beneath the delicate pastel nightgowns in which her sister dressed her. I wondered if she was remembering my father's hands upon them, if she was thinking of his touch, his kiss.

I read her the letters he wrote home, his descriptions of the English countryside, his work at the field hospital, his volunteer stints at the reception centers where Jewish children from Germany were examined before being sent on to foster homes or orphanages. " 'Yesterday I examined a girl from Frankfurt who was just about your age. She was so sad and frightened. I thought of how lucky my Sharon was to be living a happy life surrounded by family.' "

It angered me that my father thought that I was living a happy life. I had been uprooted from my Boston home, deprived of my room with its long mirror, separated from Nicole, who had been my best friend since kindergarten; my mother was dying and he was overseas and it was possible that he might be killed. I was not beautiful. I might never be beautiful. But it was true that I was surrounded by family.

And family overflowed the house when I arrived home that D Day afternoon — Death Day, I thought then and always afterward. Relatives, friends, and neighbors stood on the porch and ranged themselves mournfully on the red brick steps. Hands reached out to touch me in sympathy as Robert and Leon led me indoors.

I had studied our long shadows as we crossed Ocean Parkway. In dying, my mother had lost her shadow. Never again would it move in velvet softness before her and never again would I dance upon it as I had when I was a small girl and we walked down the broad streets of Brookline. But there was no time to think about my mother's shadow because when I reached the porch I was surrounded by my aunts and uncles and cousins. They clutched handkerchiefs and tissues like small white flags of grief and their faces were very pale. My uncles led me inside where my grandmother and grandfather sat at the dining room table, motionless, their gnarled blue-veined hands folded in defeat. My grandfather wore a dark suit, a white shirt, and a high black skullcap perched on his thick snow-colored hair. He read from the open prayer book before him, moving his lips soundlessly. He did not move when I kissed him, although my grandmother seized my hand and held me so close that the cameo which secured her navy-blue-and-white-print dress cut into my skin.

"Do you want to see your mother?" Edna asked.

"You don't have to," Dina said. She played with the gray chiffon scarf that draped her black maternity tunic and I understood that she and Edna had quarreled about this. I looked helplessly at Lottie.

"Come," she said and took me to the doorway of the room. A compromise had been reached. I did not enter but I looked at my mother, who was no longer my mother but a dead woman who had no shadow. Her eyes were closed and her skin was the color of the white roses that I had carried up to her the previous evening and which stood now on her bedside table.

The funeral was the next day — the swift, wise ritual of the Orthodox. I wore a navy blue cardigan which the rabbi ripped at the collar, just as he cut the blouses of my aunts, my grandmother's dress, the shirts of my grandfather and my uncle Samuel. I wondered if my father would rend his shirt when the news of my mother's death reached him. Was it permissible to rip a shirt that belonged to the United States Army?

At the cemetery, when the plain pine box was lowered into the chalky ground of Staten Island, I dropped two fistfuls of earth into the grave — one for myself and one for my father. My aunts stood close to my grandparents, their arms entwined, and Dina pulled me toward them, enclosing me in the intimate circle of their grief which excluded their own husbands. My grandfather and Samuel intoned the Kaddish and I too struggled with the prayer, reading the Hebrew from the mimeographed sheet which the funeral parlor had provided.

I saw that Robert was bareheaded. His skullcap had fallen off as he helped to lower the coffin and he had not bothered to retrieve it. He was a Communist and did not believe in God. Heidi had told me that Communists believed religion to be the opium of the people.

"That's a quote from Marx," she had said solemnly and I had nodded and asked Leon, who had studied pharmacy, what opium was.

"It's a narcotic. It soothes and numbs you," he replied.

At the cemetery that afternoon, I decided that Marx was wrong. The prayers did not numb me and the ritual frightened rather than soothed. I did not look back as we left. I did not want to watch as the men in green pants covered my mother's coffin with earth, consigning her forever to darkness.

The week of *shiva,* the requisite seven days of mourning, passed swiftly and tempestuously. We sat on upturned crates, and although sympathy was extended to all, I was clearly the star mourner.

"So young to be without a mother," the women murmured to each other.

"And the father?"

"Overseas. In Europe." They spoke in whispers.

"And what if he . . . ?" The question faded on their lips but their meaning was clear. What if he died? What if he was killed by a bullet, blown up by a hand grenade somewhere in Germany or in Holland or in Belgium? It was possible. Each evening we listened to the news, and despite Gabriel Heatter's gravel-voiced reassurance that "there was good news tonight," the reports of Allied gains were always tempered with reminders of the heavy casualties that they — we — had suffered. Bodies strewed the beaches of Normandy, and blood ran in scarlet rivulets through the streets of Saint-Lô and Caen.

On the fourth day of *shiva,* it was reported that a gold-star banner now hung in the window of the corner house on the street. Johnny Calderazzo, who had always asked me to buy him a *Daily Mirror* when I went to the candy store on Coney Island Avenue, had been killed on D Day. It occurred to me that he might have died within minutes of my mother and that all my life when I lit the memorial candle on the anniversary of her death I would think of him. He had been nineteen years old, a dark-haired boy still beset by acne whose muscles rippled when he played stickball in the street with his brothers.

If Johnny, who was so strong, so young, had died, then my slim, bespectacled father, his hair thinning, was doubly, triply vulnerable.

"If anything happens to him, well, it's a large family, a close family."

The answer was subtle but clear. If my father was killed in the war I would be taken in by one of my aunts or perhaps by my uncle Samuel and his wife, Dolly, who had no children of their own.

That thought filled me with dread. Samuel was a short man who wore highly polished shoes with built-up heels, double-breasted suits of fabric so sleek and electric that it appeared to have a life of its own, and boldly patterned ties held in place with a diamond stud. His hair was thick and dark, like my own, and for years he had worn a neat brush mustache. With the advent of Hitler, he had allowed the mustache to extend so that it curled about the corners of his mouth. He smoked large and fragrant cigars, removing them from their cellophane wrappers with surgical care and always offering Heidi or me the gold paper circlet that held the wrapper in place. He did not realize that we were no longer small girls who would pretend that the paper circles were wedding bands.

When he offered an opinion, he spoke with absolute certainty and his opinions were many and varied. He gave Julius business advice. Who needed furs during a war? Julius should switch over to garment manufacture. Uniforms. Even underwear.

There was a lot of money in underwear. Soldiers needed a lot of underwear.

"What do I know about underwear? Furs, I know." Julius shrugged.

Samuel's addiction to the news made him an authority on the war, on each campaign, on every general.

He thought Montgomery and Rommel evenly matched. Eisenhower was a genius.

"The highest IQ of anyone who ever went to West Point," Samuel proclaimed and his sisters looked at one another.

"Since when do they publish IQ scores in the newspaper?" Edna asked caustically.

"Who says I know it from the newspaper?" Samuel blew a smoke ring and Dolly glared at Edna.

"Samuel knows a lot of important people. Customers rely on Samuel. Businessmen. Lawyers." She paused for a moment and then delivered her demolishing salvo. "Doctors."

She touched a hand to her dyed red pompadour, smoothed the pleats of her white skirt, and moistened her lips, sliding her tongue across the layering of Revlon's Fire and Ice that matched the polish on her long dagger-shaped fingernails. She and her sisters-in-law disliked each other intensely but they were all clever women who knew precisely when to rein in that dislike so that it would not erupt into argument and estrangement.

I too loved Samuel, whose cheeks were always fragrant with lemon-scented after-shave lotion, whose mustache tickled my face when he kissed me, and who always slipped me a quarter when he visited. But I hated Dolly and I would never live with her. Not even *if* . . . I did not conclude the thought. Like our worried and whispering visitors, I could not articulate the possibility of my father's dying. It would not be fair. It could not happen. It would not happen.

At night I could hear my aunts talking softly as they sat in the living room. Lottie and Edna wore loose housecoats over their nightgowns, and Dina was enveloped in a royal blue silk kimono patterned with scarlet lions. They sat on the couch, and Dina and

Edna smoked while Lottie twisted her blue-gray hair into small pin curls and fastened each with a bobby pin. The nights of the *shiva* period were transformed into slumber parties, and my aunts did not begrudge themselves moments of laughter and gossip about the events of the day, the callers who had come to pay their condolences.

I listened to them as I lay awake. There was wry wisdom in their laughter, cynical knowledge in their derisive comments. They were women who saw beneath the surface, canny and clever, and I wanted to learn their secrets because now I had no mother to teach them to me.

Of more serious things, they spoke in sober tones.

"I wish we would hear from him."

I lay there tensely. *Him.* My father.

"The Red Cross said they reached him, so he knows. But telegrams, mail — impossible since the invasion and they can't give special priority. Mr. Weiner even called Washington." Lottie and Dina were silent. If Mr. Weiner, whose contacts with senators and congressmen had resulted in the rescue of dozens of Jewish intellectuals, had been unable to reach my father, then nothing more could be done.

"We have to know what he would want for Sharon," Lottie said. "His mother is too sick to have her and besides she lives so far away."

My father was an only son. His widowed mother lived in Cleveland, where my parents had met when my mother, while attending a tax seminar at Case Western Reserve, had fallen and twisted her ankle. My father had been on the emergency room rotation that night. "The luckiest night of my life," he often said. Did he still think so? I wondered, as I lay there in the darkness, listening to my aunts.

"Look, for now she has to finish out the term at Lincoln. Three more weeks. And she has to take the geometry Regents," Edna said.

"But what about the summer. We're near the beach. A ten-minute walk to Brighton. And Tuesday nights there are fireworks," Lottie said.

"You'll be going to business with Julius all summer," Edna protested. "She's a teenager. What will she do all day?"

Julius's bookkeeper had been drafted and it had been agreed that Lottie would fill in.

"She could come to us but she'd be bored there too. Heidi is going to the music camp in Michigan, and Bernie will be at Boy Scout camp."

Since her eighth birthday, Heidi had spent every summer at the Interlochen Music Center, where she took lessons from a distinguished pianist, practiced intensively, swam in an enormous pool, and played tennis on grass courts. She had shown me her scrapbook, full of solemn-faced young people like herself staring gravely into the camera.

"Do you like it at Interlochen?" I had asked her and she had shrugged.

"I don't know. My mother says it's a good experience. It's enriching," she had replied and I did not press her because it seemed to me for a split second that she was about to cry.

"You know, Sharon should come to us — to Woodstock. The Bassens — you know, Sarah and Teddy — they have two teenagers. She'll be in the country. There's swimming and tennis. And I'm sure she could even find a part-time job." Dina's voice gathered enthusiasm as she spoke and my heart soared.

"He would like that. I'm sure he would like that," Lottie said, meaning that they could assume my father's approval. "She'd be away from the polio and she'd be meeting young people. It would be a new experience, a change." Lottie was building her case, reinforcing the arguments she would offer to my grandparents and to Julius. "Yes. It's a good idea, if Sharon wants to do it."

I fell asleep smiling and awakened weeping because I feared that I had betrayed my mother with my joy.

Summer

1

We drove up to Woodstock in the yellow Nash convertible. Robert put the top down and the wind riffled my hair and tossed Dina's into a fiery tangle until at last she scooped it into a topknot and tied it into place with her bright green scarf.

"Are you all right, Sharon!" she called to me as we drove through the low hills of Westchester. "It's not too windy for you?"

It was too windy but I did not want them to raise the canvas roof. Children along the roadside stared at us, and passengers in other, more conservative cars glanced our way curiously. I read admiration and envy in those gazes. Dina and Robert, sitting tall in the front seat, he with his straw hat placed at a cocky angle, she with her scarf trailing in the wind, were an attractive, interesting-looking couple. I myself had dressed with care for the journey. I wore a white peasant blouse with an elasticized neck that I had pulled down to my shoulders as soon as we rolled out of sight of the Brooklyn house, and a pair of bright red pedal pushers which Lottie had bought me as a reward for getting 100 on the geometry Regents.

I sat on my knees in the back seat and imagined that those

who observed me surely thought that I was Dina and Robert's daughter, and briefly, with guilty disloyalty, I wished that to be true. It would be wonderful to have parents like Dina and Robert, bubbling with ideas, deeply involved in the social issues of the day, she so beautiful and he so handsome.

My own parents had always been serious, attentive to their work and attentive to me. My mother had been an accountant, a profession which I considered to be the height of boredom. Dina, on the other hand, told me stories of welfare mothers, pregnant teenagers, strife-riven families, all of whom turned to her for help. I imagined her driving from town to town in the foothills of the Catskills, her brightly colored scarves flaring behind her, offering solutions and solace.

My mother had never discussed her work with me. What could an accountant tell her child — that a bank reconciliation had been managed without difficulty, that a ledger had been balanced in record time? My father, who might have provided dramatic stories, had always been too tired to talk.

Robert, however, spoke of his paintings with enthusiasm. He planned to paint a series of portraits of children that summer.

"I want to focus on shared expression, shared fantasy," he said. "A Negro child. A Chinese child. The Italian greengrocers on Main Street have a gorgeous little girl."

"What about a Jewish child — a Jewish girl?" I asked. I wondered if at fifteen I could still be considered a child. Because I wanted my uncle to paint me. Perhaps if he captured me on canvas I would be able to see myself more clearly and know whether I was approaching beauty. I touched my bare shoulders. My skin was very soft. I wondered if Robert could see me in the rearview mirror and I was glad that I had spread Vaseline on my eyelashes so that they curled stiffly upward.

"I hadn't thought about a Jewish child," Robert confessed. "I was thinking about kids who have been deprived, discriminated against. Colored kids. Immigrants."

"Jews were immigrants. Buba and Zeidey. Uncle Julius. Lottie and Samuel." Lottie and Samuel had been born in Europe but Lottie had been four years old and Samuel a toddler when they arrived in

America. Still, they qualified to be part of the tired and the poor, the "huddled masses yearning to breathe free." Lottie often recited the Emma Lazarus poem as she peeled and washed vegetables.

"It's different for the Jews," Robert said.

"Why? Why is it different?" Dina asked.

"Because Jews come from a materialistic mercantile background and they adjust easily to a consumer-dominated capitalistic society," Robert replied swiftly in the smug monotone of the good student who assimilates texts with ease.

"Oh come on, Robert. This isn't a lecture hall or a meeting of the John Reed Society. Forget the dogma," Dina said impatiently.

"It's not dogma. It's truth. Look at your own family. Julius got off the boat maybe thirty years ago without knowing a word of English and now he's the cigar-smoking boss. He's got a factory with God knows how many workers sweating over sewing machines, his own showroom, and if he listens to your brother, Samuel, he'll be running a goddamn underwear factory." Robert smiled as though he had scored a point.

"Uncle Julius works very hard," I said, mysteriously spurred to defend the uncle who barely said ten sentences to me during the course of a week. Still, I was fond of the short, chubby man whose balding scalp was spattered with freckles and who waddled on tiptoe from room to room when he arrived home late at night so that he would not disturb anyone. When he did speak, his English was heavily accented, and perhaps because each word cost him a great effort, he chose them carefully.

I had seen him, at the sabbath table, the only dinner he shared with his family during the entire week, cover Lottie's hand with his own and I had seen the tears that filled his eyes during my mother's funeral. I had watched him as he sat hunched over the dining room table late at night, writing letters to his daughter, Beth, and to Aaron, who was stationed at Fort Sills. He wrote the words laboriously, mouthing them as he worked. *I hope you are well. I hope you are not working too hard. I hope you are eating good food. Remember who you are. If you can't find kosher meat, eat eggs and vegetables.*

Julius himself had survived on hard-boiled eggs, raw carrots,

and brown bread during the nine months it had taken him to reach
New York Harbor from his village in Poland. He had met Lottie
when a friend brought him to the kosher East Side restaurant
where she worked as both cashier and bookkeeper.

"Her eyes danced and her fingers flew," my uncle said, recalling his first meeting with the woman who became his wife, and I
thought that there was poetry buried within him and that Lottie,
who loved lilting verses and graceful images, had sensed that from
the start.

"Of course he works hard. He wants to be rich," Robert retorted.

"Robert, please." There was real distress in Dina's voice now
and I remembered how my mother grew upset when my father,
however good-naturedly, mocked her sisters and their husbands.

"Richard, please," she had said in the exact cadence of Dina's
voice and at that moment I missed her so much that my stomach
hurt, and tears seared my eyes. That pain comforted me because I
sometimes feared that I did not feel her death deeply enough.

"All right. All right. I forgot. Your sisters and their families
are off-limits." He laughed and placed his hand on Dina's head,
losing his fingers in the nest of bright hair. When we reached Kingston, he pulled her toward him as we stopped for a light and kissed
her on the lips.

I wondered if a man would ever love me like that. I sucked on
a strand of my own dark hair and thought that I might dye it
although I knew that no artificial coloring could re-create the color
of Dina's hair, which looked as though it had been spun from
lashings of firelight.

I fell into the light sleep that had become my refuge from
misery and awakened when Dina called out, "We're here, Sharon.
We're home."

Home. The very word pierced me with anguish, reminding
me that I had no home and would not have one until my father
returned. *If* he returned. But he would. He would. He had to.

I studied the house, which looked as though it had sprung
from the pages of my first-grade primer.

It was set back from the lush lawn; its shutters were painted black and a red brick chimney sprouted from its sloping roof. Red roses climbed the trellis next to the side door, and velvet-hearted pansies and marigolds grew in serried rows along the flagstone path. It was on a quiet street, separated by an expanse of tall grass and sweet-smelling purple clover from its neighbors on either side.

"It's wonderful," I said. "It's so . . ." I struggled to find the right word and settled on "quaint," which caused Robert and Dina to laugh just as I realized that the word I had been seeking was "American." It was the most American-looking house I had ever seen.

Dina opened the door and I entered a large room lined with bookcases. Paintings and lithographs hung on the white walls, and the polished wood floor was covered with a rug of Indian design in muted shades of blue and terra-cotta. A serape patterned in crimson and gold was tossed across the sagging beige sofa, and huge woven pillows were scattered across the floor. The pine coffee table was cluttered with ceramic bowls, oddly shaped shells, and a small wooden sculpture of a pregnant woman. A battered guitar leaned against the wall. Magazines and journals littered the low tables, and the music stand on the upright piano was laden with pages of sheet music.

The room proclaimed itself. Here books were read, art was appreciated, and music was played. I looked at the paintings on the wall and recognized Robert's work. A portrait of a farmer leaning on his tractor, the hills of the lower Catskills in the background. A study of an old woman seated on a straight-backed chair, her red, work-worn hands clasped on her lap. I preferred the gentle Monet landscapes my mother had hung in our Brookline living room and that preference seemed disloyal to me. After all, Monet was not a relation and Robert's work was surely excellent. It had been exhibited in galleries in New York and he was to have a show that summer in a Woodstock gallery.

"A bit different from Lottie and Julius's place," Dina said. "But I hope you like it."

"Oh, I do," I said and just then the phone rang and she hurried to answer it.

"How wonderful of you to call. We've just arrived," she said breathlessly to the caller. "Robert and myself and my niece." She flashed me a smile and I started out the door to help Robert with the bags, but standing on the steps, I heard her add, "Yes, Sharon. The one I told you about. Poor thing."

I wondered what Dina had told her friends about me — that my mother had died and that my father was overseas and that there had been no word from him for two weeks, not since the telegram he had managed to get through to me at the end of the *shiva* period. BE BRAVE MY BABY. I LOVE YOU. WE HAVE EACH OTHER. I carried it with me always, tucked in a pocket, and several times a day I touched it, creasing the yellow paper between my fingers as though to assure myself that it existed.

Dina's voice trailed after me as I started down the steps.

"She's lovely, very sensitive. But I suppose she'll have to adjust."

Adjust to what? I wondered as I took my valise from Robert and staggered briefly beneath its weight.

"Come on, let me get that," he said and took it from me, swinging it easily as I followed him into the house. He was a strong man although the army had rated him 4F because he had a punctured eardrum. Leon, too, was 4F because he was nearsighted. Leon had been disappointed by his rejection — "I really wanted to give those Nazi bastards a kick in the ass," he had said — but Robert had been elated.

"His being 4F saves him a lot of trouble," Edna had observed wryly. "He doesn't have to deliver his conscientious-objector routine."

"No one can be a conscientious objector in this war," Lottie had protested. "No one in his right mind. Even the Communists are now working for the war effort."

Dina's sisters treated her politics with affectionate contempt. I remembered my mother trying to explain Dina to my father after a particularly fierce quarrel when the Hitler-Stalin pact dominated the news.

"It's because Dina is so good," she had explained. "She sees so much injustice in the world and she thinks that under communism the world will be a better place."

My father, usually the most soft-spoken of men, had let an expletive fly. "You can't use that argument now," he had said angrily. "Look how many have left the party because of that pact. Imagine — to sign a treaty with Hitler. Your sister and brother-in-law have red stars in their eyes and hammers and sickles on their brains. Miriam, Hitler is killing Jews. Murdering them."

I wondered for the first time if, after all, my father would approve of my visit to Woodstock.

I followed Robert up the stairs. The room which they had given me was next to their own and would be a nursery in the fall when their baby was born. It was newly painted and bare except for a bed, an unfinished desk, and a bureau. A long mirror hung on the back of the door.

"I found that at a yard sale," Dina said, coming up behind me. "I remembered that you had one like that in your room in Brookline. The only thing is I don't want to see myself in it. Not while I look like a beached whale."

She had changed into a sleeveless jade green maternity blouse and shorts, and despite her words she studied her reflection ruefully.

"You look beautiful," I protested swiftly.

"Do I?" She twirled her gold loop earring and flashed herself a smile. "I just hope I get my figure back. Robert can't stand fat women. A lot of men can't although my friend Ellie — she's a psychotherapist — says that some men actually prefer overweight women. Something to do with a womb fantasy, losing themselves in a huge female body. Very Freudian, I guess."

I nodded. She spoke to me in the language of her generation, as though I were her contemporary, and I felt a new maturity. This summer Dina would initiate me into the secrets of a woman's world. I too would practice my smile and learn what men liked and what repelled them. The secrets of love would be revealed to me.

Dina smiled and took my hand in her own.

"Let's get dinner started. Some friends will be dropping by."

Her casualness startled me. My other aunts spent days cleaning and polishing their silver if friends were coming for dinner, and my mother would test recipes and read cookbooks for weeks in advance, always exhausted and pale when she at last opened the door to the couples who were invited. But Dina was relaxed, almost indifferent.

I followed her down to the kitchen, a large bright room that overlooked the garden. Copper pots hung on its wood-paneled walls and ropes of onions and garlic dangled from the ceiling. There was a shop on Main Street where Dina bought them.

"That's the wonderful thing about Woodstock," she said cheerfully. "It has such shops."

She foraged in the pantry and found spaghetti and tomato sauce.

"Wonderful," she said and put a huge pot of water on to boil. Her menu was set.

Robert went into the garden and picked lettuce and tomatoes and two fat cucumbers.

"Oh, you have a victory garden too," I said, holding the moist lettuce to my cheek.

My grandfather had cultivated his garden throughout my mother's illness, stooping, despite the arthritis that twisted his fingers, to thrust the tomato plants into the small wadis he dug with his trowel. With great deliberation, he had trained the cucumber vines across the fence and scattered carrot seeds. As the plants grew, he spoke to them tenderly in Yiddish, plucked the weeds, and watered the entire area with the hose. His garden offered him a refuge from the household of women and spared him, for a few sunlit hours, the agony of watching his daughter die. I wondered if there had been a garden in his home in Poland, in the small village to which he dispatched anguished letters week after week although both Edna and Julius had told him that there was no way they could be delivered, that he was wasting the postage.

"But my sisters are there. And my brothers. And their children." His gray-blue eyes filled with tears because by then the newscasters were speaking somberly of new places. Camps. Auschwitz. Treblinka. Buchenwald.

"Our garden isn't a victory garden," Robert said. "It's an

organic garden. An experiment in self-sufficiency. We were growing vegetables long before the war."

"Okay," I said, although I didn't see what made his garden
different from my grandfather's except that the Brooklyn tomatoes
were larger.

I cut up the salad and watched as Dina padded barefoot
about the kitchen, snipping at the herbs that grew in small ceramic
pots on the windowsills and adding them to the sauce. She cooked
the way she dressed, with flair and with insouciance.

I offered to set the table but it turned out there was no table
to be set. Silverware was simply tossed into a basket and plates
were piled on the sideboard in the living room where the pot of
spaghetti and the salad bowl would also be placed.

"Why don't you go out and see Robert's studio — and pick
some flowers. I want to fill that blue vase. Franchesca made it and
she's coming tonight," Dina said absently.

Robert's studio was a building in the rear and almost as large
as the house itself. It was a reconverted barn; huge windows had
been carved into its sides, and a skylight, through which sunlight
poured, had been created above the rafters. Unlike the house, it
was uncluttered, almost austere. Two easels stood on the scrubbed
pine floor, and canvases were stacked against the walls. Tubes of
paint, oversize jars of watercolor powders, were neatly arranged
on a scarred and stained worktable, flanked by brushes soaking in
old mayonnaise jars filled with alcohol and turpentine. A work in
progress stood on the easel. I stared at the pencil sketch of a hospital bed on which an emaciated form lay. Dark hair fanned its
way across the pillow. I drew closer and realized that Robert had
drawn my mother as she lay dying in Lottie's house. Fresh grief
stirred within me and I turned away.

"Do you like it?" Robert asked.

He stood in the doorway, his thick sand-colored hair damp
because he had showered quickly after the long drive. He pulled
a Lucky Strike from the pack he kept in the pocket of his blue
denim shirt, and then, discovering that he had no matches, he
replaced it.

"I don't know," I said. My cheeks were burning but he was indifferent to my discomfort.

"Let me show you some finished ones," he said and started for a group of canvases that leaned against the wall. "This is just a sketch."

It occurred to me that it did not matter to him that it was my mother he had drawn. Only his skill interested him.

"Not now," I said. "I have to pick some flowers for Aunt Dina." I turned to leave.

"Just Dina," he called after me. "And I'm just Robert. Okay?"

"Okay," I called back. "Okay, Robert," I added daringly and I forgave him for drawing my mother as she lay dying.

I picked black-eyed Susans and daisies from the profusion of wildflowers that grew in the untended swale beyond the garden and arranged them in the tall blue vase, finishing just as Franchesca Syms swept into the room, followed by her husband, Randy, a short bespectacled man with an involuntary blink.

"But I must have created that vase just for those flowers," Franchesca exclaimed in her rich musical voice. She was a tall woman, her jet black hair hugging her head. Her black slacks and loose black tunic flapped about her slender body. Her long beringed fingers toyed with a womb-shaped silver pendant that dangled from a leather thong.

Dina drifted into the room, carrying a bottle of Chianti. She touched her hand to Franchesca's cheek, handed Randy the bottle.

"Pour the wine, will you, Randy?" she asked. "You know where the glasses are."

He blinked and took the bottle from her, found the glasses in a cabinet, and poured with great care. He was a man charged with maintaining order for a careless company of friends.

"We're here!"

The door was thrust open — Dina's friends did not knock or ring bells — and the Bassens burst into the room. Sarah and Teddy Bassen were both pink and plump. Thin strands of pale hair criss-crossed their way across Teddy's scalp, and Sarah smiled cheerfully beneath a helmet of pink-gold curls. They both wore bib overalls and work shirts. Their son and daughter, in contrast, were startlingly thin. They wore dungarees rolled about the ankles and loose white men's shirts. Their fair hair was long and they were both sharp-featured. Standing in the doorway, they looked like androgynous twins rather than the older brother and younger sister I knew them to be.

"Sarah. Teddy." Dina grasped their hands in welcome, proffered her cheek to Teddy. "And Karen, Peter, I want you to meet my niece Sharon."

"Hi, Sharon." It was Karen who spoke for both of them.

"Hello." I was shy suddenly and dropped my eyes, noting that Peter was wearing scuffed penny loafers without socks and that strips of dirt snaked their way about the blue veins of his ankles. He limped slightly as he moved forward. The dirt and the defect gave me power over him and I was newly courageous.

"I'm going to be here all summer," I said.

"Great. We're right next door. The yellow house. We'll do things."

"Like what?" Peter stared his sister down but Sarah Bassen intervened.

"Really, Peter, there's so much to do in Woodstock," she said brightly and bustled into the kitchen with the garlic bread and fruit salad she had brought.

The spaghetti was marvelous and the salad was sprinkled with balsamic vinegar Franchesca made herself. Teddy mopped up spaghetti sauce with Sarah's delicious bread. Now and again, they rose from their seats and moved about, changing places like dancers in an elegant quadrille. Franchesca left her seat on the couch to sit on the floor beside Robert's chair. She spoke to him of a new glaze she had perfected.

Teddy Bassen squatted before Dina and discussed a case she was handling. He was a psychiatrist on the staff of the hospital in Kingston and often worked with Dina's clients.

"Your aunt is one of the most sensitive social workers on staff," he told me. "And that in addition to being beautiful." He kissed her hand and returned to sit beside his wife on the couch.

Randy drifted through the room, studying the books that

were scattered everywhere, plucking up a volume and setting it down. And then they assembled again in a circle, sated and content. Their conversation was urgent and fluent. The war absorbed them. They had all traveled in Europe and the battlefields whose names filled the news were the scenes of their youthful adventures. They mourned the devastation of Cherbourg, liberated for the Allies by Lightning Joe Collins.

"And it was a beautiful port," Robert said. "I used to go down to the harbor at first light to paint. Do you remember, Dina? We used to have croissants and coffee at that little café at the edge of the wharf."

"No more little cafés," Randy said bitterly. "The Nazi bastards."

"We're doing our bit for destruction. We seem to have leveled Caen," Robert said.

"We're doing what we have to do," Teddy Bassen said. "We didn't start this damn war, Robert."

The conversation was growing dangerous and the women took it over. Sarah, who taught English at the local community college, had just read *Strange Fruit* and she pronounced Lillian Smith a genius.

"I'm afraid that the level of my concentration right now is limited to *Forever Amber*," Dina said and they all laughed.

The conversation switched to films. *Henry V* with Laurence Olivier was playing at the small arts movie house in Woodstock.

"You kids ought to see it," Sarah Bassen said.

"They probably want to see that new Hitchcock, *Lifeboat*. It's playing in Kingston," Teddy said.

But all talk ceased when Dina turned the news on. They stared into their coffee cups and listened gravely. Patton was sweeping through Brittany. V2s and buzz bombs were falling on London. Edward R. Murrow, his gravelly voice newly bitter, described the rush to air-raid shelters, the deafening explosions followed by the shrill whine as the bombs whizzed through the darkness. "I ask you to believe that they travel faster than sound," Murrow advised us, as though pleading for our credulity.

I tried to remember the formula for the speed of sound as I thought of how my father grew breathless when he moved too swiftly. He could never outrun a German bomb.

"My father is in England," I told Peter and Karen. "At least I think he is."

I reached into my pocket and touched the telegram and they looked away with embarrassment. It shamed them that their father was not in the army. Teddy Bassen, I learned later, had tried to enlist, but he was too old.

"Your father will be all right," Karen said softly and our friendship was sealed. She had instinctively understood both my fear and my need for reassurance.

"Do you want to come with us tomorrow?" she asked.

"Where to?"

"We work down at the civil-defense collection center sorting out stuff. And then we go swimming. There's a whole bunch of us."

"Sure," I said. "Why not." I forced myself to sound nonchalant but my heart was soaring. Karen liked me. She was prepared to include me in her life.

Robert switched off the radio and reached for his guitar. He strummed it and they began to sing.

"I dreamed I saw Joe Hill last night . . . alive as you and me . . ."

Everyone knew all the words and they sang with great solemnity, their voices growing louder with the final chorus.

" 'But Joe, you're ten years dead,' said I. 'I never died,' said he."

Franchesca pressed her silver pendant to her cheek and sang chorus after chorus and Randy's eyes glittered as he watched her. I thought then, as I think now, that it must be very difficult for a mild and uninteresting man to be married to a fascinating and beautiful woman.

They sang in Spanish.

" 'Viva la concerbrigada . . .' "

"That's from the Spanish Civil War," Karen whispered to me.

"I know," I said, although I didn't know nor did I understand why singing a song of that war should cause Sarah Bassen's lips to tremble and her husband to hold her close.

"Hey, if we had all the great songs, how come we lost the war?" Robert asked and their responding laughter was bitter.

Everyone left early because the next day was Monday. Randy and Sarah were both teaching summer session courses.

"Another workweek for us poor uncreative slobs," Teddy said cheerfully.

Dina and I carried the dirty dishes into the kitchen and while she washed and I dried, she told me that Franchesca and Randy had met at a fund-raising party for the Abraham Lincoln Brigade — Americans who were fighting in Spain.

"Why?" I asked. "Why should Americans fight for the Spanish?"

"They were fighting for the ideal," Dina explained patiently. "The Republican ideal. Working people everywhere have to help each other. We all have to fight for justice and equality. Don't you think so?"

"Yes," I agreed vigorously. "Yes, I do." It was easy to adopt the ideals of justice and equality.

"Franchesca's beautiful," I said.

"Oh, do you think so?" Dina stared at her own reflection in the shining pot she had just washed. She wiped her hands and slipped them over the rise of her abdomen.

"But not as beautiful as you," I added quickly.

Later that night as I lay on the narrow bed, the sheets smelling of the musky potpourri Dina kept on the shelves of the linen closet, I listened as Dina and Robert talked.

"I think Sharon will have a good summer here," she said.

"Why wouldn't she?" His lack of interest pained me.

"Sharon thought Franchesca was beautiful."

"She looked sensational tonight. I'd like to paint her dressed in black."

"I'm sure she'd love that."

"Don't be bitchy, Dina."

"Robert . . ." There was a subtle plea in her voice, a throatiness I had not heard before.

"I'm tired tonight, Dina. Really tired."

They were silent then and I got out of bed and went to the window. I could see the Bassen house. A light burned in an upstairs window and I imagined that Karen Bassen was awake and reading. She had told me that she was halfway through *A Tree Grows in Brooklyn* and had promised to lend it to me when she finished it.

I went back to bed and tried to remember the words to "Joe Hill." " 'I never died,' said he. 'I never died,' said he."

I fell asleep for the first time since D Day without thinking of my mother's death, without worrying that my father would die. I was happy that first night in Woodstock, or perhaps I was anticipating happiness. Summer, after all, had just begun.

2

That first morning in Woodstock began as all the mornings of that long wartime summer would begin. Dawn broke slowly across the village, and its first tentative light filled my narrow room with a silvery luminescence. I lay awake and watched as the translucent patterns danced across the pale, newly sanded floor. A vagrant aureole briefly crowned the framed photograph of my parents which I had placed on the unfinished pine bureau. My father wore his dress uniform and the camera had caught him as he smiled shyly, like a small boy at a costume party who is both pleased and embarrassed by his disguise. His hair, thick and unruly like my own, had been tamed by the military, and the requisite crew cut gave his narrow face a vulnerable, boyish look.

My mother wore a simple white dress, and her pearl necklace was looped about her long and graceful neck. ("My beautiful swan," my father had called her in one of the love letters I read aloud to her in the room where she lay dying.)

In the half-light of dawn I studied the way my mother looked at my father, her long-lashed eyes soft as dark velvet, her lips curled into a sweet half smile. That picture had been taken on the last night of my father's last leave, just as they left for dinner at their favorite restaurant. They could not have known that night would mark their last shared intimacy, that that photograph would be their visual epitaph.

Self-pity suffused me and the cloud of sadness that weighted me down grew darker as the sounds of laughter and soft talk drifted in from the room next door. Dina and Robert were awake and whatever anger there had been between them the previous evening had been erased by the night of rest and the gentle silver-streaked morning. I listened to their languid murmuring, the lightness of their laughter.

"No," she said.

"Yes. I say yes," he countered.

There was a brief and sweet silence, then Robert's stertorous breath and Dina's sigh of joy.

I had long been a spy on love, outside my parents' closed bedroom door (yes, even on that very last night), lingering in the long dark hallway of the Brooklyn house and watching as the slat of light beneath the door vanished and the bedsprings moaned eloquently beneath the shifting weight of my aunt's and uncle's bodies. Once, Nicole and I had held glasses to the wall and listened to her parents' husky voices — their tone frighteningly feral in the darkness, their language coarse. Nicole had wept but I had continued to listen, fascinated then as I am now by all things physical.

"Shh," Dina said. "She'll hear."

"Healthy for her," Robert replied and laughed but they spoke in whispers then and I could no longer discern their words.

That transient sadness smothered my new wakefulness and I fell back to sleep, a pattern that would repeat itself throughout the long lazy daybreaks of that July and August, when I would waken briefly as darkness ended, watch the dance of silvery light, and then, assured that all was as it should be, fall back to sleep.

Dina was gone when I came down for breakfast that first morning. She began work early, Robert said, because her social service agency was assisting the wives of servicemen at the Newburgh Air Field and a nearby army base. Dina was helping them to find housing and encouraging them to battle depression by organizing them into small self-help groups.

"All this propaganda about home-front solidarity is just a lot of capitalist double-talk," Robert said with the cool cynicism that was his conversational trademark. "The bastards around here are rent gougers. They charge these kids whatever the market will bear until they go off to get their brains blown out defending democracy. They hoard and do black-market deals and the OPA makes believe it isn't happening. But Dina thinks she can still make the system work."

"But that's her job," I said reasonably as Robert poured me orange juice and filled a pretty blue-and-white ceramic bowl with Rice Krispies, blueberries, and milk.

"Franchesca's work," he said when he saw me pass my finger across the smooth glaze. "Very unique."

"It's beautiful," I said and when I finished the cereal, I carried the bowl tenderly to the sink, fearful that I might break it.

"It's going to be a really hot day." He stared moodily out the kitchen window where pools of golden sunlight swirled about grass and hedge. "Aren't you dressed a little too warm for all that cycling? Oh, your bike's outside — I even filled the tires with air because they looked a little low." He waited expectantly. He was a man who required the expression of gratitude — it validated his own concept of himself.

"Thanks. I'll be all right," I assured him. I wore rolled-up jeans and a tattered white-on-white shirt that had once belonged to Julius which I had rescued from Lottie's rag pile. I had rolled the sleeves up, working for a long time to achieve the sloppy careless look of Karen's outfit the previous evening. My white bobby socks, cuffed to the proper thickness, bulged above my saddle oxfords, and my bathing suit and a towel were stuffed into my woven shoulder bag.

"Okay then." He himself removed his paint-stained blue cambric shirt, which was already sweat-dampened.

Although it was early summer, his skin was amber-colored and I knew that by summer's end it would be a deep gold. He was one of those lean and muscular men who move with natural grace and I watched him as though hypnotized as he went from table to counter, clearing away the breakfast dishes. There was a small bite mark on his arm, the skin indented but unbroken, and I wondered if Dina had clenched her straight white teeth against his golden flesh as they came together in the mercurial light of dawn. Was that how lovers celebrated their union? I wondered. Was it such playfulness, such loving violence, that evoked the murmurs and laughter I heard through the walls that were too thin and doors that did not close tightly enough? Surely, there was more to love-making than the depiction of intercourse in a drawing which Nicole and I had found in one of my father's textbooks. We had studied with grave embarrassment the anatomical drawing of a penis inserted into a vagina. But I did not know and I had no one to ask. I was a motherless child and my father had gone off to war.

Certainly I could not ask Robert. I was content to watch him at his morning chores and my cheeks grew feverishly hot when he smiled at me because I carried the coffeepot to the garbage pail and neatly emptied the dregs into an open egg carton.

"At least tie your hair back," he said and I did, knotting it into a ponytail and feeling very pleased that he had noticed that it was loose. Perhaps he had also noticed that I had brushed it that morning until it fell into curling layers.

"Sharon!" Karen and Peter called my name in unison and I hurried to the door.

They stood leaning against their bicycles and I jumped onto the old Raleigh that Robert had readied for me and rode off with them. I looked back just as we turned the corner and saw that Robert had settled onto a lawn chair. Still bare-chested, he arched his body forward as though reaching toward the sun.

We cycled down the sun-dappled road, past the huge old houses shielded behind hedges which, in zestful patriotism, had been carved to form huge V's, wide-winged eagles, and even a Liberty Bell. We reached the village and wove our way down the narrow streets crowded with shoppers. The war had transformed routine marketing into a complicated enterprise. Housewives stood before vegetable stands and examined produce, hefting oversize heads of lettuce, holding shimmering maroon eggplants up to the sunlight. A line formed in front of the butcher shop where the plate-glass window was dominated by a huge banner that read HAVE YOUR RATION BOOKS READY. THINK BEFORE YOU BUY.

Young women convened on street corners and exchanged ration stamps. I thought of how my aunts gathered at Lottie's kitchen table and made small piles of the red-and-blue and green-and-brown stamps. Edna needed extra meat stamps because Heidi was anemic and had to eat liver twice a week. Coupons for sugar were set aside for Dina. Pregnant women had a sweet tooth, Lottie confided to me knowingly.

We stopped for a light and I saw a young woman give her ration book to a woman who wore a flowered housedress in exchange for a ten-dollar bill. I turned away and wondered about the desperation that led her to sell her stamps. Perhaps she was one of the servicemen's wives of whom Robert had spoken so bitterly that morning.

As we rode, radios blared through open windows. Newscasters vied valiantly with Frank Sinatra and Jo Stafford. "Fighting is fierce in the Pacific theater — bloody battles on the Marshall Islands, the Marianas." "Buckle down, Winsocki, buckle down! You can win, Winsocki, if you'll only buckle down." "There are reports of hand-to-hand fights in the Ardennes." "When I go to sleep, I never count sheep, I count all the charms about Linda."

The civil-defense collection center was an unmarked warehouse at the end of Main Street.

"Security," Karen explained and I nodded, imagining enemy planes circling above Woodstock, seeking out defense installations. There were still reports of German spies slipping across borders or landing on isolated beaches. It was prudent that the rambling building remained unidentified and I felt proud to be part of a patriotic conspiracy. Inside, the cinder-block walls were hung with posters. I recognized the Norman Rockwell poster of the Four Freedoms that hung in my homeroom at Lincoln High School and I grinned at the stern drawings of a saddened Uncle Sam asking, "Did you drown a sailor today because you ate a lamb chop?" Judy Bergman and I had always thought that particular poster very stupid. "Two lamb chops — two sailors?" Judy had asked sarcastically while I wondered if one steak could kill an infantry sergeant. There was also a photograph of young people working at long tables with the slogan VICTORY IS IN YOUR HANDS printed across it.

WOODSTOCK WORKS FOR VICTORY had been painted in red across a white bedsheet and hung on a wall, and it was beneath that banner that I took up my position beside Karen and struggled to hear her instructions above the cacophony of clattering metal and the voices that shouted to be heard above the inevitable bleat of the radio.

The flattened tin cans that filled cartons and pails in every garage and alleyway; the newspapers assiduously collected and roped together; the empty toothpaste tubes; the cooking grease in coffee cans, congealed into mounds of lucent whiteness; the discarded silk and nylon stockings, their rips tracked with nail polish — all were brought to the collection center. It was our job to sort through them and prepare them for shipment to the war plants and factories where they would be transformed into material for the war effort. Peter was already working the lever of a machine used to flatten the aluminum pots and pans that filled a huge bin. Opposite me at the long metal table, a smiling redheaded girl cheerfully sorted through a crate of padlocks.

"Bronze," she shouted to no one in particular and tossed a rusting padlock onto one pile. "Steel," she called and threw another into a carton.

I was at work on the stockings, rolling them into balls that would be crammed into a canvas bag.

"It's easy but smelly," Karen said, wrinkling her nose. Some of the women, Karen explained, in an excess of patriotic zeal did not wash the hosiery because a rumor had circulated that detergent weakened the fiber. I gagged but struggled for control.

"Those women get double brownie points," the redhead said. "They're also saving soap." We giggled and introduced ourselves. Her name was Lola Szimecki.

The stockings, Karen told me, would be used to make powder bags for naval guns, the cooking grease would be used in the manufacture of ammunition, the tin and metal for producing armor, bullets, and grenades. Above Peter's flattening machine was a sign that read ONE OLD SHOVEL WILL MAKE FOUR GRENADES.

"How do they know that?" I asked Karen. "Did they stand around and watch the grenades being made?"

"They don't," Karen replied cheerfully. "It's a patriotic guess."

We worked on amid talk and laughter. The cavernous room hummed with energy and activity. The sense of purpose was palpable. We were helping to win the war. It was an intergenerational army that assembled at the collection center. There were high school students like Karen, Peter, and me, and college students like redheaded Lola, who had tried to get employment at a defense plant.

"But they weren't hiring for just the summer," Lola said. "And I had to do something. So I'm waitressing at the pizzeria at night and volunteering here. Glen — he's my fiancé" — she waved the finger on which a minuscule diamond chip sparkled — "he's somewhere in the Pacific."

"My father's somewhere in Europe," I said.

We spoke the cryptic language of the patriotic civilian. We knew that loose lips sank ships and that the enemy was everywhere, listening. We averted our eyes from the frightening poster on the wall opposite us that showed a sinking American ship, the agonized face of a drowning sailor, and the legend SOMEONE TALKED.

Gray-haired men and women, too old to be employed in defense plants, boxed empty toothpaste tubes, rolling them tightly and arranging them by size. Now and again someone cut himself on the jagged edge of a can or pot, and an old woman who had been a nurse painted the small wounds with iodine and fashioned intricate bandages.

"They'll be giving out Purple Hearts next," Lola said and we laughed.

Lola relied on humor as others rely on air. She needed it in order to survive, in order to keep herself from worrying about Glen who was somewhere in the Pacific and about the fact that even when the war was over they would have very little money. With Lola, I laughed aloud that day for the first time since my mother's death and the sound of that laughter surprised me. It rang with an almost musical clarity, a joy that I had thought lost to me forever. Peter wheeled about when he heard it and he looked at me and smiled. He had a nice smile, I decided, and I wondered why it should cause me to grow uncomfortably warm and to look away.

We worked until one, when a new shift of volunteers arrived, and then we climbed on our bicycles and pedaled north to a small pond. There, we ate the sandwiches that Karen had packed, changed into our bathing suits with a great deal of giggling, and plunged into the icy water. Afterward, we sat on the granite boulders that bordered the pond, our faces turned to the sun. The heat wave which swept across the nation that last summer of the war had begun, and we welcomed it. We arched our bodies up toward the red-gold orb and turned to allow the searing rays to lash our backs. We were young in a time of death and the sun was life-giving, its radiance reassuring.

I wondered if it was hot in Europe, if my father, who was a good swimmer, ever had a chance to shed his uniform and submerge himself in the cool waters of a lake or perhaps dash into the surf as he and my mother had done each summer at Revere Beach. I remembered myself as a small girl, sitting on a blanket and watching them walk hand in hand to the water's edge. My mother wore a white one-piece suit. I began to cry because never again would they touch each other. My mother was dead and the sun's bright heat could not pierce the cold darkness of her grave. My tears startled me. Always, my sorrow took me by surprise. I did not know then how long it takes until grief is assimilated and loss is realized.

"Hey, Sharon," Peter said softly. He limped over to sit beside me. Karen had not noticed my tears. She was waving to a quartet of new arrivals who clambered over the brush and boulders to the pond.

"Karen's crowd," Peter said. "Kids from school. Meg and Melanie. Roger and Bob." He knelt to study an ant colony while I wiped the tears from my cheeks. He understood that pain requires privacy.

"Not your crowd?" I asked and I glanced quickly at the group.

Meg and Melanie wore their blond hair short, in the New Look bob, their half-bangs flopping carelessly about their foreheads. Short hair was patriotic, the newly published *Seventeen* magazine had advised in a recent issue. Bobby pins and metal curlers were scarce. The article had featured a photograph of a girl setting her hair, with the admonishing caption "Don't You Know There's a War On?"

I stared glumly at Meg and Melanie. I was not going to cut my hair. I was patriotic enough, and besides, I hardly ever set my hair, much to my aunt Edna's dismay.

Roger and Bob were tall and pleasant-looking. I recognized them at once because there are boys like them at every school. They were the easygoing, popular captains of athletic teams. One of them would be the president of the student council and the other would be vice-president. When they walked into the luncheonette after school, their names were called from every booth, and room was made for them at crowded counters. Such boys never lose that confidence, that visceral certainty that they are attractive and likable, that they will attract and be liked. I meet them now as colleagues who are always certain of their skill, indifferent about research grants, confident of success. Sometimes they come to see me as patients and face me across my desk, smiling engagingly, daring me to offer them a negative diagnosis, a pessimistic prognosis. Their eyes shine and their message is clear: bad things do not happen to them.

"Not my crowd," Peter said. "We hang out together but they move too fast for me." He pointed to his leg as though daring me to look at it but I was not afraid. I was, after all, a doctor's daughter, and even then I planned to become a doctor myself. The human body, in all its complexity, fascinated me. I had asked Judy Bergman if I could trace the pale rim of her appendix scar with my finger. When pus oozed from a sore on Nicole's knee, I pressed some of it against my finger and tasted it. When I sat beside my mother as she lay dying, even as I lied about my popularity I studied the outline of bone beneath the parchment-thin flesh of her arm and pondered the blushing bruises that surfaced like tiny islands on the rivulets of her etiolated veins. With that same abstract curiosity, I stared at Peter's deformed leg, noting its unnatural thinness, the distortion of the tibia which curved inward and accounted for his limp.

"Polio," he said. "When I was nine. Me and FDR. I was out of school for two years. But I was lucky. It was a mild case and it responded to exercise and hydrotherapy. You know, Sister Kenny stuff, just like in the movie. I'm okay. No casts or crutches or anything but I'm not going to win an athletic scholarship and when I register for the draft I'll be 4F."

"Two of my uncles are 4F," I offered consolingly. "Robert and Leon."

"I thought Robert was a CO — a conscientious objector."

"No. He believes in conscientious objection, but he couldn't go for it because he had a punctured eardrum and never got past the physical."

"I thought he said he was a CO once," Peter persisted.

I shrugged. Karen and her friends joined us, introductions were made, and we all raced to the pond. Peter trailed behind us. He could not run, but when he swam he had as much speed and power as Bob and Roger. Swimming cured my own infirmity as well. Floating on my back or cutting my way through the clear blue-green water, I experienced a wondrous lightness. The hump of grief that hobbled me vanished, and like Karen and the others, I was swift and glad-hearted, released from melancholy.

We cycled back, the five of us, our hair wet and our faces sunburnished. We sang as we pedaled, " 'Mairzy doats and doazey doats and little lambsie divy — ' " The nonsense words, rapidly repeated, made us laugh and the drivers of passing cars shot us amused glances. Perhaps they were pleased that we had rescued laughter and song and that, for the moment, the war was left far behind. Perhaps our youth and careless gaiety briefly deceived them into believing that they lived in happier times. "Mares eat oats and does eat oats and little lambs eat ivy . . ." We enunciated each word clearly and waved as one after the other Meg and Melanie, Roger and Bob disappeared up the driveways of their homes. Peter, Karen, and I did not sing as we dropped our bikes on the lawn of the Bassen house. The aroma of a sauce of wine and herbs drifted through the window, and Sarah Bassen, her plump cheeks flushed, came to the door.

"I started dinner," she called to her son and daughter. "Sharon, tell Dina and Robert that you're all invited here for dinner."

"Who else is coming?" Karen asked.

"Oh, I think the Langsams. And some other people may be dropping by," Sarah replied vaguely. In Woodstock that summer there were always other people dropping by.

The first day set the pattern for the weeks that followed. Each morning I came downstairs after Dina had left for work. Some mornings Robert was already in his studio. Other mornings the door to their bedroom was closed and I assumed he had not yet awakened. Usually he slept late after an evening when a great deal of wine and liquor had been consumed, and with each passing week, such evenings became more frequent. As the heat wave tightened its grip on the city, more and more people sought refuge in the mountains, and the evening gatherings grew more crowded, with new faces constantly appearing.

Karen, Peter, and I observed the frenetic gaiety with stoic forbearance. We watched as ponytailed women flew across smoke-filled rooms to embrace bearded men. We listened to their conversations.

They discussed FDR's most recent Fireside Chat, and there was always someone present who could imitate Churchill. But there were no imitations of the British prime minister after the speech early in July in which he reported that V1 bombs were being dropped on England, causing thousands of civilian deaths. I was seized by severe stomach cramps then — the sort of discomfort that I now routinely dismiss as "anxiety aches" and for which I prescribe Valium rather than antacid — and I allowed Robert to take me home early. I stared hard at the photograph of my father and assured myself that in all probability he was no longer in England. In my innocence, it seemed that the battlefields of France were safer than the English countryside.

"You're safe," I told my father's gently smiling visage. "You are not going to die." I covered my mother's face with my hand. She was already dead.

More often than not, Dina, who was working very hard, opted to stay at home in the evening.

"All I want to do is put my feet up," she said apologetically to Robert. "But you go on, darling. And you go with him, Sharon. Take care of your uncle."

I knew she was relieved when I accompanied Robert to the potluck dinners and the kaffeeklatsches held in the wide-windowed studios and book-filled living rooms of their friends.

"Who was there?" she asked when I came home and I rattled off the usual names. Sarah and Teddy, Liz and Hank, the Langsams, the Golds, Marcie Klein.

"And Franchesca — was Franchesca there?" Dina would ask, patting the swell of her pregnancy as she sucked on a strand of copper-colored hair. Randy had been summoned to Washington and Franchesca was often alone.

"Yeah, I think so. Yeah. She was there."

Franchesca was seldom absent. She moved sensuously through crowded rooms, her black hair carved into a helmet that closely hugged her head, her full lips brushed with whitener and her large dark eyes shadowed with kohl. Her skin was ghostly pale and now and again a man tenderly touched her cheek, as though challenged to bring color to it. She invariably dressed in black, long gauzy skirts the color of night, and close-fitting turtleneck shirts. A heavy pendant of twisted silver dangled from a leather thong between her breasts, which, I had noticed, were very large for a woman who was so slender. As my own body changed, I carefully and competitively appraised the figures of other women. Franchesca's beautiful hands flew through the air as she spoke. Her fingers were very long and her fingernails were sculpted to long points and painted with silver. I wondered that they did not break when she worked at her wheel or at the kiln. It was Karen who told me that she was almost certain the fingernails were false. Karen had a talent for discerning deception.

Each morning Karen, Peter, and I cycled to the civil-defense collection center. The first excitement had worn off and the work was tedious although we rotated positions. The coffee cans packed so tightly with congealed cooking grease emitted a sour smell that made me retch, and my arms ached after a stint at the metal bins.

"It's so much more fun to collect door to door for the Red Cross," Meg said. She wore a red-lined cape, a perky hat, and carried an important-looking receipt book.

But I loved the camaraderie at the collection center, the ambience of collegiality, the concern we all had for one another.

"Was there any mail from your father?" Mrs. Seubert, the middle-aged woman who had three sons serving in the South Pacific, asked me each morning.

On the day I told her that I had had a letter from him, there was a burst of applause. His letter was brief but loving. He could not say where he was stationed, only that he was working very hard. He was pleased that I was in Woodstock and that I was helping Dina.

Lola showed us a picture of Glen, a fair-haired young man, his good-natured face speckled with freckles, his grin wide and engaging.

"We ought to invite Lola home with us one night," I suggested to Karen.

"She wouldn't be comfortable," Karen said, but I understood that it was Karen who would be uncomfortable.

We — Karen, Peter, and I — were voyeurs at those long evenings of talk and song. We opened closed doors and wandered through workrooms and bedrooms. We peered into kitchen cabinets and checked the contents of medicine chests. Once I tasted Sal Hepatica and once Karen snapped a diaphragm case open and shut with rapid clicks.

We filled our plates with food and ate quickly, moving barefoot through smoke-filled rooms, keen eavesdroppers scavenging scraps of conversation. We were adolescent initiates, hovering at the edge of an adult world that both fascinated and repelled us.

"Are you having a good time, Sharon?" Edna and Lottie asked anxiously when they phoned.

"Yes. It's okay. Really," I assured them, knowing that it was more than okay. I was like a tourist who fortuitously stumbles onto a fantastic overview. From that secure and distant vantage I witnessed the patterns of other people's lives and wondered what course my own would take.

3

One sultry Saturday evening late in July we were all invited to a party at the Langsams' rambling hillside house. The Langsams owned an art gallery in New York and they had opened a smaller one in Woodstock. They were a pleasant couple, large-boned, ruddy-complected midwesterners whose money, it was rumored, came from a cereal dynasty, and indeed their fair hair was the color of grain. Belle Langsam wore flowing robes of brilliant colors and laughed too loudly at small witticisms. Robert, with sly malice, had said that her laughter camouflaged her ignorance.

"Belle is good-hearted," Dina had protested.

"Good-hearted does not an interesting dinner companion make," Robert had retorted and I thought his comment very clever.

Edward Langsam had been badly wounded when he served with the Eighth Army in North Africa. His left arm had been amputated, and although there was talk of a prosthesis the empty sleeve of his loose poplin shirt fluttered soundlessly when he moved. It seemed doubly cruel that such a tall, robust man should be crippled in such a way. We had not yet seen many wounded return from the war and Edward's maiming both fascinated and frightened me. I imagined my father suffering a similar wound and one night I dreamed that he walked up Lottie's Brooklyn street, but when I ran to greet him, my own arms joyously outstretched, I saw that both his sleeves were empty and he could not embrace me.

Dina had not wanted to go to the Langsams' but Robert had insisted.

"You work too hard. You'll have a good time. And they really want to see you."

"And they own an art gallery," she added dryly. Still, she put on her gold maternity dress and added a long green chiffon scarf. Her auburn hair was swept back in a soft knot at the nape of her neck and she wore the delicate jade earrings she had bought from Marcie Klein, the jewelry designer who lived in a small cottage down the road.

Her mood lightened as we walked to the Langsams'. Dina loved a party. As we neared the Langsams' house we heard the sound of a guitar.

Robert kissed the top of her head, and as though sensing the loneliness that suddenly swept over me, she reached out and pulled me close. "Sharon, walk with us. You look wonderful tonight. Really. Doesn't she look beautiful, Robert?"

I smiled shyly but I had dressed carefully, selecting a bright red peasant skirt and the white blouse with the elasticized neckline that I pulled down so that my shoulders were exposed. Those long afternoons at the pond had burnished my skin and brought out the copper tones in my dark hair. I had looked into the long mirror that night and thought that perhaps my beauty was beginning.

"She is beautiful," Robert said. "And that is why I want to paint her. Will you sit for me, Sharon? Can you fit me into your busy schedule?"

"Sure," I said, embarrassed and pleased. My heart beat rapidly as I imagined the long quiet hours in the studio, the softness of our voices as we talked, his intense concentration on my face, my body, the tentative, tender strokes of his brush. "I'd like that."

There was a rush of greetings when we entered. Karen and Peter were perched at the top of the stairwell and I threaded my way through the crowd and joined them.

"Ratatouille," Karen said. "And taboullah. A patriotic menu."

The rest of the country might be grimly meatless but the women of Woodstock were creative vegetarians. They cooked the lush regional produce into simmering vegetarian stews, fashioned croquettes out of black beans and zucchini, tossed salads with enormous zeal. Not for them the austere recipes issued by the government — meat loaf stretched with oatmeal, macaroni dotted with Spam, Protose steaks with boiled rice.

"I made up a plate for you." Peter held it out to me. His blond hair was still damp from the shower and there was a cut on his chin where he had nicked himself with the razor. I noticed for the first time the narrow cleft on his chin and how his lashes grew long and straight, almost brushing his angular cheekbones.

We ate and looked down at the crowd that swarmed through the living room as though we were theatergoers with choice seats in a secluded box. Nothing escaped our notice. We watched Franchesca steal glances at herself in the mirror opposite the couch which she shared with Edward Langsam. He was explaining something to her, gesticulating wildly with his arm, the empty sleeve limp across his chest, when Franchesca suddenly took a safety pin out of her purse and pinned the cuff of the sleeve to his shoulder. The gesture was boldly intimate. Edward Langsam smiled and touched her hand.

We listened as Dina discussed a teenage runaway she had taken to the bus station that morning.

"She came from Chicago and I arranged for an agency there to take responsibility for her. We just don't have the facilities. But the station was a nightmare. A unit shipped out of Newburgh today and their wives were following them, of course. Every bus was jammed — people standing in the aisles, babies crying. My own poor girl began crying and it was all I could do to keep from bursting into tears myself."

"This war is being fought on the backs of the working class,"

Robert said with practiced bitterness. He refilled his wineglass, swirled the crimson liquid.

"That's hardly fair, Robert. Roosevelt's doing what he can on the home front. But he has to concentrate on the war itself, on the theaters of operation," Teddy Bassen said in his patient psychiatrist's voice.

"War. The word itself is ugly, barbaric. We don't believe in war." Robert spat the words out with ideological certainty.

Dina placed a restraining hand on Robert's shoulder but I admired his courage. I too thought that war was barbaric and yet I knew that this was a war we had to fight. It confused me that I could agree with two different points of view.

"And what would happen if they gave a war and no one came? If we just declined the invitation to fight?" Robert asked, flashing his charming boyish smile.

"If it was this war, the world as we know it would come to an end," Teddy replied firmly. "If we hadn't gotten into the war, Hitler would have won in Europe and Nazism would cross the ocean. You'd have concentration camps in this country. Death camps, Robert. We're fighting a nation that rounds up Jews, that drops V1 bombs on civilian populations. And the Japanese are a whole other story."

And then, thankfully, the exchange ended because someone turned the radio on and we listened to Edward R. Murrow reporting from London.

They passed cigarettes from hand to hand, striking matches so rapidly that the room was saturated with the acrid smell of spent flint. They inhaled deeply and exhaled wearily, because the tobacco could not ease their anxiety, because the news, even when it was good, was bad. Murrow had been on a bombing run. He had been on a plane on which the navigator got hit and he had seen the man's skull come apart, exposing the spongy texture of his brain.

Dina closed her eyes. Edward Langsam left the room. I gagged and Peter put his hand on my arm, just as Dina had placed her hand on Robert's shoulder. Was that the secret language between men and women, I wondered. Was that how they comforted and cautioned each other? I shrugged Peter's hand off. I wanted neither comfort nor caution.

"Look," Karen whispered.

Franchesca was following Edward Langsam from the room.

Murrow reported on the bomb plot against Hitler. It was rumored in London that Rommel, who had organized it, had committed suicide. There was a small burst of applause. Belle switched the radio off and a guest with an accordion began to play. A wild polka. They snuffed their cigarettes out and sprang to their feet. They danced with frenetic energy, twirling and switching partners. They celebrated because Hitler had almost died. There was dissent in the ranks of the enemy. The war was speeding to an end. And Peter, Karen, and I, like the appreciative audience that we were, clapped our hands in rhythm.

Edward and Franchesca slipped in through the French doors. Karen stared at them knowingly.

"I'm bored," she said harshly. "Come on."

We followed her upstairs and into the master bedroom. She locked the door. It was a large and luxurious room, the pale gray carpet soft and thick beneath our feet. The huge double bed was unmade. Giggling, we sat amid the tangled sheets. Karen brought us Belle's jewelry box, and like small children playing with unfamiliar toys, we spread the necklaces and brooches across a pillow, dangled lengths of beads. Peter sprayed us with Belle's perfume and we smeared Edward's after-shave lotion across his cheeks. I rubbed it into the razor cut and when he winced I kissed him lightly.

Someone turned the handle of the door, knocked.

"Sorry, the bathroom is in use. Out in a minute," Karen called out sweetly and I flushed the toilet in the adjoining bathroom.

We laughed nervously, delighted by our own daring, our meaningless malice. We forgave ourselves. We were only apprentices, after all, eager to learn the secrets of the adult world which would be ours one day. We cast a brief look at their bedside reading, Belle's piles of the *Saturday Evening Post* and *Art News*, Edward's copy of *One World*. I thought of them reading in bed, side by side, and I wondered how Edward balanced the book and turned the pages with only one arm. Hysteria welled within me and I was glad when Karen motioned us to leave. We sauntered out one at a time and Peter was careful to turn the light off.

Downstairs the party had split off into two groups. One was clustered about the bearded, red-cheeked guitarist who sang love ballads and the requisite songs of peace and justice. Across the room, the inevitable discussion of the war was in progress.

"It's only a matter of time," Teddy said authoritatively. "When Patton is finished in France the Third Army is going to head east and give Stalin some muscle."

"You must be joking. The United States and Britain won't lift a finger for the Soviet Union," Robert said. "Roosevelt and Churchill would like nothing better than to see Hitler finish off Joe Stalin."

"That's ridiculous," Teddy objected. "The Allies are in a united effort against Hitler. Don't be paranoid, Robert."

"Why not? Even paranoids have enemies. Especially Jewish paranoids." Robert laughed harshly.

There was silence in the room then. No one wanted to talk about what was happening to the Jews in Europe. The rumors and dark imaginings had been exposed as facts, and my grandparents wept when they listened to the news. I looked at my watch. It was ten o'clock on a Saturday night. My uncle Julius and his *landsmannschaft* friends would be gathered around the dining room table in Brooklyn, drinking tea and sorting through their piles of lists, their checkbooks open, murmuring the terrible names: Auschwitz. Majdanek. Belsen. Treblinka. My grandparents trembled at the mention of Treblinka, which was only thirty kilometers from their village in Poland.

Dina stood up and yawned languidly.

"I think it's time for this pregnant lady to go home." She knotted the green chiffon scarf.

"Dina, you're missing an earring." Marcie Klein, who had designed the small jade scarabs, pointed and Dina's finger flew to her naked earlobe.

"I must have dropped it when I went out before," she said. "I'll find it. I was only on the patio."

"I'll go with you, Dina," I volunteered and together we made our way into the fragrant darkness.

"We should have brought a flashlight," I said.

"I have matches." She fumbled in the pocket of her golden tunic, found a book of matches, and lit three of them to form a small torch.

"There it is," she said and I stooped to pick it up. As I rose to my feet I saw a couple standing at the edge of the lawn, their faces turned to each other. The man drew the woman close and kissed her on the lips. I could not discern their faces but the woman's large silver pendant glittered in the darkness and I knew that it was Franchesca who stood there. The man moved. The pinned-up empty sleeve fluttered in the darkness like the useless wing of a wounded bird.

Dina too was staring at them.

"Silly Franchesca," she said softly. "She doesn't mean anything, you know, Sharon. She's lonely. She's just playing."

"Playing?" The word jarred and I resisted it. "It's not a good game," I said, with the arrogant certainty of the adolescent.

"No," Dina agreed sadly. "It isn't."

Neither she nor I mentioned seeing Edward and Franchesca to Robert as we walked home. Dina rested her head on her husband's shoulder and spoke to him with an almost apologetic tenderness. It occurred to me that she had been almost relieved to see Franchesca with Edward and I pondered the reason for that relief as I lay awake in my narrow bed and listened to their murmuring voices.

On Monday I began posing for Robert. I thought he had forgotten about it but he reminded me at breakfast that I had said I would be willing.

"But Sharon enjoys the afternoons at the pond," Dina said.

For once, she had slept late and was having breakfast with us. She was taking the day off because Lottie and Edna were spending the day in Woodstock. Leon, who had arranged to buy a record collection from an estate sale in a neighboring village, was driving them. The arrangement had been made during one of their frequent phone calls, sandwiched between Dina's repeated assurances that she felt well and that the baby was active, and her questions about her parents' health. At the end of each conversation she spoke to her mother in Yiddish and her fluency always surprised me. Dina, who had been born after it was assumed that my grandmother would have no other children, was at least ten years younger than Edna, and Lottie was of another generation. I thought of Yiddish as the language of the elderly and I was jolted when Dina spoke it.

"She can go to the pond and pose for me when she gets home," Robert said. "Would you mind leaving the pond a little earlier, Sharon?"

"No, I wouldn't mind at all." Heat flooded my face and I turned away because the rush of color to my cheeks embarrassed me.

"I'll expect you at four then," Robert said with professional formality.

"Sure." I wanted to ask him what I should wear but just then Leon's car drove up and I ran my fingers through my hair and sat up straighter, readying myself for my aunts' kisses and questions, for the bombardment of their concern and affection. Robert flashed me a conspiratorial grin.

"The very first thing Lottie will say is that Dina looks tired," he predicted.

"And the first thing Aunt Edna will ask me is if I've made any friends," I countered.

The sisters burst into the house like swimmers soaring on the crest of their own urgent conversations. They bit each other's words off in midsentence, anticipated questions, bubbled forth with answers. "Yes, Mama and Papa were fine — oh the victory garden — such tomatoes — Julius — works so hard, terrible — Aaron — no word — the Pacific — rumors about Guam or Saipan — God knows — Heidi, yes, learning a lot — well, you know Bernie and his *mishagass* — Beth—we didn't tell you about Beth — a boyfriend — a soldier — yes Jewish, of course Jewish . . ." Names sputtered forth in staccato crossfire; in three minutes they would communicate weeks of news. I remembered how my mother would laugh and wave them to silence, saying, "Softer. Slower."

I wondered what would happen if I waved my own hand now and said, in her quiet voice, the voice that I conjured up in the darkness of the night when I called upon my dead mother to assure me that my father would not die, "Softer, slower." They would be startled, I knew, and surely they would weep. Their sorrow for their sister Miriam, so newly lost to them, was still unmitigated but they were kind women and would not reveal their pain to her daughter. Instead they hugged me, showed me the present they had brought me — a Tommie pajama set with a plaid housecoat to match. They studied my face, my form. They were skilled maternal detectives — they could detect misery in a pimple, unhappiness in a posture. When they had looked at me for too long I turned away. I knew they were searching for their sister, my mother, in my eyes, in the tilt of my chin.

"Tell me, Sharon," Edna asked, "have you made any friends?"

I looked at Robert and we both struggled to contain our laughter.

"I have two really good friends — Karen and Peter — a brother and sister," I said. "We work together at the civil-defense collection center."

"Civil defense. Very important," Edna said. "Leon is an air-raid warden now."

"You're kidding," Robert said.

He looked at short, stocky Leon, with his unruly thick dark hair and soft large dark eyes.

"Yup. I'm an air-raid warden," Leon said cheerfully. "You should see. I have a helmet, an arm band, a big searchlight. I scare little old ladies to death because I do airplane spotting from the roof of the A & P on Ocean Avenue."

"Sure. Very necessary. The Germans are too worried about losing their asses in France and marching on Warsaw to even think about bombing Brooklyn," Robert said contemptuously.

"Probably," Leon agreed. "But four of us meet on the roof of the A & P. Moshe Rosenbaum plays the cello. Frank diNappoli on the viola and me and Abe Kass with violins. One of us mans the searchlight and the binoculars, and the others play."

"Real guardians of the republic," Robert said. Edna bit her lip angrily, and noisily began to clear the table. "So what do you play?"

"What should we play while we try to spot German aircraft? We play Bach and Beethoven, Mahler and Schubert." Leon laughed as though imagining a German fighter-bomber flying too low over Ocean Avenue and hearing the music of his homeland. "Okay, now I have to go and find this place near Annandale and see what they have for sale. The estate agent said they have some old Carusos and when this war is over there'll be a market for opera. After every war people listen to opera."

"Don't pay too much, Leon," Edna said warningly. "And when you make the check out don't forget to enter it in the book. And ask them if you can postdate the check by two days — that way we can still get the next period interest."

"Yes. Sure. Why not?" Leon kissed his wife, who sighed with resignation. He would, of course, overpay. He would forget to enter the amount of the check in the checkbook. And he would never ask if he could postdate the check. He was her *luftmentsch,* her dreamer, and she trembled to think of what would happen to him without her.

He slammed the screen door behind him and waved jauntily to Karen and Peter, who rode up on their bikes just then.

"My friends are here," I said and kissed my aunts good-bye.

As we rode away, I glanced back and saw Edna and Lottie staring out the window after us. I lifted my hand and waved. From that distance I might look like Miriam, my mother.

I left the pond early that afternoon although a group of kids from the collection center, including Lola, had joined us.

"It's a drag," I told Karen. "I don't know why he wants to paint me. But I couldn't say no."

"I'd love it if Robert would do my portrait. But my face isn't interesting enough. It's not like yours, Sharon," Karen said.

I touched my cheeks, my lips, my too-thick eyebrows and my

too-pointed chin, as though to test the truth of her words. I thought Karen, with her evenly spaced features and fair silken hair, beautiful, and I benignly envied her. She would have made cheerleader; the pretty girls in their bulky white sweaters would have given her at least a 2 if not a 1. She would not have had to lie to her dying mother.

"Oh, he just needs someone to model for him," I said.

"No. He wanted to paint you. If I were an artist, I'd paint you," Peter whispered into my ear.

I concentrated on lacing up my saddle oxfords and pretended not to hear him.

Robert was in the kitchen drinking coffee when I arrived. The table was littered with mugs and plates, the residue of the morning's breakfast.

"I volunteered to clean up," he said. "Your aunts implied that Dina is working too hard, that I don't do enough to help her, so I thought I would prove them wrong. But then I got caught up in the background detail of my portrait of Violanda and didn't have time."

"Oh, you know how they are," I said dismissively and I began to clear the table.

It was true, I acknowledged, as I plunged the dishes into hot soapy water, that I often arrived home to find the table still cluttered with breakfast dishes. Once I had to throw away margarine that had melted and congealed in the dish and often the room was sour with the smell of spoiled milk, left all day on the counter. But when Robert was absorbed in his work, he would think of nothing else. It was unfair to expect him to worry about household chores.

"Just leave them," Robert said. "Let's get to work. You came home to model, not to wash dishes."

"Should I wear anything special?" I asked.

"No. I want to paint you as a home-front teenager — blue jeans and a man's shirt, bobby socks and saddle shoes — just what you're wearing."

I was disappointed. I had just begun to accept Karen's judgment that he wanted to paint me for my interesting face or perhaps for what I hoped was the beginning of my beauty ("If I were an artist, I'd paint you," Peter had whispered into my ear). I had wanted to wear my white peasant blouse and the flowered ballerina skirt that fanned out about my knees. We all wore short skirts that summer. It was patriotic. Fabric was needed for uniforms, for bed sheets and bandages.

I did, however, brush my hair vigorously to subdue its wild curl and coax out its amber highlights. I smiled at myself in the long mirror and applied Pond's Honey to my lips.

Robert waited for me in the studio, which, even in the late afternoon, was flooded with brilliant sunlight.

"Here," he said and pointed to the tall stool where I had watched Violanda and Jennifer, the girls from town who modeled for him, pose. I sat down, feeling awkward and self-conscious.

"No. Not like that." He moved swiftly toward me. "Like this," he said and arranged my body as though he had dominion over it. He moved my legs so that the left one was poised on the rim of the stool and the right one was crossed over it. He played with my arms, now resting one hand on my lap and then, dissatisfied, allowing them to hang loosely at my sides. And I submitted to his touch with a subdued excitement that I dared not let him see. My own submission pleased me; at his will my legs bent and my arms curved. At last he settled on a pose in which my clasped hands encircled my lifted knee and my head was tilted toward the light. Tenderly, he touched my face, adjusted the angle of my chin. His fingers were soft against my skin and smelled of soap and paint.

"Can you hold that position? It's not uncomfortable?" he asked.

"No, not at all," I said bravely although already my back ached with tension and my neck was stiff with effort. The discomfort balanced the excitement and I welcomed it.

He went to the easel where a large drawing pad was already in place. I was familiar with his technique. He would make a pencil sketch first, or even several sketches, and only when he was satisfied with those would he begin work on the canvas.

He worked quickly that first day.

"When did Lottie and Edna leave?" I asked.

"Leon picked them up about an hour ago. Dina took them shopping in town and then out to lunch. I was working on Violanda's portrait and then I had to crate my paintings." He had been invited to exhibit at a Madison Avenue gallery and although he protested that he did not paint to please wealthy snobs, it was clear that the invitation gratified him.

"Please don't move, Sharon. Don't talk. It disrupts."

"Sorry."

I fell silent, disappointed. I had heard him talk softly to Violanda and Jennifer as he worked and I had anticipated conversations threaded with sharing. But I did not protest. I sat absolutely still, and when he flipped the page and indicated that he was finished I did not ask to see the drawing.

"Same time tomorrow." He did not ask a question but rather made a statement.

"All right." I slipped off the stool and walked out of the studio, my back and neck stiff.

He did not thank me but that night at dinner he told Dina that I had been a great model.

"She's really patient," he said and smiled at me. "And her face has great angles."

"Ah," Dina replied. "Angles. I think I've forgotten what an angle is. I am familiar only with great curves. Huge curves. Monstrous curves. Like this one." She patted the swell of her abdomen, and later smiled wistfully when I came downstairs after dinner wearing my red pedal pushers and a white shirt.

Karen, Peter, and I were going to the Teentown nightclub in the basement of the Unitarian church on Main Street. Teen centers had opened everywhere because gasoline rationing restricted activities. The synagogue in nearby Kingston hosted a Coke bar and the regional high school opened its gym on Saturday nights, hung red, white, and blue crepe paper streamers from the basketball hoops, and called itself "the Rec."

"Have fun," Dina called after us and we waved and adjusted the night lamps on our bicycles.

The church was brightly lit. We paid the twenty-five-cent

admission fee, dropping our quarters into the jar next to the photograph of Bob Hope and a message thanking us for our patriotism. The money would be donated to the USO.

I wondered if my father ever went into a USO club. Perhaps he sat alone at a table nursing a beer and staring at a snapshot of my mother, grief glinting in his eyes. It was an unlikely image. My serious father did not drink beer. He was a very private person and would never display his sorrow in public. Still, such thoughts comforted me. It was two years since I had last seen my father and there were times when I no longer believed in his existence.

The church basement was crowded. The flashing lights of the huge jukebox shot forth rays of magenta, gold, and chartreuse, and the dancers twirled, laughing at the radiance that flashed across their faces. Bob grabbed Karen's hand and swung her about in a fast-paced lindy. When he held her in a dramatic dip, her head almost touching the floor, the other dancers circled about them and applauded.

They jitterbugged to big-band music, gyrating to the rhythms of Harry James and Benny Goodman, Tommy Dorsey and Glenn Miller. Occasionally, soldiers in dress uniforms would edge their way in and the prettiest girls gravitated toward them. The soldiers were only a few years older than us — their faces were sometimes blotched with acne and they blushed when they danced. When we next gathered to feed coins into the jukebox and tap our feet, they might be in a trench in Europe, a swamp in Asia. The pretty girls were aware of that as they walked with them through the soft summer evening and kissed them with sweet tenderness in the graveyard of the Unitarian church.

Peter did not dance because of his limp and I was happy to sit with him at the makeshift bar. We sipped cherry Cokes through paper straws that grew flat between our lips. Karen remained on the dance floor, her long hair sweeping across her face, her body writhing as she passed from partner to partner.

"Why so serious?" Karen joined us, her face flushed, her eyes bright. The jukebox was playing "They're Either Too Young or Too Old" and she sang along with Jo Stafford. " 'They're either too shy or too bold.' "

"Oh, we're just talking," I replied. "I don't feel like dancing.
I'm tired from posing for Robert."

"How was it?" Karen asked.

"Hard," I replied honestly. "I have to stay in this one position.
And a little boring."

"Isn't it creepy being all alone with him in the studio? Just you
and him. Doesn't it make you nervous?" Karen giggled and I
remembered that she had underlined all the sex scenes in the copy
of *A Tree Grows in Brooklyn* she had lent to me. She was imma-
ture, I decided, and I relished the word.

"Karen, Robert's my uncle," I retorted indignantly.

My indignation was directed as much at myself as it was at
Karen. It was precisely because Robert was married to Dina that I
felt safe when I quivered at the softness of his touch against my
skin, and experienced a nervous thrill when his eyes studied my face
and body so carefully. Our familial relationship protected me. My
fantasies would not become reality.

"Oh, I was just kidding. Don't get mad."

"I'm not mad. I'm tired and I want to go home."

But of course everyone was ready to leave by then. The church
closed Teentown at ten on weeknights. The conservation of electricity was part of the war effort. We walked home in a crowd,
except for blond Meg, who disappeared in the opposite direction
walking hand in hand with a tall young soldier whom we had never
seen before and would never see again.

There were two letters from my father that week. He wrote
carefully, cryptically, but it was clear that he was no longer in
England. One sentence read: "It is so noisy here that it is difficult for
me to collect my thoughts." I decided that he was somewhere in
Normandy and the noise came from the intense bombardment
launched by General Bradley.

I bought a map of France and hung it in my bedroom next to
the long mirror. I studied my reflection and concentrated on the
names of the villages through which my father might be passing.
"Dieppe," I said aloud. "Rouen. Beauvais." I imagined him kneeling beside wounded soldiers, shouting commands to the medics,
giving directions to his nurses.

My letters to him were determinedly cheerful. I wrote him of my work at the collection center, the afternoons at the pond. I did not tell him that Robert was painting my portrait, and my own reticence puzzled me.

The sessions with Robert were pleasant. He talked easily once the pencil sketches were completed and he had begun work on the canvas. I asked him about my father, about his memories of my parents.

"I always liked Richard. I was sorry we didn't get to know each other better but your family was living in Boston when Dina and I met. The first time I ever saw you was at our wedding."

"I remember. I wore a pink silk dress and a pink headband. My mother's dress was pink also."

"Yes. Miriam looked beautiful that day." Unlike the rest of the family, Robert spoke comfortably about my mother. He did not lower his voice mournfully when he mentioned her name or recalled experiences they had shared. We played gin rummy one evening and when I won and exulted over my victory, he remarked wryly, "Miriam loved playing gin, Sharon, and she was just like you — she loved to win."

Dina had shot him a warning glance but I was grateful to him. His words brought my mother to life and briefly the memory of a laughing young woman rejoicing over a winning hand of gin replaced the mental image of a wasted and blanched invalid lying in a hospital bed.

"She was beautiful, wasn't she?" I asked now.

"Don't change position." He waved his brush in warning. "Hold your head perfectly still. I'm working on your eyes now. You have fantastic brows. What did you ask me? Oh — yes, she was beautiful. A different look than Dina's — or yours. Miriam had great serenity. I thought that I could never paint her because I could never capture the peace in her expression."

"But you did draw her."

"When she was dying. That was different."

Of course it had been different. Her serenity had been vanquished then by the agony of her illness. I looked at him bitterly and I realized that Robert could be unintentionally cruel. I did not understand then the artist's egotism — the greed that defied conventional boundaries and allowed him to sketch a dying woman because he needed her pain upon his pad.

"Are you and your father close?" he asked because he had sensed my mood and wanted to change the subject.

"I think so. And what about you? Are you and your father close?" I asked daringly.

"No." His answer was clipped, hard.

"What are they like, your parents?" I was persistent.

And he told me, sliding the brush across his palette, blending his paints with angry thrusts and then leaning forward to study the canvas, moving his brush with all the delicacy of a surgeon wielding a scalpel, each stroke exact and decisive.

He had grown up in a cavernous apartment on Park Avenue. His father was a stockbroker who spent long hours downtown, leaving before his son awakened in the morning and arriving home when he was already asleep. His mother spent much of her life shopping, talking on the phone, and traveling. When he thought of her he imagined a woman with blond marcelled hair, wearing a fur stole over her dark suit and speaking rapidly, surrounded by suitcases and boxes. When she kissed him good-bye, her lips never touched his face. He was cared for by a succession of nursemaids, all of whom smelled of carbolic soap, while his mother sprayed herself with the scent of wild orchids.

One of his nursemaids took him to visit her family in a tenement not far from the river. He still remembered the dimly lit, narrow rooms of the railroad flat, rank with the stink of river sewage and the sweat of too many people huddled together. He had not forgotten the pale barefoot girl his own age who touched his velvet jacket with trembling fingers. When they returned to the Park Avenue apartment, he asked the nursemaid why her family could not come and live with them since they had so many rooms and so much food and clothing. She had laughed at him, bitterly, harshly.

"I guess I became a Communist that afternoon," he told me cheerfully.

His father beamed when Robert was accepted at Yale. He had

been right to change his name from Weiss to White. The admissions officer had probably not even suspected that Robert was Jewish. He congratulated himself and his son in a single breath, but he did not embrace him. Even at his commencement, his mother had only touched her finger to her own lips and then his cheek.

"She has a fear of intimacy," Robert said. His words echoed the after-dinner conversations when the new Freudian idioms were uttered with authority and intensity.

I pitied Robert that afternoon, because he had grown up amid wealth and coldness. I pitied him because his name had been changed and he did not know who he was, and because his parents disapproved of his vocation. They had not sent him to Yale so that he might become a painter. Still, they underwrote his life. They had bought him the Woodstock house, the yellow Nash, and had arranged for the interest of a generous trust to be paid to him. Their money embarrassed him. It was tainted, earned through the capitalist exploitation of families like the one he had visited in the railroad flat near the river. But he was an artist, and because artists had to make sacrifices, he used it. His parents did not approve of Dina, whom he had met at a fund-raising concert. She had sat beside him and wept when Paul Robeson sang "There's a man goin' round takin' names." He had fallen in love with her tears, he told me gravely. But to his parents, Dina was a social worker from an immigrant family. Grudgingly, his father had pressed my grandfather's hand at the wedding. His mother had smiled politely and touched her manicured fingers to the blaze of Dina's hair. She never forgot their birthdays or their anniversary but neither she nor his father had ever visited Woodstock or viewed his paintings.

"So I guess you could say we were never close, Sharon," he said finally. He wiped his brush across his sleeve. "We're through for today."

I slid off the stool and went up to him, stood on tiptoe, and kissed him on the cheek.

"I'm sorry," I said, and he looked at me in surprise. He did not know that I was apologizing for my question, that I was expressing my sorrow for the sadness of his youth.

4

It was Belle Langsam's idea to establish a fund for the families of Woodstock servicemen.

"What sort of fund?" Franchesca asked languidly.

She leaned back in her deck chair and lifted her arms so that the loose sleeves of her pale green silk tunic fluttered in a mild August breeze. With her lacquered helmet of dark hair and her burnished leathery skin, she resembled a mysterious winged insect poised for flight.

We sat on her terrace. We had been invited for Sunday brunch, but in Woodstock fashion the meal had stretched out into the afternoon. It was pleasant to sit in the sunlight lazily talking and listening to music. Dina, wearing a bright blue cotton tent dress, reclined on a chaise longue and turned the pages of the *Saturday Evening Post*. Her ankles had swelled during the past week and her doctor had suggested that she stop working, but she was stubbornly resistant.

"My clients need me," she had told Lottie on the phone and then added irritably, "Oh, you wouldn't understand. How could you understand?" Minutes later, she had called Lottie back to apologize. That was the pattern of the sisters' relationship — anger, apology, and reconciliation. Each conversation was a verbal seesaw on which affection and irritation struggled for balance.

Peter, Karen, and I sat on the back steps at Franchesca's house, out of view but listening to their conversations as we passed the pages of the Sunday comics to each other. Peter handed me the section in which Terry fought fiercely grimacing Japanese commandos. He had given up pirates for the duration. I turned the page and followed Smilin' Jack's air force exploits and admired Daddy Warbucks's new uniform.

"He got to be a general awfully quickly," I whispered to Karen. My father, who after all headed a medical unit, was only a major.

It pleased us to think that the others were not aware of our presence. We were spies gathering clues about the adult world. Like clever Terry, we would enter it armed with knowledge clandestinely obtained. That morning we had patrolled Randy and Franchesca's second floor and discovered that although Randy was home for the weekend, his pajamas, his reading glasses, and the detective story which he was in the midst of reading were in the small spare room.

"They don't sleep together," Karen had concluded with satisfaction and she had tried on Franchesca's coral-colored robe while I applied the kohl eye shadow that gave Franchesca's bice-colored eyes such an elongated mysterious look.

We waited expectantly for Belle to explain her fund, for Franchesca to belittle it, for the others to align themselves on either side. Like my aunts' conversations, Woodstock exchanges followed a predictable pattern.

"A lot of families here are having a hard time," Belle said. "I thought it could be a sort of interest-free loan fund. People around here would be too proud to accept charity but they need ready cash and a loan would be something that they could live with. It's hard for a family to manage on a serviceman's check." She blushed and spoke with the embarrassment of a woman who has always

been wealthy; she reminded me of Robert's shame when he discussed his family's prosperity. "And then, of course, there are
going to be widows. There are already widows."

"And where there are widows, can orphans be far behind?"
Franchesca asked sardonically and there was an uncomfortable silence.

Karen and Peter moved closer to me but I did not lift my eyes
from the funny papers. I was not going to be an orphan. Franchesca was an idiot. I moistened my finger with saliva and wiped
away any traces of the kohl. Anything that had touched her skin
was tainted, poisonous.

"You might think occasionally before you speak," Randy
said dryly. Franchesca brought a clenched fist to her breast.

"Mea culpa. Mea maxima culpa," she intoned. "But a loan
fund means a fair amount of money. I presume you're not propos-
ing to underwrite it yourself, Belle?" Deftly she turned the conversation away from herself.

"I was thinking in terms of an art show and a craft sale. The
artists and sculptors from the colony and the people we know —
the potters and jewelry makers, the leather workers and
weavers — Marcie Klein and her group. Everyone would set up
tables and sell their stuff. And either the entire amount or a per-
centage could go into the fund. You know, it's sort of embarrass-
ing to pass the bake sales and the produce sales that locals run for
the Red Cross and the USO and to consider that we haven't done
anything at all," Belle said.

"I think it's a marvelous idea," Dina said. "I'd like to feel I
was doing something. This war goes on and on and I feel so help-
less, so useless."

"You're doing more than most of us." Robert rose and went
to sit at the edge of Dina's chaise, to slowly and rhythmically mas-
sage her distorted ankles.

Edward nodded and wiped the sweat from his face with his
empty sleeve.

The gesture filled me with a sudden hysteria, followed swiftly
by a wave of sadness. I understand both the hysteria and the sadness now, with hard-gained professional hindsight, but then they

bewildered and frightened me. Edward might have lost his arm in the war, I told myself fiercely, but my father would not lose his life. *I would not be orphaned.*

"Where would we have it?" Teddy asked.

"We can have it on our property," Sarah said decisively. "On ours and yours." She turned eagerly to Robert and Dina.

Their properties were adjacent, and together they encompassed several acres of grassy swale set back from the road. The ground was level and shaded by an enormous oak and a scattering of maple trees. It was an ideal location.

"That's fine," Dina said. "The tables can be set up on the lawns and the paintings can be displayed in the studio. That's all right, isn't it, Robert?" She deferred to him almost as an afterthought, in the familial tradition. The women made decisions but did not proceed without the approval of their husbands.

"Yes," he agreed. "Of course it's all right. I could exhibit the portraits of the children. A first showing. And I'll speak to the others at the colony about it. Maybe we could even lure some New York critics to come up."

"I'll make the contacts," Belle said. "It could be a wonderful angle for them. Artists doing their bit for the war effort, that sort of thing."

A new enthusiasm energized them. They talked rapidly and made plans. Even Franchesca was caught up in the excitement. She produced pads and pencils. We stole away as they began to make lists. There had to be committees for invitations, refreshments. Their excitement trailed after us, their voices not unlike the voices of children planning a party.

"It will be fun," I said as we cycled toward the pond.

"It will be interesting," Peter corrected me.

Preparations for the sale were absorbed into the routine of our days and evenings. Karen, Peter, and I talked about it at the civil-defense collection center. We obtained promises of tables, attendance, and even contributions. Mrs. Seubert would bake cookies. Our elderly nurse volunteered to make lemonade. She had a large quantity of ration stamps for sugar. Robert designed a poster which featured a canvas on an easel set in a flowering meadow, with the message JOIN WOODSTOCK ARTISTS AND CRAFTSMEN IN SUPPORT OF OUR SERVICEMEN. There had been much arguing over that legend. Robert had protested the use of the words *war effort.*

"It implies a belief in war," he claimed.

"If you don't believe in war, just turn the radio on." Teddy was impatient, angry.

"Will you come?" I asked Lola when I saw her looking at the poster.

"I can't afford to buy anything," she said but she was cheerful that day because she had received a letter from Glen. He sounded good, she said, but she wished she knew where he was.

"Make it up," I advised.

Each night I made up a new location for my father. I lay awake and imagined him in a field hospital in France, bent over a dying soldier, saving the wounded man with a daring act of surgery performed with a bayonet rather than a scalpel. Blood spurted across my father's uniform, pebbled his spectacles, but against all odds he saved the soldier's life.

"I did it for my daughter, Sharon," he told the admiring nurses who stood beside him. "She believes in me."

Another night I envisioned him at a hospital in Italy, tending to dark-eyed children. He lifted a small girl in his arms and told her that she resembled his beautiful daughter, his Sharon.

I shared these imaginings with Lola and she looked at me in surprise.

"I couldn't do that," she said. "Anyway, it's enough that he's okay. I have the letter."

Mrs. Seubert smiled at her.

"Mail is important," she said. Her own sons wrote to her regularly and she wrote to each of them every night although she admitted that she found it difficult to think of enough news to fill the V-letter forms.

I liked the grave-eyed woman who wore neatly ironed plaid housedresses to the center each day and who showed me a new method for balling the stockings. When I developed a small blister on my hand she noticed it and brought a salve to apply to it.

"Hold still," she said and I did, pleased to feel her fingers on my skin. Her touch signified her concern. My mother's hand too had been light. I closed my eyes as Mrs. Seubert worked the salve into my skin and I mourned my mother anew.

I told Robert about Mrs. Seubert and her three soldier sons when I posed for him that afternoon. Our sittings were going well. He worked rapidly, his brush dancing from palette to canvas, his gaze steady as his eye moved from my face, my body, to the work at hand. He wanted to finish the portrait in time for the show on Labor Day. It would round out his series on children.

"You are my American Teenager, Sharon," he said. "My home-front girl. Your Mrs. Seubert will be proud of you."

"Why should I care if she's proud of me?" I asked. It was hot and I was restless. It angered me that he did not understand what I was telling him and I wondered if I understood it myself. I wanted him to know that the middle-aged woman who worked beside me was the mother of three sons who had gone to war and that I welcomed her mothering because I was the daughter of a woman whose battle was done and who would never return. My thoughts were confused. I was still unprepared for the way in which the grief of loss amazed me, taking me by surprise when I thought I had vanquished it. *Mama,* I said to myself. *Mama.*

"Hold still."

He crossed the studio and approached me. I had moved my arm, released my fingers from their tight clasp. Impatiently, he corrected my pose. He had taken his shirt off as he often did on a hot afternoon and his body smelled of grass and sweat and paint. A streak of blue sliced his arm, quivered on the golden rise of his biceps.

"Why do you smell of grass?" I asked daringly.

"Because I mowed the lawn. Your head — you've got the angle wrong."

He bent his face close to me, his hand upon my hair.

I held my breath. I dared not breathe. An unfamiliar moisture slithered through my body and I feared that it had an odor, that Robert would smell it as I had smelled the scent of grass upon his skin. But he turned and went back to the easel. I relaxed and calmed myself. I was safe. He was my uncle, Dina's husband. I had worn a pink dress at his wedding.

"I know it's hot," he said apologetically. "But try to be patient. Only a few more sittings."

We finished early that day. He had promised to go over to Franchesca's to look at a new glaze she had developed.

"Robert, I want to apologize for being so cranky," I said and I kissed him on the cheek to demonstrate my courage and my gratitude.

"That's all right." He smiled and ran his fingers through my hair.

That night Dina phoned Lottie and asked her to come to Woodstock for Labor Day weekend.

"I'm asking Edna and Leon to come too. With Bernie. Heidi won't be back from Michigan yet. And Mama and Papa too. You can all stay at Fleishman's, the kosher hotel near Kingston. It will be a good change for everyone. The whole family together, except for Samuel and Dolly." Dolly lived the entire year for the last two weeks in August which she and Samuel spent at Grossinger's.

Dina was persuasive, her arguments steady and reasonable.

"It will help you keep your mind off Aaron and Beth. I hope I don't worry about my children the way you worry about those two." She smiled and touched her abdomen.

Then Dina talked so softly that I could not hear her from my bedroom. I knew that they were talking about me. Dina was reporting on my emotional temperature, telling Lottie that I seemed less tense, that my friends were wonderful young people, and that at last I seemed to be assimilating the loss. "Assimilating the loss" was a social-work school term and she used it often.

"Everyone's coming for Labor Day," she said when she hung up.

"Terrific." Robert's voice was flat. "Can you skip going to the pond tomorrow, Sharon? I want to start working on the portrait earlier. I have to nail and frame the other portraits and begin to figure out space for the other artists."

"Sure, I don't mind," I said and it was not until later that I realized Robert had not asked if I minded.

But although I did not go to the pond the next day, I did not go to the studio immediately after working at the collection center. Just as we were about to leave, the Western Union messenger rode up the pathway to the center. Lola clutched the package wrapped in brown paper and tied with string — her waitress uniform fresh from the laundry — close to her chest, as though it might afford her protection. Mrs. Seubert took my hand but I felt her own fingers flutter.

The messenger was an old man; his iron gray hair pushed its way out of his visored cap, his uniform jacket was unevenly buttoned, and his face was mottled with the effort of pedaling the bicycle with its balloon tires up and down the village hills. He was a familiar figure. We saw him all over town, his leather pouch slung over his shoulder, his expression sober. He was engaged in serious business. The yellow envelopes he carried to the front doors of quiet, tree-shaded houses contained important news, news that changed lives, altered destinies. Women fainted and men wept when they opened them. He had grown used to fetching glasses of water from neat kitchens and calling doctors from phones in unfamiliar rooms. He was a kind man who had lived in Woodstock all his life, but the war had turned him into the angel of death. We stood as still as statues and watched him rummage nervously through his pouch.

"I knew you'd be here," he said, and because he did not raise his head, we had no way of knowing to whom he spoke. "I didn't want you to be home alone when you got this."

The envelope was in his hand and he walked up to us, his arm extended.

"No," Lola said. "Oh, no." She slipped to the ground. Her body fell soundlessly. Her freckles were very bright against her chalk white skin. The brown paper wrapping ripped as she dropped the package and the newly laundered white uniform spread like a shroud across the rich red earth.

But the yellow envelope was not for her. It was for Mrs. Seubert, who held it in her trembling hand and stared at the three stars next to the address. We all knew that telegrams marked with three stars meant a death.

Karen knelt beside Lola and I stood close to Mrs. Seubert. She opened the envelope. She had cut herself on the jagged edge of a can that morning and the open scratch patterned the yellow envelope with a thin scarlet line of blood. She unfolded the telegram, read it, neatly refolded it, and replaced it in the envelope.

"It's Joey," she said. "My youngest. It's my baby."

"I'm sorry," the elderly Western Union messenger said. "Oh, Grace, I'm so sorry." He called her by name. They had known each other always. He put his hands on her shoulders and she stood there quietly, as though he were blessing her. Then the silver-haired nurse came forward. Together the two old people walked Mrs. Seubert to her car. We observed the slowness of their steps, the tenderness of their touch upon her arms, the gentleness of their murmuring voices. They were accomplished escorts to the grief-stricken and we watched them so that we might learn their secrets. We too would be called upon to behave like that through the passing years, as we comforted others and accepted their comfort in turn.

Karen brought Lola a glass of water and she looked at us and said, "It wasn't Glen. Glen is all right."

There was relief and triumph in her voice and guiltily, disloyally, we shared that relief, saw ourselves as victors. We all went into town together and ate lunch at the Woolworth's counter. Lola removed all her pictures of Glen from her wallet and passed them around. I looked down at the smiling soldier, and I wondered if Mrs. Seubert was passing pictures of Joey to those gathered about her in her living room.

"Poor Joey," I said.

"Poor Joey." Their voices were a chorus of sorrow.

I ordered another cherry Coke. I needed sweetness to neutralize the biliousness that had soured my mouth and throat the moment I saw the Western Union messenger. Like Lola, I too had been reprieved. The three-starred yellow envelope might have been addressed to me.

Slowly, very slowly, although I knew that Robert was waiting for me, I rode my bicycle home.

He was in the studio as I had known he would be and he called my name as I rode up.

"I'm ready for you, Sharon." Irritation rimmed his tone.

"I have to change," I shouted back.

But I did not simply change into the jeans and the white man's shirt, the bobby socks and saddle oxfords I wore for posing. I took a very long hot shower and scrubbed myself with the concentrated intensity of a visitor returned from a hospital who vigorously washes away all possibility of infection. I had been exposed to the virus of fear, to the dangerous game of death. I dressed and hurried to the studio, my face flushed, the ends of my long hair dampened. Robert looked at me quizzically as I assumed my pose, but said nothing.

He had the radio on and we did not speak as a newscaster described the thrust of Patton's Third Army.

"The general believes that France will be liberated within weeks," he said.

Within weeks. I turned the words over in my mind. My father could be coming home. *Within weeks.* It was possible. The Allies were on the offensive and soon a world of peace might be restored to us. *Within weeks.* As I sat on the stool, frozen in my pose, the words became a hypnotic mantra that blocked out the memory of Mrs. Seubert's telegram, the memory of her words and of her tears. *Within weeks.* I have learned through years of practice that my most desperate patients cling to the slightest expression of optimism. "It is hopeful," I might say cautiously, and throughout the day and into a delirium, my words would be repeated: *It is hopeful. It is hopeful. It is hopeful.*

"What do you think, Sharon?" Robert's voice broke through, arrested the whirling alliterative words. *Within weeks. Within weeks. Within weeks.*

"I'm sorry. What do I think about what?"

"Do you think Dewey has a chance against Roosevelt?"

The newscaster was discussing the political conventions. Names blared forth — Dewey, Wallace, Truman. Of course

Dewey could not win against FDR, our presidential saint. We listened to his Fireside Chats on the radio as though they were benedictions. His picture hung in my grandparents' dining room, on the eastern wall, and my grandfather faced it when he murmured his morning prayers.

I shrugged.

"I don't think so," I said and suddenly I began to cry. My shoulders shook in a paroxysm of sobs and my tears were hot upon my cheeks.

"Sharon."

Swiftly, he crossed the sun-spangled room, his face sober with worry. Gently, he helped me down from the stool. He took a paint-stained handkerchief from the pocket of his jeans, turned it until he found a clean spot, and wiped away my tears.

"What is it? What happened?"

"Oh, Robert." I pressed my head against his chest as Mrs. Seubert had pressed her head against the chest of the elderly messenger. I told him about the telegram.

"I thought it was my father," I said. "And I was so glad it was for her and not for me. Oh, I'm so bad."

"No, you're just human," he said. His hand rested on my hand, smoothed my hair, played with the still-damp tendrils. "Very human." His voice was husky, his face very close to mine.

"Oh, I'm so ashamed." I pressed closer to him, seeking the comfort of his embrace, wanting to be held.

"There's nothing to be ashamed of," he said and silenced me by pressing his lips against mine.

"No!" The protest exploded from my throat. My mouth opened and his tongue thrust its way in, as though to smother my scream. His penis swelled and throbbed against my thigh and I broke loose and ran from the studio.

"Stop!" he shouted. "Sharon, stop!"

But I ran desperately, breathlessly to the house and then up to my room. I slammed the door behind me, and for the first time I hooked the latch I had noticed but never used.

I lay on the narrow bed and allowed the waves of misery to sweep over me, to drown me in their relentless assault, until, at last, I slept. The brief, unsettled dreams of restless afternoon sleep came and went.

I sat beside my mother's bed and slowly I became so small that I could slip into her mouth when she opened it to rant against the pain. My father held a girl in his arms but although she wore my white peasant blouse and my red flowered skirt, she was not me. Her hair was blond and her blue eyes were like those of a china doll, inanimate and thus innocent.

A phone rang again and again. I wanted to answer it but my limbs were so heavy I could not move. And still it rang. There was a knock at the door. It was repeated. I stirred, writhed against the constraints of drowsiness. The knock persisted, grew louder.

"Sharon. Sharon. Open the door. Come downstairs. We must talk." His voice was at once imploring and imperious. I did not move.

"Please. Before Dina gets home."

Dina. What could I say to Dina? Nausea welled and I sat up to fight it, startled to find that my shirt was soaked with sweat but my eyes were dry.

"In a few minutes," I said. "Wait downstairs."

I heard his step on the stairs and then I rose from the bed and studied myself in the long mirror, the mirror that Dina had bought me. How kind she was, how good she had been to me. I stared hard at my reflection, surprised that my face was unchanged, that my eyes were not rimmed with red but stared back at me with a new calm. I changed my shirt and rolled up the cuffs of my socks, bemused that I should bother about such details.

I went to the bathroom and brushed my teeth. I clutched the tin of Dr. Lyons' Tooth Powder, shook the powder onto my palm, and rubbed the brush against it as my father had taught me. "Work very slowly," he had advised. I worked very slowly. Slowly, I scoured the taste of Robert's saliva from my mouth, my teeth. I even moved the brush across my lips, against my tongue. I washed my face with cold water, tied my hair back, and went downstairs.

He sat at the kitchen table, his shoulders sloped, his head down, like a penitent schoolboy. I slid into the chair opposite him. I felt, for the first time, the power of the victim.

"I'm sorry," he said. "Very sorry."

I said nothing.

"I should have known better but I thought — you seemed to be sending me messages."

"No," I said.

"My mistake. My very great mistake." I pitied him for the misery in his voice and I hated him for making me pity him.

"You're my uncle." My words were a simple statement. I had spoken them before. To Karen. "He's my uncle," I had said and she had understood that I meant "I trust him, he will protect me."

"You're a beautiful girl. I thought you were — I don't know — inviting me — teasing me. Kissing, touching."

My heart turned. Yes. I had kissed his cheek, in compassion, in commiseration. Yes. I had submitted to his touch, allowed him to handle my body as though it belonged to him — here an arm raised, there a leg lifted and dropped. I had delighted in that submission, welcomed it, known myself to be aroused, and surrendered to that arousal. Because he was family and family was haven. I had been stupid and I had been wrong.

"No," I said. "I wasn't inviting. I wasn't teasing."

"What will we do now?"

"I'll go back to Brooklyn. To Lottie and Julius, my grandparents," I said.

"How would we explain that?" How frightened he sounded. His fear triggered my own.

"I don't know." Anger replaced fear. I was too young to have such answers. I relied on others for my answers. It was unfair of him to thrust such decisions upon me.

"Stay," he said. "Please. You don't have to finish posing. I'll finish the portrait on my own. And I will never touch you again. Believe that."

"I don't know," I said again.

"Think of what it would do to your aunt Dina if she found out. And it was just a moment, a weak moment. A mistake." He repeated the word as though it could absolve him. "A terrible mistake."

"I wanted . . ." The words froze on my tongue.

"What did you want?" He looked at me, my handsome uncle Robert, the boy-man whose paintbrush was a magic wand, who pitied the poor and sped up mountain roads in his yellow convertible.

"I don't know."

I could not tell him that I wanted him to be father and friend to me, that I yearned for his tenderness, his understanding, and yes, his forbearance. He had been my phantom lover but he had betrayed me by asserting his corporeality; he had trespassed and violated my dream.

"You'll stay?" he said pleadingly.

"I'll stay. But now I'm going over to the Bassens'. I'll have dinner there."

"All right. And Sharon. I'm sorry. Truly sorry."

He buried his head in his hands but I refused to pity him. I left the house, closing the screen door softly behind me.

5

We managed somehow to get through the next few weeks. I tried hard to persuade myself that nothing terrible had happened. "A moment of weakness," he had said (a weakness that I had provoked), and I determined to take him at his word. I fought back shame at the memory of my careless touch, my lighthearted kiss on his cheek. I practiced forgiving him. I smiled and thought of kind things to say. His gratitude for these concessions, expressed in wistful smiles and appreciative glances, gave me a strange thrill. I mentioned a book I wanted to read and he went to the library and took it out. One night I had a craving for chocolate ice cream and he drove into town and bought a pint. I exulted in my power over him and reproved myself for that exultation. Dina, caught up in her work, did not notice any tension between Robert and me. Instead, she was pleased by what she discerned to be a new closeness.

"The wonderful thing about having Sharon here this summer is that she has really gotten to know Robert," she said to Edna during one of their long phone conversations. "It's been good for her. Robert is sort of a substitute for Richard — a father figure, I suppose."

Listening from my room, I trembled with outrage. Robert could never substitute for my father. No one could. But especially not Dina's husband, whom I now perceived to be a cripple of a kind, a man who could not fight weakness and was thus as disabled as Edward Langsam, whose empty sleeve dangled at his side.

Excitement mounted as the sale drew near. Robert finished my portrait and I went to see it with Karen and Peter. It was very good, I acknowledged. In my dungarees and white man's shirt, my hands tightly clasped, my pale eyes searching and my mouth unsmiling, I typified my generation; I was an androgynous adolescent girl waiting for the war to be over. The tension of my expression contrasted dramatically with the innocence and joy in the faces of the children he had painted — they were too young to understand the pain and loss of war.

"It's wonderful," Peter said. "I wish I could afford to buy it."

I looked at him in surprise but his gaze was still riveted to the portrait.

"I'm not sure it's for sale," Robert replied casually and his words frightened me. I wanted him to sell my portrait. I did not want him to keep it in his studio or in his house where it would give him dominion of a kind over me.

The studio was cleared of the paraphernalia of painting. A crew of volunteers whitewashed the walls and cleaned the skylight's huge windows, transforming the huge area into a gallery.

The weavers erected a tent on the lawn, a gay enclosure of green-and-white-striped canvas, and within it they set up long tables on which they spread their brightly threaded purses, their tablecloths and place mats, their bolts of batik and swatches of fabric in the intricate subtle weaves of Guatemala and Andalusia. One of them crowned my dark hair with a shawl woven of different threads of white wool — eggshell and alabaster, ivory and oyster — and there was a brief silence as they looked at me.

"You have such a wonderful distinct look," the weaver said at last and I removed the shawl and folded it carefully. I did not want to have a "distinct" look. I wanted to be like Meg and Melanie, pert blond girls who resembled the models whose smiling faces filled the pages of my *Seventeen* magazine, girls who would always be remembered for their careless gaiety, not for their dark and brooding sadness.

The silversmiths and potters, the metalworkers who pounded copper and brass into pins and bracelets, the ceramicists whose works shimmered with brilliant glazes — each group occupied an island of grass and they arranged the long tables on which they would spread their work. A coppersmith dangled bracelets and necklaces from the low-hanging branches of an apple tree and when a gentle wind blew they swayed and chimed softly.

My family arrived late on Friday afternoon — Lottie, Julius, and my grandparents in Julius's gray Studebaker, and Edna, Leon, Bernie, and a bearded stranger in Leon's wood-paneled station wagon. My grandparents looked old and frail, the lines of grief and age etched into their life-worn skin. A black straw hat fringed with small cherries perched on my grandmother's white hair and although the day was warm, she wore a long black cotton coat over her blue-and-white-patterned dress.

My grandfather wore his black suit, and as always, his shoes were highly polished, his shirt snow white, a match for his thick hair and carefully shaped Vandyke beard. He did not remove his black fedora as he stared at the displays through his very thick glasses.

"When you come home, you'll help me with the victory garden, Shaindel," he said and I nodded vigorously. Only my mother, my grandmother, and my grandfather had ever called me by my Yiddish name, and now my mother was dead. When my grandparents died that name would be forever lost to me. It troubled me that I should think of their deaths as they stood beside me on the sun-drenched lawn but such thoughts were my companions that summer.

"How are the tomatoes?" I asked.

"Such tomatoes." He shook his head proudly and I squeezed his hand.

Edna kissed me, her sharp eyes scanning my face, my form, a maternal drill sergeant making an inspection.

"You look good, Sharon," she said approvingly and introduced me to the tall, bearded man whose thick jet black hair, shot through with a single silver arrow, contrasted with his parchment pale skin. His avian features were expressionless but his blue eyes were electric; they registered the busy scene, the faces, the ambience of energy and excitement.

He was Nachum Adler, a world-famous artist whose work was on exhibit at the Museum of Modern Art, at the Tate Gallery, at the Venetian Guggenheim collection. Robert and his friends shook hands with him respectfully and escorted him to the studio to view their own work. He had been interned in a concentration camp called Terezin, Edna told us. "I went to Washington twice to deliver letters and petitions to senators. We had a mountain of affidavits. But we did it. We got him out."

"What about his family?" Dina asked.

"His wife and daughter were killed." Her voice was flat but her eyes were closed.

Lottie and Dina glanced nervously at their parents. They wanted to protect the elderly couple from their own dark imaginings, to avoid the questions to which there were no answers.

"This is so exciting. This is wonderful," Edna said. "Heidi is sorry she had to miss it but she's having such a great time in Michigan — she just didn't want to leave early. And this weekend is the piano competition. She didn't want to miss that. You can't blame her."

"No," I replied. "Of course not."

I did not tell my aunt that I had received several letters from Heidi that summer; sad, wistful ramblings in Heidi's perfect Palmer penmanship, for which she had won one of her many academic awards. She wrote that she hated practicing while the sun burned so brightly, that there did not seem to be any point in her working so hard because she would never be that good. "Of course my mother won't believe that. It seems crazy to be practicing scales while people are being killed," she wrote, and then, remembering my father, she swiftly added that she just knew he was all right. "He has to be." The intimacy of Heidi's letters startled me. We had never been close. It was years before I learned that distance often grants the license for confidence.

Nachum Adler walked toward us, squinting against the assault of the sunlight.

"This is a wonderful thing you are doing here," he said to Dina.

"Oh, I have very little to do with it," she protested. "I'm just a social worker. My husband is the artist — the creative member of the family." She thrust her hands into the deep pockets of the rust-colored maternity dress that almost exactly matched her hair.

"I would say that you are being creative enough," he replied and for a fraction of a moment, he rested his hand on the rise of her pregnancy.

Her eyes met his and sadness and understanding flickered between them. She understood his need to touch her, to feel the miracle of a new life growing. He was so newly arrived from the shores of death. I remembered my mother's bone-thin fingers passing across Dina's maternity smock as though contact with that approaching life could stave off her own approaching death.

I was put in charge of my cousin Bernie, who wore his Boy Scout uniform although the day was hot. Two Junior Commando medals were affixed to his shirt pocket. He had earned one for filling a barrel with the narrow strips of wire that were twined about the caps of milk bottles, and the other for hanging blackout curtains in the windows of an old-age home. Freckled and plump, with his sandy hair combed damply back, he patrolled the lawn as though he were a duty officer reviewing a garrison.

"This whole lawn should have been planted with vegetables," he said officiously.

"Dina and Robert have a garden," I protested.

"So what? The whole lawn could have been planted with lettuces and peppers. Cucumbers too. They need sunlight," he insisted stubbornly.

"Oh, Bernie, you're such a jerk. What do you know about lettuce and peppers except what you read in *Boys' Life?*" I asked jeeringly. "Why don't you go ahead and find some empty tin cans and win the war."

His cheeks blazed fiery red and I was immediately sorry. Poor Bernie, too young to fight, had missed the war, and I deprived him of the valor of his home-front battles. I did not apologize to him until years later, when he wore a different uniform, that of the Israel Defense Forces, and we met in a Jerusalem café, middle-aged cousins who had not seen each other for many years exchanging photos of our children across tepid cups of espresso. I told him then that I was sorry for my impatient cruelty of that August afternoon and he looked at me in bewilderment. He recalled neither my words nor that weekend in Woodstock.

My grandparents and Lottie and Julius left for Fleishman's Hotel. They would return on Sunday morning.

"It would have been nice for all of us to have *shabbas* together, Dinala," my grandmother said as she kissed her youngest daughter. "But it would be too much work for you."

Peace, in our family, was preserved through silence and pretense, words unsaid and assumptions uncontradicted. We did not lie. We just did not speak the truth.

Nachum Adler and Bernie would stay at the Bassens' and Edna and Leon would have the sleep-away sofa in Dina and Robert's living room. The flurry of arrangements excited me. I loved being surrounded by family, feeling myself an integral part of a protective unit. That was what family meant. It was a bastion against loneliness. It was a fortress of kindness in a world beset by cruelty. I closed my mind against the remembered image on newsreel footage of a dark-haired, wide-eyed girl in an oversize coat on which a Jewish star had been sewn walking with her head down, all alone. My mother was dead, my father was off to war, but I was not alone. I had my family.

My arms loaded with linens, I passed Robert in the narrow hallway.

"Everything all right, Sharon?" he asked in the stiff, hesitant tone he used in addressing me ever since that afternoon in the studio.

"Everything is fine, great. Really," I replied and I flashed him a smile of forgiveness. Whatever had happened that day had been, perhaps, as much my fault as his. I understood how he had seen my actions, my words, as provocative, presumptuous.

"She got what she asked for," Karen had said contemptuously when blond Meg had complained of the advances of a young soldier. I too, I decided, had asked for it and I determined to place the entire incident behind me.

"Okay then." Robert smiled and hurried away.

Crowds thronged the lawn as soon as the craft fair was opened. Tourists and locals moved eagerly from table to table. Wartime austerity had whetted their appetites and every purchase was justified because the proceeds went toward the war effort. The shoppers filled their bags with purchases, and the potters and weavers, the jewelry makers and ceramicists hastily replenished their displays. Critics drove up from New York and Belle Langsam guided them through the exhibit in the studio. By noon, three paintings had been sold and it was rumored that several others were marked with the small blue seal that meant "hold." I wondered if my portrait was among them.

The accordionist and the guitarist who had played at the Langsam party strolled across the lawn singing and playing their instruments. Even Franchesca was caught up in the excitement. She lifted her work to demonstrate the effect of light on each glaze and she flushed with pride as item after item was bought. Bernie, wearing a freshly ironed uniform, patrolled the grounds plucking up discarded pieces of paper and the mimeographed circulars announcing the sale that we had distributed throughout the town.

"We're in it so let's win it!" Teddy Bassen shouted from a makeshift podium. He was selling raffles and the prize was a fifty-dollar war bond.

Dina and Sarah manned a table that sold lemonade, root beer, and sandwiches.

Peter, Karen, and I helped where we were needed. At one table I made change, at another I wrapped ceramic planters in newspaper.

Nachum Adler wandered about, a bemused and admiring tourist. He knelt to help a small boy tie his shoelace and then went to stand beside Dina at the refreshment table.

"You must not stand too long on your feet," he said.

He brought her a folding chair, holding it steady as she lowered herself into it. It was a practiced gesture. He had done as much for his wife during her pregnancy. She and the child she had borne had been killed. I turned away. I did not want to think about Nachum Adler and his dead wife and his dead daughter any more than I wanted to think of the war or of my dead mother or of my father from whom I had not heard for weeks. I ran across the lawn to the weavers' tent, where I bought a tie of forest green weave for my father and a cherry red cape with a voluminous hood for myself.

I twirled about in it, laughing as everyone exclaimed at how marvelous it looked, how the color exactly suited my dark hair. I was Red Riding Hood, embarked on a dangerous journey, but in the end I would be saved. I would live happily ever after. I pirouetted joyously and curtsied as the weavers applauded.

The crowds thinned as sunlight waned, and when the last of the visitors left we repacked everything in cartons, ready to be taken out and displayed for sale the next day. Belle counted the receipts. We had made more than two thousand dollars, an enormous sum. The produce and cake sales seldom made even a hundred dollars.

Franchesca's work had sold extremely well. A New York critic had interviewed her and photographed the long slender vase with the emerald glaze, and the delicate perfume vials in muted blues and purples.

"He said he would come back tomorrow. I'll display the small sculptures then. They should photograph well."

"They take a lot of photographs, they make a lot of promises," Randy said dryly, maliciously. I looked at him in surprise and saw that his face was stony with dislike. Was it possible for a man to dislike his own wife? I wondered, and I was grateful that Leon's arm rested affectionately on Edna's shoulder, that Dina was stretched out on the couch with her feet in Robert's hands. He massaged them gently, tenderly. My family, at least, was intact, safe.

Exhausted, Karen, Peter, and I nibbled at the leftover sandwiches and drank the lukewarm lemonade.

"Summer's over," Karen said.

"Almost." I was reluctant to surrender the season.

The screen door slammed and we fell silent. Nachum Adler stood on the porch. He looked up at the starlit sky and then covered his face with his hands. Tears like liquid diamonds stole through the ivory wands of his fingers. We sat very still. We had never before seen a grown man cry.

The craft sale was even more crowded the next day. Word had spread and the hotels in the lower Catskills dispatched vans loaded with guests. It was difficult to entertain vacationers in wartime — good cuts of meat were rationed and the handsome young boys who made up the corps of waiters, busboys, and lifeguards were off fighting the Germans and the Japanese. Women in high heels, their legs patriotically painted with tan makeup to simulate stockings, walked uneasily across the grass and fingered silver pins, batik scarves, leather belts. They called to their husbands and children, seeking smiles, approval. It was virtuous to shop here. The proceeds of the sale would go to the families of fighting men. They repeated this to one another as they filled brown paper sacks with their purchases.

Our friends from the pond and civil-defense collection center came. Meg and Melanie giggled slyly as they examined the displays.

They went to the studio to see the paintings.

"Hey, Sharon, that portrait of you is great," Melanie said and she looked at me with new interest.

"And there's a guy from some magazine taking pictures of your uncle's paintings," Meg added. There was awe in her voice. Magazine articles signified fame, success.

"Yeah. So?" Feigning indifference I left them and went to greet Mrs. Seubert, pleased that she had come.

Her face was still blanched with grief, and loss lines were etched about her eyes. She had returned to work at the center only two days after the receipt of the telegram. There had been no funeral. Not yet. The war violated even the rites of loss, the rituals of grief. I introduced her to Dina, to Robert, to Lottie and Julius, to my grandparents.

"I am a gold-star mother," she said. She would wrest pride from sorrow.

My grandparents looked at her sadly and Lottie gripped her hand tightly.

"Please, I'm sorry," my grandfather said. "It is a terrible thing to bury a child. The Talmud says it is the worst thing that can happen to a person." His own faded blue eyes were rheumy.

"Ah, you see." Mrs. Seubert's eyes filled with tears. An ancient text of a religion not her own validated the enormity of her loss. She had license to weep.

"My Joey," she said.

"My Miriam." My grandmother's words converged; the names of the son lost to war and the daughter lost to cancer melded. "Sharon's mother," my grandmother added.

"Sharon's mother," Mrs. Seubert echoed.

I looked from one grief-worn woman to the other and experienced the onset of misery, the tightness at my throat, the heaviness at my heart. But I disclaimed my anguish. My mother had died between clean sheets in her parents' home. How could I compare her death to that of Joey, lost on a mud-covered battlefield, to the deaths of Nachum Adler's wife and daughter, who had been victims of hatred? My misery seemed selfish and I banished it.

"Buba, don't," I said because my grandmother too was weeping.

"Lola!" I broke free of the circle of their sadness and ran to greet my redheaded friend, who was already armed with laughter.

Skipping gaily, we wandered the grounds. I tried on Marcie Klein's zaniest earrings and looped a wide brass-buckled leather belt about my narrow waist.

In the weavers' tent I helped her to pick out a woven rug in the russet hues of autumn. She paid for it with quarters and one-dollar bills, counting the money out carefully.

"My tips," she said. "But it's a great rug. Glen loves those colors."

I imagined them standing barefoot upon it, their shadows

darkening the brilliant weave. I thought that they might place it near the hearth and lie across it, their faces brushed by firelight.

"He'll come back and you'll live happily ever after," I said.

"I know. I know." She was impatient with me; I was treading on dangerous territory, giving voice to dangerous thoughts.

We mounted a grassy incline and joined Karen and Peter, who had scavenged sandwiches and narrow-necked, green glass bottles of Coca-Cola. We spread the rug out and sprawled on it, eating and drinking and watching the gay and colorful scene on the lawn below. Slowly, the crowds dwindled and the crafts people examined one another's handiwork. Marcie Klein tried on a turquoise serape. Lottie and Edna emerged from the weavers' tent with a rainbow-colored bedspread that they held up to the light.

The long slow sunset of summer's end began. The sky was stippled with pink, brushed with violet.

"Summer's over," Peter said. "Tomorrow's Labor Day and then real life begins again."

I twisted long strands of grass into a braid. My mother had plaited my hair each morning, and often my father had watched her intently, as though he would commit the serenity of her expression, the grace of her movements to memory. Did he summon that memory now, I wondered, wherever he was? Did he withdraw it slowly, carefully, as clever depositors withdraw their interest?

"We'll see each other during the year, Sharon," Peter said, as though he sensed my mood. "You'll come to visit Woodstock. And we come into the city a lot."

"I know," I replied, but I heard the sadness and uncertainty in my own voice.

We sat on in the silence as the violet deepened into purple, and streaks of crimson slashed their way across the darkening sky. The tables were being cleared and Bernie scurried importantly about with cartons and shopping bags. Dina and Nachum Adler stood beneath a tree and talked intently.

"I have to go," Lola said. "I'm due at the pizza place at six. But it was fun. Thanks for helping me pick out the rug, Sharon."

"We'll write," I promised. "I have your address."

"Sure. Terrific."

She hugged each of us and hurried down, clutching the furled rug. It was the talisman of her optimism. Its purchase underscored her belief that Glen would come safely home and that they would build a life together. I imagined myself knotting the green tie I had bought for my father, sliding my fingers across his cheek. One did not purchase gifts for the dead.

We left that grassy incline at last, walking hand in hand, moving slowly, not because of Peter's limp but because we were reluctant to see the day end. Peter and Karen went home and I wove my way though the after-sale debris, skirting the dismantled tables that littered the lawn, and went into the house.

"Sharon. We wondered where you were," Dina said.

She sat between Lottie and Edna on the couch and they moved over to make room for me where once my mother would have sat.

"You have grown beautiful this summer," Edna said. "Mama," she called across the room to my grandmother, "you have a beautiful granddaughter."

My grandmother adjusted her black straw hat, her fingers toying with the cherries.

"Why shouldn't I have a pretty granddaughter? My daughters aren't pretty?" She spoke in the Yiddish that I could understand but could not speak.

"We're going to Fleishman's Hotel for dinner," Lottie said. "The food is very good there and we don't want Dina to go to the trouble of cooking."

What she meant, of course, was that she and Julius and my grandparents could not eat in Dina's house because it was not kosher.

"Listen, do you mind if I don't go?" I asked. "I just ate sandwiches with my friends so I'm not hungry. And I could use the time to pack. I'm feeling kind of tired."

"You're all right?" From opposite sides of the couch Edna and Lottie stretched out their hands and felt my forehead.

"I'm fine."

"She's fine. She's tired, she's not hungry, and she wants to pack." It was Robert who came to my defense. I smiled at him gratefully and he smiled back. We were friends again.

I watched from the window as they climbed into the cars and drove off, and then I wandered through the house and restored it to order. I put the Sunday papers into a pile and collected the mugs and washed them. A person who kept a house clean and organized had a claim on it.

I went up to my room and took my suitcase out of the closet but a heavy lassitude overcame me and I lay down on the bed. Within minutes I was asleep. When I awakened, the room was webbed with the silver shadows of early evening. I lay quietly in the half darkness and surrendered to a tender melancholy. Tonight I would sleep in this narrow bed for the last time. Within a month this room would be transformed into a nursery for Dina and Robert's new baby. I would be back in Brooklyn, my summer self vanished, my golden tan faded. Instead of dungarees and men's shirts, I would wear plaid skirts and matching sweater sets, the cardigans with lines of tiny pearl buttons. The orphan as chameleon — her colors changed, her personality adjusted. The girl who had cycled down the sun-dappled road with Karen and Peter would be gone. Would anyone remember her? I wondered, with the indulgent narcissism of adolescence. Would I even remember myself?

I thought of Robert's portrait. My summer self was safe, captured on canvas. It occurred to me that I had never really studied the portrait in solitude. I did not bother to put on my saddle oxfords but wearing only my thick white bobby socks I hurried through the darkened house and across the grass, damp with evening dew, to the studio. I regretted not bringing a flashlight, but a small light was on in the huge room. The lamp that Robert used when he worked late glowed softly and I was relieved.

I moved into the doorway and paused in the shadow. White drop cloths carpeted the floor and Robert and Franchesca lay on them, their naked bodies ambered by the lamplight. He was upon her, his eyes closed, a shock of fair hair damp against his forehead.

She writhed beneath him, held him close, clawed at his back with her nails. She moaned loudly, luxuriously, and called his name.

"Robert. Oh, Robert."

Mesmerized, I watched as their bodies moved as one. His large hands encircled the black helmet of her hair and his face pressed against hers.

Swiftly, soundlessly, I glided through the door and ran back to the house. I did not vomit until I reached the upstairs bathroom. It was there that the others found me when they returned home, kneeling as I wiped up the spongy detritus of my illness from the rim of the toilet bowl.

"Something must be going around, some virus," Edna said as she relieved me of the cleaning rag and the can of Bon Ami and finished the job herself. "Robert felt sick before we even ordered dinner and went home. Didn't you hear him come in, Sharon?"

"I was probably asleep," I said. "I didn't hear anything."

And Robert, his hand on Dina's shoulder, his face pale, turned away so that our eyes would not meet.

We left the next day. Amid the flurry of farewells, the exchange of gifts and embraces, Robert and I artfully avoided each other. Perhaps he knew that I had seen him with Franchesca and perhaps he didn't, but it no longer mattered. I could not rationalize a second forgiveness.

Karen and Peter gave me a photo album in which they had already pasted some of our snapshots from the pond and from the collection center. The Langsams gave me a beautiful crystal paperweight.

"For ballast," Belle said and I marveled that she had discerned my need for an anchor. I would place my father's letters beneath its shining weight. In my mind's eye, I saw the pile of flimsy V-forms growing, although again weeks had gone by without a letter.

Sarah and Teddy gave me a copy of Kahlil Gibran's *The Prophet* because I had so often borrowed Peter's and I smiled gratefully at them. But when Franchesca pressed a small white box into my hand I did not open it although I thanked her gravely.

Somewhere south of Kingston, I opened Franchesca's gift.

Dangling earrings in her distinctive oyster glaze, nestled on white cotton. I held them to my ears, felt the cold metal against the soft flesh of my lobe. And then, without thinking, I dropped them one by one from the car's open window. I looked back and saw them on the black tarmac, exquisitely shaped white snowdrops oddly angled on the busy roadway.

Autumn

6

Rumors wafted through the air that autumn as swiftly and as colorfully as the falling leaves that crunched beneath our feet. Teachers clustered in the corridors of Lincoln High School and compared news stories in the *Times,* the *Herald Tribune,* the *Journal American.* The voices of newscasters drifted through the open door of the teachers' lounge. Predictions abounded. The Japanese were on the run. No, the Japanese were reinforcing their positions. The Germans were crushed. No, the Germans were garnering their strength, waiting for the construction of a secret weapon. We stopped for frankfurters on Brighton Beach Avenue after school and listened to retirees at the counter analyze the news of the Allied paratroop assault on Holland. The general consensus was that the war in Europe was almost over. Some said it would end in months, others predicted weeks, and there were even those, like Judy Bergman's mother, who were certain that it would be only a matter of days.

Her hair had turned white with stunning suddenness when Judy's brother, Marvin, had been shipped overseas, but now she went to the beauty parlor and had it colored a chestnut brown in anticipation of his return. She listened expectantly to each hourly news broadcast because she did not want to miss the declaration of peace. Recipes cut from *Woman's Day* and the *Woman's Home Companion* littered her kitchen table as she considered the Thanksgiving dinner she would prepare for Marvin when he marched triumphantly home. She had no doubt that he would arrive in time for the holiday and she read out recipes for sweet potatoes topped with marshmallow, cranberry sauce simmered with apples.

"Will Marvin like that?" she asked Judy anxiously.

"I guess." Judy, a tall, serious girl, had fought with her brother the night before he left. A stupid fight, she said. Something about space in a hall closet, but he had shouted and she had wept. She had thought to make up with him early in the morning but when she awakened, he was gone.

"If he dies," Judy said, her gray eyes marble smooth, as though polished by misery, "he will die angry with me."

My own family was less sanguine about the prospects for an immediate peace in Europe. Refugees referred by the Hebrew Immigrant Aid Society made their way to our house and sat huddled in their ill-fitting clothing at the dining room table. They came from my grandparents' village and from the small town that bordered a woodland where Julius had been born and spent his boyhood. Some sat in silence while Julius explained job opportunities, advised them about housing. Others talked with a rapidity that I recognize now to be barely controlled hysteria. Their words tumbled out in a tangle of Yiddish and tears that plunged my grandparents into a nameless misery, caused Julius, Samuel, and Leon to clench their fists, and sent Lottie into the kitchen, her eyes bright with tears and anger. Sometimes they stayed only an hour, long enough to tell their stories, eat a slice of sponge cake, and sip their tea and cognac before they disappeared, clutching a check from Julius and leaving their horror neatly suspended in our dining room. None of them believed that the war in Europe would be over by Thanksgiving.

Nor did Emanuel Weiner, Edna's powerful boss, to whom our family turned for all wisdom and guidance. Occasionally on

Sundays I went to his office in Long Island City to help Edna with the filing. The aroma of freshly baked cakes and muffins permeated the building, breathed its welcome to us through the long factory windows covered with blue cellophane against air raids. The radio played all day in the office, and Emanuel Weiner switched stations nervously, greedy for every scrap of war news, pounding his fists at the Allied defeats, beaming at mention of a victory. He was a large florid-faced man whose steel-rimmed spectacles perched precariously on the tip of his fleshy nose. Like many obese men he moved with grace and speed, and he seemed always to be in motion. His bald head shone with perspiration and he spoke raspingly with a thick German accent.

He was a wealthy man who had never been poor. His money vested him with power and authority but he understood that influence had to be cultivated and he worked at that cultivation as assiduously as he worked at his business. I filed letters to congressmen and senators, to governors and state legislators. He addressed all of them by their first names and assured all of them of his support. Always, he waited for the last paragraph of a letter to ask a favor. His brother's family, living in Switzerland for the duration of the war, required some documents. Could they be included in a diplomatic pouch? A distinguished painter needed an exit visa, a symphony conductor required safe escort through dangerous territory.

He was not in awe of money, which after all had come to him so easily, but he worshipped talent. Music and art were the fulcrum of his life. He and his wife collected paintings and sculpture and had a box at the opera and season tickets to the symphony. And they worked together to rescue writers and artists, painters and musicians from war-torn Europe. It was through their efforts that Nachum Adler had come to America.

"Have you heard from your father, Sharon?" Emanuel Weiner asked me each Sunday.

And because letters from my father were rare that autumn, more often than not I shook my head.

"Be patient," he advised. "This will be a long war." And I believed him because he was our family's oracle.

One Sunday, when Edna herself did not go to the office, we all went to the Oceana Theater to see Rita Hayworth in *Cover Girl*. The feature was preceded by Movietone News and we sucked our Jujubes and watched clips of General Mark Clark marching triumphantly into Rome and Charles de Gaulle striding down the Champs Elysées. As always, I leaned forward in my seat when the camera focused on American units. There was always the infinitesimal chance that I would see my father, and his would be the face looking out at me from the army truck marked with the insignia of the medical corps.

Heidi clutched my hand as we watched an interview with two large-eyed Jewish girls who told of how their parents had been rounded up by the Gestapo and taken to a huge stadium. The girls themselves had escaped because they were hidden by gentile families in a Paris suburb.

"And now your parents are free?" the correspondent asked.

We read the subtitles breathlessly.

"But no. Our parents are dead." They spoke in unison, their tones flat.

We closed our eyes against their misery and opened them to see a wooden cross that marked the grave of a GI who had fallen in France. A helmet hung on the marker and flowers had been placed on the coverlet of fresh earth. I imagined my father lying in such a lonely, narrow grave and I wondered if those who buried Jewish soldiers knew how to fashion a Star of David out of sticks of wood. I slumped in my seat, the candies sticky in my hand as the booming voice of the Movietone narrator rumbled through the theater. "The battles have been strenuous and the losses grievous but clearly the Hun is on the run."

"Well, he ain't running fast enough," Leon said as we made our way out of the theater and into the disorienting brightness of Coney Island Avenue.

We stopped to buy potato knishes for the ritual Sunday evening delicatessen dinner at Lottie's house. Samuel and Dolly usually came and Nachum Adler occasionally joined us. The tall, lean artist had rented a studio in Sea Gate and spent much of his time painting on the promontory. In Europe he had earned fame as a portrait painter but now he concentrated on capturing turbulent oceanscapes and the skies of autumn. Still, he could not keep from sketching; his drawing pencil danced across scraps of paper and napkins to render Heidi and me in profile, Bernie pulling down the blackout curtain, my grandfather reading the Yiddish paper.

"Do you think anyone in our building would hide us?" Heidi asked Bernie as we waited for the knishes to be wrapped in waxed paper. "I mean, like if it happened here."

"It can't happen here. It won't happen here," Bernie replied. "This is the United States of America. This is Brooklyn, New York." He stood very straight in his neatly pressed Junior Commando uniform, his merit badges dangling.

"Hurry, let's get home before the knishes get cold," Edna urged us, and hugging the brown bags, we dashed to the car.

But the knishes did grow cold before we could eat them that evening, because the house was in turmoil. Dina had given birth while we were at the movies, three weeks before her due date. Teddy Bassen, who had phoned from Woodstock with the news, assured Lottie that it was not unusual for first babies to arrive a few weeks before term.

"What does he know about babies? He's a psychiatrist," Lottie said.

"Psychiatrists go to medical school," Dolly retorted authoritatively and patted her red cloth hat. The hat marked her transient presence in this house, her status as "company." It exempted her from setting the table and clearing it, from washing and drying the dishes. Her own contribution was limited to bringing coffee cake from Ebinger's, neatly encased in a white box tied with narrow red string. Always when she handed the cake to Lottie she told her how she had to stand on line at the bakery, how she had refused a cake that was not freshly baked.

"The important thing," she added now, "is that the baby is healthy."

"A boy or a girl?" Edna's voice quivered.

"A little girl. A beautiful little girl. Six pounds two ounces. A good size." The worry in Lottie's voice was replaced with exuberance and she, Edna, and Samuel embraced and encircled their parents with their joy.

"Mama, Papa, another granddaughter, a new *einiekel*." They offered this new birth as compensation for the grief and loss my grandparents had suffered. My mother, their daughter, had died but a granddaughter had been born. I willed my own self to joy but felt only grief and an odd sense of betrayal.

My grandparents took each other's hands, an awkward gesture because they were never demonstrative in front of us. My grandmother smiled and I realized that she had not smiled since my mother's death. Tears streaked my grandfather's face. His high black skullcap was askew on his thick white hair and I reached up to straighten it and held my hand there as though my touch might staunch his tears.

"My Dina," he said and I wondered if he had wept when I was born and said in that same mystified tone, "My Miriam," awed that his daughter had become a mother. I began to cry then and it occurred to me, not erroneously, that all my life I would punctuate joy with sadness.

"Come on. Enough crying," Leon intervened. "We have something to celebrate here. Hey, why did Teddy call? Where was Robert?"

The taut silence of adults who are reluctant to speak in front of children stretched across the room. Lottie coughed nervously.

"Before we eat, you kids go and wash your hands," Edna commanded and Heidi, Bernie, and I looked at her incredulously. We were not babies; we knew when to wash our hands. Still, we went into my bedroom, slammed the door loudly, and then opened it a crack so that we could hear their conversation.

"They don't know where Robert is. He left the house early this morning. Dina was feeling fine and he said he had some business to take care of. And then the pains began and they couldn't find him." Lottie spoke slowly as though still trying to comprehend the situation.

"And no one has any idea of where he might be? The

Bassens? Their other friends?" Edna, ever the competent investigator, asked.

"The Bassens — thank God they were home and able to get Dina to the hospital — they called everyone they could think of. It could be he had a flat tire or maybe an accident." Lottie used her own lexicon of experience. Only dire circumstances could keep a man away from his wife at such a time.

The doorbell rang and Nachum Adler's deep voice augmented the chorus of their concern and excitement.

"A little girl. Wonderful! Mazel tov!"

Heidi and I looked at each other. The previous Sunday, Nachum had tossed his tweed jacket on the bed in my room and his wallet had fallen out and fluttered open. We had stared down at a snapshot of a beautiful blond woman holding a fair-haired small girl on her lap. Nachum's wife and daughter, we knew, the wife and daughter he would never see again. Fascinated, we studied the tender curve of the woman's lips, the wispy hair of the child. The mother wore pearls and the child a ribbon, exquisitely tied. They had dressed in their best summer dresses and smiled charmingly for the photographer and Nachum Adler had surely kissed them both. Now they were dead, the pearls and the ribbon ground into dust.

Nachum was drawn into the web of their conjectures. *Where could Robert be?* He offered tentative explanations. Artists sometimes traveled great distances if they were intrigued by a particular subject. Often they lost track of time as they worked. He himself had spent the afternoon painting a formation of shells washed up on the surf, unaware of the passage of hours until he realized that he was hungry and his fingers were chilled. Surely the same thing had happened to Robert.

"Heidi, come set the table," Edna called. "Sharon, help her."

"You go ahead, I'll be there in a minute," I told her. "Bernie, you help."

"I have to fix a rip in the blackout curtain downstairs," he said. He fished the black masking tape that he carried everywhere out of his pocket and disappeared down the staircase into our grandparents' apartment.

"What's Bernie going to do when the war is over?" Heidi asked sarcastically.

"Oh, he'll find another war," I replied carelessly. I could not have known then that my words were prescient, that Bernie would wear uniforms all the days of his life.

When Heidi left I closed the door and dialed Information. I held my breath as I dialed the newly obtained phone number but my voice was firm when I spoke to her.

"Franchesca," I said, "this is Sharon Grossberg. I would like to speak to my uncle Robert."

There was only the briefest of pauses.

"Sharon?" He spoke my name with questioning bewilderment.

"Dina had the baby. She's in the hospital in Kingston. No one knows where you are." My tone was calm but not conspiratorial. I meant him to know that I would not betray him but I also meant him to sense my cool disapproval.

"She's all right? The baby's all right?" It pleased me that his voice trembled. His anxiety excited and aroused me.

"Yes."

"Thanks, Sharon. For everything." How swiftly he was restored to calm. I understood that his gratitude extended to my discretion, that I was newly ensnared in the maze of his deception. I hung up and it was not until I was in the bathroom washing my face that I realized that Robert had not asked me if the baby was a boy or a girl. The omission did not surprise me.

As we ate dinner the phone rang. It was Teddy Bassen calling to tell us that Robert had called. He had traveled upstate to paint a waterfall and had not realized how late it was. Alarmed when there was no reply after repeated calls to Dina, he had phoned the Bassens and was now speeding toward the hospital in Kingston.

"You see," Nachum Adler said. "It is as I told you." But his eyes rested on me as Julius filled small crystal glasses with the rich golden brandy he kept for special occasions.

"L'chaim," my grandfather said and we laughed as he downed his drink, his head thrown back so that the black silk skullcap slid to the floor.

"*L'chaim!*" we all shouted back. Heidi, Bernie, and I raised our tall glasses of cream soda and tilted our own heads back in mimetic frenzy.

"What will she name the baby, I wonder," Edna said as she passed the platter of cold cuts and then fashioned a thick pastrami sandwich for Bernie, carefully cutting away the crusts because he disliked caraway seeds. I remembered how my mother had always skimmed the top of my oatmeal because I had an aversion to the slightest curdling, and I was gripped by an irrational and fierce jealousy. I jostled Bernie's arm and watched as the cream soda flooded his plate.

"We never spoke about names," Lottie said. "Did she talk to you about it, Sharon?"

"No." I took a bite of the coffee cake Dolly had selected with such care. "This tastes a little stale. I guess they gave you what was left from yesterday, Aunt Dolly," I said. Malice brightened my smile.

"Nonsense. It's delicious." Dolly chewed her own piece vigorously. "I should imagine they would want to name the baby for Miriam," she added.

Everyone grew quiet and my grandmother put her face in her hands and sat very still. Perhaps if she did not move, her grief would not overflow.

"Dolly, that was a foolish thing to say." Samuel's tone was monitory but his wife stared at him defiantly and licked at a crumb that clung to her very white, slightly protruding front tooth.

"Why?" she asked.

I too wanted to know why. It seemed to me that a baby born into our family only months after my mother's death should, by all rights, be named for her. A teacher in my Brookline Hebrew school had told us once that the spirits of the dead float restlessly until a baby is named for them and they know that they will not be forgotten.

"It's bad luck to name a child for someone who died young," Julius said. "An *ayin hora* — an evil eye."

"You don't really believe that." Dolly was persistent. Our family irritated her with our Old World superstitions and customs.

She knew that Samuel's family in turn eyed her fussy apartment with its pastel walls and carefully matched furniture suspiciously. They perched awkwardly on the armless chairs upholstered in coral satin and picked at the elegant casseroles she served as though searching for forbidden foods among the mushrooms and artichoke hearts. Their dislike hovered closer to pity as they waited, year after year, for her to become pregnant. Samuel delighted in children and had always brought us extravagant gifts when we were little, dolls that came with their own carrying cases and wardrobes for Heidi and me, baseball bats and ice skates for Bernie. The pity rocketed into near hatred when Edna told her of a physician who was a fertility expert, a close friend of Emanuel Weiner's. "He's done wonders for couples like you," she had said. "Listen, Mrs. Take Charge of the World, I don't want children," Dolly had told her angrily and watched with satisfaction as Edna blanched and bit her lip.

"I believe that a child should be named for someone who lived a long life. Such a name gives hope, promise." Julius struggled for words to explain the inexplicable, for a rationale to express the unreasonable. Defeated, he poured another glass of brandy and emptied it into his tea.

"It's a belief that if you name a baby for someone who died young, you raise the fear that that child will also die young. It's just superstition, I know, but still . . ." Edna shrugged her shoulders, acknowledging that superstitions had their own value in a world where so much was beyond our control, where danger erupted without warning and destinies were altered by biological imbalances and capricious accidents.

My family practiced their small rites against such unforeseen dangers because they knew themselves to be vulnerable and because they lived then, as I do now, with fear that cannot be assuaged. They spilled salt over their shoulders, chewed bits of thread when they sewed, and were careful never to step over anyone sprawled across the floor. And I, trained scientist that I am, have not forgotten their lessons. Only last night my daughter laughed at me because her small son lay on the floor and after I stepped over him I hurriedly reversed my steps, thus canceling out my indiscretion.

"It's just a superstition, that if you step over a child he won't grow," I said to my daughter apologetically. "But still . . ." And my aunt Edna's voice resonated in memory.

I knew that night that Dina's baby would not be named for my mother and I knew too that if my father was killed in the war, no child of our family would bear his name.

"I'll name my baby for my mother," I announced, my cheeks burning. "When I am grown and married."

They laughed that I had thought to amend my declaration and Lottie kissed my cheek. Julius turned on the radio and we smiled as Jack Benny harangued Rochester.

Relieved that good humor had been restored, we sat around the table longer than usual that night, unwilling to forfeit the last hours of the weekend. Reluctantly, Lottie removed the delicatessen platters with their meager residue of smoked and roasted meats. Julius scraped the golden scabs of mustard from the white cloth and slid the half-sour pickles back into the large jar. My grandmother divided the rye bread into three piles and placed two of them in brown paper bags which she handed to Samuel and Edna.

"You'll make sandwiches tomorrow," she said. "Always Lottie buys too much bread."

Although a soft autumn rain was falling, I stood on the porch as they left and remained there until I could no longer see the headlights of their cars. I wondered if it was raining in Kingston and if Dina was awake, watching the drops stream down the windows of her hospital room. Shivering, I went inside to read the first chapter of *Beowulf* for my honors English class.

7

Dina named her baby Anna, for Robert's grandmother, although it was unlikely that Robert's family worried about wandering spirits or uneasy souls. Still, Heidi and I agreed that it was a pretty name. We all drove up to Woodstock the next weekend, laden with presents and breathless with excitement. Things were happening swiftly in our family. A baby had been born and soon there would be a wedding. Or at least I hoped there would be a wedding.

"My cousin Beth is getting married," I told Peter and Karen as we sat together at the pond. "Maybe."

We had cycled to the pond to escape the friends and relatives who crowded Dina and Robert's living room. It was strange to be sitting in our summer refuge swathed in sweaters and scarves, to kick aside leaves of crimson and gold and to see the cobalt sky through the barren branches of the maple trees. The season of sunlight was over and we shivered in this place where once we had lifted our arms to radiant heat and sought shelter from brightness in patterned shadows.

"Your cousin? How old is she?" Karen asked.

"She's twenty. She goes to college in Arizona. That's where she met him — at a synagogue dance for Jewish servicemen. He comes from Chicago. Alfred Levine. He's really good-looking." I leaned back on a boulder and stretched languidly.

In the photo she had sent, Alfred Levine, tall and sandy-haired, smiled shyly down at Beth, who wrinkled her button nose as she stared into the camera. As always, she wore her blond hair in a pageboy, carefully cut so that a silken fall of hair covered the right side of her face in the style Veronica Lake had made famous. But my cousin was not emulating the movie star. She was conceal-ing the small red birthmark that puckered like a strawberry against her pearl white skin. She wore a strapless white dress, and Alfred Levine's arm rested protectively on her bare shoulder. He was in dress uniform, his dark jacket studded with buttons, epaulets at his shoulders and two small badges pinned above his breast pocket. The uniform vested him with authority and drama and accounted for the anxious sadness I perceived in his light eyes. He was a soldier in wartime, poised at the edge of danger. Beth had written that his unit would soon be shipped overseas. His vulnerability afforded him privilege and gave him the right to rest his hand so possessively on Beth's shoulder and to smile at her with such wist-ful yearning. It gave him the right to ask her to marry him only four months after they met.

"I think that's marvelous," Karen said. "So romantic."

"My aunt and uncle don't think so," I responded. "It's been nothing but screaming and arguments all week."

"Why are they so against it?" Karen asked. "He's Jewish."

"Sure." Alfred's religious credentials had been fully vali-dated. Julius had called a cousin in Chicago and through an intri-cate network of synagogue and organizational connections, it had been established that Alfred's father was a plumbing contractor and his mother a kindergarten teacher. They belonged to a syna-gogue. There were two younger daughters but Alfred's older brother had died of polio some years earlier.

"Is she pregnant?" Peter tossed a stone into the water and watched it skip across the surface.

The question angered me, perhaps because it had occurred to

me when Beth called to say they wanted to be married at once. I thought my conjecture disloyal.

I had always looked up to Beth, my pretty cousin for whom the phone rang with reassuring frequency. She was popular, an epithet to be yearned for and envied. *Popular.* The word itself was lyrical. Beth's laughter was musical, her skirts were always exactly the right length, her sweaters exactly the right cut. She had always been kind when I came to visit from Brookline. She allowed me to sit at her skirted dressing table and touch her perfumes and makeup while she spoke to her friends on the white phone which Lottie and Julius had installed in her room on her sixteenth birthday. She set my hair in tiny pin curls, took me shopping with her, and read poetry aloud to me — not the classical poetry her mother favored, but works by poets whose words were published in slender volumes with rainbow-colored endpapers. *This Is My Beloved* was on her bedside table and she copied verses out of Kahlil Gibran's *The Prophet* and hung them about her room.

She awakened one night gasping for breath. Tears filled her eyes as she struggled, and her pale skin shone with sweat in the darkness as she writhed from side to side. Frightened, I ran to waken my father, who ran barefoot through the house in his striped pajamas, clutching his medical bag. That night I learned that Beth had asthma.

It was my father who told Lottie and Julius that the climate of Arizona was beneficial to asthma sufferers and it was at his suggestion that they sent Beth to the university at Tempe, a daring decision for an Orthodox Jewish family. My father did not tell Lottie and Julius that he believed Beth's asthma to be psychogenic, that she had difficulty breathing because she was asphyxiated by the overwhelming affection and obsessive concern of her parents. She was their American princess and they willed her to live in the kingdom of safety and plenty. His diagnosis was simplistic, I think now, but not erroneous, and in retrospect I am impressed by his intuition and sensitivity.

"I'm sure she's not pregnant," I told Peter. "But we'll know tomorrow when she gets home."

"Probably when your aunt and uncle meet her fiancé, they'll

like him," Karen said hopefully. She was a reader who always leapt to the last chapter in search of a happy ending and she has lived her life as an adventure in optimism. "Oh, everything will work out," she assures me even now during our infrequent long-distance conversations. Although the news we have shared is devastating — a friend has a terrifying illness, a longtime marriage is foundering — Karen fantasizes a miraculous cure, a loving reconciliation, an unexpected outbreak of joy.

"Even if they like him they won't want them to get married now. He's supposed to be shipped overseas and they're afraid of what might happen."

I could not say that they were afraid that Alfred Levine might be killed or maimed in the war that raged on despite all the hopeful rumors, despite Mrs. Bergman's energetic hopes and her ambitious recipes. To say that Alfred might die was to acknowledge my father's terrible vulnerability and I could not give voice to my deepest fears. It was sad enough that I thought such things, that wild terror weighted my heart and blocked my capacity for joy as surely as the constriction of her lungs had blocked Beth's capacity for breath.

"And besides," I added, "they're afraid she hasn't known him long enough. There's never been a divorce in my family. They think that marriage is forever."

"They ought to spend more time in Woodstock," Peter said and he laughed bitterly.

"Let's go back." I sprang to my feet and they did not protest. Our shared confidence had carried us to dangerous territory. A cold autumn wind slashed its way across the pond causing the quiet waters to ripple angrily.

Dina, Lottie, and Edna were talking quietly in the kitchen when I arrived back at the house. Fragments of their conversation drifted out to the living room, where Heidi stood looking moodily out the window while Bernie officiously roped piles of newspapers together.

"My Beth — she's so young . . ." Lottie's words were a maternal threnody.

"Reason with her, understand her." Dina spoke in her rational social worker's tone.

"What's to reason? What's to understand? There's a war and he's a soldier being sent overseas. And even without the war — they know each other, what, three months, four months? How well can they know each other?"

"So, how well did you know Julius? How well did I know Robert? The truth only comes with marriage." Weariness edged Dina's voice and she said no more.

"Still, if there's going to be a wedding we'll have to make arrangements quickly, a catering hall, gowns, flowers," Edna said.

I went up to the room that had been my own only a few weeks ago and was now transformed into a nursery. It saddened me that my presence had been so swiftly erased, and I knew, with melancholic certainty, that through the years to come many rooms would be my own only for a length of months and years and then they would be taken over by strangers. Transience came early into my life. Perhaps that is why my own family has always lived in the same house and why I insisted that my husband add extensions as our family grew when others opted for new homes in new neighborhoods. The fears of my girlhood are etched into the blueprint of my maturity.

The baby, Anna, was not in her crib. She was in Nachum Adler's arms, held close against his chest. His dark beard brushed the wispy, copper-colored cap of her hair and he sang softly to her in a language I did not recognize. He turned when he heard my step.

"Ah, Sharon. Your cousin Anna is beautiful. Like her mother. Like you."

"I'm not beautiful," I replied sullenly.

He did not answer but handed Anna to me and left the room. I carried her to the window, moved by her lightness, and looked down at the grassy swale below. Within minutes I saw Dina and Nachum walk across it, their heads bent close, her hands clenched and his tucked into the pockets of his brown corduroy trousers as though they feared each other's touch.

I put Anna back in her crib and went downstairs. Robert, Leon, and Julius sat in the living room drinking coffee out of large mugs. Unlike the women who had spoken so softly of love and weddings as they sat at the kitchen table, the voices of the men were verberent, almost harsh. They spoke of war and death. They spat out the names of battles and foreign terrain with authoritative precision.

"Operation Anvil was a success," Leon stated. "Look, the First Army is at the Siegfried Line and Patton's heading for the Saar Basin."

"If it's such a success why aren't they bombing the railroad lines?" Julius countered. He lowered his voice and glanced across the room where my grandparents sat side by side on a small sofa. My grandfather turned the sepia-colored rotogravure section of the *Jewish Morning Journal* weekend edition, his gnarled finger pointing to a photograph. Now and again he read a paragraph to my grandmother, his voice low and tender, as though he were reading a letter from a friend. And my grandmother folded her arms on her chest and rocked slowly as she listened.

Heidi and I understood that Julius was talking about the railroad lines that led to the concentration camps. We had seen the film clips of the sealed boxcars; we had shifted nervously in our seats and turned our eyes away from the faces of bewildered men, women, and children who clutched small valises and descended the uneven steps to stand wearily in the shadows of extended rifles and barren trees.

"Because the world doesn't give a damn about the Jews," Robert replied angrily. "The great Allied leaders are more concerned about crushing Joe Stalin. What do you think Churchill and Roosevelt were talking about in Quebec last week — saving Jews or containing communism? They're two old men who are afraid of the future. But we can't afford their fear. We have to plan for a new world, new ideas."

I was offended by his reference to the president and the prime minister. Their understated elegance, FDR's deftness with his cigarette holder, Churchill's meticulously buttoned vest, reassured me. The fluid silver sentences they uttered so effortlessly thrilled me and I harvested words that I repeated to myself in the darkness of the night. There was nothing to fear but fear itself. We were living through our finest hour.

"I don't worry about the future," Julius said firmly. "I don't worry about a new world. I worry about now and I worry about Jews. Now, this minute, they are killing Jews and shipping them to their deaths. And it can be stopped." He pounded the coffee table with his fist, and an accumulation of magazines thundered to the floor.

"Stop! Be quiet!" Heidi sprang to her feet. Her voice was strangulated and tears stood in her eyes. She rushed from the room, slamming the door behind her.

I left the room in search of my cousin because I remembered how she had stood in the knish store and asked so plaintively where she would find refuge if "it" happened here. I wanted to assure her yet again that we were safe, on a continent removed from danger.

She was in the bathroom and the door was locked.

"Heidi," I called.

"I'm all right." Her voice was muffled, but as though to prove her well-being, she flushed the toilet. When she emerged her eyes were red-rimmed and her thin-featured face was very pale.

We did not speak of her outburst during the long ride home and not for a long time afterward. Not until it became necessary.

Beth had arrived when I came home from school the next day. Her luggage filled the hallway and her laughter rippled through the living room.

"Sharon!" She ran toward me, hugged me, and kissed me on the cheek. She smelled of baby powder and jasmine. I hugged her back and deeply inhaled what I was certain must be the scent of love. A pear-shaped diamond glittered on her finger. "Will you be a bridesmaid at my wedding — you and Heidi?"

"Sure, I guess," I said. I did not want to be disloyal to Lottie, whose lips formed a thin line of disapproval. Still, Lottie's eyes were soft when she looked at Beth, and she crossed the room to lift a silken swath of her daughter's golden hair and to kiss the rise of the strawberry birthmark that puckered the smooth creaminess of Beth's skin.

Beth was even prettier than I remembered her. She wore a

pink angora sweater that hugged her slender torso and the gentle rise of her firm breasts. Her gray box-pleated skirt, cut short in the fashion of the new fabric-saving patriotism, swirled about her knees, and her shapely legs were encased in shining silk stockings. A black leather belt cinched in her tiny waist. She was definitely not pregnant.

"You must see this picture of Alfred," she insisted and she dashed across the room to open her suitcase and remove the framed portrait. "Isn't he handsome? Isn't he good-looking? Isn't he wonderful?"

He smiled out at us, an even-featured young man, the concavity of his cheekbones shadowed by the leather brim of his military hat. As in the snapshots she had sent, he wore the dress uniform of the infantry, the dark belted jacket with its double pockets and rows of glistening buttons, the crisp khaki shirt with its matching neatly knotted tie. It seemed strange to me that men who trained for battle should knot their ties so expertly and polish their buttons and badges with such care.

I remembered suddenly the last night of my father's last leave. He had sat on the edge of the bed and polished his shoes while my mother ironed his khaki shirt. They had talked softly as they concentrated on their small tasks. It was winter and the scent of the shoe polish and steam commingled in the overheated apartment. I sat cross-legged on the floor reading my social studies text, soothed by the rhythm of their movements, the knowledge that I was the daughter of conscientious parents who cared for their possessions in time of crisis and so would surely take care of me.

I handed the framed portrait back to Beth, smiling with a forced brightness because I did not want the shadow of my sadness to encroach upon her joy.

"He's really good-looking," I said. "Sort of like Dane Clark."

Lottie took the picture and studied it gravely.

"He's very handsome," she said. She did not want to seem miserly in her praise; she wanted Beth to understand that at another time she would surely have delighted in her daughter's choice.

"And he's smart. He graduated at the top of his class from

Northwestern and he's going to go to law school there. After the war." She waltzed about the room, hugging the picture close. "He's handsome. He's smart. He loves me," she sang out. "And we're getting married." She stretched out her hand and pulled me into her dance, into the swirling circle of her happiness. And then my grandparents came upstairs and we danced with them as well, moving more slowly and finally persuading Lottie to link hands with us. Beth smiled, certain that with each step she drew her mother closer to acquiescence. Her parents, who had never denied her anything, would not deny her such happiness.

Edna's family came for dinner that night, ostensibly to celebrate Beth's homecoming, but Heidi and I knew, of course, that Edna and Leon were backup artillery for Lottie and Julius. They would agree that Alfred was a wonderful young man but he was a soldier about to be shipped overseas and this was a time of war. Edna would punctuate her advice with insights gained from Emanuel Weiner. Heidi and I predicted the scenario. We had seen the sisters in action before.

It was Bernie, however, who carried the dinner-table conversation. He wanted to know Alfred's rank.

"Lieutenant." Beth twirled her ring, lifted her finger to study it in the light, and held it beneath the cloth to watch it shimmer in the darkness.

"What's his division?"

"Armored infantry."

"Does he think he'll see action?" Bernie's eyes were wide with envy.

My aunts and uncles looked unhappily at one another, and my grandmother shuffled into the kitchen and brought out freshly baked strudel. Always when conversations grew awkward in our family, we were encouraged to eat our way into silence.

"Of course. He's being sent overseas. That's why we want to get married right away."

"When? When is he being shipped out?" Bernie was persistent. "And where's he going? To Europe? The Pacific?" Bernie had tacked operational maps of both war theaters to his bedroom wall.

"Hey, loose lips sink ships." Beth laughed. "How do I know you're not a spy, Bernie."

"Enough nonsense. Enough questions. You have no homework?" Edna asked and we knew it was our cue to leave the table.

We trooped into my room, slammed the door behind us, and then opened it slightly. We crouched in the doorway listening. Their voices, soft at first and then raised in a crescendo of persuasion and protest, trailed down the hallway.

"Why can't you wait until the war is over, until he comes home? Be engaged. Wear his ring. But wait."

"We have no time to wait. We love each other."

"But what if something happens?" Julius asked miserably.

"You mean, if Alfred is wounded? Or killed?"

Heidi and I held each other's hands and marveled at our cousin's courage. She said the words we dared not utter.

"All right. You said it so I'll say it. In wars, soldiers get wounded. Crippled. Blinded. They die. And their wives become widows."

Was Julius looking at Beth as he spoke? How could he bear to hurt her like that? We hated him for his cruelty, for speaking the words we left unsaid.

"That's why it's even more important that we get married now," Beth replied firmly. "At least we'll have had something, shared something. But Daddy, nothing will happen to Alfred. He'll be fine. I know it."

"How can you know it?" Edna sounded exhausted. "The war in Europe isn't going to be over tomorrow. Look what happened in Holland. The Germans had their panzers waiting for our paratroopers. Mr. Weiner says that Hitler isn't about to roll over because Patton is marching on the Saar."

We shivered at her mention of Holland. We were close enough to our childhoods to think of it as the land of Hans Brinker and his silver skates, of wooden shoes and tulips and windmills. It was not a country where men were cremated alive by flamethrowers and macerated by mortars. But Movietone News had shown no tulips or windmills on the flat fields where young men plunged through the air to their deaths. We had heard General Urquhart of the First British Airborne say, in his flat war-weary voice, "Eight thousand Red Devils came down at Arnhem, two thousand came out alive." Many thousands more would lose their lives before the war ended. And one of them might be Alfred Levine, the lean-featured young man whom Beth loved, whom she had loved from the moment of their meeting.

Beth had told me that afternoon how she and Alfred had met at a dance for Jewish servicemen, sponsored by a Phoenix synagogue.

"It was a big room. He was on one side and I was on the other. We walked toward each other. He opened his arms and I stepped into them." Her voice had been dreamy. She spoke as though recounting a fairy tale and I listened, like a small girl, with rapture and envy. I too yearned to glide into my lover's outstretched arms.

They had been together whenever possible after that first night. Often, late in the afternoon, they drove into the desert and watched the brilliant sunsets that stained the sky mauve and crimson. They plucked cactus fruit and fed each other tiny bits of the sweet pink flesh. They spread picnics beneath a Joshua tree, and when they had eaten, Alfred turned the car radio to a big-band station and opened his arms. Barefoot, she sailed into them and they danced upon the cool sand as the sun set.

"Alfred will be all right," Beth insisted. "*His* parents aren't against our marrying," she added accusingly. Of course he would be all right. He was her prince, her fairy tale lover. They were destined to live happily ever after.

I remembered that Alfred's brother had died of polio. Perhaps his parents thought they had already paid their dues, that on some huge celestial ledger, their debit column outweighed the credit and they would be recompensed. I understood them. I, too, relied on divine equity. I hugged the belief that because my mother had died, my father would be safe. "You would not do that to me," I said fiercely to God on the nights when I could not sleep, when I stayed awake reading and rereading my father's letters and hissing my angry prayers into the darkness.

"Of course *they're* not against. For them what would there be to lose?" Julius asked in his businessman's tone of bitter reasonableness. Married or unmarried, Alfred would go to war. Married or unmarried, he would survive or he would be killed. It was Beth who might be widowed or condemned to a lifetime as a nurse for a badly wounded veteran. It was Beth who might have to raise a fatherless child or a child whose father would be cruelly incapacitated.

"Daddy, this isn't a business deal. No one's losing and no one's gaining. We love each other and we want to be married. We'd like a real wedding, with friends and family and music and food, but if you don't want to make us a wedding, we'll go to a rabbi's study or even to City Hall. But Alfred is coming here when his leave begins and we're going to be married." Beth was firm and decisive. I realized that she spoke as a woman in charge of her own life, not as a willful daughter. The war had catapulted her into a new maturity.

Everyone was quiet then and so it was easy to hear my grandmother when she began to speak, softly, hesitantly, with her voice gathering strength as her story unfolded. She spoke in Yiddish and told of a cousin, a beautiful young girl, gentle and soft-voiced, whose family had refused to allow her to marry the young man whom she loved and who loved her. They objected because the young man was a merchant who frequently traveled great distances on business. Such journeys were hazardous in Poland because Jews who ventured into unfamiliar environments were vulnerable and such itinerant Jewish merchants sometimes disappeared. The young girl's parents advised their daughter not to marry until her fiancé had saved enough money to go into business in their own town. And because daughters listened to their parents in those days, my grandmother's cousin agreed. There was no marriage.

"You see," Lottie said triumphantly, but the story was not yet over.

Our grandmother continued her story. The young merchant never returned and was never heard from again. But his beautiful fiancée never married. The life had dried up within her. Her laughter was stilled and the voice that had once been so soft and pleasing crackled with anger and bitterness.

"You know her. Bracha Liebe. She came to our Miriam's funeral," my grandmother reminded Lottie and Edna.

Even I knew who Bracha Liebe was — an old woman whose
skin was webbed with age and whose words were always harsh.
She was thin, almost wraithlike. Her body had never softened into
womanhood and seemed, even when she was seated, coiled and
braced for assault and disappointment. Bracha Liebe's parents had
triumphed but their daughter's happiness had been forfeit. Her
passion had remained frozen and her tenderness had withered.

There was a brief silence and then Beth's laughter, lightly
laced with hysteria, trilled through the room.

"But I'm Beth — I'm not Bracha Liebe," she said.

She knew, of course, as Heidi and I did, that it was my grandmother's story which would allow for a wedding to be celebrated.
Lottie and Julius would not allow Beth to grow frightened and
bitter, mourning a marriage that had never taken place and a lover
who had never had an opportunity to prove his ardor. Our family
also had something to lose.

It was decided then, and with the decision came a storm of
activity and arrangements that energized us and invoked our
laughter and our hope. Planning a wartime wedding, we briefly
and blessedly forgot the war.

The Manhattan Beach Jewish Center was reserved for the
wedding and the reception.

"There's no time to shop around," Lottie explained to Dina
on the phone. "We were just lucky they had the date open."

There was no time to print and mail invitations. Phone calls
were made. Relatives and friends were asked to call other relatives
and friends.

Beth, Heidi, and I traveled uptown, sandwiched on the
wicker seats of the Brighton Express between Lottie and Edna, to
select our gowns. Uncle Julius's friend Abe Rosenstein owned a
company called Only for Brides which manufactured bridal gowns
and bridesmaid dresses.

"We're lucky," Lottie said. "In these days it's hard to get
fabric. From Abe we'll get special treatment."

With the wedding a foregone conclusion, she congratulated

herself on her luck as each hurdle in its preparation was vaulted. She was lucky to have secured the synagogue, lucky to have found a caterer who despite rationing could put together a decent meal, and she was lucky that Abe Rosenstein had a nice selection of gowns.

"Do you have an idea of what you want, Beth?" Edna asked.

"Puff sleeves, long, and a high neck. Shirred. A tulip-shaped bouffant skirt and a long train. A very soft fabric, maybe peau de soie," Beth replied without hesitation.

"What colors for Heidi and Sharon?" Lottie asked.

"Blue." I answered for myself, shouting above the whir of the train. "Powder blue. A short dress. You know. Because of the war. A bride needs a long gown but I don't mind."

I spoke virtuously but the truth was that Judy Bergman had informed me that I had very good legs.

"Show them off," Judy had advised. "Marvin once told me that a lot of men think legs are more important than breasts. Although you're doing okay in that department too."

We had been standing naked in front of the long mirror in her bedroom, staring at our reflected bodies with critical absorption. I studied my firm dark-nippled breasts and noted that Judy's pubic hair formed a soft ash-colored cloud while my own was black and wiry. Like dancers in a carefully choreographed duet, we turned slowly, lifted our arms, and extended our legs. And then we dressed hastily, suddenly embarrassed by our daring, and hurried downstairs to help Mrs. Bergman go through wallpaper patterns. She had decided to have the house newly painted and papered before Thanksgiving. It would be a homecoming surprise for Marvin.

"What about you, Heidi?" Edna turned to her daughter, who had not spoken throughout the journey.

A copy of *The Voyage Out* was open on Heidi's lap but she had not turned a single page. Heidi adored Virginia Woolf. A picture of the novelist, clipped from a magazine, was taped to her bedroom wall, and the novels were neatly arranged on her shelf. She had wept when she learned of Woolf's suicide and she and her two best friends at the High School of Music and Art had dressed in black for a week.

"I don't care." Indifference weighted her words.

Beth closed her *Bride* magazine and looked at Heidi and then at me, but I did not meet her eyes. I did not want her to see the reflection of my own worry and I feared that if I exposed and articulated my anxiety, I would endow it with reality.

The truth was that I had been troubled about Heidi since summer's end.

The weeks at the Michigan music camp had left Heidi pale because she had spent a great deal of time indoors practicing for a competition, which, in the end, she had lost, attaining only an honorable mention.

"Which for my mother is really dishonorable," she reported with a harsh laugh.

"You should tell her that you don't want to concentrate so much on the piano, that you don't want to go back to music camp next summer," I advised.

"It doesn't matter. There are more important things to worry about."

It was the war that Heidi worried about. She read the *New York Times* each morning during the long subway ride to school. Then she read the *PM* on the way home. She asked my grandfather to translate the war stories from the Yiddish press. And from all these newspapers she clipped stories and photographs and filed them away in an oak-tag folder.

"Heidi is so interested in current events," Edna said proudly but I knew that the clippings Heidi saved referred only to what was happening to the Jews as the war in Europe raged on. In that year of our war, the concentration camps and the deportations were common knowledge. We knew that Jews were dying and that Jews were on the run and that they had no place to go. But this knowledge formed yet another discrete block in the vast mosaic of a world at war. We concentrated on specific patterns of that mosaic, selecting a cross section where we had vested interests. Because of my father, I focused on stories about the European theater, and Judy Bergman followed stories about air action over the Pacific because that was where Marvin flew. We made such choices because a war fought on so many fronts was bewildering, incomprehensible. We pitied the newscasters who struggled to pronounce the names of battlefields in distant lands, stuttering as they verbally leapt across the globe. Cotentin, Caen, Nijmegen, Eindhoven, Leyte Gulf, Sansapor, the Vogelkop Peninsula. The names formed clumsily on their tongues, wounded our ears, and very occasionally caused us to giggle with mild hysteria. For Heidi, only the concentration camps were of significance in that far-reaching mosaic. She slept lightly, I knew, and wakened often in the night moaning and murmuring pleas and protests. "*I didn't.*" "*Oh stop.*" "*Don't hurt me.*" I feared her dark dreams and when we shared a room I slept at a remove from her because even then I knew that terror was contagious.

Heidi had grown several inches during the summer but she had gained little weight. Her skirts, which were too short, and her blouses, with sleeves that ended at midarm, hung forlornly on her bony frame. She could not be persuaded to go shopping for new clothing. She ate so little that Edna, in exasperation, shouted that she had begun to resemble an internee in a concentration camp. Briefly, an expression of satisfaction drifted across Heidi's thin face and I realized that was precisely what she wanted. Unvictimized, she would transform herself into a victim. She too would become skeletal and ill-clothed, imprisoned behind the barbed wire of her own fear and fantasy.

Only for Brides was located on Seventh Avenue and Thirty-fourth Street. We hurried past the Macy's window, draped in red, white, and blue bunting, slowing our steps briefly to admire the mannequins in clinging evening gowns who floated in the arms of papier-mâché Allied officers. Mr. Rosenstein, rotund and dapper in his double-breasted suit, snuffed out his cigar on the showroom desk and hurried forward to greet us.

He was a man who made his living pleasing women and he understood the words and gestures that invoked their trust, the subtle deference that restored older women to youth and endowed adolescent girls with a new and sensual maturity.

"You're in luck, such luck," he said with great enthusiasm. "I thought I had only three gowns to show you, but just today I have another one. And this one, I know, is perfect for your Beth. Look, tell me if I'm not right."

He led us into the factory where round-shouldered men and women in worn cardigans bent over sewing machines and worked at cutting tables.

"Here, look. I hung it already on the dummy."

We looked. The dress was of ivory peau de soie, high-necked and puff-sleeved. Its long skirt belled out like the petals of a tulip and it trailed a long train. Beth gasped.

"I dreamed it and here it is," she said.

Proudly, Mr. Rosenstein carried the dress into the plywood cubicle that served as a dressing room and I closed the door behind him. Dutiful ladies-in-waiting, Heidi and I helped to lift the gown, heavy as a small child, over Beth's head. I knelt to arrange the train and Heidi stood on tiptoe to fasten the tiny buttons that paraded up the back of the dress.

"Oh, Beth, you look beautiful, really beautiful." We spoke in unison and circled her, adjusting the skirt, setting the Juliet cap with its flowing veil on her golden hair. The dress was almost a perfect fit. It transformed our cousin into a princess bride stepped from the pages of a fairy tale book.

"Once upon a time . . ." Heidi said softly.

"And they lived happily ever after," I concluded gaily.

Holding the train between us, Heidi and I followed Beth into the factory. The sewing machines whirred into silence and the cutters lifted their silver scissors as though they were magic wands.

"Mazel tov," a seamstress called from across the room.

"A beautiful bride." "Mazel tov." "She should only know happiness." The blessings of luck reverberated throughout the factory, punctuated by laughter. They turned back to their work with renewed vigor as Beth moved toward Lottie and Edna.

"What do you think?" she asked shyly.

"Ah, it's perfect, perfect," Lottie said and her eyes were wet with tears.

"It needs the tiniest tuck at the waist, Abe," Edna told Mr. Rosenstein, who was already darting forward, a pincushion braceleted to his wrist. Deftly, he pinched the fabric at the waist and held it firm with a straight pin.

"Better. Turn around, Beth."

Slowly Beth turned. Edna touched the buttons.

"You'll have to resew the buttons."

"The buttons are tight. I checked them myself."

"No. They have to be resewn. See?" Magically, Edna had found the single button that needed reinforcement and he nodded in defeat. Always Edna could be relied on to ferret out obscure imperfections and ensure against disaster.

"So I'll resew them. But look, the hem is perfect. The sleeves also."

"Perfect. So you have a wedding dress," Lottie said. "Edna, help her change. I want Heidi and Sharon to see what Abe has for them. Bridesmaid dresses we need, Abe. My nieces want short dresses. In the same style as the wedding dress, if you have."

"I have. Short dresses in that style. One blue. One yellow." I glanced at him curiously. The coincidence was odd but he bustled off and returned with the dresses on his arm, removing tags from them before he handed them to us. Heidi and I were directed to a fitting room. My dress fit well and I liked the shade of blue — as quiet as a summer sky. The skirt flared out just at my knees and I plucked it higher and studied my legs in the mirror. Somehow, I would get silk stockings for the wedding and they would shimmer as I danced. I swept my hair back, twisted it into a single dark curl that I tossed over my shoulder. Yes, I would wear it that way, tied with a blue silk ribbon. I rejoiced because I no longer looked like the androgynous adolescent in jeans and an oversize man's shirt whom Robert had captured in his portrait. I saw the sensuous curve of my lips, the new fullness of my figure. And then grief tumbled after joy. Lottie had wept at Beth's beauty. But who would weep for mine?

I turned to Heidi, who had struggled into her dress. Yellow was the wrong color for her. It jaundiced her already pale skin. The dress had been made for a large-breasted girl, cut to measurement, I suspected. The bodice tented on Heidi's flat chest and the high collar cut into her slender neck, almost cupping her chin.

"It's not for you, Heidi," I said. "It's the wrong color, the wrong cut."

"It doesn't matter. Beth wants them to be the same. And yours looks swell."

She scowled angrily at her reflection, at the narrow-featured face that gave her no pleasure, at the body that was taking too long to develop.

"My neck is so long." Misery muffled her voice.

"My mother had a long neck — a swan's neck, my father called it," I said.

I offered her emotional bribery; I would shame her out of self-pity.

"Your mother was beautiful," Heidi said. "But I don't care. It doesn't matter. It shouldn't matter. Not with what's happening to other people."

Her lips set in firm resolve. She would not allow it to matter.

"Girls, let's have a look," Edna called and I opened the door of the cubicle and pirouetted in front of my aunts and my cousin.

"Oh, Sharon, good. Perfect." Beth clapped her hands and nodded in approval. "We'll have to get shoes dyed to match. And silk stockings. Aunt Edna, you're going to have to come up with silk stockings."

Edna nodded. Somewhere, among Emanuel Weiner's vast acquaintances, there was someone who would come through with silk stockings.

But Beth shook her head when Heidi stepped forward.

"Uh-oh. It's all wrong. The color, the style, everything."

"Come. You must have something else, Abe. Something in a dark rose color, a lilac — cut narrower," Lottie said. "Don't worry, Heidi, Mr. Rosenstein has a big stock."

"It's not important."

"It is important." Already Mr. Rosenstein had three new dresses looped over his arm.

"Look, primrose pink. More tailored but with a nice flared skirt. And here is a very classy number in raspberry taffeta. And look, this lilac silk is pre-war stock. A scoop neck. Perfect for her."

It was the lilac pre-war stock that we settled on at last. Heidi herself smiled to see how the fabric fell in graceful folds and the bolero jacket with its winged sleeves afforded her a layer of fullness and such easy grace that she lifted her arms as she turned slowly before the mirror.

"You see. You see how pretty you can look," Beth said triumphantly. Even then she was determined to share her joy, to allow her happiness to spill over into the lives of others. That generosity of her girlhood has endured throughout her life.

Swiftly, Heidi pulled the dress over her head and dressed again in her plain white blouse and the gray skirt that hung too loosely at her waist.

We thanked Mr. Rosenstein, who packed up my dress and Heidi's. The wedding gown would be altered and delivered within days. He beamed at us, beamed at the check Lottie gave him, and cheerfully bobbed us out into the showroom and then to the elevator.

But when we reached the street, I turned.

"I left my book up there," I said. "I'll be back in a minute."

I darted back into the elevator before they could remember that I had not carried a book.

"Mr. Rosenstein," I said breathlessly when I was back in the showroom, "I have to know. For whose wedding was my cousin Beth's gown and my blue dress made? And how come we were able to get them? Was the engagement broken?"

He reddened and looked away.

"Not a broken engagement," he said. "A sad thing. A terrible thing."

"Why sad? Why terrible?" My own persistence surprised me.

"The groom was killed. He was an army officer but he was set to come home. From where I don't know. Maybe Europe. Maybe the Pacific. One day before he was set to leave he was riding in a jeep that was booby-trapped. This is what the bride's father told me when he came to cancel the order for the dresses. He cried when he told me. Cried and cursed. He planned for a wedding and went instead to a funeral. That we should live to go to such funerals. That we should bury our children. They were babies. He was twenty-three. She was twenty." He swayed from side to side, his grief become a prayer.

My heart swelled and my cheeks burned. Beth was twenty. Alfred was twenty-three.

"I'm sorry," I said. "But I had to know."

"Why?" He looked at me and all affability vanished from his face. "Why did you have to know?"

I had no answer to offer him. I turned and took the elevator down to the street where my aunts and my cousins waited for me. I walked very slowly, hobbled by the sad knowledge I would not share with them. I was glad that I did not know the name of the bride whose wedding night had never come or that of the bridesmaid who had never danced in the soft silk dress the color of a summer sky.

8

Alfred arrived and we were all relieved that he was so pleasant, that he laughed with such ease, that he looked at Beth with such tenderness and love. They went out every night. Julius bought them orchestra seats for *Oklahoma!* and Leon got them tickets for the New York Philharmonic at Carnegie Hall. Emanuel Weiner invited them to have dinner with him and his wife at the Waldorf-Astoria. Although the weather had turned chilly, Alfred and Beth went to Coney Island and rode the Cyclone and ate hot dogs at Nathan's. They strolled through the Brooklyn Botanic Garden and walked the aisles of Fifth Avenue stores hand in hand. Alfred carried a Brownie box camera and he took pictures of Beth, and Beth took pictures of him, and strangers took pictures of both of them together. They were a handsome couple and passersby looked at them with wistful affection and wished the tall lean soldier and the blond girl whose face was bright with joy good fortune.

Beth returned from each excursion with a souvenir — a program, a ticket stub, a menu, a mustard-stained paper napkin — all of which she pasted into a leather-covered scrapbook.

"You're going out again?" I asked one evening as I watched Beth dress.

"There'll be plenty of time to sit home after Alfred's shipped out," she said as she buckled the ankle strap of her black platform heels. They were going to a nightclub called Leon and Eddie's to listen to jazz. "We'll have only a couple of days together after the wedding.

"But I'll be home tomorrow night," she promised. "Alfred's buddies are taking him out for a sort of bachelor party. And my parents are taking Bubbie and Zeidey to the Yiddish theater so we'll have the house to ourselves. We can have a party too. We'll ask Heidi and maybe some other girls. A hen party."

But Heidi was hesitant when I called to invite her to spend the evening with us.

"I have so much to do. There's a big chemistry exam. And I have a paper due."

"Oh come on," I argued vigorously. "Beth's getting married. What difference does all that school stuff make? Judy will be here. And Karen."

There was a long silence and then she said, "You're right, Sharon. You're absolutely right. What difference does it make? What difference does anything make?" She spoke in a monotone and there was an intake of breath that was neither sigh nor laughter.

Lottie left dinner for us the next night, a festive delicatessen meal to be served on paper plates. But Heidi did not arrive until we were halfway through and she waved away the platters of meat and potato salad.

"I ate," she said. "I had to make dinner for Bernie."

I did not tell her that Bernie had called from a friend's house. He had been invited for dinner, he said, and he wanted Heidi to know her piano teacher had called to ask why she had missed her lesson.

Karen, who by happy chance was visiting her grandparents, brought a bottle of champagne.

"From my enlightened mother," she said. "She insists that it's good for the bride to have a champagne dream just before her wedding. And what's good for the bride is good for the brides-maids and their friends."

Beth laughed and lined up the glasses while Karen opened the bottle. She was a Woodstock child, a skilled observer of adult rituals, and she worked quickly and expertly. The cork flew up and the frothy liquid foamed and bubbled, overflowing the glasses which we raised in a toast.

"To Beth and Alfred — our once-upon-a-time lovers," I said. "We hope they live happily ever after."

The wine tickled our throats and caused us to smile. Judy giggled. She was, then and forever after, a silly drunk. Even now when she calls me at the sunset hour I can tell by the merriment in her voice that she has had a glass of Chablis.

"Another toast," she said. "First comes love, then comes marriage, then comes Beth with a baby carriage."

We laughed. We had scrawled those words into autograph albums and jumped rope to them but Beth and Alfred had vested them with reality. There was love, there would be marriage, and there could be, with the passage of time, Beth with a baby carriage. The nonsense rhyme of childhood trilled with reality and we felt ourselves newly grown up.

Judy passed around a package of cigarettes, the red-tipped Debs that we sometimes smoked as we sat on the esplanades, and we each took one and leaned forward as she lit them with a long kitchen match. Heidi inhaled deeply and reached for the champagne bottle. She filled another glass and sipped it slowly.

"I like champagne," she said wonderingly, as though surprised that anything at all could give her pleasure.

"There's nothing wrong with champagne," Beth agreed. "When Alfred comes home from overseas, we're going to buy us a bottle and drink it all by ourselves." She smiled happily and began to clear the table. We all helped her, gliding across the kitchen as though in a dream. We laughed softly as we drifted through the clouds of smoke and felt the champagne course sweetly through our bodies.

We went to Beth's room and viewed her wedding presents. Like small girls playing house, we spread her desk with the elegant lace tablecloth that had been Emanuel Weiner's gift and arranged a place setting using her white china ribbed with gold, the shining new flatware, a slender-stemmed wineglass, and a linen napkin.

"Shall I pour?" Beth asked and waved a nut brown ceramic teapot over the cup. I recognized the glaze.

"Who gave you that?" I asked.

"Robert. It comes with a set of mugs. A friend of his made them."

Karen looked at me and I wondered if she knew about Robert and Franchesca.

Beth lifted the lid of a large white box.

"My negligee and peignoir. For my wedding night," she said and lifted a sheer golden cloud of fabric from the cushion of tissue paper. We gasped in admiration.

"Try it on," Judy said.

"All right."

She undressed and slipped the negligee on. Her skin shone rose-gold through the gossamer sunlit fabric that almost matched her hair. The gown fell in graceful folds, pleated and narrowed about the luminous globes of her breasts, billowing gently at her ankles. The peignoir was wide-sleeved and high-collared. Caped within it, she was a sun maiden, radiant and innocent, sensuous and elusive.

"Gorgeous."

"Beautiful."

We circled her like admiring acolytes, reaching out to touch her golden wings, to trail our fingers across the translucent fabric.

"Do you want to try it on?"

We giggled and swiftly unbuttoned and unzipped our school-girl clothing, tossed the patterned sweaters and woolen skirts of autumn to the floor.

"Careful, careful," Beth cautioned and we handled the delicate garments tenderly. Judy and Karen each in turn tried on the peignoir, but I held my breath as Beth slipped the negligee over my head. Karen and I each pirouetted in front of the mirror, dreaming ourselves into the future. We imagined a man's strong hands slipping beneath the golden folds to touch our breasts, our arms, the secret moist cavity of our pleasure. We caressed our own hips and thighs and then, very carefully, we slipped out of the gown and robe and handed them back to Beth. She shrouded them once again in tissue paper and replaced them in the box.

"Where's Heidi?" Judy asked.

"She's probably in the bathroom," I said and I helped Beth replace the china and the silver. I handled the ceramic teapot with special care, careful even then to contain and control my anger — an essential talent for those who live in other people's homes.

Karen and Judy, in white panties and bras, sat opposite each other on the bed and painted their toenails. Beth turned the radio on and we sang along with Frank Sinatra.

" 'It was only a paper moon, sailing high in a cardboard sky . . .' "

His voice, so mellow and caressing, crooned us into the make-believe world of his song. He soothed us into tranquillity and we forgot for a few moments that our world was at war.

Beth and I, in our plaid cotton pajama coats, danced with each other. Barefoot, we executed intricate twists and dips until at last we collapsed onto the bed.

"I have to pee," Beth said. "Isn't Heidi ever coming out of the bathroom? Heidi!" she shouted.

There was no answer.

She's probably in the shower," Judy suggested. She lifted her leg. Her toenails glowed like rubies.

"Do mine next. With the pale pink polish," Beth said. "Alfred loves my toes." She smiled and I imagined Alfred kneeling before her, her foot in his hand, kissing each painted toe. "I'll be back."

She went down the hall to the bathroom. "Heidi!" she called again and tapped on the door.

Seconds later, she was back.

"She wasn't in the bathroom," she said.

"Maybe she's in the kitchen getting something to eat. She hardly had anything at dinner." Karen waved the brush in the air and began to paint her fingernails.

"No. I looked. She's not anywhere in the house. Not upstairs, at least." Beth spoke very slowly and an icy sheath of fear coated my body.

Wordlessly, I went to the staircase that led to our grandparents' apartment. Beth followed me. Karen and Judy remained in the hallway, their laughter silenced, their faces pale. They were frightened but they would not follow. This was family business, a complicity of cousins.

A dim orange light illuminated the staircase and we made our way down, past the mops and brooms which Lottie stored on the broad middle step. There was no light beneath the closed door that opened into my grandparents' apartment and I was fearful, suddenly, that the door would be locked. Julius had installed a small latch — "They should have privacy if they want," he had said with the insight of a man who had known very little privacy in his own life — but it was rarely secured. Let it be unhooked, I prayed, and turned the knob. The door opened and we stepped into the darkened dinette area.

"Oh, God," Beth said. "Oh my God." And then she could say no more because her hands flew up to cover her mouth and nose, to block the noxious odor of gas that filled the room.

My own eyes were burning and I clamped my lips shut and felt along the wall for the light switch.

"Heidi."

We spoke in a single voice and sprinted together into the kitchen where Heidi knelt before the open oven. Her head was pillowed by the soft white towel that she had placed on the oven door. A thread of spittle dangled from her mouth. Her eyes were closed and her skin was waxen.

We seized her by the shoulder, frantic because she was a dead weight and it took all our combined strength to pull her away from the yawning oven and lay her down on the kitchen floor.

"Open the windows. All the windows," I said tersely.

"Is she dead?" Beth spoke in a whisper.

"I don't know. Open the windows."

I lay across Heidi and breathed into her mouth, in and out. My heart pounded and I pushed at her chest with my open palms.

Once at Revere Beach I had watched my father revive a man who had been rescued from the sea, and I willed that memory into action. In and out. In and out. My arms ached and my body seethed with pain. The man on the beach had vomited, I remembered, a refulgence of pale green phlegm that layered my father's lips and spurted onto his cheeks. Afterward my mother had wiped his face with a handkerchief and tossed the linen square into a wastebasket. But Heidi did not move. My own breath came in stertorous gasps. Sweat beaded my arms. I was light-headed and felt my strength ebbing.

"Will she be all right?" Beth's voice trembled with nervousness.

As though in answer to her question, Heidi stirred and her eyes fluttered open. She stared at me and a single tear formed in the corner of her right eye and trickled down her cheek. She turned her head and retched. Yellow mucus rimmed her lips, the residue of the champagne.

"Is everything okay?" Karen called down to us.

"It will be okay," I yelled back with an assurance I did not feel.

I helped Heidi to sit up and Beth wiped her face with a wet cloth.

"I'm cold," she said and she began to shiver.

Beth moved to close the window but I motioned her away.

"Breathe deeply," I ordered Heidi, and like a small girl, she opened her mouth and gulped in the cold air.

"Again." I was insistent and she obeyed me without protest. After a few minutes I helped her up and walked her to the window. Beth draped my grandmother's pale blue cardigan over her shoulders. There was a strange sweetness in the air that night, a melancholy commingling of seasonal scents, the heady fragrance of the brief-lived zinnias blending with the earthy aroma of decaying leaves in rich dark earth.

We walked Heidi back and forth beneath that window, urging her forward even when she leaned back against us in exhaustion.

"I'm so tired," she said.

"Just a bit more," I promised. "Fill the tub with hot water," I called up to Judy and Karen.

The color returned to Heidi's cheeks. Her eyes lost their glazed look and she moved more easily.

"I'm sorry," she murmured over and over but I could not tell if she was sorry she had tried to kill herself or sorry that she had not succeeded.

Beth lit the pilot light on the oven and I switched off the lights. We helped Heidi upstairs and together we bathed her, using Beth's milled soap and her purple bath salts. We would wash our cousin clean of despair and scrub her pale skin free of the scent of death. Vigorously, Beth washed her hair. The odor of gas lingered in the fine pale tendrils, and a piece of white fluff from the towel she had used as a pillow nestled behind her ear.

"Why, Heidi, why did you do it?" It was Beth who asked the question as we all gathered again in the bedroom.

Heidi leaned against the pillows. In her white, flower-sprigged seersucker nightgown, she looked like a child, and like a child she began to cry.

"I'm sorry," she said yet again. "I didn't mean to do it — at least not now, before your wedding, Beth. But I drank the champagne and I felt so dizzy, so confused. And sad. So terribly sad. It was as though all the bad feelings I've had since the summer came together into one big weight that pressed down on me. An awful dark pressure that made it too hard to think, too hard to breathe, too hard to be." Her voice cracked. "Oh, I'm so unhappy. And I know I have no right." She spoke in plaintive protest. "How can I be that unhappy, that sad — nothing bad is happening to me, nothing at all compared to what's happening to other people."

"What other people?" Karen asked gently. She was her father's daughter. She scanned the professional journals that littered his desk, and lurked beside the closed door of his consulting room, listening to the reassuring cadence of his voice, the sobs of his patients. She understood that words emancipated, that talking was often akin to touching. It brought comfort; it brought relief.

"Like the children in Europe. The Jewish children. I keep

thinking that it could have been us. It's just an accident of history that we're safe in this country and they're over there. If Bubbie and Zeidey hadn't gotten on a ship and come to the United States, it would be us in those pictures, us behind the barbed wire, in the ghettos, yellow stars sewn on our clothing. Without enough to eat, without sweaters and winter coats, without families." She shivered; her eyes glittered feverishly. "I look at their pictures in the newspapers. I watch them in the newsreels and I think — they're me. And I am them. And I worry that I could become them. What if Hitler wins the war in Europe — what if he crosses the Atlantic? Who would take care of us, who would hide us? I think about it all the time. I make lists and then I throw them away and I make new lists. Two nights ago an ambulance went down our street and the siren sounded. I woke up and ran to the window. I was sure that I'd see cars with swastikas on them, that Gestapo officers were going to march up the steps of our house. Doesn't that sound crazy?"

She looked imploringly at us. She wanted us to reassure her, to understand her fears and then to dismiss them.

We turned to one another helplessly. We were novices at grief, uneasy still with irrational fears. In our hearts, we agreed with Heidi that she had not earned her desperate unhappiness. The wide-eyed and bewildered children whose pictures had become familiar to us — the small boy in the large broad-brimmed cap, the yellow star sewn to the jacket of his coat, his arms raised; the girl with straight short hair who hugged a rag doll to her chest — they were entitled to such misery, such desperation. Even I, because of my mother's death and my father's absence, was forgiven sudden changes of mood and allowed to hide behind the veil of sadness that occasionally fell over me without warning or explanation. I was allowed such a margin because any day a telegram with three stars on the envelope might arrive and I would find myself an orphan. My itinerant moods were installment payments against losses yet to come, and as such were forgiven.

But the war had not hit Heidi in the face. It had merely tapped her on the shoulder. Her immediate family was intact and the Gestapo was not coming to Brooklyn.

"Look, Heidi, nothing like that is going to happen here," Beth said patiently. "We're in the United States."

"I read that Virginia Woolf killed herself because her husband was a Jew and she was afraid of what would happen if he was taken prisoner by the Germans." She spoke so softly that we had to draw close to hear her.

I shook my head, struck by a sudden insight. The British novelist, I knew, had filled her pockets with pebbles so that she would sink rapidly and drown in the river. Heidi had left the door to my grandparents' apartment unlatched. She did not recognize it yet, but she had not wanted to die. The thought comforted me.

"Heidi, the war is going to be over. Soon. Very soon. A few weeks. A few months." Judy spoke in her mother's voice. She lived in a house that was being repainted in anticipation of her brother's homecoming. A welcoming feast was in preparation. "And you have your music, your writing. Oh Heidi, everything is just beginning."

Judy spoke to Heidi but her words were meant for all of us. Caught in the nether years between childhood and womanhood, we desperately wanted everything to begin for us. Impatient, we willed ourselves into the future and longed for love to happen. We too wanted to glide into our lovers' arms as Beth had glided into Alfred's. We too wanted to go forth into the night, our high heels clicking, to dance to the music of Count Basie in a smoke-filled nightclub — independent women, beloved by men, responsible to no one but ourselves.

"My music?" Heidi laughed harshly. "I'm not that good. I just go on practicing and pretending so that I don't disappoint my mother. Like I pretend that I don't care how I look — that it doesn't bother me that I'm flat-chested and my skin is too pale. I'm not supposed to care about things like that when there's a war on and people are dying and suffering. But I do care. What kind of a selfish person am I to care about such stupid things at a time like this?" Her voice faded and she closed her eyes. The heavy fatigue of depression had settled upon her but we would not allow her to submit to it.

Beth and I went into the kitchen and poured Coca-Cola into tall glasses.

"Come on, Heidi. Drink something," I said but I was startled when she took a sip.

"I suppose you could say I was selfish for wanting a beautiful wedding," Beth said softly. "But it's not bad or selfish to want everything to be beautiful just for one night."

We were quiet, our silence a cocoon of regret. The apprehensions of our girlhood, the unrevealed mysteries of those years of discovery, were like floating shadows against the all-encompassing canvas of that year of our war.

" 'It's only a paper moon, sailing high in a cardboard sky,' " Beth sang softly, inviting us to reenter the world of make-believe, to move again to the rhythm of fantasy.

We sang with her and danced, our hands light upon one another's waists and shoulders. I danced alone in the circlet of light cast by the standing lamp. Karen and Judy sailed ballroom-style across the rug, and Beth and Heidi, bridesmaid and bride, held each other's wrists and swayed to their own song.

9

We awakened early on Beth's wedding day, surprised that we had slept at all. The phone rang incessantly — friends and relatives asking for directions; the florist and the caterer calling for instructions, to announce calamities, and then to announce their solutions. The front door opened and closed in an almost rhythmic pattern. Telegrams were delivered and for once we did not panic at the sight of the Western Union car. Neighbors popped in to express congratulations and offer their help. A huge bouquet of red roses arrived from Alfred's company commander.

I looked out into the backyard and saw my grandfather at work in his victory garden. He wore his dark suit, the white shirt which my grandmother had soaked for hours in Clorox and ironed with painstaking care, and the striped satin tie he reserved for Rosh Hashana. As always, his white Vandyke beard was neatly trimmed and his black fedora was perched on his thick white hair. He carried a battered red tin sand pail patterned with blue dolphins which he slowly filled with the small green tomatoes plucked from darkening vines. The small, deformed fruit had been ambushed by autumn and would never ripen, but my grandmother would pickle them in brine and we would eat them at our Sunday evening delicatessen feasts. His lips moved as he worked and it occurred to me that he might be praying. He plucked a single red tomato, held it up to the pale autumn sunlight, and nodded with satisfaction. His optimism had been validated.

I wandered into the kitchen. Lottie sat at the Formica table weeping into a crumpled white handkerchief while Julius took a bagel spread with cream cheese and broke it into small pieces, which he held out to her.

"Come, Lottie," he urged, "eat something. Beth will see you crying and she'll be upset."

"What's wrong?" I asked, taking one of the small pieces of bagel. I too wanted to be cared for and comforted.

"That Aaron shouldn't be at his sister's wedding. That I should have two children and one should miss the other's *simcha*," Lottie said plaintively. A snapshot of Aaron in uniform was propped up against her coffee cup. He smiled self-consciously, his hands in the pockets of his Eisenhower jacket.

"So send your complaint to Mr. Hitler," Julius replied tartly.

"Aaron will see the pictures from the wedding," Lottie said. "And the movie." She wiped her eyes and looked at me, ashamed because I had been witness to her grief. "Your father too will watch the movie. We'll have a wedding party after the war, when everyone is home."

"But with a different caterer," Julius said as the phone rang yet again.

But it was not the caterer. It was Alfred calling to tell Beth again that he loved her. Standing on tiptoe in her white terry-cloth robe, she whispered into the black receiver. She laughed and lifted her hand to the birthmark beside her eye as though even at a distance on this, her wedding morning, she would conceal it from him.

The whirl of activity continued. Dina and Robert arrived with a sleeping Anna, whom I carried down to my grandparents' apartment where a small crib had been set up. They were arguing when I came back upstairs, not with passion or with anger but with a cold reasonableness that frightened me. I stood in the hallway and listened, as I had listened to them before, during the long nights of my Woodstock summer.

"It's inappropriate for her to come. This is a family occasion. She was not invited."

"She's interested. She's never seen a Jewish wedding."

"This is not an ethnic show-and-tell."

"She's our friend."

"She's *your* friend. No. You're *her* friend. She's no one's friend."

"I want her at the wedding." He spoke with a sullen insistence, the rich boy who had always gotten his way.

"If you go to her now, today, don't come back here."

"I'll do as I please."

"As you always have."

The front door slammed and I went to the window to watch him drive away. The yellow Nash was spattered with dust, its front fender was dented, and its muffler trailed dangerously low. Although the day was warm, Robert had not put the top down. I no longer saw it as whimsical and romantic. It looked like an ill-kept car, dirty and too small.

No one asked Dina where Robert had gone or when he would be back. Theresa, the hairdresser who worked at Remo's Beauty Shop in Sheepshead Bay, arrived to do our hair and we turned our attention to her.

She had come as a special favor to our family, she reminded us as she set out her combs and brushes, her pomades and sprays on the huge white bath towel which Lottie had spread across the dining room table. She was doing our hair at home because Beth was a soldier's bride and Theresa's own husband was stationed in the Pacific.

"My Aaron is in Europe," Lottie said. She held Aaron's picture in her hand as she sat at the dining room table, and Theresa released her blue-gray hair from the metal rollers which encircled her head. "I worry so much about him."

"I don't worry," Theresa said scornfully. "The Japs are sneaks and cowards. We have MacArthur. We have Halsey. We're the free world. The war will be over by Christmas. You'll see." She brushed Lottie's hair loose and fashioned it into an elegant up-sweep.

Edna and Heidi arrived and took their turns at the table. A sensible pageboy for Edna, and a French braid for Heidi, interwoven with a ribbon of lilac silk that matched her dress. A strand of pearls was draped around her long thin neck.

"You look terrific," I said.

"Do I?" She studied her reflection and smiled at herself, that secret smile women reserve for private moments of self-admiration. A masturbatory smile, a friend of mine wryly calls it and I resent her contempt because I remember still how Heidi smiled that day and how it signified a new beginning for her.

At last it was Beth's turn.

She sat at the table, already wearing her bridal gown, shy as a child in a school play transformed by a beautiful and unfamiliar costume. Theresa sculpted her golden hair into silken lengths that framed her delicate features and curtained the outpouching of her birthmark. She pinned the white Juliet cap into place and arranged the veil in gossamer folds. Beth turned to face us and we gasped at her radiant beauty. Theresa stepped aside as we moved forward to encircle her in our own joy. We were, at that moment, a family of women, exhilarated by the happiness of one of our own.

The neighbors stood on their porches and lined the street as we left for the wedding. Mrs. Calderazzo, whose son Johnny had been killed on D Day, came up to us and took Beth's hands in her own. She wore the black dress and black stockings that had been her costume from the moment she heard the news of Johnny's death and which she wore until the day of her own.

"Such a brave thing you are doing, Beth," she said. "Such a wonderful thing. My Johnny did not know such happiness." She grieved that her son had died before he had lived, that he had never been husband or father. He had died a boy, a mother's son but no man's wife.

Bernie, who had his Brownie camera at hand, snapped a picture of Mrs. Calderazzo standing beside Beth and we have the

photograph still. The young girl in her wedding gown and the
older woman in the black garments of mourning stand together in
a pool of sunlight.

A photographer waited for us at the Manhattan Beach Jewish
Center. Flashbulbs exploded into brightness, and we smiled in
confusion, stood still on command, smiled yet again as we made
our way inside.

Music played. A flautist practiced the medley that would set
the pace for the bridal party during the wedding procession. The
band hired for the reception tuned their instruments behind the
closed doors of the ballroom. A piano trilled, a violin sang, and
drumsticks clattered happily. We were swept through the crowd,
through the admiring gasps and outbursts of excitement, into the
bride's room. Beth was settled on a red velvet chair, but she sprang
up at once to peer into the mirror above the dressing table, to
check a vagrant tendril and freshen her lipstick. She regained her
seat and I knelt to arrange her skirt so that it spread in soft white
tulip petals across the royal blue carpet. Lottie, Edna, and my
grandmother surrounded her, and Dina, with Anna in her arms,
leaned against the wall. They all looked expectantly toward the
door.

"What happens now?" I asked Beth.

"You'll see," she replied. Mystery heightened her majesty.
She knew secrets, understood rituals. Within minutes she would
cross the threshold of maidenhood and become a soldier's wife.
Within days her husband would go to war.

The sound of the flute drew near. A lyrical tune, light and
exuberant. Footsteps pounded down the hallway and men's voices
were raised, half talking, half singing. It was time for the ancient
ritual of the unveiling of the bride.

Lottie drew the veil over Beth's face, and Alfred, in dress uniform, followed by his father and a laughing group of young men,
some in uniforms, some in tuxedos, entered. Alfred licked his lips
and touched the visor of his military hat like a shy boy at his first
dance.

He moved toward his bride as the men clapped and the
women smiled. Gently, he lifted the veil and they looked at each

other gravely, although their faces were brushed bright with joy. She lifted her hands and he covered them with his own. Each gesture was magically anticipated, magically reciprocated. He had, after all, opened his arms on the night of their first meeting and she had floated into them. The flute sounded again and the men left, Alfred lingering briefly to stare back at Beth, who smiled and waved.

Lottie kissed Beth's cheek.

"You see, Mama, I'm doing the right thing," Beth said and her mother nodded and again drew the veil over her daughter's face.

We took our positions at the sanctuary portal, ready to march toward the wedding canopy on cue. We listened to the cantor's mellifluous tones and although we did not understand the prayer we were moved by the power of his voice. We watched as Alfred proceeded down the aisle, walking between his parents, a man and a woman as thin and sharp-featured as their son, she in a rose red dress and he in a tuxedo, their heads high, their backs erect. They had been disciplined by grief. They had buried one son and soon would send another into danger.

The ushers wore the uniforms of the army, the navy, the marine corps. Buckles and buttons glinted, beribboned medals flashed. Their smiles were at once bashful and proud. Heidi was escorted by a naval lieutenant and I matched my own steps to the pace of Marty Feldman, a marine officer whose white dress cap covered his carrot red crew cut. He had been Alfred's fraternity brother at Northwestern.

The sanctuary was crowded. The guests, summoned by telegram and telephone, had made strenuous efforts to attend this dramatic and hastily organized wedding. Relatives and friends had traveled from distant cities and they beamed at one another, telegraphed their delight with flashing eyes and brilliant smiles. They were pleased to be participants in a *simcha*, a celebration of happiness, hope, and stubborn romance. They forgot, for those brief hours of celebration, that the optimism of the late summer and early fall had been premature. Most of them did not believe that the war would soon be over. They knew about the German flying bombs, the incursion into Hurtgen Forest, and the unrelenting bombing over strongholds in the Pacific. The dark and terrible stories about what was happening to the Jews of Europe weighed heavily upon the guests. The young men of their families wore uniforms, and they haunted their mailboxes and answered their phones with quivering voices.

But this marriage energized them and they seized the joy of the moment. They whispered excitedly to one another, marveled at the beauty of the flowers, the red, white, and blue carnations set in silver urns at each row of seats. They hummed as the flautist played selections from the Song of Songs. "I am my beloved's, and my beloved is mine." "Come with me from Lebanon, my lovely, my bride."

There was a hushed silence when the first four ushers made their way down the aisle. Alfred's friends — a marine, an ensign, and two officers from his infantry division — each held a single pole of the wedding canopy, an American flag fashioned of shimmering satin stars and stripes. Slowly, with military precision, they marched up to the ark and lifted the canopy over the rabbi and the cantor.

Alfred and his parents moved beneath its shelter. He escorted them gently, supporting them as surely as he had supported them all his life with his good behavior, his good grades, his quiet achievements. He was the surviving son and it was incumbent upon him to compensate them for their loss. They smiled because their soldier son was such a handsome groom and his bride was sweet-voiced and gentle.

I smiled as I entered the sanctuary, although I clutched my bouquet of red, white, and blue roses — the florist had gone to great lengths to obtain the blue dye, he had told us proudly — so tightly that the wire that linked the flowers cut into my palms. A flashbulb exploded and I tilted my chin — my best angle, Robert had assured me as I perched on the stool in his studio. I would send the picture to my father and startle him with my new maturity. He would show it proudly to his colleagues, his nurses, to the wounded soldiers he tended. *My daughter,* he would say. *She's grown so beautiful I hardly recognize her.* He would place that photograph in the inner pocket of his Eisenhower jacket where he kept the snapshot of my mother in her wedding dress and a love letter she had written him after his induction. I knew this because I had gone through his pockets on that last night of his last leave when he and my mother went out to dinner. I had even read her letter, angered that night because they had left me home alone, excluding me from their last farewell. She loved him more than her own life, she had written in her neat accountant's hand, and now her own life was gone. I wondered if he wept over her words when he reread that letter, training his flashlight on it in the darkness of a European night.

Marty Feldman and I took our places and turned as the violinist played the Wedding March, and Beth, walking between Lottie and Julius, started down the aisle. Lottie was flushed and her eyes were very bright. I knew she was reciting poetry to herself, the favorites that she invoked as mental sedatives: "How do I love thee? Let me count the ways . . ." "That time of year thou mayst in me behold / When yellow leaves, or none, or few, do hang . . ." Her lips moved almost imperceptibly and she nodded as she passed the row in which her sisters and brother sat — Edna ramrod-straight beside Leon, Dina with Anna in her arms, Samuel beside Dolly, who had neatly spread three lace handkerchiefs on the lap of her jade green satin dress. Dolly was one of those women who cry at weddings and remain dry-eyed at funerals.

Julius was red-faced and beads of sweat dewed that part of his bald pate left exposed by his white satin skullcap. The wedding, like the war, had caught him off guard and undermined his plans. He had spent his life working for his family's happiness and well-being. He would shelter his son and daughter from the poverty and uncertainty that had defined his own immigrant youth and young manhood. But history had ruthlessly intervened and left him impotent. Aaron was somewhere in Europe, and Beth was the bride of a man who would soon be shipped overseas.

Beth floated between them, a fairy tale bride, her face shining through the sheer white veil. A hushed silence stole over the room, a communal intake of breath followed by a shared gasp of wonder. Dolly lifted the first of her handkerchiefs to her eyes.

Beth stood beneath the wedding canopy, glanced briefly up at the American flag held taut by the uniformed ushers, and then turned her head to Alfred as the cantor began the cantillation.

I listened as though in a dream to the melodious chanting of the prayers. Heidi and I lifted Beth's train and followed her as she circled Alfred, walking about her groom seven times in accordance with tradition. A baby cried and I glanced out to where Dina sat. She shifted Anna to her other shoulder. Nachum Adler sat beside her, a sketch pad on his lap, the white cloud of Anna's small sweater on his arm.

Heidi lifted Beth's veil so that she could drink from the cups of sacramental wine and I held her bouquet of white orchids so that Alfred could place the gold marriage band on her finger, which, strangely, trembled at his touch.

"Behold, you are consecrated unto me with this ring according to the laws of Moses and of Israel."

I wondered that God was not mentioned in that marriage vow. It seemed to me a dangerous omission. God, if He existed at all, and I had entered into the first season of my doubting, needed reminders, the urgent memoranda of prayers.

But there was no time to brood over that. The ceremony moved swiftly forward. Alfred stamped upon a glass wrapped in a white napkin, and amid the joyous outcry, the burst of applause, he drew Beth to him. Her veil was flung back and he kissed her on the lips and then lifted the lock of hair placed so carefully over the birthmark and kissed the wine-colored nevus. There was no part of her that he did not love; there was no fault or imperfection that he would have her conceal from him.

Their parents encircled them and the sanctuary filled with cries of congratulations.

"Mazel tov!" The words were a mighty shout, a joyous chorus of beneficence.

"Such a wedding."

"Such a beautiful bride."

"Such a handsome groom."

They were effusive in their praise and they laughed and

clapped as Beth and Alfred, bride and groom become man and wife, dashed back down the aisle.

How we danced at that wedding. Danced and ate and drank. Huge hora circles formed and the dancers stamped and sang with rhythmic strength. Leon and Julius crouched on the floor in the midst of a whirling circle of dancers and kicked their feet out in a *chazatska,* their white satin skullcaps slipping down over their sweating foreheads. The men, whom I recognized from their somber Saturday night discussions at the dining room table, hugged one another's shoulders and danced in a rollicking line. I had thought them skilled only in worry and sorrow. I had not known that these dark-suited businessmen had such a talent for joy. Beth sat on a chair in the midst of a circle of dancers, beaming happily. Other chairs were brought for Lottie and my grandmother, and Beth sat between them until she was lifted high in her chair and Alfred was lifted high in another by exuberant men and boys. Laughing, they held hands as they sat on their airborne thrones, king and queen of their joyous wedding feast.

A conga line formed and we snaked through the room, weaving our way through the laden buffet tables. Hands on one another's hips, we wiggled and giggled, balancing our heads like Carmen Miranda. " 'There's a song in the air but the fair senorita does not seem to care for the song in the air,' " we sang.

The band struck up a *debka*. Dina, Lottie, and Edna linked arms and danced toward their parents, kicking their legs out, bobbing their heads. My grandmother smiled, then laughed, and finally covered her face with her handkerchief because she was crying. Her tears were for my mother, I knew, and I felt guilty because I had not remembered how she had loved to dance the *debka* with her sisters.

I danced a slow dance with Marty Feldman.

" 'Stormy weather — since you went away, the blues walked in, and they're here to stay — stormy weather,' " the vocalist crooned.

My head rested on his shoulder and he danced me out of the ballroom and into the deserted sanctuary, where he placed a hand on my breast and kissed me with tender urgency. His tongue circled my mouth and I did not stop him because he too would soon be shipped overseas, because I loved the way the sweet moistures of our mouths mingled, and because I felt safe in this flower-filled room, now lit only by the dull red glow of the eternal light above the ark that contained the scrolls of the law.

"Will you write to me?" he asked.

"Of course," I promised and he kissed me again and danced me back into the ballroom.

There were speeches. Alfred's friends told jokes about their student days, their basic training. They pressed their military dress hats across their hearts and sang "Beth o' my heart, I love you . . ." and everyone clapped.

Julius and Alfred's father lifted glasses to each other.

"To our children."

"To peace."

"Amen."

The band played "The White Cliffs of Dover" and I circled the room with Marty, who held me so close that his badges cut into my flesh. Beth danced with Alfred, her arms looped about his neck. At the far end of the room, Dina and Nachum Adler slowly circled the same patch of dance floor. He lifted her challis scarf to his cheek then gently draped it once again about her neck. I looked up at Marty and said brightly that not only would I write to him but I would also send him packages. I imagined myself smiling wanly at the postal clerk, accepting her sympathetic glance. *Yes,* I would say sadly, *my boyfriend is serving overseas and so is my father.*

And then Beth and Alfred were cutting their wedding cake, a huge many-layered white confection baked in Emanuel Weiner's industrial bakery. We dared not ask how Edna had obtained the ration coupons for that much sugar, that many eggs. The cake was a testimony to the great man's power, and indeed he stood close by as Beth cut it. He was a rotund and balding fairy godfather who impatiently patted the gold watch that dangled from a double-linked chain at his vest.

The bride and groom fed each other pieces of cake and then

scurried away. Emanuel Weiner had a car waiting for them. He had arranged for them to spend their honeymoon at a small Catskill hotel. They had three days until Alfred's furlough ended and his war began.

The bandleader announced the last dance.

"I'll be seeing you in all the old familiar places . . ."

"I really like you," Marty whispered in my ear. I wondered what he would think of the portrait Robert had painted of me. Would he, like Peter, want to buy it? But I said nothing. I smiled and hummed along with the vocalist, a tired pale girl in a shabby black dress studded with sequins, who looked as though she could not wait for the wedding to be over.

Small children cried with exhaustion. Dina fed Anna her bottle. Robert had not arrived and no one had mentioned his absence. The last lingering guests left reluctantly.

"Such a beautiful wedding. Such a wonderful party."

"They make such a nice couple. Everything will be all right. You'll see."

"Of course. We know. We hope."

Lottie and Julius stood beside Alfred's parents. They all smiled bravely but I knew that Lottie would weep again that night and that Julius would stand at the front window staring down into the darkness.

I picked up my bouquet and saw that the red, white, and blue flowers were already wilting. The caterer folded the flag that had served as the wedding canopy and handed it to Lottie. But it was my grandmother who held it on her lap as we drove home.

10

The wedding euphoria sustained us through the chill gray days of late autumn. It was diminished but not depleted by Alfred's departure. We vested his leave-taking with a patina of romantic drama. My grandmother, Lottie, and I sat very still as he kissed each of us on the cheek and then gravely shook hands with my grandfather and Julius. We did not follow Beth and Alfred out to the porch but we watched them through the glass-paned storm door. The neighbors who had flocked to the street to admire Beth in her wedding dress also remained discreetly inside. They peered through lifted window shades and parted draperies as Beth and Alfred embraced. Beth looked like a schoolgirl in her pale blue sweater and plaid skirt, but Alfred was dressed for a wintry war in his heavy khaki wool uniform, his combat boots shined, his garrison cap perched on his brush-cut hair.

They stood together in a circlet of sunlight, holding each other so close that they seemed as one, merged lovers reluctant to part. I wondered if my father had held my mother that close at their final parting. Perhaps he, like Alfred, had at last moved slightly away, taken her hands in his own, lifted them to his lips, and kissed her fingers one by one as Alfred kissed Beth's. And had my mother, like Beth, stood so appealingly on her toes and kissed his brow, brushed her cheek across his chin? Perhaps, like Beth, my mother had watched as he heaved his duffel bag to his shoulder and made his way haltingly down the steps.

A car waited for Alfred at the curb, crowded with servicemen and driven by an older man, a father who had volunteered to drive to the embarkation point. Alfred's buddies sounded the horn in a staccato summons, so impatient were they to begin their war, and Alfred shrugged, stowed his duffel bag in the trunk, blew Beth a kiss, and was gone. Beth waved as the car pulled away. She remained on the porch, bravely smiling, her hand lifted in salute, a golden-haired poster girl. When the car could no longer be seen, that same hand flew to her mouth and she bit down on her fingers and then ran into the house, tears streaking her cheeks as she rushed to her bedroom and slammed the door behind her.

And had my mother also wept? I wondered with odd dispassion, carefully distancing myself from my cousin's grief. I would never know. I had been in bed when my father left. I remembered that he knelt beside me, smoothed my hair, and kissed me on the cheek. I smelled the mint on his breath, the Aqua Velva on his cheeks, and I knew that my mother stood close by because the scent of her lilac toilet water wafted toward me. And I had remained curled beneath the blankets as they left my room, walking hand in hand, talking softly. I had not sprinted to the window to watch them walk together into the street and so I had not witnessed their last farewell. I had, in fact, held my hands to my ears so that I would not hear the opening and the closing of the front door. I believed, with a child's magical thinking, that what I did not see and did not hear did not actually happen. Perhaps my father would still be there when I emerged from my room. I fell back into a light sleep and I was enraged when I awakened to find that despite all my precautions, he had really left.

I did not wait for Beth to open her door and accept the cup of hot chocolate that Lottie kept in readiness for the moment when her grief would be spent. I went to Judy Bergman's house and described Alfred's departure, emphasizing the kisses he had placed on her fingers.

"If I were Beth," Judy asserted, "I wouldn't wash my hands for the duration."

"Romantic but impractical," I replied. "Who knows how long the duration will be?"

I read the newspaper each day with a sinking heart, and listened to the nightly newscast. Leyte Gulf was ablaze and the Allies were fighting hard against formidable odds in Belgium and Holland.

"Thanksgiving. I have my eyes on Thanksgiving. That's when we should see a turnaround," Mrs. Bergman said. She was embroidering a new tablecloth for the Thanksgiving table — the design of a huge V emblazoned in red and blue cross-stitches across white linen. It was a popular pattern that year. Beth had received two such cloths with matching napkins as wedding gifts.

"I'll tell Hitler and Tojo you said so," Judy said and her mother snipped a length of red satin thread and glared at her.

"Marvin will be home for Thanksgiving, no matter what you say. You were always jealous of your brother, Judy." Her tone was harsh and Judy burst into tears and fled the room.

Beth did not cry after that first afternoon, at least not in front of the family. She went into her room early each night, explaining that she had so much to do. She wrote to Alfred every day and sent a weekly letter to his parents. There were thank-you notes for the wedding gifts that continued to arrive, sterling silver dessert forks, Venetian glass fruit bowls, a carving board of polished wood, and wineglasses balanced on delicate stems. Such gifts conveyed optimism, and Beth saw each small item, each fruit knife and demitasse, as a pledge of allegiance to the future.

"Oh, this will be wonderful when we have company," she said, lifting a glass ice bucket from its tissue paper wrapping. She saw herself and Alfred welcoming guests to their home. Their living room, she had decided, would be decorated in shades of green and blue. She would glide across a deep blue carpet carrying a fruit arrangement in a Venetian glass bowl while Alfred reached into the ice bucket and made drinks for their guests. She was keeping yet another scrapbook, I knew, in which she pasted pictures of furniture clipped from catalogues and magazines. Green easy chairs stared across the oatmeal-colored page at blue couches, and swatches of fabric taken from the upholstery counters at Abraham and Straus were pasted next to them. I had accompanied her on shopping expeditions to De Kalb Avenue.

"I just got married," she would tell the saleswoman with the assurance, peculiar to pampered only daughters, that the intimate details of her life were of interest to all. "My husband and I want to begin furnishing our home as soon as he is released from the army," she told the clerk as she fingered the fabrics and held them to the light.

She did not tell the helpful clerks that Alfred was somewhere in Europe and that their home existed only on the pages of a scrapbook.

Beth went to work with Lottie and Julius each morning. She greeted customers, draping their shoulders with stoles, showing them how fur collars could be sewn onto their dressy cardigans. She had an eye for design, a pleasant manner. Julius boasted about her sales success at a Sunday night dinner.

"She has a talent," he said proudly.

"Of course. Just like Samuel," Dolly replied smugly and Samuel blushed like a small boy, embarrassed by an unexpected compliment. He patted his wife's hand. My mother's only brother and his wife had no need for children of their own. They were child to each other, protective and proud.

Beth read a portion of a letter from Alfred aloud. It had been mailed from the States because Alfred had given it to a soldier who was being shipped home. I wondered that my father never found such emissaries and I was briefly angry with him. It was the end of October and I had not had a letter since the beginning of the month.

"I won't read the personal parts," Beth said and blushed.

She skipped the long first paragraph in which Alfred wrote of his longing for her and told her how he lay awake in his barracks and remembered the night they had gone dancing at Leon and

Eddie's nightclub. "Even now I can feel you against me," he wrote in the even penmanship of the conscientious student. "I remember how well our bodies fit together. I remember your perfume, your lipstick. I can smell them here in the dark."

I had read that letter while Beth was at work, sliding it out of the scrapbook in which she kept the mementoes of their courtship — the pressed flower of a cactus plant, theater programs, and menus. I knew that I was wrong to read Beth's love letters. But Alfred's words were my primer for love. I too wanted a man to lie awake in the dark and remember the touch of my body, the scent of my perfume. I wondered what it would be like to receive a letter like that.

Peter's letters, written on looseleaf paper during classes, were wry and cynical. He wrote that a new sign hung at the collection center, where he continued to work after school. It read BRING YOUR FAT CANS HERE. Peter thought this hilarious and I smiled too. But I really wanted a letter that would cause my cheeks to burn and my heart to swell.

Beth did read Alfred's description of the cold. A cruel winter had descended early on war-torn Europe. He could not say where he was but the area was gripped by a strange frost that was even more severe than those he recalled from his Chicago youth. He could only say that his unit was undergoing rigorous training. "We figure that there will be one more big push and then the Huns will have had it," he wrote cheerfully. He worried about the elections. This was the first year he would have been eligible to vote for a president. "I would have liked to cast a ballot for FDR — some of the guys here have absentee ballots, but not me. I'll just have to vote for a peacetime president the next time around."

"Roosevelt will probably still be running then," Leon said. "He'll probably be president for the rest of our lives."

"And so what's wrong with that?" My grandfather's question was terse. He loved Roosevelt. Robert had remarked once, with typical cynicism, that if Judaism allowed for saints, our family would have beatified Roosevelt. His picture hung on the wall of my grandparents' dinette, beside their framed citizenship papers. Once, watching my grandmother light her Sabbath candles, I saw that she looked toward that picture as she encircled her arms about the flickering flames. It occurred to me that she might be praying to the president as fervently as she prayed to God. She relied on him, as she relied on the deity, to keep my father, Aaron, and Alfred safe, to protect her family in Europe.

"What's wrong with that is that he's not doing anything for us — for the Jews in Europe," Leon replied. "It's not enough that he gets his picture taken with Rabbi Wise and calls him Steven on the radio. It's not enough that he has Morgenthau in the cabinet so he can say some of his best secretaries are Jews. It's not enough that he calls conferences in Evian and Bermuda to discuss the Jewish problem. Talk is cheap. Everyone talks. We need some action. We need bombs dropped on the railway lines in Eastern Europe so that the damn trains can't get to the concentration camps. We need he should twist Churchill's arm and get rid of that stupid White Paper so Jews can get into Palestine. And these things he doesn't do. So I'm going to pull the lever for Tom Dewey, the little man on the wedding cake, the fellow no one would ever buy a used car from."

"And will Dewey be any better?" Julius sounded very tired. "Will he care about the Jews?"

He picked up the *Brooklyn Eagle*. There was a front-page story about Jews being deported en masse from Hungary. A Swiss reporter had wired an eyewitness account of six hundred Jews being shot and thrown into the Danube by the Arrow Cross. Julius covered his face with his hands. Neither Roosevelt nor Dewey could bring dead Jews back to life.

"Someone has to care," Nachum Adler said, his voice enervated by exhaustion. He had driven upstate that day and was wearied by the journey. No one had asked him whether "upstate" meant Woodstock. He did not speak of Dina and she did not speak of him. As though by tacit agreement, parameters of silence were observed. Lottie and Edna continued to speak to Dina on the phone several times a week but their conversations were limited to exchanges about Anna's development and household matters.

They did not ask Dina about Robert. They knew that he was not living in the Woodstock house. Emanuel Weiner, who wandered through art galleries in search of new talent, had met Robert at an exhibition and learned that he was living in New York. Edna had reported this to Lottie, and the two sisters had ruminated over the news, which did not surprise them, shuffling it through a variety of permutations and scenarios.

The door to my bedroom was, as always, slightly ajar, and Heidi and I listened to the murmuring voices as we gave each other Toni home permanents and exchanged our own speculations.

"Do you think Dina and Robert will get a divorce?" Heidi asked. She dipped the comb into the noxious liquid and twisted my dampened hair around the curler.

"He could be working in New York for now. He did that before. When he had a show. Maybe he has a commission or something and he has to be in the city to work on it."

"Maybe."

We did not want Dina and Robert to divorce. Any instability in the family threatened us.

I bit down on a bobby pin worn thin by repeated use.

"This home permanent stuff stinks," I said. "And the war better end soon. Lottie's running out of bobby pins."

But Nachum Adler did not think that the war would end soon, and we knew from the deadness of his tone that he did not believe that anyone, anywhere, cared about the Jews of Europe.

"You vote for Dewey then," Samuel told Leon with the affectionate impatience he reserved for his impractical brother-in-law. "But we're voting for Roosevelt, right, my doll?" He fed his wife a bit of cake, and her lacquered curls trembled beneath the royal blue hat that matched her dress as she nodded vigorously.

"I just wish that Eleanor wasn't so ugly," she said and giggled.

"She's not ugly. She's beautiful," Lottie objected sternly. She never missed the First Lady's "My Day" column in the *PM*. She reported to us nightly on Eleanor's tours of defense plants and army hospitals and nurseries that baby-sat the children of war workers. "And I'll tell you who does care about the Jews in Europe," she added with rare authority. "She does. She really does."

And even Leon was silent, as though he knew that to be true.

Our house was very quiet on Election Day. Lottie and Julius

talked softly because Beth, who had awakened early, had gone back to bed. She was tired, she said, and a little achy. Lottie brought her a roll and a cup of coffee.

"You're sure you're all right?" she asked Beth worriedly. "No trouble breathing?"

"Mom, I haven't had an asthma attack for months," Beth replied irritably. "I'm just tired. You look nice."

Lottie did look nice. She and Julius and my grandparents took Election Day very seriously. Voting was a ritual to be observed with reverence and respect. They dressed for the two-block excursion to Public School 209 as though they were going to synagogue or to the theater. Lottie wore her good dark green winter coat with its stone marten collar clipped shut. The head of the small animal, with its brilliant hard eyes, brushed her chin. Her matching green hat was also fur-trimmed and she carried a large black leather purse.

Julius, wearing his double-breasted dark suit and the wide red silk tie he had purchased for Beth's wedding, set the American flag in place on the porch.

"We vote the straight Democrat ticket," he instructed my grandparents and showed them the diagram of the ballot which the Democratic party block captain left at our house before each election. "See, like always, you press the levers of the first column all the way down."

My grandmother nodded and the cherries on her black felt hat bobbed up and down. She plunged yet another silver hairpin into the neat white bun that rested at the nape of her neck so intricately webbed with wrinkles, and sat beside my grandfather at Lottie's kitchen table. Painstakingly, she practiced signing her name, clutching the pencil tightly between her arthritically twisted fingers. My grandfather brushed a bit of lint from the sleeve of his dark jacket and watched as she wrote.

"Good," he said approvingly. "But make the letters a little smaller — they have to fit on the line." He passed his hand across his carefully sculpted silver Vandyke beard and tightened the knot of his cravat. He was in all things fastidious, a man who struggled for order amid the turmoil of a household of women.

"Remember, the first column, all the way down," Julius repeated. "Democratic party."

"The first column," my grandmother said.

I watched from the front window as Julius and Lottie and my grandparents made their way down Avenue Z toward Coney Island Avenue. They progressed with stately gait, their heads erect, their shy smiles proud. They nodded to the neighbors they passed and to those who waved to them from porches or windows but they did not pause. They had a purpose, a destination.

"Are they gone?"

Beth wandered into the kitchen carrying the coffee cup, which was still full, and the buttered roll. She poured the coffee into the sink and offered me the roll.

"No thanks. I had one already."

"Okay, then."

She tore the roll into strips and shrouded them in paper napkins before placing them in the kitchen garbage.

"No sense in getting my mother upset," she said apologetically. She was very pale.

"Well, if you're sick, she doesn't expect you to eat."

"I'm not sick." But her eyes took on a glazed look and she bolted for the bathroom. Minutes later I heard her retching. Then the toilet flushed and Beth emerged, wiping her face with a damp washcloth.

"You probably have a stomach virus," I offered helpfully.

"No, I don't have a virus." She put the kettle on and plunged her hands into the pockets of her faded blue chenille robe. The golden negligee and peignoir of her brief honeymoon had been consigned to a garment bag in the rear of the storage closet. I wondered that she did not yearn to touch the silken fabric, perhaps even to wear it and feel it against her skin as she thought of the few but magical nights she had spent with Alfred. *Magical* was Beth's word.

"How was your honeymoon?" I had asked her shyly when she returned. I was acutely conscious that she had crossed a mysterious border and her world was now different from my own.

"Magical," she had replied, her eyes shining.

Magical. I pondered the word and it soared in memory when

I became a bride. I worried then that my honeymoon would be less than magical, and that I would not recognize enchantment when I encountered it.

"Maybe you're getting your period," I suggested.

"Or maybe it's because I haven't gotten my period," Beth retorted and the color rushed to her cheeks. She made herself a cup of very weak tea and rummaged in the pantry for Saltines.

"You don't mean . . ." I let my question dangle. I could not bring myself to utter the word that sprang to mind at once, but Beth laughed.

"Yes, I do. That's exactly what I do mean, Sharon. I'm pregnant. I'm going to have a baby." Her face blossomed into brightness and she hugged her abdomen as though that bit of protoplasm, that infinitesimal zygote that had formed in her womb could feel her embrace.

"And they don't know?" I motioned toward the street down which Lottie and Julius and our grandparents had walked in dignified, patriotic procession.

"No. And I don't want to tell them. Not yet. This is just what they didn't want to happen. My mother kept saying that she hoped we would 'be careful' until Alfred came home from the army. She even took me to see Dr. Schorr. In all that rush before the wedding, she found time to get me to a gynecologist. Even my father — you know how he is, he can't talk about things like that — he came into my room on the morning of my wedding day and blushed and said, 'Now, don't be foolish.' " Beth giggled. She was a mischievous child again. Her parents had tried their best but she had circumvented them. They had tried to impress her with the wisdom of their judgment but she had tossed their arguments into the air, replaced reason with romance, and once again, she had done just as she pleased. And they would forgive her. She was their princess, their golden-haired darling.

"Then why didn't you — you know — take precautions?" I blushed. The expression came from the *Merck Marriage Manual* which Judy had discovered in her parents' bedroom and carried to the esplanade one afternoon. She had read aloud from it and we had giggled together as we puffed on our red-tipped Debs cigarettes.

"Because we didn't want to. We wanted everything to be — oh, I don't know — spontaneous, romantic." Beth hesitated as though searching for yet another word.

"Magical," I suggested.

"Yes, yes. Magical." She seized on the word as though it were new to her, as though it were not the word she herself had used a scant few weeks ago. Reality had too swiftly supplanted romance for my cousin. She was a married woman who slept again in her narrow student bed and wore the tattered robe of her late adolescence.

"So we decided to take our chances," she continued. "And we thought, well, even if I became pregnant, it wouldn't be so terrible. Alfred would have a baby to come home to. And if things went wrong..." She stirred her tea and stared at the window where three white satin banners embossed with blue stars hung — one for Aaron, one for my father, and one for Alfred.

I knew what she was thinking. If things went wrong, horribly wrong — if Alfred's blue star became a gold star — he would have left something of himself with her: his child. We had seen so many romantic movies that ended that way. Yes, the hero was lost (sometimes in battle, sometimes to an illness) but a shared love had not been in vain. His wife was pregnant or a child had been born. And in that child's life their own love lived on. Deanna Durbin, Greer Garson, Merle Oberon — all smiled bravely and looked to the future. A crescendo of music. Tears. Applause. We exited the theater clutching our damp tissues, limp with the catharsis of cinematic tragedy and celluloid hope.

"And so I became pregnant. And it's not so terrible. Except in the morning. Something like today."

"Are you sure you're pregnant?" I asked.

"I'm three weeks late. And I was always exactly on time. And there's the way I feel in the mornings. And my breasts — they're very tender." Dreamily, proudly, she chronicled her symptoms. "Besides, I feel it. I feel that I'm carrying Alfred's baby, that I have a part of him within me." She said this very softly, as though she were sharing the deepest secret of her heart with me.

"Beth, you must see a doctor. To be sure," I insisted. Our

roles were reversed; I, the younger cousin, spoke with a monitory firmness that would not be denied.

"But I don't want to go to Dr. Schorr. He'd tell my mother." Her voice was plaintive. Within seconds, she had drifted from pride to fear. She was her husband's wife, but she was her parents' daughter and they had dominion over her.

"I'll find another doctor," I promised.

I called Karen in Woodstock but it was Peter who answered the phone. And Peter asked no questions. He promised to call me back with the name of a New York gynecologist. His father had classmates who practiced in the city, he assured me. I could rely on him. But of course I knew that then, as I know it now.

We waited then, for Lottie and Julius and our grandparents to return from the polls. We turned the radio on and listened to the early election returns. It was clear, even at that hour, that Roosevelt would be elected for a fourth term.

"It's because Bubbie remembered to pull down the lever on the first column," I said wryly. "Roosevelt owes it all to her."

Beth grinned. Quite suddenly, she was ravenously hungry; she lathered a roll with peanut butter and poured herself a huge glass of orange juice.

The news report switched to international events. Germany's rail lines were so crippled that it was now relying heavily on its canals and inland waterways.

Beth clapped her hands softly. Such news items convinced her that the war in Europe was almost over. And when it ended, Alfred would return to her and the gold negligee and peignoir would be removed from the rear of the closet. She would glide into his arms once again, her golden wings spread wide, to embrace him and press him against her body that fit his own so well and wherein his child grew.

But a more somber note crept into the newscaster's voice. Reuters' dispatches revealed that that very morning, even as Americans were surging to the polls to reelect their wartime president, the Japanese had executed Richard Sorge, one of Russia's most successful wartime spies. And in the courtyard of a Budapest prison that same day a young Jewish woman from Palestine,

Hannah Szenes, who had parachuted behind enemy lines in an effort to help the Jews of her native Hungary, had been shot by a firing squad.

"Hannah Szenes." Beth repeated the unfamiliar name aloud, and forever afterward when I thought of that Election Day of 1944, that name, uttered in Beth's sweet voice, echoed in my memory.

The phone rang even as Lottie, Julius, and my grandparents paused at the corner to speak to Mrs. Calderazzo. She too was on her way to vote for Roosevelt. A huge poster with a portrait of the president smiling out of an American flag hung in the front window, just below her gold-star banner. She did not blame the president because her son Johnny had been killed on D Day.

I picked up the receiver. It was Peter and he gave me the name and phone number of a Dr. Greenberg who had offices near Gramercy Park. Even before Lottie and Julius had started up the steps, I had called Dr. Greenberg's office and made an appointment for Beth that Friday morning at eleven-thirty. I took a piece of Lottie's personal stationery on which I would write a note over her signature, excusing my absence from school at that time. Beth's confidence had vested me with responsibility.

We all stayed up late that night listening to the final election results and then to Roosevelt's brief remarks on his victory. The president's voice was thin, and twice, it seemed to me, he lost his place. "We shall have peace in our time," he promised, but despite his brave words his voice was threaded with fatigue.

"He sounds sick," Edna said worriedly.

"He's exhausted. It's been a long war. He's tired of it. We're all tired of it. Except maybe Bernie." Leon grinned at his son, who held his fingers up in a V for Victory signal.

"And it's going to be even longer," Nachum Adler said. He did not look at Beth as he spoke. He did not see her grow pale and clasp her hands protectively across her abdomen.

Dr. Greenberg was a friend of Teddy Bassen's and often visited Woodstock. He knew Dina and Robert, and Robert's portrait of a dark-haired pregnant woman in a black maternity smock hung in his waiting room.

"I bought it at a gallery two years ago. My patients like it very much," the thin gynecologist told us. His hands reminded me of my father's. His fingers, too, were long and tapered, the nail cut short and scrubbed to a pale pinkness.

Dr. Greenberg examined Beth although he told us that the physical examination would reveal nothing.

"Too early to tell. The urine test will give us the answer," he said.

"When will we have the results of that?" Beth asked.

"Oh, two days, three days."

"Because I want to write my husband about it. He'll be so pleased. So excited." Beth twisted her engagement ring, her wide gold wedding band.

"I'll call you at the beginning of the week. Monday, Tuesday."

"No, I'll call you," Beth said swiftly.

On Tuesday, as the first snow of the year fell, Beth and I walked to Sheepshead Bay. I waited outside the phone booth until Beth emerged, smiling, her color high.

"Well?" I asked impatiently although I already knew the answer.

"It's wonderful, Sharon. I'm going to have a baby. Alfred's baby."

"It is wonderful." I hugged her. "You'll tell your parents tonight?"

"No. Not yet. Not until Alfred knows. I want to share the secret only with him, for now. Promise you won't tell."

"I promise," I said and my heart fluttered.

Arm in arm, we walked home, our heads uncovered so that the snowflakes pearled our hair. Laughing, we opened our mouths and the fresh cold flakes fell upon our tongues. We were children still, happy with the new snow and our wondrous secret. At Remo's Beauty Shop we waved to Theresa and then, holding hands, we skipped across Sheepshead Bay Road, our striped woolen scarves flapping wildly in a sudden gust of wind.

11

Frost spangled the windowpanes, then vaporized into a mist onto which I wrote my name with my finger as I spoke to Peter, who'd called to invite me to Karen's sweet-sixteen. A surprise party because Karen insisted that she did not want a party. She thought it would be unpatriotic.

"She has delusions of grandeur," Peter said wryly. "She thinks the course of the war is going to be changed if we mix a fruit punch and serve hot dogs. Anyway, it's not going to be your typical regional high school party. Not with my parents. They're planning a sleigh ride, marshmallows roasted over an open fire. Corny stuff like that."

"I think it sounds great," I said and I drew a birthday candle on the window.

"Then you'll come," Peter said with relief. "It's been a long time since I've seen you."

Although Karen had visited me in Brooklyn, Peter and I had not seen each other since Anna's birth. We had, of course, written and spoken on the phone. Our letters and conversations were laced with sarcasm and cynical observations that compensated for our weaknesses: Peter was lame and I felt myself abandoned. We viewed solitude as an infirmity, silence as an enemy. Our friendship was an alliance and our sharp exchanges were meant to fill the quietude of loneliness.

"I think so. But I'll have to ask my aunt," I said and because he did not reply, I knew that my reluctance hurt him.

I could not tell him that I feared to leave Beth. She relied on me each morning to carry a cup of tea and three Saltines to her bedside table. This simple operation required delicacy and cunning. I waited until Lottie rose to use the bathroom and then sprinted down the hall to the kitchen to make the tea. The kettle had to be removed from the gas jet before it whistled. In that house, that bastion of family intimacy and awareness, every sound was accounted for. Lottie would hear the water running in the kitchen through the thickness of sleep and appear in her nightgown to make sure we were all right. My grandmother was mindful of footsteps in the night. We walked barefoot from room to room and left doors slightly ajar to avoid the sounds of opening and closing. We protected ourselves from the vigilance of their love.

I was also concerned about Heidi, who worked with me, most Sundays, at Emanuel Weiner's office. It was true that she was less depressed. She continued to wear her hair as Theresa had fashioned it for the wedding, the wisps of pixie bangs falling across her high forehead and the French braid a fair luxuriant thickness between her shoulders. She gained weight and we went shopping for new clothes. She seldom practiced the piano but she had not yet told Edna that she no longer wanted to take lessons.

"She'd act as though I were putting a knife through her heart," she said bitterly.

"Then tell your father," I suggested. Leon, the *luftmentsch*, would take her decision in stride.

"Yeah. Maybe I'll do that. Thanks for understanding, Sharon."

I basked in the glow of her gratitude and I battled the despondency that threatened to overcome her. I coaxed her to go to the movies when we had finished filing Emanuel Weiner's voluminous correspondence. Desperately, I tried to make her laugh.

With the arrogance of adolescence, I considered myself indispensable to my cousins. Motherless myself, I mothered them.

"Well, try to come," Peter said. "I think everyone in Brooklyn can survive without you for one weekend."

"I'll see," I replied.

To punish Peter for his accurate perception, I wrote yet another letter to Marty Feldman. I was neither clever nor cynical when I wrote to the redheaded marine who had kissed me in the sanctuary of the Manhattan Beach Jewish Center. I described the first snow of the season and told him how I had held my tongue out and felt the icy freshness of the falling flakes upon it. "I wish you could have tasted the cold smoothness of my tongue," I wrote him daringly. "You would warm it. You would warm me." I sealed the envelope, coated my lips with Beth's Victory Red lipstick, and pressed them against the flap. I had read in *Coronet* magazine that servicemen loved getting mail sealed with the impression of a girlfriend's lips.

My aunts could not see any reason why I should not go to Woodstock for Karen's party.

"It will be good for her," Edna said, although I sat beside her at Lottie's kitchen table. It occurred to me that she even spoke of her own children in the third person while they were in the same room. She was a woman capable of dedication yet fearful of intimacy, although I did not recognize that for a long time.

"You'll stay with Dina," Lottie said. "You'll be able to tell us how things are with her. If she's all right. If she's not lonely. How she manages with Anna."

I would be their emissary, their spy.

"Sure," I said, and I thought with satisfaction of all the secrets I concealed from them — Robert's betrayal, Beth's pregnancy, Heidi's depression, my own dark fears. Those secrets gave me power over them and afforded me independence. I was not who they thought I was, poor Miriam's deserted child who had to be cosseted and pitied, who waited for mail that did not come from a father who might be dead. No, I was stronger than that. I felt myself engorged with responsibility. I was Sharon, on whom others relied, a keeper of confidences and, by extension, a controller of lives.

We all suffered from an excess of self-imposed obligation that year. Wearied and cast adrift by the vagaries of the war that would not end, we clutched the compass of responsibility. We undertook tasks that gave us direction. Powerful Emanuel Weiner intensified his efforts to rescue artists and intellectuals from Europe and drew us into the vortex of his passionate concern. A man might die if a letter was misfiled. A child might perish if a mailing was delayed. Feverishly, my uncle Julius and his friends filed affidavits and wrote checks. They were responsible for the lives of friends and relations in the villages of their childhood, the towns and hamlets now become battlefields. Bernie with his black masking tape, forever repairing blackout curtains; Leon playing his violin on the roof of the supermarket while he searched the skies for enemy aircraft; Judy Bergman spending long hours stripping the wallpaper in her brother's bedroom (he would not be shot down over the Pacific if his room was newly decorated) — they all accepted the tasks that gave them purpose. And I took care of my cousins, studied hard, and wrote to my father three times a week.

I called Peter back and told him that I would be coming. I bought Karen a set of Prince Matchabelli toilet water and dusting powder because I loved the midnight blue crown-shaped containers. I got excused from my afternoon classes and told Dina I would be arriving on the late bus.

"Don't meet me," I cautioned her. "I can walk from the bus station."

But when I arrived at school that Friday morning, I learned that the double period of Spanish which was my only morning class was canceled. There was time enough for me to dash home, pick up my suitcase, and reach the bus terminal in time for the early bus.

No one was at home. Lottie, Julius, and Beth were at work and my grandparents spent each Friday morning on Brighton Beach Avenue.

I dialed Dina's number but the line was busy and there was

no time to try again. I decided to call from the bus terminal but I knew that even if I did not reach her to explain that I was taking the earlier bus, there would be no problem. Dina never locked the front door.

It was, of course, impossible to call from the station. The cavernous terminal teemed with wartime turmoil. Servicemen were lined up in front of each phone booth, nervously jiggling their coins, kicking their duffel bags forward. USO and Red Cross volunteers shook their canisters at me and I surrendered the change I had meant to use to call Dina. A young blond woman holding a baby asked me how to get to the IRT subway. Tears clouded her pale blue eyes.

"My husband's just been shipped out," she said. "And I'm going to stay with my cousin in the Bronx. Is the Bronx far? Will my husband be all right?" I imagined her asking that question of everyone she met until the war ended. Because she was crying, I carried the baby part of the way to the subway and pressed my own nickel into her hand so that she would not have to fumble for change at the turnstile. I ran back just in time to board the bus to Woodstock.

I slept part of the trip and then wrote letters. I wrote to my father and told him that I had an A average in biology. "I'm sure I want to be a doctor," I wrote, hoping that the words would please him. I imagined him reading them and turning to a colleague to say *Listen to this, my daughter is a top bio student. She wants to be a doctor.* But why didn't he write? Worry congealed in my throat, formed a knot of misery which caused me to gag. "Write soon," I added. "We are all so worried."

We were worried enough for Julius to have called the Red Cross, who had assured him that mail from the European theater was very slow, backlogged. Evacuating soldiers took precedence over mail sacks. "There's a war on, you know," the weary Red Cross official had reminded Julius, who replied bitterly, "I heard. I heard there's a war on."

My bus pulled into Woodstock.

I walked from the village to Dina's house, slowed by the

weight of my suitcase but feeling very independent and self-sufficient.

I huddled deep into my red woolen cape and drew the hood up. The valise grew heavier and I switched it from hand to hand. Cars slowed as they passed me and I imagined that I made an appealing picture evoking curiosity and sympathy. Little Red Riding Hood — perhaps they thought me a runaway or a refugee. I imagined what it might be like to walk so burdened down an unfamiliar road, uncertain of destination or welcome.

A family from Julius's village in Poland, a mother and father and their daughter who was perhaps a year younger than me, had visited our house the previous week. The parents, pale-skinned and stooped by sorrow, sought Julius's advice about a business venture. Appreciatively, they sipped their tea, munched on their sponge cake, and listened to my uncle as though he were an oracle and the figures and percentages he scrawled on the back of an envelope were inspired calculations. But their daughter sat very still and stared down at the floor. She refused, even at Lottie's gentle urging, to take her coat off. The heels of her brown walking shoes were worn down, as though she had trekked in them for countless miles. She did not eat her cake but wrapped it in a paper napkin and thrust it into her pocket.

I was sorry now that I had not tried to befriend her, that I had not understood her fear and loneliness. Quite suddenly, I walked more swiftly. I could see Dina's house from the road and I knew that warmth and welcome were near. I would be nicer to the next such visitor, I promised myself. Much nicer. I turned into Dina's path.

Anna's large coach carriage stood beneath the apple tree. I paused beside it and watched my infant cousin as she slept in the cold late-autumn air. The wind rouged her tiny face and a soft tuft of copper-colored hair inched out of her thick white woolen blanket. Her fragility fascinated me and I rocked the carriage gently before going up to the house.

The front door was open, left ajar, I supposed, so that Dina might hear Anna if she wakened and cried. I entered quietly.

Dina and Nachum Adler sat on the worn tweed couch. She had fallen asleep and her head was on his chest, her auburn hair blanketing his plaid shirt. His paint-stained hand rested protectively on her shoulder. He smiled when he saw me and lifted his finger to his lips. I nodded and set my valise down very softly so that the sound would not waken her. My face was flushed and my heart hammered out a timpani of apologetic regret. I had intruded on their peaceful intimacy and inadvertently trespassed upon a closeness more profound than the furtive coupling between Franchesca and Robert that I had witnessed that last afternoon of my Woodstock summer.

I went upstairs and lay down on the daybed in the little room that Dina laughingly called her office. I drifted into the brief, refreshing sleep peculiar to exhausted youth, and I awakened to the murmur of their voices. The front door opened and closed. I went to the window and saw that Nachum stood beside the baby's carriage. He rocked it gently and turned it so that a shaft of sunlight vaulted across Anna's face. He understood how to scavenge wisps of radiance to warm an infant on a wintry day.

I went downstairs and kissed Dina on the cheek. She had not moved from the couch, although she opened her arms to embrace me. Her feet were tucked beneath her long paisley skirt; she held the tiger's-eye pendant, the one she always wore with her black turtleneck sweater, to her cheek as though its coolness might soothe her. I sat in the rocking chair opposite her, resuming the familiar pattern of our summer evenings.

"Nachum comes to visit me, to help me and to keep me company," she said very quietly. "He comes once or twice a week. When he has the time. When he has gas stamps."

"That's good." My voice trembled with shyness. I wanted her to know that I would handle her confidence with care, that I did not judge her.

"Yes. It's good. I've been very lonely."

I nodded, not needing to speak. Loneliness had been my companion since the onset of my mother's illness. Did Dina awaken in the night, as I did, teased by the echo of vanished voices? Did she too shiver in the grip of a forgotten dream, fearful that she would always be alone, untouched, unheard, her own words frozen, unspoken, because there was no one to hear them?

"Because of Robert?" I asked. "Because he's not here?" The question was wrenched from me but I wanted her answer to confirm what I already knew.

"No. I was lonely even when Robert was here. Lonelier. I know that's hard for you to understand, Sharon."

"But I do understand," I said miserably and my words revealed my knowledge.

"I see. I'm sorry." Regret tinged her voice.

She was saddened because my innocence had been betrayed. We stretched our hands out to each other. I felt the warm clasp of my aunt's ringless fingers, the faint beat of her pulse.

"Will you and Robert divorce then?" I asked.

"Perhaps," she said.

"And will you and Nachum marry?"

She dropped my hands and looked at me in surprise.

"We are friends, Sharon. For now we are friends. And this is enough. Neither of us is ready for anything more."

She told me then how Nachum had told her about his wife and daughter the afternoon of their first meeting at the craft fair. It had been natural that he had been placed in her care. She was the hostess and he was the distinguished guest from abroad, distinguished by his talent and his pain.

They had walked across the lawn, pausing at the various displays, their pace slowed by the great weight of her pregnancy. A small blond girl had raced past them in pursuit of a red balloon. Laughing, she had waved her arms, jumped to grasp the dangling string, and, missing, hurried after it, overjoyed by her race against the airborne scarlet orb.

"How old do you think she is?" he had asked Dina.

"Five. Perhaps six."

"My daughter, Rachel — she would have been six. Her birthday comes in March. The fifteenth. How does one celebrate the birthday of a child who has died?"

"Perhaps by remembering her life." Her suggestion had been shy but she felt it to be audacious. How dared she counsel a man who had passed through the gates of hell?

They reached a maple tree beneath which two chairs had been placed and they sat side by side in the circlet of shadow. They felt themselves spectators at a rustic theater, observing the scene; from their seats they smiled at the craft fair in all its sunlit festivity, the visitors and the artists in their light pastel clothing, the children who hurtled across the lawn, drunk with gaiety and freedom. The small blond girl passed them once again. She had caught her red balloon and she held it proudly by its string.

"She is taller than Rachel would have been, I think. Because Rachel was small-boned, like her mother — my Manya," he mused.

He told Dina that he and Manya had met in Paris. They were both art students from Czechoslovakia, Nachum from Prague and Manya from a neighboring suburb. They met at a Purim carnival given by a Jewish students' association. Manya was an improbable Vashti, in a daring flesh-colored leotard, and Nachum a villainous Haman, with a black mustache and a black cowboy hat. They laughed when they first saw each other and laughter sustained them as they drank coffee at the small cafés of Montparnasse and strolled along the Seine. Everything amused them. They had an eye for absurdity and a talent for joy. They bought black bread at one shop, vegetable pâté at another, and made sandwiches, which they ate on the banks of the river. She was small and blond, her features chiseled; he was tall and lean and dark-haired. They stood side by side in a long mirror and laughed at the contrast in their height, their coloring. They laughed at the abstract paintings of their fellow students. They laughed in the cinema and laughed again as they walked back to their student lodgings, amused by passersby, shop-window displays, snippets of overheard conversations.

They were delighted to have discovered each other, to have been emancipated from loneliness, to be young in Paris in the springtime. It was irrelevant to them that the Nazi party won the elections in Danzig that year and that a boycott of Jewish businesses in Germany had begun. They were artists, and artists did

not worry about politics and hatred. The foolish sputtering occurred across the border. They were in Paris, insulated by their
laughter and their love. They were married when they returned to
Prague, and Nachum's work received miraculously swift recognition. Curators from London and Paris, collectors from the United
States and Canada visited his gallery and purchased his portraits
and landscapes. Emanuel Weiner, on his last trip to Europe, was
one such collector. He bought a watercolor of a narrow Prague
bridge and gave Nachum his card.

"Should you ever need my help," he said and blushed because
Emanuel Weiner was always shy in the presence of artists. "These
are treacherous times," he added and Nachum slipped the card
into his wallet.

Still, he was not worried. Art critics wrote of his unusual im-
plementation of light, his daring brush strokes, the incandescence
of his pastoral scenes. He and Manya laughed when they read the
critiques. They had graduated from loneliness and obscurity.

Manya drew cartoons and caricatures reflecting the humor
and merriment that came to her so naturally, but when she became
pregnant, she set aside her pens and sketch pads and reveled in the
new life growing within her body. Nachum painted her and pampered her. He bought her flowers each day, their damp stems
wrapped in the newspapers that screamed of Hitler's demands for
Czech territory. Rose petals fell on photographs of Mussolini and
Hitler. Small, blond, pregnant Manya snipped a lock of Nachum's
black hair and placed it above her lip.

"*Achtung! Heil* Hitler!" she shouted and their friends roared
with laughter.

Rachel was born the day Hitler marched into the Sudeten-
land. Manya took up her pen and drew cartoons that were published in clandestine underground newspapers — sharp, angry
caricatures of Hitler, of those Czech leaders who collaborated with
the Germans, sketches of the Skoda armament works with death
masks painted on each window. Her drawings were unsigned and
mailed from distant cities. She and Nachum laughed at their clev-
erness and watched Rachel begin to crawl and then to toddle on
her fat dimpled legs.

Friends and family advised Manya to stop drawing the cartoons.

"It's dangerous," they said.

"But they're unsigned. They can't be traced."

Nachum himself felt uneasy. Still, he thought himself protected by his own fame and the sheer luck that had been with him all the years of his life. Czechoslovakia was occupied, the war raged on, but he and his family survived. He and Manya told their small daughter stories, taught her songs, and hugged each other because her laughter was as spontaneous and melodic as their own. On Rachel's fourth birthday, although the deportation of Jews had already begun and the streets of the Jewish quarter were wrapped in the silence of fear, he arranged for a photographer to come to their home. Manya wore a crepe de chine dress of pale violet and the pearls he had bought for her when the Tate bought his mountainscape of the Pyrenees. Her blond hair fell to her shoulders. Rachel wore a smock of pale green organdy, and a satin ribbon the color of new grass was tied about her hair. They went into the small garden behind their house and he kissed his wife and daughter as the photographer arranged his camera, glancing nervously at his watch. A Gestapo car had been seen on the corner. He feared an *action*, a random roundup of Jews, and he wanted to return to his studio.

And so Manya and Rachel were posed swiftly, the child sitting on her mother's lap, both their heads tilted to the sunlight. That was the photograph that had fallen from his wallet, the photograph Heidi and I had examined with such piercing curiosity.

Nachum walked the photographer back to his studio and arranged to pick up the photographs the following week. A Gestapo van, its siren screaming, passed him as he walked home. Anxiety gripped him and his leisurely stroll became a run. The moment he turned the corner, he saw the crowd that had gathered in front of his house.

His neighbors stepped aside as he approached, fell silent as he passed over his threshold. Manya, with Rachel in her arms, lay dead in the entryway. A single bullet had passed through the child's body and into the mother's heart.

The neighbors had seen the uniformed officers pound on the door. Manya had opened it, Rachel standing beside her. Papers had been brandished and she had shaken her head and lifted her child into her arms. More papers were waved and she brushed them away as though they were bothersome insects. She whispered something to the child and laughed — the melodic laughter that had enticed Nachum on the streets of Paris, in their student quarters, in the charming home where they had thought they would live their charmed lives. The child laughed too; a sweet duet of merriment mocked the men who goose-stepped down sunlit streets in uniforms decorated with the death's-head insignia. Perhaps it was that laughter that caused the arresting officer to lose control, to reach into his holster for his pistol and then to tighten his finger on the trigger. The sound of the single shot splintered the crystalline laughter, shattered it into shards. A child, weeping herself, said that she had heard Rachel moan softly, but the adults had heard nothing at all. Manya and Rachel were dead when they reached them minutes after the Gestapo van sped away from the house.

Nachum had knelt beside their bodies. He had touched their fine, fair hair, placed a trembling finger on the blood that trickled in delicate moist scarlet threads at the corners of their mouths. Bewildered, disoriented, he looked at his weeping neighbors, and when his own scream came women clasped their hands over their ears, and men turned away.

On the last day of the week of mourning, the photographer delivered the photographs. Nachum carried them with him when he was sent, at last, to Terezin, the concentration camp the Germans had built for the artists, writers, and intellectuals — the elite of the Jewish community. It was from Terezin that he wrote to Emanuel Weiner, whose card remained in his wallet, miraculously unconfiscated.

"I need your help," he wrote, echoing the words the collector from America had spoken in the vanished past when Nachum had painted with such energy and fervor, and his wife and daughter had laughed in the lamp-lit, carpeted rooms beyond his studio.

A member of the Red Cross team that visited Terezin, perhaps the same team that praised conditions in the camp, carried the letter away with him, and against all odds it was delivered to Emanuel Weiner. Edna immediately contacted a senator, a congressman, a federal judge, and the chairman of the board of the Museum of Modern Art where two of Nachum's portraits formed part of the permanent collection.

It took months to negotiate his release and then his odyssey to freedom. But he arrived in New York at last, gaunt and grief-haunted, possessed of the gentle, contemplative patience of those who have abandoned all hope and thus all urgency. I have recognized that resigned forbearance in the terminally ill patients who cease to ask me about experimental treatments and alternative drugs. Their voices, too, are very soft and they move, as Nachum did that first year, with slow grace and solemn gesture. There is no longer anything of enough importance to impel their haste or command their intensity. Like Nachum during that year, they are neither hopeful nor desperate. Life is simply something that happens to them as they wait for death.

Dina told me all this as the swirling shadows of twilight deepened into darkness.

"You understand, Sharon, that it is not easy for a man to recover from such a tragedy." Her voice faltered. She regretted that she had shared so much with me. I too was newly bereft, struggling, as she was, toward recuperation after the wrenching debility of loss.

"I understand," I said and it surprised me that I did. But even then, I recognized the healing power of friendship. It was natural for Dina and Nachum to reach out to each other, to reveal their wounds, and to take comfort from the sound of each other's voices — the light touch of a hand upon a shoulder, her head against his chest. Loneliness shared became comradeship; friendship nurtured might tremble into love.

Nachum left after dinner. He seldom stayed the night, Dina said. He needed the solitude of his studio, the comforting silence of his small apartment. I wondered if the other pictures the photographer had taken on that day of his small daughter's birthday — the last day of her gentle, laughing life — hung in his seaside bedroom. Perhaps he spoke to the portraits of Manya and Rachel, as I sometimes spoke to the photograph of my dead mother and my absent and silent father. *Why did you leave me? Will I ever be happy again?*

I lay awake that night and thought of Nachum Adler driving through the darkness, speaking softly to his wife and daughter.

12

It snowed that night. The flakes fell with such thickness and rapidity that by morning the ground was shrouded in a deep and crusty whiteness. An exuberant Peter burst in as Dina and I ate breakfast.

"Come on out," he commanded. "The coast is clear." We had worried that my presence in Woodstock on the weekend of Karen's birthday might betray the surprise party.

"What about Karen?" I asked.

"My mother arranged everything. She set it up with Meg and Melanie. They'll go shopping with Karen and then to lunch and a movie. When they get back, the party will be all set. She thought of everything. She even arranged the snow. There'll be a sleigh ride after all. My mother's a witch, you know."

I laughed. Peter was more relaxed than he had been during the summer. I thought him very handsome in his heavy argyle sweater and his gray corduroy slacks. His fair hair, always too long, fell into his eyes and playfully I brushed the renegade cowlick back.

"Hey, don't do that," he protested and pushed my hand away.

"Why not?" I asked teasingly.

"Because I'm not a kid — I'm not a toy. Listen, you may be looking at a Harvard man. I had my interview and the guy said that it was practically certain that I'll get early admission."

"Peter, that's wonderful."

He beamed.

"You'll come to visit me?"

"Sure. I have friends in Boston."

I did not add that I might have a home in Boston, when the war ended. Surely my father would want to return to the staff of the Massachusetts General Hospital, where he had worked since his residency. But superstition constrained me to silence. I did not want to tempt a malicious God by revealing my secret hopes to Him.

Peter and I built a snowman that morning, dressing it in a paint-stained blue cambric shirt of Robert's and crowning it with a felt hat plucked from a cluttered chest in the Bassens' front hall.

Dina made us hot chocolate and grilled cheese sandwiches for lunch. I thought that in Brooklyn, at this hour, my grandparents and Julius and Lottie would be walking home from synagogue and Beth would be staring out the window, waiting for the mailman.

"How is Beth?" Dina asked as though reading my thoughts.

"Fine. Terrific," I said. I was an initiate into the adult world of well-meant lies and unrevealed truths. "I mean, she's lonely and sometimes she gets really worried, of course."

"Of course," Dina said. Worry and loneliness were familiar to her.

That afternoon we sledded down the hill upon whose crest we had munched sandwiches on hot summer days. I knelt behind Peter and we careened down, laughing and gasping as we gathered speed and the cold air frosted our faces, stung our eyes. The newly fallen snow fragmented beneath the rudders of the sled and danced upward, falling again in a brilliant shower that pelted our skin and settled in diamond chips of moisture on our bulky snow pants and jackets. I climbed on Peter's back and stretched across him; we took the hill again, only to roll off the sled near the bottom.

"Your fault!" Peter shouted.

"Your fault!" I retorted joyously and tossed a snowball at him.

"Hey, no fair." He crawled toward me across the glittering white expanse but I was ready for him. I fashioned another snowball and when he reached me I rubbed it across his face.

"Hey, hey." Laughing and sputtering, he twisted my hand behind my back and threw himself across me. I struggled beneath his weight, pummeled his shoulders. Two crows flying in tandem soared by, shrilling lustily in flight. The wild sound triggered our gaiety and we called back in mocking unison, "Caw. Caw."

The huge black birds disappeared into a distant thicket and we lay still. I felt the cold of the snow beneath me and the heavy warmth of Peter's body upon my own. He pressed his face against mine, bruising my cheeks, my chin. But his breath was warm and his lips melted the granules of snow that had settled on my own. He kissed me, not with Marty Feldman's force and urgency but with a petal softness, a sweet unfurling. I closed my eyes. The frost on my lashes trickled down my cheeks, mingling with the hot tears that inexplicably began to fall. Gently, he released me.

"I missed you, Sharon," Peter said quietly. He lay beside me.

I did not reply. I did not want to lose the sweet taste of his breath, the softness of his lips. And I had no words. I was certain that anything I might say would be wrong.

The crows flew back, their wide-winged shadows darkening the plain of whiteness. I sat up.

"We should go," I said.

"Yes."

Slowly, pulling the sled, we started back to Dina's house. As always when he was tired, Peter's limp became more pronounced. He paused to rest and we sat together on the sled.

"I'm sorry, Sharon," he said, his eyes cast downward.

"Oh no. Don't be sorry." I searched for words that would comfort him, that would cauterize my own melancholy. Instead of speaking I leaned toward him and kissed him lightly on the lips.

Karen was surprised. We were all waiting for her when she returned from Kingston with Meg and Melanie, singing "As Time

Goes By" because they had sat through *Casablanca* twice that afternoon.

"Happy birthday! Surprise!" we shouted, jumping up from behind the sofa and armchairs, waving streamers of green and gold crepe paper and green and gold balloons.

Karen burbled with joy.

"You shouldn't have. Oh, you're all such traitors. How could you fool me like that? Oh, but it's wonderful. Sharon — I just spoke to you and you never let on. Melanie, Meg — you were in on it too . . ."

She was aglow with pleasure. She is, even now in late middle age, one of those women on whom happiness settles in a patina of transforming beauty.

In true Woodstock style, there was a pot of cheese fondue and another of chocolate and we giggled a great deal as we twirled the long forks, dipping slices of toast and apple into the simmering mixtures. We toasted marshmallows in front of the open fire, seated in a circle about the stone fireplace. Lola was there with her Glen, who had been returned stateside after being wounded in the onslaught at Peleliu Island. He was still in uniform, his arm supported by a khaki sling.

"Hey, I was lucky," he said, his other arm around Lola's shoulder, his toothy smile as wide and friendly as in the snapshots we had studied that summer at the Woolworth's soda fountain. "A bullet grazed me, that's all."

We knew that the bullet had, in fact, shattered his wrist bone but even in that he had been lucky. Almost ten thousand American soldiers had been killed in the amphibious attack on Peleliu in the western Carolines. Lowell Thomas's voice, usually so smooth and businesslike, had quivered when he reported the casualty figures on Movietone News. I had closed my eyes as the film clips showed the flag-covered coffins that were returned for burial in the United States. But my imagination would not be shuttered. I dreamed of Alfred's uniformed friends cold and still in pine boxes that were lowered to the ground as a young marine played taps.

I did not dream of my father in such a pale wood box. I saw him tending the wounded in a field hospital, riding bravely into fire in a military ambulance. He was too busy and too important to be killed.

"You were on Peleliu, right?" Bob asked. "That must have been some battle." He looked enviously at Glen. The tall, handsome athlete was a senior but he had accelerated his program so that he would graduate in January. He was impatient to join the army, fearful that he would miss the war.

"Yeah. It was some battle," Glen agreed. His smile remained frozen in place as though he feared that if he relaxed his lips, his face would collapse into a mask of misery.

There was an uneasy silence. We were still shy with returning veterans. Their wounds shamed and embarrassed us. We did not meet their eyes lest we be seared by their memories. At the bus station I had avoided a marine on crutches and averted my eyes from a sailor whose left cheek was glazed to the purple incandescence that I now know is the scarring caused by phosphorus burns. We were relieved then when the sleighs arrived, the bells clanging merrily to the tune of "Happy Birthday."

"Oh, Mom, Dad, really, this is so corny," Karen said, but she was radiant with joy.

We bundled up and clambered onto the sleighs, hired from neighboring farmers. Peter and I crawled beneath a horse blanket that smelled of straw and manure. Lola and Glen followed us.

"Hey, isn't this fun?" I called to them and Lola nodded. She plucked a long straw out of the blanket and tickled Glen's cheek.

"Hey, cut it out," he protested but she persisted. She would teach him how to laugh again, how to play. She would unfreeze his desperate smile. She would spread the russet-colored rug that she had bought at the craft fair in front of the fire and they would lie on it together. She pulled him to her, careful of his wound, cradling his head in her arms, sliding deeper and deeper into the cocoon of the blanket. They had been so long separated, and now, at last, they were together.

"Oh Lola, my Lola." His voice was muffled and Peter and I smiled at each other, as though we were tolerant adults amused by the antics of willful children.

The sleighs glided forward amid laughter and singing. We

sang "Chattanooga Choo Choo," and "In the Mood," and "The Caissons Go Rolling Along." Patriotism and nonsense were interspersed. We bellowed "Mairzy Doats" at high speed and segued into "Praise the Lord and Pass the Ammunition" with equal vigor.

"Look up," Peter said and I lifted my eyes to the dark velvet sky of late fall, ablaze with stars so clearly limned that we could trace each constellation.

"The Big Dipper, the Little Dipper, Orion," Peter said and he rested his hand on my head.

A fresh wind lashed across us and I buried my face in his chest. I sought protection and claimed tenderness.

His arms came around me and I remained very still.

"Sirius," he said. "Capella. Castor." The names of the stars fell musically from his lips. He offered them to me as small verbal gifts and I repeated them in a voice muffled by his body. "Sirius, Capella. Castor."

"Look up at the stars," he commanded, "and make a wish."

"And will you make a wish too?"

"Yes."

"But I need more than one wish." My tone was playful but my heart was heavy.

"Then make as many as you like," he said. "There are enough stars."

And so I lifted my eyes to the star-spangled canyon of the dark, cold sky and I wished for my father's safety, for the safe return of Aaron and Alfred, for the health of Beth's unborn child, and for the happiness of my small cousin, Anna. I wished for my own happiness as well, and because that last wish seemed too selfish, I wished finally that peace would come and that this would be the last year of our terrible war.

"You're supposed to keep your eyes closed when you make a wish," Peter reproved me gently.

"And you're not supposed to look at a person when they're wishing on the stars," I rejoined.

"I couldn't help it. You looked so beautiful."

He kissed me and then I did close my eyes and feared to open them again, lest the stars be dimmed and my happiness vanished.

13

Brown-and-orange crepe-paper turkeys with paper American flags in their beaks crouched in the windows of Woolworth's. Indian corn dangled from front doors, and the Pilgrim fathers smiled benignly down from posters and urged us to give thanks and buy war bonds. The Lincoln High School student council sponsored a raffle for a twenty-one-pound turkey, the proceeds to go to the USO. Judy and I sold tickets outside the auditorium before the Friday assembly, thus avoiding the weekly roll call of Lincoln graduates who had been killed, wounded, or reported missing in action. The principal read their names, his voice choked by the sorrow he could not express; the color guard strained to balance their flags at half mast; and the students stood at solemn attention, their heads bowed. Now and again a girl would giggle nervously, a brief spurt of hysteria that was wisely ignored. We sold a record number of raffles on the morning the principal announced that Ben Rosenberg of the class of 1939 had died at La Spezia and Donald Fallone of the class of 1942 had been wounded at Leyte Gulf. It sobered us that a boy who had so recently walked the corridors of our school was a casualty of the war.

Each evening, our family gathered about the Stromberg Carlson radio and listened to the prophets of the airwaves deliver their sermons of optimism. Douglas MacArthur was the messiah of the Pacific theater and Dwight Eisenhower and George Patton were the patron saints of European operations. We spoke their names reverently. Their predictions were our catechism.

Beth and I gave each other manicures as Gabriel Heatter assured us that "Ah yes, there was good news tonight." He urged us to offer thanksgiving for the sinking of the *Ushio*, the last surviving warship of the Japanese fleet which had struck at Pearl Harbor.

"Yes, my fellow Americans, that day of infamy is being avenged."

He spoke to the darkness of our hearts. We wanted revenge; we wanted those who had not played fair, who had started this terrible war, to be punished and we were grateful to him for speaking our truth. It consoled us that the British were deepening their advance into Burma. Soon the Chindwin River would be crossed. It was true that the Japanese were gaining a foothold in mainland China, heading toward Kwei-yang, but then French forces had reached the Rhine at Rosenau. Our geographic scoreboard was crowded and confusing.

"Where *are* these places?" Beth murmured and waved her emery board at the globe that rested on the piano.

Julius twirled it thoughtfully during each newscast, laboriously seeking out cities and islands, mountain ranges and obscure archipelagoes. The war had exposed us to our own provincialism, made us aware of borders and boundaries with mysterious names, across distant oceans. Men like my uncle Samuel, who considered crossing the George Washington Bridge into New Jersey a great adventure, who consulted three different road maps for a drive to Monticello, now spoke knowledgeably about Skopje and Karelia, Bologna and Imphal.

Jinx Falkenburg interviewed Eleanor Roosevelt and we learned the size of the White House turkey, which the First Lady had selected herself. But there would be no dessert on the presidential table.

"I've used up all my sugar coupons," Eleanor Roosevelt told us cheerfully.

"I didn't even know Alfred last Thanksgiving," Beth said and passed her hand across her abdomen, as though to caress the unborn child of the young husband who had not even glided through her dreams a scarce year ago.

"Yes — a lot has happened since last Thanksgiving," I agreed and I turned away so that Beth would not see my face collapse against the wave of sadness that swept over me.

My mother had been alive the previous year, and still strong enough to bake the apple pies that had always been her contribution to the family feast.

My father had always arranged to be off duty on Thanksgiving Day and at the first light of dawn we drove south from our Brookline apartment to the house on Avenue Z. Always I sat in the rear seat, next to the carton of pies which I had helped to bake, inhaling the sweetness of cinnamon and sugar, of spiced apples and newly baked crusts. My parents sang softly as we drove — the popular songs of their courtship, "Smoke Gets in Your Eyes," "Blue Moon," "Walking My Baby Back Home." Lulled into drowsy contentment, soothed by song and scent, I fell asleep somewhere in Connecticut and awakened as we approached Ocean Parkway. It was then that my mother always said, "Oh, we're there, we're almost there."

She would never say it again. Her voice was forever stilled. I submitted to a brief melancholy, startled anew that a fleeting memory could cause such a heavy sadness.

Judy Bergman's mother set her table four days before the holiday. The newly laundered and starched white tablecloth with its huge V embroidered in scarlet satin thread, flanked by doves of peace, anchored in royal blue French knots, was spread with the best china and gleaming cutlery.

"All that's missing is the 'Welcome Home, Marvin' banner," Judy said wryly but she narrowed her eyes as her mother frosted a chocolate cake — Marvin's favorite.

Mrs. Bergman's hope that her son would be home for Thanksgiving had been nurtured with such care, reinforced by such yearning, that it was vested with reality. She had stocked the pantry with his favorite foods; his sweaters, freshly washed, were in the top drawer of his bureau. Always a nervous woman, she jumped when the phone rang, sprang to the door at each tentative knock, her fingers flying to her hair, which she had dyed to a chestnut color because she did not want her son to know that she had worried herself into a premature gray. She was always dressed, her face made up. Marvin had hated to see her pale and wearing a housedress. She was determined to look her best when he came marching home, his war over and her terror ended.

"What happens when he doesn't come?" Judy asked me. Her voice was hollow. She and her father stared at each other worriedly across the living room that was newly vacuumed each day because Marvin had such a low tolerance for dust. Silently, they braced themselves for the sadness, or perhaps the madness, that would follow a disappointment so profound.

"My mother has a history," Judy hinted darkly when I tried to reassure her.

Still, she no longer argued with her mother, understanding that irrational expectations defied all reason and reasonableness. And I fingered the embroidered cloth and envied Mrs. Bergman her fanatic radiant hope which contrasted so starkly with my own nocturnal fears.

"Perhaps he will come home after all," I said softly, and averted my eyes from Judy's angry frown.

Lottie, too, began her preparations early that year. I went with her to the live poultry market in Brighton Beach and watched as she selected her turkey and counted out her ration coupons. I turned away as the ritual slaughterer approached, although I was not then and, of course, am not squeamish now about the spurting of blood. Still, I thought that I might be tempting fate if I witnessed the death of a living creature and I needed every infinitesimal weight I could muster on the scales of luck. I did, however, carry it home, swathed in a shroud of newspapers, the headlines screaming the news of the Allied advance into Alsace and Lorraine, France. My father was in France. He had hinted as much in his letter. GERMAN CASUALTIES HIGH the *Herald Tribune* proclaimed,

but this did not mean that Allied casualties were low. I was familiar with the euphemistic journalism of the home front that announced enemy losses in lead paragraphs and did not mention
Allied deaths until the end of the story.

Lottie proudly settled the turkey on the counter which my
grandmother had spread with copies of the Yiddish paper and
completed plucking it — she never trusted the wizened old woman
at the market — while vigorously reciting "O Captain! My Captain!" She thought of Lincoln as the Thanksgiving president and
Walt Whitman the poet of the holiday.

" 'The ship has weather'd every rack, the prize we sought is
won!' " she emoted as she reached into the yawning stomach cavity of the large bird to bring forth the huge maroon liver. Droplets
of blood speckled the newspaper and coursed down the columns
of Hebrew letters. Beth, who had been dutifully stemming cranber-
ries at the kitchen table, gagged, covered her mouth with her hand,
and ran to the bathroom.

A frown creased Lottie's brow and her eyes flew to the calendar.

"It's because she has her period. She got it this morning," I
said quickly. The lie came effortlessly. I lied to protect Beth's secret, to shield Lottie from worry, to spare myself an unsettling
confrontation.

Lottie accepted my lie with relief.

"That must be it. She always gets nauseous on the first day,"
she said and thrust the turkey liver into the broiler.

I chased after Beth and knocked lightly on the bathroom
door.

She opened it, her face pale, spittle clinging to her lips.

"I'm all right," she said. "Really I am."

And I believed her because I wanted to, because I could not
sustain another worry.

Nachum Adler came to dinner that night and it was arranged
that he would drive to Woodstock and pick up Dina and Anna.

"Will you bake the pies, Sharon?" Lottie asked.

I looked at Nachum.

"Yes," I said. "I baked them with my mother last year."

"She made wonderful pies. Miriam didn't like to cook, but she loved to bake," Lottie reflected.

"Oh, she liked to cook some things. Casseroles and soups," I protested. I remembered my mother slicing vegetables, her face flushed, the steam rising fragrantly from the large yellow pot she favored, filling our kitchen with the garden scent of nurturing love. "But it was hard because she never knew when Daddy would be getting home from the hospital and she hated for things to be ruined. She used to get so mad."

A sweet relief stole over me. A ban had been lifted. For the first time since her death, I spoke of my mother as she had been before her illness transformed her into an emaciated and suffering invalid.

I read her recipe book. The measurements of ingredients and instructions were recorded in her firm accountant's hand; the blue Waterman's ink shimmered silkily on the lined pages. *Three cups of flour, well sifted. Two cups of sugar. Ten apples, peeled and cored.* I wondered if my mother had written so carefully, so precisely, because she knew that the calico-covered notebook was her legacy to me, each recipe a codicil to her domestic will.

I recalled how I stood beside her in our overheated Brookline kitchen and watched as she mixed and stirred, as she moved her rolling pin across the soft white flesh of the dough. She dangled long strands of apple peel and wound them into bracelets about my wrists. Flurries of flour whitened our dark hair and we laughed and pressed our fingers against the edge of the mixing bowl and licked them like mischievous small girls.

I smiled at the mental image. It was safe, at last, to remember my mother as she had been, to accept her loss.

"We are planning a terrific Thanksgiving. I am using Mommy's apple pie recipe. Practice for next year when you will be with us," I wrote my father.

I had, at last, received a letter from him, an odd, disjointed communication made almost unreadable by the censor's angry slashes. Still, I knew that he was well, that he was pleased with the men in the mobile medical unit he now commanded, that he thought of me constantly and was proud of me.

"Someday we will travel together in this country which you have always wanted to visit," he wrote cautiously and that was how I knew that he was in France. When I was a small girl he had read the Madeline stories to me and heard me promise sleepily that I too one day would stroll down the Champs Elysées.

I listened carefully to the war news from Europe. My father might be close to the border between France and Switzerland where Allied troops were fighting fiercely. Or perhaps he was at Saint Dié, in the foothills of the Vosges, where American armor was forcing the Germans into retreat.

"Probably he is at Saint Dié," Bernie, our military consultant, ventured wisely. He wore his Junior Commando uniform, and a flashlight dangled from his belt. During blackouts, after checking the curtains, he crawled beneath the dining room table and read Classic Comics by the thin beam of light.

"Probably not," Heidi retorted and tossed her pillow at him. Half a dozen V-letters fluttered from the pillowcase, and she gathered them up, her face beet red.

" 'Anchors away,' " Bernie sang tauntingly. "Heidi's got a sailor boyfriend — bell-bottom trousers, coat of navy blue . . ."

I was glad that Steven, Alfred's ensign friend with whom Heidi had danced at the wedding, wrote to her so faithfully, although my gladness was shadowed by a narrow patch of jealousy. I had received only one letter from Marty Feldman, a shy and brief message that spoke of his impatience to see action.

"So far the only enemies I've killed are these damn mosquitoes," he wrote, and so I knew that he was somewhere in the South Pacific. The newspapers wrote of the clouds of mosquitoes that darkened the skies over Leyte. Our class at Lincoln had launched Project Calamine and each week I faithfully deposited a bottle of the pink lotion into the huge carton that stood next to the gym. A letter from the Red Cross thanking us for our efforts had been read aloud in our homeroom.

I was disappointed that Marty did not write of our romantic moment together in the synagogue sanctuary and it disturbed me that even as I read his letter I remembered the smell of straw and manure and the touch of Peter's lips against my own. A sweet, unfamiliar moisture slithered through my body, suffusing me with pleasure and with fear.

I wrote my father about the holiday preparations, about my induction into Arista — the academic honor society — about my friendships with Judy and with Karen and Peter. I wanted him to know that I was learning, that I was stretching my way into adulthood. It was perhaps the first time that I thought of comforting him rather than indulging my own fantasies and assuaging my own fear and loneliness.

Beth and I walked to the mailbox together to post our letters. She opened and closed the mailbox twice because she had read somewhere that sometimes letters got caught in the chute. In a world where we had so little control, we concentrated on small acts which offered us small guarantees.

In the glow of the streetlamp that stood above the mailbox, I saw the tears that webbed her thick lashes like silver threads. I did not mention them. Beth's moods grew increasingly unpredictable. She wept because she ran out of shampoo. She wept because there was a letter from Alfred and she wept because there wasn't a letter from Alfred. She wept because a customer was rude to her and she wept when a sanitation truck ran over a squirrel on our street. The source of her tears, of course, was the terror that grew daily within her heart, even as the small secret life she carried grew within her womb. When she undressed that night, I saw the almost imperceptible rise of her abdomen and I pressed my hand gently against it as though to comfort her, although truly I was comforting myself.

We gathered in the kitchen on the Wednesday before Thanksgiving. I assembled the ingredients for my pies and Lottie worked beside me, slicing and peeling sweet potatoes for her special casserole. Beth chopped herbs vigorously and then abruptly abandoned the task and carried her stationery and pen to the kitchen table. She wrote to Alfred amid the scents and sounds of holiday preparations as though willing him to share in the gay domestic frenzy. A tiny flake of parsley adhered to her engagement ring and she licked it off and pressed the ring to her cheek. The phone rang. It was Peter, calling from Woodstock to say that he wanted to come to Brooklyn with Nachum and Dina — was that all right?

"That's fine," I said, careful to contain my pleasure. I could not rejoice openly over Peter's presence at our family's dinner when Beth grieved over Alfred's absence.

How carefully we monitored our joys and sorrows during those treacherous days when the ringing of a phone, a knock at the door could alter lives forever. Mothers whose sons had returned safely from the war crossed the street to avoid black-clad Mrs. Calderazzo. Women whose husbands and sons were still overseas nodded gravely to her at the bank or the markets. They spoke to her of the weather, of the shortages of canned goods, of the lines at the OPA center, but they never discussed the war itself or their men still in uniform. They asked solicitously about her health. Their courtesy filled them with shame and they were white-faced with effort when they parted from her, averting their eyes when they passed her house so that they would not see the gold-star banner that hung in her front window.

I understood their discomfort; I recognized their fear. I myself had moved my seat in study hall so that I would not sit near Leatrice and Letitia, the black twins with the heart-shaped faces whose father had been reported missing in action. I did not know what to say to them and I feared the contagion of their misfortune.

The principal had announced during a Friday assembly that the twins' father was missing in action. Leatrice and Letitia stared straight ahead, their expressions frozen, impervious to our sympathy. They were doubly isolated now — loss and race had conspired against them.

That afternoon Judy and I walked to the esplanades in Manhattan Beach and scrambled onto the promontory. We leaned back against the sharp-pronged rocks, their micaceous surfaces cold against our backs even through the thick layers of our sweaters and plaid hooded coats, and we lit our red-tipped Deb cigarettes and debated, in troubled voices, the mysterious dimensions of "missing in action."

"The twins are in limbo," Judy said. "Okay, killed in action is terrible but at least you know where you are. It's final. There's been a death so you can grieve legitimately. You hang a gold star in the window and you don't lay awake nights wondering and worrying."

"But killed in action is final," I protested. " 'Missing' means there's still hope." I chose to forget the article in the *New York Times* which estimated that 85 percent of those reported missing in action would eventually be declared dead. Hope had only a 15 percent margin. "All sorts of things might have happened," I continued. "The twins' father could be wounded — his dog tags may have been stolen. He could be a prisoner of war. The Germans don't always declare their prisoners of war. Maybe he has amnesia." Novels, films, and radio drama about amnesiac soldiers were very popular that year. Audiences wept as the sound of a voice, the color of a flower triggered memory and the handsome hero repeated his name with verberent wonder as his faithful and tenacious girlfriend pressed his hand to her lips. Silently I prayed that should a telegram ever come for me, it would report that my father was either missing or wounded. I had had enough of what Judy called "legitimate grief." I knew that the finality of death did not mean an end to wakeful nights and the frightening turbulence of nocturnal sorrow.

"Letitia and Leatrice don't look very hopeful," Judy said wryly and dropped her cigarette stub into a moss-grown crevice between the rocks. "Maybe they should speak to my mother. She has enough hope to go around. She's absolutely convinced that Marvin is going to walk through our front door on Thanksgiving Day, if not before. God, I don't know what's going to happen when he doesn't." Her voice was strained, almost faint with worry. And that worry was not unfounded.

I had learned that Mrs. Bergman had had a nervous breakdown some years ago, a collapse brought on by an excess of hope and a heart-wrenching disappointment. She had been pregnant, exuberant in her anticipation of a third child.

Then she ranted and raved against the injustice of it all, shouted at the doctor who insisted that the miscarriage was "nature's way." She cut the layette into pieces with her kitchen shears.

One afternoon she thrust the proud coach carriage down the high brick steps of her house. The white mattress lay like a small coffin in the street until a horse-drawn vegetable wagon ran it over. Neighbors summoned her husband from work and stood on their porches watching for Judy and Marvin, who were diverted to the home of school friends so that they would not see their mother being led from the house by a doctor and a corpulent nurse who assured her loudly that she would be all right.

Now, again, Bella Bergman had written a scenario of fantastic hope and she focused all her energy on a single event: Marvin's homecoming on Thanksgiving Day, which was at worst impossible and at best improbable. Judy feared that disappointment would shatter the fragile balance which enabled her mother to make her way cautiously through each day.

"She'll go nuts again, I know she will," Judy said and her voice was hard because she did not then, and not for many years afterward, forgive her mother for her illness. Adolescents are harsh judges of things they do not understand. "I'm scared, really scared."

"I know." I covered Judy's hand with my own and we stared out at the waves, dark green now and crowned by turrets of foam.

"Okay — missing in action is better than killed in action," she conceded and we collapsed into paroxysms of the nervous laughter that I would recognize now as incipient hysteria.

But I never talked with Beth as honestly as I talked with Judy. Beth smiled at me now as I hung up after talking with Peter.

"He's coming then?" she asked.

I nodded.

"Aren't you glad?"

"Sure," I replied casually and reached over her shoulder for the paring knife. I could easily read the letter she was writing to Alfred. "Next year, we will be together in our own home — and just think, darling, there will be three of us!" She drew a little heart after the exclamation point and I averted my eyes and tried not to think of all the things that could happen during the course of a year, especially during a year of war.

I concentrated on my pies, sifting, slicing, and stirring, moving systematically through the steps my mother had specified in ink the color of sapphires. I dotted the apple slices with cinnamon and frowned because the container was almost empty and I was not sure it would suffice.

Lottie looked at me, sighed, and then smiled.

"You looked just like your mother for a minute," she said. Sadness and love mingled in her voice. "Just like Miriam. You had her expression. She worried. She wanted everything to be perfect."

"But I'm not like that," I protested. "I don't want everything perfect. I just don't want some things to change." My own words confused me. The truth was that I wanted everything to change and everything to stay the same.

Lottie looked at me seriously.

"But that can't be," she said gravely. "Do you know what I sometimes think — I think life is like a theater and every day a new curtain goes up. Some days a tragedy, some days a comedy." She was a woman who recited poetry and thought in metaphors. "But everything changes. It has to."

"Why?" I asked petulantly, suddenly exhausted. I thrust the last of my pies into the oven and went into my bedroom, where I fell into a deep sleep.

It was dark when I awakened. I sniffed the fragrance of my newly baked pies, heard the ringing of the phone, the buzz of the doorbell. I glanced at the clock. I had slept for nearly three hours.

I sprinted down the hallway to the phone.

"Hello."

"Is that you, Sharon?"

I recognized Robert's voice at once.

"Yes, it's me," I said as the door opened and Dina, wearing her black cape draped with a scarf of golden silk and a black beret perched jauntily on her copper-colored hair, swept into the room. Nachum Adler followed her, cradling a sleeping Anna, and behind them came Peter, limping slightly, smiling shyly, his fair hair, as always, falling across his high pale forehead. "How are you, Robert?" I said this loudly, and Dina froze for a moment. The gaiety fled her face and then, swiftly, she walked toward me, kissed me on the cheek, and took the receiver.

"How funny, Robert, that you should call just as I walked in. Yes — of course Anna's with me. Where would she be?" She laughed, although she was very pale, and waited for his reply. We too listened, like an audience transfixed by a drama whose first act was familiar but whose ending was still unpredictable.

I admired the way Dina kept her voice friendly although the receiver trembled ever so slightly in her grasp.

"Tomorrow will be fine. Oh, we'll eat about two, I suppose. Come sometime after four."

Robert was not invited to Thanksgiving dinner and it surprised me that I felt sorry for him. I had not yet learned that emotions commingled, that contempt and compassion are often interwoven, that rage and pity contract in a single heartbeat.

"Hi, Peter." I moved toward him, held my hands out. "It's great that you could come."

"I think so too." His hands were very cold and instinctively I pressed them to my cheeks to warm them.

"Bubbie, Zeidey — you remember my friend Peter?"

My grandparents nodded and smiled but their attention was focused on Anna. Nachum Adler placed the baby in my grandmother's outstretched arms and I watched as she held the infant while Lottie slowly undid the ribbons of her tiny hat, peeled off the layers of clothing. Anna cooed softly and there was an exchange of smiles. My grandfather placed his finger on the baby's palm, so soft and as pale as a flower, and beamed as she closed her small fingers about his gnarled knuckle, gripping it tightly as though she could feel his love and wonder radiate through it. Beth stood close by.

"She's a miracle," she said softly and we did not think her words an exaggeration.

Anna *was* a miracle for the family that year. We dreamed of Jewish children in jeopardy, read news stories about the deaths of toddlers and infants in ghettos and camps; in Antwerp the week before Thanksgiving, thirty-two children died when a flying bomb hit an orphanage. Yet our Anna was safe and healthy, encircled by the protection of our love, her tiny life a tender promise.

"A miracle," I repeated softly after Beth and I saw that my

grandfather's eyes were closed and his lips moved as though in prayer.

Peter and I went to a movie that night, Claudette Colbert in *Since You Went Away*. We held hands in the rear of the theater and when I wept at the heroine's courage, Peter wiped my eyes with his large white handkerchief and then kissed my cheeks, licking them lightly with his tongue.

"You have powerful tears," he said. "I can still taste the salt."

14

Snow fell lightly on Thanksgiving morning but slowly gathered momentum, the flakes thickening and whirling in wind-tossed flurries. Cars drove silently and slowly down streets carpeted with brittle frost.

Nachum Adler, when he arrived, told us of the icy roads that had slowed his progress from Sea Gate.

"A gift for you."

He held out a large envelope and Lottie removed a stiff sheet of paper. She spread it on the dining room table and we studied Nachum's watercolor sketch of Anna in my grandmother's arms as Lottie deftly untied the infant's hat and my grandfather placed his finger in her tiny palm. He had captured the tender scene in all its detail, the subtle differences in skin textures — my grandparents' faces lined and life-worn, the baby's face white and petal soft. The pale blue hat ribbons were entwined about Lottie's finger, on which a scab of orange sweet potato clung. Nothing had escaped his eye.

"It's wonderful," Lottie said. "We'll have to frame it, hang it up."

"I call it *Thanksgiving*," Nachum Adler said and smiled at Dina, who stared first at the sketch and then at Anna, whose head rested sleepily on her shoulder.

"Yes, a good name for it." Surprisingly, it was Julius who spoke. He had always been drawn to Nachum Adler's work and he studied this new watercolor carefully.

"Yes," he said. "That's what we must give thanks for — for *mishpacha*; for family, and for a *neie kind*, a new child that is part of us." Sorrow softened his voice, accented the commingling of Yiddish and English. He had no family other than Lottie's. The village of his birth had been singed off the map, and the lives of his brother and sisters, his cousins and the friends of his childhood had disappeared in swirls of smoke. Years later when Beth's daughter led a group of students on a tour of Eastern Europe, she could not find even a trace of the hamlet where Julius had been born.

I looked at Beth. This was the moment to tell her father that she was pregnant, that a baby, his grandchild, would be born to her. A *neie kind*, a newborn child; an extension of *mishpacha*, of family. She would relieve herself of the weight of her secret and offer him comfort at the same time.

But Beth said nothing and continued to shape the linen napkins into smooth rosettes. As though reading the appeal in my eyes, she shook her head.

I looked out the window and watched as the falling snowflakes swirled dizzily in a sudden gust of wind.

"If you're going to bring one of these pies to your friend Judy, you'd better start now," Lottie said.

"I'll call her," I said. "Do you feel like a walk?" I asked Peter, who was still looking at Nachum's drawing.

"Sure," he said. "This really isn't much of a snowfall, not for us. Right, Dina?"

"Absolutely. In Woodstock we'd consider this a dusting. Remember the snow two weeks ago, Peter? I could hardly dig my car out of the driveway."

I looked at my aunt with new respect, recognizing for the first time the courage it took for her to live alone with Anna in the

Woodstock house, the house Robert's parents had purchased but never visited. They rarely saw their son, just as Robert rarely saw his daughter. Was such a legacy of indifference passed from one generation to another? I wondered then, as I often wonder now. Cold fear gripped me. Who would teach me the secrets of motherhood? Where would I learn the mysteries of marriage? *Daddy, come home.* I willed my father into survival and turned away from Dina.

I dialed the Bergmans' number for perhaps the tenth time that morning. The line was busy, as it had been at each previous try.

"Well, at least you know they're home so we can go over there," Peter said.

I nodded and packed the cake into a corrugated carton. I did not think that the constantly busy phone was a good sign. I imagined Judy and her father frantically making phone calls, trying to locate a doctor on Thanksgiving, a psychiatrist who could respond to an emergency. Or perhaps Bella Bergman in the panic of her disappointment had knocked the phone to the floor and damaged it. She had, after all, pushed a baby carriage down a flight of brick steps.

Booted and bundled into our heavy winter jackets, Peter and I made our way to Manhattan Beach, the cold wind blowing frostily into our faces. We passed children on sleds and toddlers in bright snowsuits fashioning snow angels on the white expanse of narrow lawns. I spotted four boys from my class in a snowball fight. Flags fluttered from porches and windows. It had become a national habit to fly the flag when the news was good, and the news had been very good that Thanksgiving morning. French and American troops had entered Strasbourg and liberated the city which Hitler had named the capital of annexed Alsace.

"You see," Peter said, "it's almost over. They're on the run."

"Alfred wrote Beth that he's sure there's going to be one last big battle in Europe," I said.

Two soldiers stood on the corner where Brighton Beach Avenue and Coney Island Avenue intersected. They wore army greatcoats and leather-brimmed dress hats but they were so young that they reminded me of my cousin Bernie in his Junior Commando uniform. One of them carried a cake box and the other a bouquet of flowers which he held with embarrassed awkwardness. Their faces were wind-reddened, and they stared in confusion at the street signs. I stopped.

"Can we help you?" I asked.

"Excuse me, ma'am, but we're looking for Corbin Place." The freckled soldier spoke in the slow accent of the Deep South.

"Just walk along with us. I'll show you where to turn," I said, and they fell in step gratefully.

They told us that they were stationed at Fort Hamilton and the chaplain there had arranged for them to have Thanksgiving dinner with a local family.

"Real nice of them," the soldier with acne said. "My mother — she's in Iowa — I spoke to her this morning and she's having two boys from California for dinner."

"Musical Thanksgivings," Peter said and we all laughed bitterly at the vagaries of a world that scattered young men about the country and transformed them into guests at the tables of strangers.

The four of us stopped to help two small girls make a head for their snowman and roll it onto the body. The soldier who carried the bouquet took a rose from it and plunged the flower into the snowman's trunk, and we stood back to admire the effect.

"Have a good time," I said when we reached Corbin Place.

"We'll sure try," they replied in unison and we watched them walk on, raising the collars of their coats and hunching their shoulders against the snow.

"Are we almost there?" Peter asked and I realized that it was difficult for him to walk in the snow.

"Another block," I said. "I'm almost afraid to get there." I had told Peter about Mrs. Bergman's irrational hope, about Judy's dark fear.

"Hey, Sharon, you can't take on everyone's problems and make them your own," he said warningly and put his arm around my shoulders.

"Do I do that?" I asked.

"All the time. You worry about Dina and you worry about Beth and you worry about Judy."

"Is that so bad, to worry about people you care about?"

"My father says that sometimes it's easier to worry about other people's problems than to face your own," he replied carefully. "Actually, he was talking about me when he said it. Do you think it's easy to have a psychiatrist for a father?"

I did not reply. It was, I acknowledged, easier to worry about whether Marvin Bergman would come home for Thanksgiving than to wonder whether my father would ever again rest his hands on my head, his lips on my cheek.

Judy lived in a house not unlike our own. High brick steps led to a porch, and like Lottie, Bella Bergman kept the front door closed in all seasons. They were both women who had grown up in tenements and valued their privacy. But even from the street I saw that the door was open although the venetian blinds at the front window were drawn. I had anticipated that Mrs. Bergman, who regularly sat at that window, scanning the street, would be stationed there today of all days, watching for Marvin. ("He may be late," she had said the previous week. "But we'll just wait dinner for him. The other relatives won't mind.") Something else about the house was unusual — the blue-star banner no longer hung in the window.

"Something's happened," I said to Peter, and because my hands were trembling he took the carton that contained the pie from me.

Slowly, carefully, we made our way up the snow-covered steps. I noticed other footprints on the snow and I imagined wild flights to the street, a grieving pursuit, Judy and her father chasing after her mother.

We reached the porch and I heard the phone ring and then a woman's shrill voice, words tumbling over each other in a feverish monologue, rising to a hysterical pitch. Bella Bergman's voice —
"He didn't — you can't believe it. . . . That such things happen . . .
I almost fainted. . . . Believe me, I don't know how I didn't fall

down. . . . So I'm crying — why shouldn't I cry — I can't stop crying. . . ."

And then Judy's calming tone cut across her mother's voice. "Please, Mama, let me talk to Aunt Irene — we'll call you back when we're calmer, Aunt Irene. Yes, I promise."

My heart turned with sympathy for my friend, forced to mother her own mother. And then at once the weight of self-pity catapulted into place: *At least she has a mother.*

Hesitantly, I pressed the doorbell. Through the storm-door window I saw Mrs. Bergman seated at the kitchen table, her eyes red, her carefully marcelled hair in disarray. Her husband stood beside her, his skin mottled, his hands resting on her shoulders. Judy was still on the phone, calming her aunt. It was her father who came to the door, stared at us, and then released the latch.

"Oh, Mr. Bergman," I said. "I'm so sorry to be intruding at a time like this . . ." My voice faltered and Peter steadied me, his hand firm against my back.

"Don't be sorry. It's good that you came. Come in."

Judy replaced the receiver. She too had been crying. I bit my lip and struggled to remember the words that had been offered to me as comfort when my mother died. *It was for the best. She's released from her suffering. It's hard now but soon it will be easier. You're young.*

Those remembered utterances, all well-meant and all useless, were like ashes in my mouth. I could not repeat them to my friend, who rushed toward me and hugged me. I closed my eyes against her misery and opened them to see that she was smiling, her tear-streaked face alight with joy.

"Oh, Sharon, isn't it wonderful?" she asked breathlessly as Marvin Bergman, whom I recognized from his photographs, came into the kitchen.

I stared at him as though he were an apparition, a figment of my wild imaginings.

He put his hand on his mother's shoulder, his face close to her own.

"Ma, if you're going to cry like that, I'm going to rethink this entire furlough," he said in a deep voice hoarsened by embarrassment.

My heart soared. It did not matter that his arm was in a khaki sling, that because he had lost so much weight his uniform was ill fitting, or that his face was too thin and etched with worry lines that furrowed his forehead.

Nor did it matter that Marvin moved awkwardly, with the shifting gait that I now know to be peculiar to patients who have been so long bedridden that they walk unsteadily as they convalesce, resembling passengers on land after a long sea voyage. What mattered was that he was home — that he had miraculously arrived on Thanksgiving Day to sit down at the table set in his honor, covered with a cloth that his mother had embroidered in celebration of victory, the victory of survival.

Judy and I grasped hands and danced around the room.

"He just walked in — about two hours ago. He used his own key. Just walked in. I thought I was dreaming . . ."

"She means she thought she was having a nightmare," Marvin said, laughing, kneading his mother's shoulder because she was crying again, her body racked with sobs although her mouth was curled into a smile. "Believe me, the surprise wasn't my idea. You can blame the Red Cross. We landed in Seattle two days ago, walking wounded evacuated from the Pacific, and they flew us east. Operation Thanksgiving Day, they called it. Never gave us a minute to telegraph our families. They were going to do it but there was some foul-up. I hope not too many moms got heart attacks when Johnny came marching home."

Judy and her father exchanged glances — better a minor heart attack than a nervous breakdown, their eyes flashed.

"What do the doctors say about your arm?" Bella Bergman asked the question urgently although surely it had been asked and answered often since his arrival.

"I told you, Ma. Just some shrapnel. I was lucky."

"Lucky." Mr. Bergman's voice was bitter. "Your right arm."

"It'll be okay, Dad. Look, the important thing is that I'm home."

"Of course. That's what's important. But I told you he was

coming," Mrs. Bergman said and now her face was serene. "Didn't I tell you he'd be home for Thanksgiving? You know what I did after I hugged him — I took the star out of the window. I don't need a banner with a star. I have my son." She smiled, proud of her prescience, of her own good fortune. She looked at Peter. "I don't know your friend, Sharon."

"This is Peter Bassen. He lives next door to my aunt in Woodstock."

He crossed the room to shake her hand and she stared at him through narrowed eyes, assessing him as mothers of daughters assess available young men, as I myself have judged the young men my daughters' friends have brought to visit — critically and competitively.

"You're a lucky boy," she told him. "You'll never have to go into the army."

We all gasped and Judy blushed, but Peter merely nodded.

"That's exactly why I decided to get polio, Mrs. Bergman," he said, and then he laughed to show us that he understood and that he was a good sport, although his face was pale and his hands were clenched into fists.

Judy walked us to the door.

"I hope you don't mind my mother, Peter," she said apologetically.

He smiled and shrugged.

We walked in silence for a while. The snow had stopped but we made our way across the quiet whiteness. We passed a lawn on which a snowman crouched, a garrison cap on his frosty head, a khaki scarf around his neck. Peter saluted, his mouth twisted bitterly.

"She didn't mean anything. I told you, she's a little crazy," I said.

"No brakes," he replied.

"What do you mean?"

"My father says that he sometimes thinks that the only difference between the sane and the patients he sees is that his people have no brakes. They don't know when to stop. No inhibitions. He says that their honesty is sometimes refreshing."

"I didn't think her honesty was so refreshing," I retorted angrily.

"Hey, Sharon."

We broke our pace, stood very still. He took my face into his gloved hands, pressed his lips against my own. I felt the frigid sweep of his eyelashes upon my cheeks. I was glad, very glad, that he would never be called to the army.

Our own Thanksgiving dinner was a happy one, each course energetically punctuated with laughter and talk. Our family was buoyed by the Bergmans' good fortune.

" 'Home is the sailor, home from sea / And the hunter home from the hill,' " Lottie intoned and we toasted Marvin Bergman, who had returned safely from the jungles of the Pacific theater.

"And soon," Julius said, "Alfred and Aaron and Richard will be with us — God willing."

"*Got villik*. God willing." We repeated the words aloud in Yiddish and in English. Samuel told us jokes that he had heard as he fitted customers for suits.

"Some of Samuel's customers are professional comedians," Dolly reported proudly. "Henny Youngman. Eddie Cantor. He bought a blazer two weeks ago. A navy blue blazer. He had dinner at the White House. He told Samuel about it."

"Anyway," Samuel said, "you know how Jews used to believe in two worlds — *dos velt*, this world, and *yener velt,* the next world. Now we believe in a third world — Roosevelt."

We all laughed appreciatively.

"All right, here's another," Samuel said. "In Hungary just before the Nazis took over, a Jew goes to a travel agent and asks him where he can go to avoid danger. The agent takes out a globe, but with each country he points to, there are problems. Cuba wants special visas. For England you have to have ten thousand pounds. The United States has quotas. Who wants to go to Africa, where you could get maybe yellow fever? So the Jew says to the agent, 'You have maybe another globe?' "

This time the laughter was hesitant, nervous. Nachum Adler studied his plate, speared a bit of turkey with his fork, and set it down again. Julius put his head in his hands. He could not laugh at jokes about Jews who had no place to run, no country that would offer them refuge. He had spent too many hours soliciting affidavits, asking for contributions.

Samuel rushed to repair the damage. In lilting falsetto, he imitated Princess Elizabeth. "Don't be frightened, children. I'm not frightened. Are you frightened, Margaret Rose?" He fashioned his linen napkin into a crown, held out his fork as a scepter, pursed his lips in imitation of the British princess's beatific smiles.

My grandmother patted her only son's cheek.

"Ah, Shmulik — with you, everything is a joke."

But I looked at my uncle and realized that while laughter came from his lips, there was no joy in his eyes. I had begun to perceive the secrets that adults concealed from one another, to recognize that tears did not always signify sorrow and that laughter did not always mean merriment.

"Enough with the jokes. It's time for music. Between dinner and dessert, there should be music," Leon said and Edna immediately began to organize us.

"Yes. Leon's right. Everyone go into the living room. Wait. There aren't enough chairs. Bernie, bring chairs from the dining room. Heidi, you'll be at the piano. You'll play too. Now, Sharon, Beth, help me clear the table."

We assembled in the living room, that deeply carpeted, over-furnished, brightly lit room that testified to Julius's success and Lottie's homemaking. My grandparents, white-haired and dignified — he in his black suit and high black skullcap, she in her navy blue crepe dress, her cameo carefully affixed to her lace collar, sat on the high-backed brocade occasional chairs.

Dina, Anna in her arms, sat on the burgundy velvet easy chair in the corner, and Nachum Adler perched on the ottoman at her feet, studying the room. Would he do another drawing of us? I wondered, and I envied him his artist's eye. Peter and I sat on the floor. I spread the wide folds of my kelly green skirt across the thick gold carpet.

"You look like a flower," Peter whispered, and I smiled because that was what I had wanted him to say.

Heidi sat obediently at the piano. Her hair was twisted into a ponytail and she wore a navy blue skirt and a navy blue turtleneck sweater draped with a soft silk scarf of pale violet.

"I think Heidi has discovered her style," Dina had said earlier that day and I had nodded. I had not added that I thought Heidi had begun to discover herself.

"So play already," Samuel said.

He patted Dolly's hand. He was so proud of her; she was so pretty in her bright clothing, her hands so smooth, her nails so wonderfully colored and shaped. She was so modern, so American. She kept him safe, at a remove from the turmoil of the immigrant world, from the memory of his early years in New York when he, his parents, and Lottie had lived in a single room and ventured down a dark hallway to a toilet that they shared with two other families. Samuel now rarely used a public bathroom. He had tried to enlist in the army when the war began and was relieved when he was rejected because he was too old. He had not feared the danger; he had feared the communal bathrooms of the barracks, the latrines of the battlefield. Oh, he would have liked children — even one child. His heart turned when he held Dina's infant daughter. But he had his Dolly. He took care of her and she took care of him. All this I read in his sad eyes and in his impatient voice.

"You play first," Leon said to Heidi and she shrugged.

"Play the piece you won the prize for in Michigan," Edna said. She leaned against the wall, a dish towel draped over her arm.

"All right," Heidi said. "But I didn't win a prize. I only got an honorable mention."

She bent over the keyboard, her face intent. She played a Bach étude, the fingering complex, the mood compelling. We clapped when she finished and she smiled, her face flushed with the effort.

"Next year you'll win first prize," Edna said. "Next year."

"No, Ma. There isn't going to be a next year. I'm not going to take piano lessons for a while." Her voice was strong but her fingers were knotted and a small vein pulsed at her neck.

We waited for Edna's reply, her objections, her anger. But we had underestimated her.

"So you won't take piano lessons. Where is it written in stone that you should be a pianist?"

She left the living room and when I went into the kitchen for a drink of water a few minutes later, I saw her at the sink, washing her face. Her eyes were red but she had found her purse and carefully applied powder to conceal the traces of her disappointment. I was ashamed that I had judged her so harshly, that I had thought her ambition for Heidi was stronger than her love.

"Everything's going to be all right, Aunt Edna," I said in apology.

"Of course everything's going to be all right."

We stared at each other for a split second of mutual recognition that bridged the generations. We acknowledged each other's truth but we did not touch.

"Help me set the table for dessert," she said brusquely.

We set the cutlery and china in place as the strains of Leon's violin drifted in from the living room.

Leon played the klezmer tunes that my grandparents loved. He played a *debka* and Heidi picked up the tune on the piano, and Dina danced about the room, Anna in her arms, the skirt of her peacock blue dress swirling about her slender black-stockinged legs. Nachum's eyes followed her; he smiled as she bent and swayed. And then the tune was over and the dance was done. We applauded and Bernie put two fingers to his lips and whistled. Dina blushed, curtsied, and returned to the burgundy velvet chair. Once again, Nachum sat at her feet on the ottoman.

"You are tired?" he asked Dina softly.

"No. It was fun. I love to dance," she replied breathlessly and she shifted Anna, who had fallen asleep, from one shoulder to the other.

"My daughter, my little Rachel, used to say that dancing was like magic. When she danced with me and Manya — we would hold hands, the three of us, and dance across the rug — she said that she felt as though she was floating. Always Manya and Rachel took their shoes off." Dreamily, his voice almost atonal, he continued, speaking more to himself than to Dina. "We danced to the music from the radio and to our gramophone records. We had so many records." He closed his eyes as though straining to visualize that room where music had played and he and his wife and daughter had danced with magical movement across a carpet the color of sunlight.

I studied his face and saw the pain that shadowed his features, clouded his blue eyes. I thought that it matched my own anguish on the nights when I lay awake and struggled to recall our Brookline apartment: the rolltop desk where my mother worked, the floral-patterned easy chair where my father read his medical journals, my own rocking chair with the coral corduroy cushion that matched the carpeting my father had laid himself. And then the arrogance of that comparison shamed me. Our furniture was in storage. Nachum's home was forever lost.

Leon took up his bow, turned the pages of his sheet music. He played Bartók, the Humoresque. Nachum rose and went into the dining room. Dina handed me the sleeping Anna and followed him. Surely she had seen the tears that glinted in his eyes as he heard the music of his homeland.

She was comforting him then when the front door opened and Robert entered. He stood in the vestibule between the living room and the dining room and turned instinctively to the source of the music. His lips were curved in a smile, his face ruddy with the cold. He was prepared to charm us, to present the huge bouquet of yellow roses he carried to Dina, the potted orange tree in his other hand to Lottie. But at once his eyes veered to the dining room and he saw Dina and Nachum. The smile froze on his lips, then twisted into a grimace, a scowl of anger. I clutched Peter's hand, suddenly fearful.

We sat in silence, our ears keyed to the rumble of voices from the dining room — Robert's deep with anger, Dina's soft, almost pleading, Nachum's calm and cold. In my arms, Anna cried, a plaintive infant wail of fear and hunger. Lottie stood but Julius shook his head and she sat down again.

And Leon again took up his violin. Oddly, he chose tunes

from *Oklahoma!* and Heidi plucked out the melodies on the piano. Beth began to sing. She knew all the words. She and Alfred had sat in the orchestra and held hands as the chorus sang of cattle standing like statues and corn that was as high as an elephant's eye. It was the most popular musical of that year of our war, a patriotic pageant that captured America in all its optimism and innocence and offered us an alternative to the dark reality of the war being fought across our oceans.

Above Beth's high sweet voice, we heard the fragments of Robert's fury, of Dina's tremulous explanation.

"I was going to apologize to you — imagine — when it was you and him — all along I felt guilty — while you — "

"Robert, you don't understand . . ." She was right, I knew. Robert was a foreigner to the intimacy of silence, the comfort of a light touch, a soft voice. He had been schooled by rhetoric, governed by physical impulse, seduced by his own desires.

"You cannot talk this way to her."

" 'Chicks and ducks and geese better scurry . . .' " Beth sang and Bernie and Heidi, Peter and I joined in, raising our voices to drown out the staccato of accusation from the room next door.

My grandmother sighed deeply and murmured something in Yiddish, and my grandfather covered her hand with his own. I envied my grandparents, who could comfort each other against their daughter's pain.

We did not stop singing even when the front door slammed behind Robert. Dina took Anna from me and carried her down the staircase to my grandparents' apartment. Nor did we stop when Nachum entered the room, pale but calm, as though he had come to a painful but correct decision. We reached the final chorus of "Pore Jud Is Daid" as Dina returned.

"Anna's asleep in the crib," she said. "Let's have dessert."

We gathered again around the table and it was agreed that my pies were delicious.

"As good as Miriam's," Leon said daringly.

There was a moment of silence and then a murmur of assent.

"Yes, yes. As good as Miriam's." They said my mother's name lovingly and I was grateful to them.

I tasted my own slice and remembered my mother's laughter, the snow of flour upon her dark hair. Tears burned my eyes. She had been restored to me. Mysteriously, anger had been sifted from my grief.

Dina returned to the table, poured herself a cup of tea.

"Robert asked for a divorce," she said quietly, "and I agreed."

"A divorce." Dolly's tone was shocked but Samuel placed his finger on the bright red bow of her lips.

"A divorce," he repeated. "People do get divorced, you know."

"Emanuel Weiner will know the name of a good divorce lawyer." Edna's tone was brusque but she pressed her cheek against Dina's and briefly placed a comforting hand on her mother's shoulder.

"It was not a boring Thanksgiving," I said to Judy Bergman on the phone that Sunday evening after Peter had left, smiling but tired, sandwiched in the back seat of Nachum's car between Anna's bassinet and a carton of food.

"No," she agreed. "Not boring at all."

I hung up then and listened to the muffled sounds from the room next door, Beth's choking sobs of fear and loneliness. I could not comfort her. I closed my eyes and pressed my hands to my ears, against her pain and my own sudden terror.

15

Beth's second visit to Dr. Greenberg was scheduled for mid-December and once again I skipped school so that I could go with her.

"Really, I can manage alone," she protested weakly.

"But I want to go," I insisted.

I saw myself as her accomplice, her confidante, a vital ingenue in the cast of her wartime drama.

We waited on the platform of Sheepshead Bay station, she in her pale blue coat with its soft silver fur collar, a matching hat set fashionably on her blond hair. She stood tall in the platform-soled high heels whose straps cut into her slender ankles. I wore my plaid wool hooded coat, saddle oxfords, and bobby socks. Our clothes defined us. I was a schoolgirl still but Beth, only four years older than me, wore the uniform of a young matron, a soldier's wife. The war had accelerated her life. Within weeks she had been transformed from a carefree coed into an expectant mother.

"Isn't that Theresa?" Beth asked, staring at the south end of the station.

I followed her gaze and my heart sank as I saw the thin beauti-

cian. I remembered how her carmine-tipped fingers had flashed
across bobby pins and combs the morning of Beth's wedding as she
confidently assured us that the war would be over by Christmas.

"We have MacArthur. We have Halsey," she had chanted as
she wielded hair spray and conditioner.

Her husband had been in the navy and he swore by Halsey
and Nimitz. But now October and November had come and gone;
it was two weeks before Christmas and the war was not over nor
did we believe that it would be over soon. Theresa's sailor husband
was dead, killed by a Japanese attack as the destroyer on which he
was stationed approached the Philippines. Peter Remo, the proprietor of the beauty shop where Theresa worked, had whispered the
news to Lottie the previous week and Lottie had contributed two
dollars to the wreath which patrons of the shop had sent to
Theresa.

"That poor girl," Lottie had said to me. "We won't tell
Beth — all right?" She touched my hand, inviting my understanding, my complicity.

I nodded. Of course we would not tell Beth. The news of
another young woman's loss would shadow Beth's hopes, pierce
her with arrows of fear. Theresa's widowhood might presage her
own.

"Yes. Yes, it is Theresa," I said miserably now.

Theresa wore a belted black coat and she seemed thinner and
paler than I remembered her. Her hair, unpermed and badly colored, hung lankly about her face. She leaned against a pole, indifferent to the lateness of the train. She was, I realize now, newly
bereaved, her identity and her future destroyed. Holiday wreaths
hung in windows and the radio played Christmas carols but time
stretched like a desert before her and she was in no hurry to go
anywhere.

"We should go over and talk to her," Beth said, but even as
she spoke the Brighton Express roared its way into the station and
we hurried on. Theresa entered two cars forward and I was relieved when I saw her leave the train at De Kalb Avenue. She
plunged into the crowd with her head down and I saw that her fair
skin was mottled by her grief. I felt guilty then and turned swiftly

back to my book, pursing my lips as Edna did when she did not want to be disturbed.

I was reading Elliot Paul's *The Last Time I Saw Paris* and I imagined my father walking down the streets of the City of Light, pausing at a jewelry shop on St. Honoré (Paul's favorite street) to buy me a brooch, showing my picture to the proprietor. It comforted me to know that I was special to him — words that he repeated in each letter. It terrified me to think that if he died — if he were killed (the thought curdled in my mind but I willed myself to think it), there would be no one in the world for whom I would come first. It did not disturb my imagining to know that in all probability my father was no longer in Paris. The cryptic clue in his last letter indicated that his medical unit had been transferred to a wooded area. He wrote of waking to the scent of a wintry forest.

"Stay safe," I commanded him fiercely and I turned a page of my book although I was so consumed by fantasy and fear that I had hardly read a single word.

We were early for Beth's appointment and we walked slowly from the subway station at Union Square to Gramercy Park, pausing at the black wrought iron gate of the park to watch a group of small girls jumping rope. They wore leggings and snow pants against the cold and jumped awkwardly but their singsong voices were loud and clear as they chanted a nonsense rhyme in rhythm to the turning rope.

> Whistle while you work
> Hitler is a jerk
> Mussolini is a meanie
> And the Japs are worse.

Beth and I laughed.

"Do you think they know who Hitler and Mussolini are?" she asked.

"I wish we didn't," I replied. I thought of the dictators of Italy, Germany, and Japan, those small men who wore elaborate uniforms and gave themselves titles that proclaimed their omniscience. It was because of them that Theresa was widowed, that

Mrs. Seubert mourned her son, that Leatrice and Letitia were balanced on the seesaw of terror.

The singsong ridicule of small girls did not diminish the power of their evil intent. Hitler, Mussolini, Hirohito.

"I hope they die," Beth said. "All of them." She spoke very calmly. The curse floated from her soft lips painted the color of watermelon, and vanished in the frosted cloud of her breath.

It frightened me that a woman who carried life within her should speak of death, and it frightened me too that I agreed with her. I also wanted them dead.

We were early initiates into hatred. The war had violated our innocence and burdened us with a fury that sapped the optimism and hope that is the natural mind-set of youth.

We walked very slowly then and we were both tired when we reached Dr. Greenberg's office.

Beth was called into the examination room and I sat opposite the portrait of the pregnant woman that Robert had painted.

A young woman who sat diagonally across from me, pixie-faced and dark-haired, her maternity dress a daring scarlet, smiled at me.

"You're a little young to be here," she said.

I saw the curiosity in her eyes and I resented her patronizing tone.

"I'm waiting for my cousin," I said. "Her husband is overseas."

"Oh." She took out her compact, powdered her cheeks, smiled at herself.

I jumped to the next question. I knew just what to ask her. "Is your husband in the service?"

"No." She hesitated. "No. He's not. He has a deferment."

"Oh, is he 4F?"

She had invaded my privacy and so I would invade hers. I wanted to hurt her, to make her pay for looking so well, for smiling into the mirror, for waking in the morning beside her husband, his hand on the gentle rise of her abdomen, while Beth slept alone in the narrow bed of her girlhood and trembled each time the doorbell rang.

"No. He's in essential industry." She blushed painfully and turned back to her copy of *Look* magazine — a feature spread on Betty Grable and Harry James looking cheerfully patriotic as they counted out ration stamps, studied war bonds.

The door opened and Dr. Greenberg beckoned me into his consulting room. I sat on a leather chair beside Beth, who was very pale. She wore a pink wool dress that Alfred favored — she had worn it, I recalled, when they went to see *Oklahoma!* She held her coat, although the fur hat was neatly in place and the usual long smooth lock of golden hair covered her birthmark.

"I wanted you to hear what I say to Beth," Dr. Greenberg said, speaking very slowly as though he feared we might not understand his words. "She is now at the beginning of her second trimester and I think she is doing well. But Beth tells me she experiences mild cramps and nausea from time to time and this concerns me a little."

"It's because I'm so worried about Alfred," Beth said plaintively.

"That may well be. But if those cramps are accompanied by asthmatic symptoms, there may be complications and we have to be aware of that.

"I rely on you, Sharon," he continued, "to help your cousin, to call me if you become aware of any difficulty. Beth tells me that you are a doctor's daughter, that you plan to become a doctor."

My heart beat too rapidly. I was a doctor's daughter. I did plan to become a doctor. But I was only a high school girl. Still, I nodded with grave acquiescence.

"I understand," I said. "But Beth hasn't had an asthma attack since she was married."

"Just some very mild symptoms," she said and guiltily dropped her eyes.

I remembered then the labored breathing, the nervous gasps that sometimes accompanied her nocturnal grief. I had heard them as I hovered outside her door and I blamed myself for not having questioned her about them, for trying so intensely to ignore them. I had not wanted to know about those symptoms because such knowledge might have impelled me to reveal Beth's secret to

Lottie, to end my role as Beth's faithful ally. And I had not wanted to be burdened with more responsibility.

"That's really all. I'll see you both next month," Dr. Greenberg said and I was grateful to him for including me.

The woman in the scarlet maternity dress passed us in the narrow hallway. We did not look at each other. Beth paused at the secretary's desk and wrote a check to pay for the office visit. I watched as she made it out, her signature, in her round schoolgirl handwriting, firm. The simple act placed her in a world apart from my own, among adults who paid their own bills. Of course, Alfred's allotment check was mailed to her each month and she drew a salary for her work in the fur store. Still, her independence startled me and filled me with envy.

"You must be careful, Beth," I said severely as we walked toward the subway.

"I am careful." She spoke loudly because the street had grown suddenly noisy, abuzz with a nervous excitement, an electric energy. Drivers hooted their horns impatiently, pedestrians dashed across the broad avenue against the light. A newsboy rushed past us shouting a headline, but we could not discern the words. Crowds clustered about the corner newsstand. We edged ourselves forward and stared at the banner headline of the *Journal American*. HUN NO LONGER ON THE RUN! The *New York Post* read: HITLER LAUNCHES MASSIVE ASSAULT ON TRAPPED ALLIED TROOPS! Beth put down a quarter and gathered up all the afternoon papers. The news dealer made change rapidly. A line formed and each customer plucked up more than one paper, as though hopeful that one headline might cancel out another, one news story might provide a glimmer of hope absent from other dispatches. News was our addiction throughout the war, especially on days when reports from the battlefields were very good or very bad. And they were very bad that December day on which the assault that we would call the Battle of the Bulge began.

"This is awful," a woman who stood beside me said. Three ribbons, red, white, and blue, dangled from the collar of her dark coat. She had three sons in the service. Her hands trembled and her newspaper fluttered in the wind.

"Terrible," her companion agreed. They stood in the middle of the sidewalk, the paper stretched open between them, their eyes riveted to the columns of print.

"The Ardennes," the first woman said, mispronouncing the word so that it rhymed with *mean* rather than with *men*. "What is that?" she asked desperately. It was hard that her sons might fall in a forest whose name she could not pronounce, whose location was unknown to her.

Julius found it for us on the globe that night, in France, close to the Belgian border. Beth and I stared hard at the patch of green on the blue orb. My father might be there. Alfred might be there.

All the newscasters were sober, their voices constrained by anxiety. We turned the radio dial from station to station, gleaning the same news everywhere. The assault on the Ardennes had been unexpected, although in retrospect there had been clues that the Germans had been planning a counteroffensive.

"Alfred has been writing for weeks that the Germans had something up their sleeve," Beth said.

Irritation edged her voice. Surely if Alfred had sensed the imminence of such an attack, Patton, Marshall, and Eisenhower should not have been unprepared. It was incredible that 80,000 unprepared and unsuspecting American troops were exposed to an assault by 200,000 Germans. Anger was safer than fear and she aimed her rage at the carelessness of the American generals, the ineptitude of the Allied high command. It relieved her to make accusations, to levy blame.

I envied her that solace. I myself was too constricted by terror to be diverted. I knew with dead certainty that my father was in the Ardennes. He had, after all, written of the beauty of the forest, of the sound of pine needles falling softly on his tent. And, although he had not named the woodland where his medical unit had set up camp, I knew it was on the Belgian border because he had written cryptically that if all went well he might be able to cross into another country and buy me some lace. The censor had ignored that but it had not been lost on me. I read each letter like a detective, seizing on the slightest clue.

"We were too comfortable, too confident. We did not read

the signs," Nachum Adler said sadly. He turned the pages of the *Aufbau,* the German-language paper of the Jewish community of New York City. "We should have realized when Hitler lowered the draft age to sixteen that he had a plan for those conscripts."

"He's drafting sixteen-year-olds?" I asked incredulously.

"He has no conscience," Nachum said and went to the window. A light snow fell. The thin flakes adhered to the glass pane and became crystalline tears that wept their way down the frosted surface. In the Ardennes, Edward R. Murrow's raspy voice advised us, a heavy fog blanketed the countryside, obscuring visibility and weakening the position of the Allies. I shivered and wiped the window with my sleeve.

"I don't think Alfred is in the Ardennes," Beth said that night as she brushed her hair.

"Why not?"

I watched as she studied her face in the mirror, as she draped a long lock of hair over her birthmark and then lifted it. She touched the strawberry-colored outpouching with her fingers as Alfred had touched it so gently with his lips on their wedding day.

"He must be in Italy. Because he knows Italian. He had three years of Italian at Northwestern. He wanted to learn it because he wanted to understand operas. He loves opera, you know."

I didn't know. I knew very little about Alfred. He had drifted into my life for a brief few weeks, married my cousin, and gone off to war, leaving her with a scrapbook of souvenir menus and theater programs on her bookshelf, a wedding band on her finger, and a child in her womb. Occasionally when I looked at the wedding photographs in the large white satin-covered album which Lottie kept proudly on the marble-topped living room coffee table, I had difficulty picking Alfred out from among his ushers in their group portrait. They were all smiling young men in uniform, hands on one another's shoulders. Alfred leaned slightly forward, as though he might break free of this circle of men and reach for his bride. He had no time to waste. He would soon be off to war.

"So what does that mean?"

"They'd use Alfred to do intelligence work in Italy. I figured it all out," she said and her voice was determinedly confident.

"It's not as though they don't have thousands of Italian Americans in the army," I retorted harshly, "who all understand Italian perfectly and speak it perfectly. Even dialects. Why would they need Alfred?"

I recognized the cruelty in my words but I wanted to deflate her optimism, to thrust her into reality.

Her face collapsed in misery. Her hand flew to the wen, which seemed to have turned darker suddenly.

"But maybe you're right, Beth. Maybe he is in Italy. Or somewhere else in Europe. He's probably not in the Ardennes." Swiftly, I contradicted myself, begging her, with that rush of words, to forgive me.

"Maybe." But her voice broke and I knew that she would weep into her pillow that night.

Julius and Lottie stayed up late, talking softly, falling silent for the hourly newscast. Twice the staircase door opened and my grandfather shuffled into the living room. Julius translated the more complicated portions of the news into Yiddish.

"*Oy*," my grandfather said. "*Oy veh*." It seemed to me that all the sorrow of our times trembled in those two words, uttered so softly with such desolation.

Hitler was calling his new campaign the Watch on the Rhine. We were calling it the Battle of the Bulge. But names were irrelevant. No matter what the battle was called, the bodies of soldiers lay on cold forest floors. I remembered the young soldiers whom Peter and I had directed to Corbin Place on Thanksgiving Day and I wondered where they were. In my mind's eye, I saw my father, pale with fatigue and slight of build, pressing his very clean long fingers to a soldier's wound, stanching a flow of blood, his own life spared so that he could save the lives of others.

"Daddy," I whispered into the night silence. "You must stay safe. You must not die."

I dreamed that night that I was lost in a fogbound forest. Swirling masses of mist hung like heavy vines from snow-laden branches. Whipped by the wind, they flailed in the darkness, and as I stumbled about, they lashed my arms, my legs. My cousin Bernie, wearing the gray uniform of the Wehrmacht, drifted before me. "That way, Sharon. That way." A ribbon of blood trickled from his lips but I did not stop to tend him. I walked on in the direction he had pointed me until I reached a clearing, a quiet glen where no trees grew although the forest encroached on every side. And there my father stood, smiling thinly, his garrison cap slightly askew on the brush-cut of his fair hair as it had been slightly askew the morning he kissed me good-bye and went off to war.

"Daddy!" I said the word loudly, and as I spoke it a huge cloud of mist rushed in, hovered briefly between us, then swirled about, growing thicker and thicker. We lurched toward each other, my father and I, our arms outstretched, our bodies buffeted by a restraining wind.

"Sharon."

"Daddy."

Helplessly, hopelessly, we struggled on, but we were entangled in the vines of fog, blinded by the thick mist. When at last the fog lifted, I was alone. My father had vanished. Where he had stood, a freestanding marriage canopy was in place: a prayer shawl draped across slender bamboo poles. Beth stood beneath it, dressed in black. Through the veil that covered her face, her birthmark flashed with an electric glow, a rosy light like that of the eternal light in the sanctuary where she had been married. Her mouth opened but before she could utter a word I hurled myself toward her.

"No, Beth, no!"

I awakened then and sat up in bed, shivering. My face was wet and when I lifted my hands to my cheeks, I was startled by the heat of my newly fallen tears — I had thought I would touch the chill residue of the mist that wove its way through my dream. I crept out of bed and stood for a moment outside the closed door of Beth's room. And then I opened it and peered in. My cousin was asleep, her breathing even, her face turned toward the night table where Alfred's picture was in place. He smiled down at her as she slept. I left the door slightly ajar and twice more that night I awakened and went again to stand in her doorway, newly vigilant, newly fearful.

On the sabbath eve of that first week of the German strike

across the Siegfried Line, Beth stood beside Lottie at sunset and fingered the white cloth that covered the table. The house was fragrant with the aromas of the sabbath — the newly baked braided loaves of challah, simmering chicken soup, brisket juices dripping onto thinly sliced onions. It reassured us to know that the war had not interfered with that weekly ritual. Beth covered her fair hair with a kerchief and struck a match to light the wick of the squat white candle; with this she ignited the other candles that stood in slender silver candlesticks that had been our grandmother's wedding gift to her. She held her hands over the newly kindled flames so that they danced in linear patterns of light between her fingers.

She mouthed her prayer silently, as Lottie did, as my grandmother did in her own dinette below us. I thought that silence increased the intensity and potency of their benedictions and I watched from the doorway and willed them to remain still. Their hands, warmed by the flames, were held to their eyes, and their unspoken prayers wafted through the sabbath stillness. Such quiet concentration surely had chimeric power. They were women praying over sanctified lights for the safety and survival of men who fought a war. Beth's cheeks were flushed. I noticed that her skirt was unbuttoned and I wondered how much longer she would be able to conceal her condition from her parents.

We took shelter on the sabbath day from the tumult and terror of the war. We could neither buy a newspaper nor listen to the news on the radio and we accepted those restrictions with gratitude. Heidi spent the sabbath with us, as she often did, and we walked together through the quiet streets to the small synagogue in Brighton Beach, where we sat in the women's section, pleased to be at a remove from the dark presence of the men who murmured to one another throughout the service. Surely they spoke of the war, of the casualties, of the German surge across the Meuse. When the memorial prayer for the dead was read, three men who were new to the synagogue stood. They were Belgian Jews and they mourned relatives killed when a V2 rocket hit a cinema in Antwerp. Almost six hundred people had been killed by the rocket fired from Holland across a distance of more than 130 miles. This was a war fought against civilian populations, a war that invaded the lives of men, women, and children who bought tickets to a cinema and died as the theater was incinerated by an explosive fired across a distant border.

"War from a distance," Heidi said bitterly. "The new age."

We could not see the men who said the prayer for the dead because a thin gauze curtain separated the men's section of the synagogue from the women's, but we could discern their silhouettes, their bowed heads, the manner in which the tallest of the trio lifted his hand quite suddenly to his face as though to shield other worshippers from the sight of his terrible grief.

We were grateful that afternoon to feel ourselves insulated by the sabbath stillness. We did not speak of the war as we ate Lottie's delicious lunch — the chopped egg mashed with fried onions, the smooth cold gefilte fish, the cold chicken and salad. Julius spoke of the Torah portion. He pondered the intricacies of Moses' character, the reluctance of the children of Israel to leave the land of Egypt. My grandfather spoke of the close relationship between Moses and his brother Aaron, his sister Miriam. The men's voices were gentle, dreamy.

It was easy at that sabbath table to imagine that we lived in a time of peace, that the days of our childhood, sweet and untroubled, were restored to us. I closed my eyes as I ate the compote which my grandmother made each Friday afternoon. Perhaps when I opened them, my mother and father, holding hands, would walk into the dining room and stand behind my chair. My mother would be flushed with health, her dark hair caught up in a pale blue ribbon that matched her simple dress. And my father would not be in uniform. He would wear the rumpled gray serge suit of his civilian days, his stethoscope plunged into his jacket pocket. Their hands, radiating love, would rest upon my shoulders.

A plum pit slithered about my tongue, slid to the back of my throat; I coughed violently.

"Sharon." Lottie leaned forward. There was fear in her voice.

I spit the pit onto my plate.

"I'm all right," I said. But my voice was thick with sadness.

Winter

16

Huge red mesh stockings hung in our homerooms at Lincoln High, and we filled them with gaily wrapped bars of Lifebuoy soap, tubes of shaving cream, small bottles of Vitalis, hand-knit socks and woolen scarves rolled into small balls. The girls who had done the knitting pinned affectionate messages to their handiwork. "This is to keep you warm wherever you are. I don't want you to have cold feet. Ha ha." Red, white, and blue ribbons dangled from holiday wreaths. Patriotism and religion mingled and reinforced our hope, and hope was in short supply that preholiday week as the news from Europe grew increasingly darker. The Germans had surrounded Bastogne, trapping several thousand American soldiers. I read the headline but not the news story.

The school corridors were reverberant with Christmas music carried by loudspeaker as we changed classes. The words of the carols took on new meaning. "O come all ye faithful, joyful and triumphant." I sang along. I too wanted to be joyful and triumphant.

I felt deprived because our house was not decorated. Hanukkah had come early that year. The slender orange candles had all

been lit and the menorah polished and put away before the first
Christmas trees were hauled out of car trunks.

"Next year," Lottie had said, "we will have a Hanukkah
party. When everyone is home."

Next year — when the war was over, when Aaron and Alfred
and my father were returned from its dangers. I envisaged that
Hanukkah a year away. Beth's baby would be chortling in a high
chair, Anna would be toddling about the house. Peter would be on
vacation from Harvard and my own desk would be piled high with
college catalogues. My own desk in my own home. I would be
back in Boston, living with my father, our furniture redeemed
from storage, our lives redeemed from terror. With desperate eagerness, I contemplated that happy future as I stood at the window
and rested my fingers on the smooth blue satin star.

Beth fashioned a dove of peace out of layers of white tissue
paper, and Heidi painted a red, white, and blue V for Victory on a
large piece of oak tag. We lashed the dove to the oak tag with
strips of adhesive tape and hung it on the front door. We waited,
half expecting Julius to protest, but he did not.

"All right," he said. "So now we have decorations too —
we're regular Americans." He smiled and touched his daughter's
fair hair. He would not object to anything that made Beth happy,
that brought her respite from fear.

And, of course, there was so much to be sad and fearful about
as the Germans continued to press forward. A broadcast of the
"Lux Radio Theater" was interrupted with the news that nine
thousand Americans surrendered at Schnee Eifel after being hopelessly outnumbered and outgunned. The Japanese perpetuated terrible brutality against the Filipinos. German rockets fell on
Antwerp.

I did my homework as we listened to the news reports, thrust-
ing the point of my compass onto the sheet of graph paper as
though it were a bayonet piercing the heart of an enemy, pressing
the nub of my pen so hard that droplets of blue ink showered my
French conjugations.

Beth, who had just learned to knit, clicked her steel needles in
fierce staccato beat. She was making a scarf for Alfred and she

worked very rapidly, as though she had a deadline to meet. It was urgent that she complete the scarf, that she mail it to Alfred so that it would keep him warm against the biting cold of the European winter. Each click of the needle affirmed her hope. One did not knit scarves for dead men.

On the last day of classes before winter recess, Leatrice and Letitia were absent. We stared at their empty seats and averted our eyes. I remembered how tears had silvered their dark cheeks on D Day and I was regretful and ashamed because I had never dared to talk with them about their father. I had never told them that I shared their sadness, that I prayed that he would be found, that he would be all right.

"What do you think happened?" I asked Judy as we filed into the auditorium.

The twins had never been absent before. They came to school even when they had colds. They were both honor students, propelled to excellence by their mother, who occasionally appeared at school carrying a textbook or an assignment that had been forgotten at home. She was a tall and beautiful woman, her skin darker than her daughters', her features finely chiseled.

"You know what I think," Judy replied bleakly. Marvin's safe return had not vanquished her natural pessimism, a pessimism that would haunt her all the days of her life. Even now, so many decades later, her heart sinks when the phone rings. "What's the matter?" she asks as others say hello. She still greets each dawn fortified against sorrow although her life has been surprisingly happy. "I think their father's dead."

"Yes. I think so too," I said and my heart swelled with grief. If the twins' father was dead, the chances of my own father's survival were somehow diminished.

We stood, staring at the twins' empty seats as the color guard proceeded down the aisle, their flags dangling at half-mast and draped with black. We stood at attention for the Pledge of Allegiance, the singing of the "Star-Spangled Banner." The principal rose from his maroon leather chair and shuffled to the podium.

"There is some bad news for our school today," he said in his gruff monotone and we stiffened.

"Howard Arnstein and Jordan White, both Lincoln graduates of the class of 1940, were seriously wounded in the Philippines. Let us pray for them."

Dutifully, we bowed our heads. Judy and I nudged each
other, shifted our weight from one leg to the other. How were they
wounded? Were they blinded? Had one lost a leg? A nascent hysteria stirred within us. If we looked at each other we would laugh
uncontrollably.

"But I have some good news as well," he said. "Captain John
Newling, the father of your schoolmates Leatrice and Letitia, is
alive and convalescing in a military hospital near Washington. The
Red Cross advised the family of this yesterday and Letitia, Leatrice, and their mother will spend the holiday with the captain."

The news of the twins' father's safety elated us. Lightheart-
edly, we raced through the rest of the school day. There were holiday parties in every homeroom. The glee club practiced in the
auditorium and their voices wafted sweetly through the open door.
" 'There'll be bluebirds over the white cliffs of Dover / Tomorrow,
just you wait and see.' " The phonograph in the girls' gymnasium
was piled high with records, and girls danced with one another as
Bing Crosby and Frank Sinatra crooned the songs of the season.
Our bodies twitched and our lips mouthed the words as our dancing feet tapped out the rhythm.

" 'Oh the weather outside is frightful,' " we sang in chorus
and our skirts flared about our knees; we clapped our hands and
stamped the pink rubber soles of our saddle shoes.

We helped to pile the red mesh stockings, which we had been
dutifully filling since Thanksgiving, into large cartons. The principal was to drive them to an army hospital that afternoon.

"Hey, I thought they were for boys overseas," I complained
to Judy.

"How would they get there in time?" she asked sensibly.

"Well, I just hope the stocking with the socks you knit
doesn't go to anyone who lost a leg. Or two legs," I said.

"And I hope that whoever gets the one with Andrea's scarf
has a neck," she retorted and we both giggled, humor diluting our
anxiety.

Judy and I did not go directly home from school. She avoided her house because Marvin sat in the darkened living room idly turning the pages of a magazine although his eyes were locked in a glassy stare. He jerked forward at the slightest sound as he surely must have jerked forward when the tall wild grass of the jungle moved and he feared that death approached him from behind the luxuriant foliage. His furlough was almost over and each time Judy arrived home her mother pulled her by the wrist into the kitchen.

"They won't send him back to the front, will they?" she would ask. "He's wounded. How could they send him back?" Her fingernails carved their way into Judy's flesh and her eyes were wild with worry.

And I avoided the house on Avenue Z because I feared to open the door to the thick silence of midafternoon. I feared to pluck up the mail thrust through the brass slot and scattered like a thickly petaled flower across the tiled floor of the vestibule. My hands trembled as I gathered up the envelopes and studied each return address, exulting at the sight of a V-letter but more often sinking into a depression because there was no mail from overseas.

I felt very alone at that hour, a stranger in my aunt's house, an interloper in Aaron's bedroom although Lottie had removed his brown drapes and bought me a Bates bedspread and curtains in a cheerful plaid. I wondered where I would sleep if Aaron returned from the war before my father. Would he reclaim his room and would I then be exiled to the very small bedroom in my grandparents' apartment?

Judy and I postponed going home by walking to Brighton Beach Avenue. The war being fought a world away energized the busy Brooklyn thoroughfare. Harried housewives shuffled their ration coupons. The posters at the Lincoln Savings Bank urged the purchase of war bonds, the conservation of fuel and electricity. Coastguardsmen from the base at Manhattan Beach strutted down the street, the collars of their pea jackets turned up, their faces wind-ruddied, their blue wool berets at jaunty angles. They grinned at girls, who smiled shyly back.

"Excuse me, miss, would you care for a soda?"

Their invitations were daring and occasionally a girl would nod and follow the uniformed boy into Meyer's Sweet Shoppe, her head held defiantly high. She was not allowing herself to be picked up. She was being patriotic, entertaining a boy in uniform. Tomorrow he might be shipped out. Within weeks he might drown in icy ocean waters.

We stopped at the Hebrew National Delicatessen for frankfurters with mustard and sauerkraut, which we clutched awkwardly between our mittened fingers so that the meat tasted of wet wool.

"Is that good?" asked a soldier descending from the Brighton Beach station, his duffel bag on his shoulder.

"Delicious," I replied. "Here. Finish it," I added daringly and thrust the last bite into his mouth.

Giggling, Judy and I dashed away, pausing at the newsstand on the corner of Coney Island Avenue to scan the headlines of the *New York Post*. The news was good. The low-lying fog over the Ardennes had lifted and the Germans had lost their advantage. Already an American counterattack had been launched on the southern flank of the Ardennes. The tide of the Battle of the Bulge was turning. It would be a happy holiday season after all.

Still laughing, we turned toward my house. Judy and I linked arms. Our books were heavy but our hearts were wonderfully light for the first time in days. The headlines were optimistic and the safety of the twins' father was a happy omen. The principal had concluded that morning's assembly by reading from a recent Order of the Day issued by General Eisenhower to all Allied troops in the Ardennes. "Let everyone hold before him a single thought. To destroy the enemy on the ground, in the air, everywhere to destroy him." Now Eisenhower's troops were following his command. We trusted the architect of D Day, who smiled paternally as he rode his command jeep and waved to his men.

"Stay for dinner," I invited Judy.

"I don't know. I'll have to call my mother," she said.

"Hey, anyone home?" I opened the door with my key and shouted into what I believed to be an empty house. It was still too early for Lottie, Julius, and Beth to be home or for my grandparents to have wakened from the long afternoon naps of the elderly.

But my grandparents were awake — awake and seated side by side at the dining room table, my grandfather with a prayer book open before him, my grandmother with her hands folded on the white cloth. So she had sat after my mother's death, her clasped fingers indicating that she had surrendered, that she could do no more. The last rays of late-afternoon sunlight penciled the cloth and brushed their soft white hair with patinas of gold. My grandfather, as always, wore his dark suit, a soft white shirt, and dark tie, his gold watch dangling from a chain across his vest. He was a man who seldom left the house but dressed each day as though for momentous events.

But my grandmother, who favored cotton housedresses on ordinary days, wore her black crepe dress, its long sleeves and collar trimmed with narrow ruffles of lace. A black shawl draped her shoulders. I recognized that dress. She reserved it for funerals and condolence calls. It was her uniform of grief. It was too big for her. She was much diminished since Lottie had first bought it for her.

She pulled her black shawl closer about her as Judy and I moved toward her.

"Buba, Zeidey, what's wrong?" The smile faded from my lips, all joy left my heart. My mood plummeted, shattered into discrete shards of terror. Nausea washed over me in a sickening wave. I dropped my book bag, heard its thud on the floor.

My grandmother pointed to the telegram placed squarely on the center of the clean white cloth. She had distanced herself from it, as though fearful that its message might contaminate her. "I signed for it, Shaindel," my grandfather said miserably. "They brought it to our door, because there was no one home upstairs." He had not wanted to sign for it. He had not wanted to bear the message of grief to his daughter's home. He looked at me from behind his thick-lensed glasses as though begging for forgiveness.

The envelope lay facedown. I could not see to whom it was addressed.

"Look, maybe it's nothing. Maybe it's good news," Judy said without conviction.

"No. It's something. It's bad news," I replied. My voice was flat.

I turned the envelope over. My eyes were closed. *Don't let it be. Don't let it be.* The words ricocheted through my mind, circled back, began again. I did not know what they meant, to whom they were addressed. *Don't let it be. Don't let it be.* The mental plea had a life of its own, a rhythm beyond my control. It has recurred so many times through the years, at moments of crisis and danger, at moments of sadness and loss. It is my secret mantra, automatic but ineffective, a verbal anchor that restrains me against waves of panic.

I opened my eyes, saw the three stars on the envelope. The telegram was addressed to Mrs. Alfred Levine. I trembled. Relief and sorrow melded. Vomit spurted into my throat, receded, soured my body. My father was alive but Alfred was dead. I clenched my hand into a fist and pounded the unopened envelope.

"Shaindel?" My grandmother's voice was questioning, imploring.

I knelt beside her, placed my head on her lap, felt her gnarled fingers smooth the tumulus of my hair.

"It's Beth's Alfred," I said, my voice grief-muffled. "It's her Alfred."

My grandfather went to the phone and called Edna at Emanuel Weiner's office. In that curious amalgam of Yiddish and English which he used to address his children, he told Edna about the telegram.

"You should come," he said. "You'll know what to do."

Organizational skills are necessary at a time of death. We would need Edna, who would know what to do, whom to call. Judy filled the kettle, placed it on the stove, kindled the gas jet. She left and I took up my seat at the table between my grandparents. When the kettle whistled I made each of us a cup of tea and although we did not drink we circled the cups with our hands and warmed our fingers as we waited for Lottie, Julius, and Beth to come home from work, as we waited for their sorrow to overflow, for their mourning to begin.

We saw them from the window as they walked up Avenue Z.

They moved through the early evening darkness with energy and determination; Lottie and Julius in their pale heavy coats flanked Beth, who wore her fur-collared cape, her soft fur hat. They each leaned slightly toward her in an attitude of protection, as they had leaned toward her as she walked between them down the aisle of the synagogue on her wedding day. They did not know that they now escorted her to her widowhood. Lottie carried a white paper bag. Fresh bread from the bakery at Sheepshead Bay. Julius held a heavy briefcase, his ledgers, carried home each night for review at the dining room table when dinner was done and the dishes cleared. But Beth's hands swung freely at her side and her face was radiant in the soft darkness. She was telling a story that reached its end as they passed the Calderazzo house. Julius smiled. Lottie took Beth's gloved hand. I willed them to halt, to stand frozen in their rare and brief gaiety, to postpone the moment when all smiles would cease and the avalanche of grief would overwhelm them. But steadily they advanced toward the house, Julius pausing for a moment to shift the weight of his briefcase from one hand to the other, Lottie plunging her hand into the bag of bread and plucking out the top small rounded slice, which she passed to Beth.

They mounted the brick steps, Beth munching like a small girl, chewing and amending her story, Lottie and Julius laughing again.

"Ah, Sharon must be home," Julius said. He had seen the light from the street.

I covered the telegram with my hand as the knob turned and the door opened. They rushed in, flushed with the cold, pleased at the welcoming warmth of the house, pleased because they had talked and laughed and because the news that day had been extraordinarily good. Julius carried all the afternoon papers with their banner headlines: FOG OVER ARDENNES LIFTS! ALLIED BOMBERS STRIKE RAILWAY YARDS AT KOBLENZ, GEROLSTEIN, AND BINGEN!

But the pleasure faded from their faces when they saw us, seated in our patient gloom around the dining room table.

"Sharon?" Lottie uttered my name as a hesitant question, her voice so soft that it was barely audible.

I removed my hand from the telegram.

"No!" she screamed and her heavy black purse and the white bag of bread dropped to the floor. Slices of fresh rye bread skittered across the red linoleum floor. "Not Aaron! Not Aaron!" Her first fear was for her son, as my first fear had been for my father. She swayed from side to side and Julius stood beside her, still clutching his worn brown leather briefcase, as though it gave him ballast, prevented him from sinking deep into the pain that grayed his face and blurred his eyes with the mist of misery peculiar to men who have been taught they must not ever weep.

"No, not Aaron," I said miserably.

I did not look at my cousin. I dared not confront the pain that darkened her eyes, blanched her skin.

Beth took her gloves off. Crumbs of bread lingered on her lips and she licked at them impatiently as though they hampered her understanding. Very slowly, she removed her hat and set it down before the telegram, which she lifted gingerly, as though its very touch was poisonous. She opened it, read it, folded it, and placed it on the table.

"Oh, Beth, I'm so sorry." My voice broke.

"He's dead," she said. "My Alfred. He's dead. Alfred is dead." She spoke in a monotone, each syllable clipped and muted, as though the words were incomprehensible.

Lottie moved toward her, her arms outstretched, but Beth stepped back, shook her head, and again reached for the telegram.

"He's dead," she repeated. "Killed in action. Dead."

The telegram fluttered from her hand onto the table and sobs racked her body. Still wearing her fur-collared cape, she hugged herself and tears flowed down her cheeks in a steady, unceasing stream.

It was Edna, coming in just then, grim-faced and breathless, who removed Beth's cape and led her into her bedroom. Lottie sank into a chair and Julius stood behind her, his hands on her shoulders. They could not comfort their daughter but they could comfort each other.

My grandfather stooped and gathered up the slices of bread, brushing each piece carefully with his fingers and handing them to my grandmother, who replaced them in the bag, one by one, although of course in the end we placed the entire loaf into the garbage. And I lifted the telegram signed by the adjutant general and read it, memorizing the heartless sequence of words, allowing the strange cadence to echo rhythmically in my mind — an atonal poem I would never forget and never recite.

> The Secretary of War
> Desires me
> To express his deep regret
> That your husband, Lieutenant Alfred Levine,
> Was killed
> In action
> In France
> Seventeen December, Nineteen Forty-Four

December 17. Only one day after Beth and I had stood on Union Square, our eyes riveted to the headlines. Why then had it taken almost a week for the news to reach us? My grief turned into fury. It was not right that family was not notified immediately, that the government should clutch its secret lists of the dead and the maimed while the families of the fallen imagined them alive and wrote them loving letters. It was cruel that Beth should have continued to knit the long khaki scarf that was to have wrapped Alfred's neck in its warmth while his body was already lifeless and cold. *Unfair. Unfair. Unfair.* I slammed my hands against the table again and again until my grandfather clenched my wrists between his fingers and pulled me to him. He held me close as I wept out my sorrow and my rage, my hot tears moistening his white shirt front.

Edna came out of Beth's room and nodded to Lottie and Julius. Hand in hand, their faces set in masks of misery, they walked down the hall and knocked tentatively at the door, like concerned visitors to a sickroom who are uncertain how the invalid will receive their attentions.

"Oh, Mama. Oh, Papa." Beth's voice, childlike, high-pitched and grief-rimmed, broke my heart.

I stood at the doorway and saw that her head was buried in

Lottie's bosom, that Julius held her hand, lifted it to his lips. The room was dark except for the ribbon of light cast by the bedside lamp. Its gentle glow illuminated the picture of Alfred that was on Beth's night table. The slender young man in dress uniform, soft-eyed and smiling, looked at his bride through the polished glass.

Edna made her parents fresh cups of tea. She called Leon and told him to pick up cold cuts and to drive over with Bernie and Heidi. She called Nachum Adler and asked him to go to Wood-stock so that Dina would not be alone when she received the news. She called Dolly and, too harshly, I thought, told her about the telegram.

"We want Samuel here," she said.

For the first time I felt sorry for Dolly, who must surely have felt the cold breath of her husband's family's dislike. They did not want her. They wanted Samuel.

Edna called Emanuel Weiner and read the telegram to him, slowly enunciating each word as she often did when she read cor-respondence aloud to him.

"If he died on December seventeenth," she said, "why should it have taken so long to notify Beth?"

She translated her distress into annoyance at government in-competence. That was something she could cope with.

"Mr. Weiner will find out," she told me. "He'll find out why it took so long."

I shivered. I decided, with mysterious prescience, that I did not want to know.

I called Peter.

"There was a telegram when I came home from school," I said.

"Oh, Sharon." I imagined him tense with concern, his hand gripping the receiver, worrying about me, for me. "Not — " The question he could not bear to ask froze on his lips.

"No, no. It wasn't my father. It was Alfred. He was killed in action. Last week."

"Last week." He too was upset about the lapse of time be-tween Alfred's death and our knowledge of it. We had thought him alive, spoken cheerfully of him as a man who would return from the war, who would kiss his wife, coddle his newborn child, fill out applications to law school. But even as we spoke he was lost in the sleep of death. He had been lowered into his grave by strangers who could not know that once he had danced across twilight desert sands with the soft-voiced blond girl who became his bride, that always he had been the good son, the honor student, that his parents, who had already buried one son, would now sit on the low benches of mourning for another.

"Sharon, I'm sorry," Peter said. "I'll call you tomorrow."

"Yes. Tomorrow." I wondered how we would get through the evening and then the night — whether Beth would sleep at all, whether she would tell her parents of her pregnancy and thus relieve me of my solitary stewardship, my fearful responsibility.

But, of course, we managed through the evening. The house filled with people as Beth lay in her dimly lit room, emerging only to speak to Alfred's parents, who called from Chicago.

"Yes," she said, her voice as gentle with them as Lottie's voice had been with her, "I'm glad about that too — glad that we married. Yes — we had happy days, Alfred and I. Oh — I am — I am grateful." Tears filled her eyes, coursed down her cheeks; she trembled but she continued to speak, calming the thin and fragile man and woman, her husband's parents, grandparents to the child she carried. She rocked back and forth upon her heels as though to soothe the fragile life within her womb, Alfred's legacy to her.

Lottie and Julius, too, spoke to the man and woman whose son had married their daughter, who would sit in mourning for him for seven days in Chicago as Beth would sit in mourning for him in Brooklyn. The rabbi, a gaunt man with a narrow black beard and sorrowing eyes, had already visited and explained the ritual of grief when death occurred far away at a time of war. The seven-day mourning period began when notification of death was received. He told Beth this as she lay on her girlhood bed, exhausted after her conversation with Alfred's parents.

"Of course, if you are not strong enough," he began hesitantly, because her pallor and lassitude frightened him.

"But I want to sit *shiva*," she insisted. "Of course I want to."

She spoke with an almost breathless eagerness. The act of *shiva* would validate her loss, place a parameter about her grief.

We ate the cold cuts Leon had dutifully bought, boiled kettle after kettle of tea that grew cold in our cups, answered the phone that rang continuously. It was astonishing to me that the news should have spread so quickly to relatives, neighbors, and friends. I did not know then that news of death and disaster must be quickly blurted from one person to another so that the pain may be mitigated and diluted. In disbelief, we confide to others. *He is dead. He who was is no longer.* The words, spoken so wonderingly, release us from the limbo of denial.

As a physician with years of practice, I have seen many patients die, and yet with each death I am seized anew with despairing disbelief. How can it be that the pulse I felt only moments before no longer throbs, that the heartbeat that resonated through my stethoscope, however weakly, has ceased?

"Gone," I say to the attending nurse, so that she may nod, agree, and restore me to credulity and thus to reality. Often my signature on a death certificate wavers, as though even at that final moment I am resistant to the reality of death.

Heidi and I did the dishes. Bernie repaired the blackout curtains. We, who ordinarily resisted household tasks, searched out chores, rushed to answer the doorbell, the telephone. Edna and Lottie talked softly with my grandmother. Beth was strong, resilient, and so beautiful. She was still only a girl. Surely she would remarry. It shocked me that they could speak of remarriage when Beth was so newly widowed. I did not recognize the pragmatic optimism of their words, nor did I understand that they looked to the future to sustain them against the crushing weight of the sorrowful present.

"It's lucky she didn't become pregnant," Edna said in her harsh, practical tone, and Heidi shot me a sharp glance. Heidi had her suspicions but she did not know the truth. I looked away. I would speak to Beth in the morning, urge her to confide in her parents.

"It was such a beautiful wedding," Lottie said dreamily. "She looked like an angel. That dress. I made the dry cleaner put it away in a sealed bag. Maybe one day Heidi will wear it. Or Sharon."

"Never," I muttered and sunk my hands deep into the scalding soapy water.

Beth's beautiful wedding dress was death-tainted. It had been fashioned for a girl whose fiancé had died, then worn by a bride widowed only three months after her wedding day.

"That dress — that wedding dress — we should give away," my grandmother said quietly and I marveled at her wisdom.

In the living room the men talked. My grandfather and Julius planned the *shiva* minyan, the quorum of ten men who would pray at our house morning and evening while Beth observed the week of mourning. And although music is prohibited in a house of mourning no one objected when Leon sat down at the piano. He played a medley of Yiddish songs, a lullaby that sang soothingly of almonds and raisins, a mournful prayer to a vigilant God who caused the winds of heaven to gently rock a child's cradle and ruffle the hair of strolling lovers. The tender musical phrases caused us to sit very quietly and briefly lightened the terrible heaviness of our hearts. Heidi and I gripped each other's hands and listened to the musical elegy for the soldier father so newly dead, to the lullaby for the child as yet unborn.

I slept in Beth's room that night, creating a nest for myself with the blankets and pillows I carried in from my own bed. She slept fitfully while I lay wakeful, fearful of each change in her breathing, of each small sound. Twice she wakened. Each time she sat up in bed, took Alfred's picture from her night table, and pressed her face against it. When she replaced it, the glass was aglitter with her tears.

The week of Beth's sorrow passed slowly, long days that began early in the morning with the arrival of the prayer quorum and the singsong murmuring of the morning service. I stood in the arched entry to the living room and watched the ten dark-suited men — their snow white prayer shawls hooding their heads and draping their shoulders, their phylacteries wound around their arms and strapped to their foreheads — sway as they turned the pages of their prayer books. I listened as they recited the Kaddish, the hymn of praise to God who made peace in the firmament and who would surely send peace to them and to all of Israel. Their prayer seemed maniacal to me. Our world was at war, and we exalted a God who allowed the fires of Auschwitz to burn, who did not care that Alfred had died and Beth was bereft.

I stared at the worshippers, scorning their words, envying their faith, and because I could not pray, I wrote two letters each day to my father — letters that I did not mail. The closely written pages chronicled my bewilderment.

On the last night of the week of mourning, Emanuel Weiner and his wife came. Lottie brought Mrs. Weiner a cup of tea and Dina urged her into a more comfortable chair. My aunts' obsequiousness irritated me. It was years before I understood that the Weiners represented power and influence to a vulnerable immigrant family. And we, in turn, provided Emanuel Weiner with a fiefdom for his paternalism and his natural kindness.

He disappeared into the kitchen with Edna, and I knew that he had come to tell us how Alfred had died. Edna was pale when she joined us, and Leon walked down the hall with her, allowed her to lean against him, smoothed her hair. My competent aunt was thus gently soothed by her *luftmentsch* husband, who, I recognized with sudden clarity, was a strongly intuitive man, a man who knew when to play music and when to place his hands gently upon his wife's head.

"It is terrible but you must tell her. It is better that Beth know," he said softly. "Otherwise what she imagines may be even worse."

"But what could be worse?" Edna asked bleakly.

Still, she followed Leon's advice. When the last of our visitors had left, when only our family sat in the living room surrounding Beth, Edna told us, in halting tones, that Alfred had been part of a contingent of seventy-two soldiers who were captured by a German SS unit somewhere south of the Ardennes town of Malmédy. Malmédy. I thought the name of the town very pretty, almost musical, and I repeated it to myself. Malmédy.

The American soldiers had been marched into an open field and forced to line up. The Germans had trained their machine guns on them and systematically killed the defenseless prisoners. A dozen men, including Alfred, escaped the massacre and fled into the village, where they sought refuge in a café. The Germans pursued them, placed petrol cans around the café, and ignited them. As the men fled the fire, their clothing ablaze, screaming with pain, they were shot by the SS men who then moved on, continuing their march southward, tightening their grip on the Bulge. The frightened villagers dared not approach the bodies, and the corpses lay sprawled upon the ground for days, shrouded by the mountain mist, the stink of their putrefaction carried by the wind to hamlets both north and south. It was not until Allied troops reached Malmédy that the bodies were discovered and the grim story of the American soldiers' deaths was revealed. And then, of course, there were the problems of identification, the transmission of the news of the death to the company, then the battalion, then the regiment, and finally to the division — the adjutant general in charge of personnel. It was he who notified the Secretary of War and only then had the telegram been sent to Beth.

Beth sat very still on the low stool of mourning, one hand covering her mouth, the other resting on her birthmark. The chalky whiteness of her face was accentuated by the black sweater she wore that entire week. She closed her eyes and I thought that she must be imagining Alfred darting out of the café, his arms flailing in wings of flame, his thin, gentle face black with soot. Did she imagine that he called her name as he ran, that her face danced before his eyes, that he remembered then how she had smiled at him on their wedding day? I assigned my own dark images to her and so I was startled when she bolted from her seat and ran into the bathroom. We did not look at each other as we listened to the sound of the retching, her moans.

"I shouldn't have told her," Edna said.

"She had to know." Nachum Adler spoke softly, reassuringly. He was then, and remained all the days of his life, a fierce believer in truth. He was a man who had knelt beside the bodies of his wife and his small daughter. He understood the dangers of dissimulation, the recuperative powers of the mourner.

Lottie tapped on the bathroom door.

"Beth," she called gently. "Bethie."

There was no answer. Lottie opened the door and we heard Beth's muffled sobs. She closed the door behind her and we heard the rush of water as she filled the bathtub. I took a large white bath towel from the linen closet and a clean flannel nightgown from Beth's drawer. I carried them into the bathroom where Lottie knelt beside the tub in which Beth sat, her head tilted back, her eyes closed. Lottie soaped her body, washed her hair, gently passed a washcloth across her shoulders and neck as though she were a small girl rather than a young woman whose breasts rested like nacreous bulbs upon the sudsy water and whose abdomen was slightly swelled by the protuberance of beginning life.

"Beth, my Beth, it will be all right. It will be all right," Lottie crooned softly and I left the steam-filled bathroom and lay down on my bed.

It would not be all right. It would never be all right again. Alfred was dead and the nightmare of his death would haunt us always. And if he had died horribly, mercilessly, so might others die in horror, without mercy. I looked at my father's picture but I dared not touch it. I feared to upset a mysterious balance. I feared that my very love might endanger him, make him more vulnerable — and I understood that there was madness in fear.

Again that night I carried my blankets and pillows into Beth's room and slept at the foot of her bed. I awakened at dawn to the sound of her closet door opening and I saw Beth reach up to the top shelf and take down a large white box. She removed the gold negligee, unworn since her return from her honeymoon. I did not stir as she pulled the flannel nightgown over her head and then slipped on the shimmering garment. The gossamer sun-colored fabric clung to her body, swirled about her legs. She shrugged into the peignoir, adjusted the collar, fluttered her arms to loosen the wide winged sleeves. She brushed her hair until it framed her face in a golden cloud.

She studied herself in the long mirror, arranged the folds of gown and robe, and smiled at herself with the secret satisfaction of a woman who recognizes her own beauty. And then she glided across the room, plucked Alfred's picture from the night table, and, humming softly to herself, held it close against her body as she danced slowly around the room, her golden wings fluttering, her eyes closed.

Motionless, I watched through narrowed eyes as the pace of her solitary dance increased, as she lifted the framed photograph to her lips, as tears flowed down her cheeks, although she did not break the rhythm of her movement. As last, she sat down at the edge of her bed, replaced the picture, and looked at it for a long moment before sinking back against the pillows.

Her breath came in shallow gasps but so fearful was I of invading the privacy of her grief that I did not move until I heard her moan softly.

"Beth." I waited for her to invite me into her suffering.

She did not answer but moaned again. I leapt up and leaned over her. Pain twisted her features, contorted her body. Her soft lips curled and whistled strenuously with each breath. Her hands clutched her abdomen, and as she writhed, great flowers of blood petaled the golden folds of her gown, trickled about her pale ankles, formed viscous scarlet puddles on the sheets. She twisted from side to side as though warring with the unformed life that struggled to break free, to crash through the restraining wall of placental blood.

"No. Oh no." Beth struggled to breathe; pain vied with pain, effort with agony.

"Lottie! Julius!"

My throat ached with the effort of the scream and they rushed into the room. Lottie called Dr. Kaplan, who lived a few doors away, and he was there within minutes, a winter coat flung over his striped pajamas, his worn black bag in his hand.

I was sent out of the room. The door closed behind me and I stood in the hallway with Dina and my grandparents, trembling and crying.

"I should have known. I should have done something. But it all happened so quickly," I said over and over.

I had been charged with responsibility, with vigilance. Beth and Dr. Greenberg had relied on me. But I had failed my cousin and now she might die. The blood. There had been so much blood.

I know now that spontaneous abortions rocket through the body in minutes, that the blood cascades forth in a swift onslaught, but then the suddenness of it all frightened and overwhelmed me.

"You did everything you could," Dina assured me. "It was good that you went to sleep in her room. If you hadn't been there . . ." She did not finish the sentence.

My grandmother led me into the kitchen, made me a cup of tea.

"She will be all right, Shaindel."

"How do you know?"

"I know."

She spoke in Yiddish. I replied in English. But our sorrow had a common language, our sadness spanned generations. She placed her hand on my forehead and in the dryness of her touch I felt the ancient sorrow of women, the shared wisdom that had become mine too soon.

Lottie came into the kitchen, her face drained, her eyes red-rimmed.

"She's resting. Dr. Kaplan gave her a shot for the asthma."

"But the baby?"

Lottie stared sharply at me.

"You knew?"

I nodded. She leaned against the refrigerator and covered her face with her hands. My grandmother led her to a chair, moistened a dish towel, and washed her eldest daughter's face. Her own dark eyes, so burning and bright in the withered folds of her life-worn skin, were moist, although she did not weep. Her long white hair, twisted into a single silken braid, floated down the plaid flannel fabric of her faded pink chenille bathrobe.

"It will be all right, Mama?" The question broke from Lottie's lips. Daughters always ask their mothers if it will be all right. And mothers always reassure them.

I listened for my grandmother's answer so that I would know what to say to my own daughter in my turn.

"It will be all right," she murmured.

Lottie stood. She did not look at me; she filled a basin with water and carried it into Beth's room. Dr. Kaplan and Julius stood in the hallway, speaking softly, urgently.

Dr. Kaplan hitched up his pajamas, buttoned his coat. I saw that he wore sneakers without laces and this seemed wildly funny to me. I struggled not to laugh and instead began to cry.

"She'll sleep now," the doctor said reassuringly. "She's young. She's strong. She'll be fine."

"Fine. She'll be fine." Julius echoed him, as though the repetition of the words reinforced their truth. "It's all right, Sharon."

He placed his hand on my shoulder and at his touch my tears flowed anew. I turned my face to the wall and wept because Alfred was dead and because he had died a cruel and inhuman death, because Beth had lost her baby, because I had failed her and deceived my family. I wept because in my mind's eye I saw my father running through the ensnaring mists and because I had no mother who would bathe me and cover my hands with her own and assure me that everything would be all right.

Awkwardly, tenderly, my uncle stroked my hair until Dina at last led me off to bed.

17

My aunts quarreled. Their dissonance hissed through the house the next morning like the compressed steam that forced its way through the radiators. They spoke softly because they feared to waken Beth and because they did not want me to hear their bitter exchanges. But I, the experienced eavesdropper, stood with my ear to the door of my room and listened. I heard Lottie's subdued anger and my heart twisted with remorse.

"Sharon should have told me that Beth was pregnant. How could she have lied — how could she have deceived me?"

"She didn't lie. Beth probably made her promise not to tell you." Edna spoke calmly, in the reasonable tone with which she soothed disgruntled customers, reluctant suppliers, resistant congressmen. Logic and organization made her indispensable to Emanuel Weiner and empowered her within the family.

"Sharon had no right to make such a promise." Lottie was firm, her anger congealed.

"But Sharon's had so much to cope with. So many traumas. Miriam's death. Not knowing from day to day whether Richard is alive or dead, whether he'll survive the war. She's been so alone. Beth was like an older sister to her. She needed Beth's love, her approval." Dina pleaded my case blending affection and the language of her profession.

"And I didn't do everything for her after Miriam died? I didn't treat her like my own daughter? And how did she pay me back — she sneaks around. She found the doctor. Did you know that? Beth told me. Sharon's only sixteen but she knew how to find a gynecologist," Lottie said accusingly.

"This is crazy, Lottie." Edna's tolerance was spent. "This is not Sharon's fault. She did what she could to help Beth. I know you're upset but you're being ridiculous."

"I think Edna is right," Dina said softly.

They did not say that it had been Beth's responsibility to confide in her mother. They would not add to Lottie's burden of guilt. *How could I not have noticed?* she had muttered over and over to herself as she paced the hallway throughout the long night.

"You know everything, Edna. Mrs. Know-it-all. Mrs. I'll Take Care of Everything. But it's not your daughter who lost a husband and lost a baby. It's my Beth who's crying, who's bleeding. Just like it's always been my children who suffered. Their whole childhoods they worried about Mama and Papa. They were the ones who were home when Papa had the heart attack, when Mama had the pneumonia that winter. That's when Beth's asthma began — did you know that? It began when she saw that Mama had trouble breathing. She used to tiptoe downstairs and make sure that she was all right and then she began having asthma attacks." Lottie spat the words out in verbal bullets of blame that ricocheted through the house.

"What are you saying — you're saying that your kids suffered because Papa and Mama lived in this house? But you always said you wouldn't have it any other way. You made Julius buy a two-family house." Again Edna raised the voice of reason, but she spoke too quickly and grief rimmed her words.

"All right. Yes. We wanted them to live here. But my children suffered. Especially Beth. And now this business with Sharon . . ." Lottie's voice trailed off.

"You're not being fair, Lottie. Sharon helped Beth," Dina answered quietly.

"Helped? Helped? You see how my Beth was helped."

They did not answer. Words were dangerous. They slammed the doors of the cabinets, banged pots, turned the faucets on full blast. I went back to bed and fell into a deep sleep. I had slept fitfully throughout the week of mourning, and the compounded fatigue overtook me. Later, much later, I realized that I slept because I could not bear to be awake.

It was almost noon when I opened my door and peered into Beth's room. She was not there. Her bed was neatly made and Alfred's picture had been moved to the bureau. Dina and my grandmother sat on the living room sofa, playfully passing Anna back and forth. The baby smiled, loving the movement, sucking at the red fringes of Dina's paisley shawl, clawing at my grandmother's glasses with her tiny hands.

"You had a good sleep," Dina said brightly.

"I guess. Where is everyone?" I asked.

"Edna was here earlier but she went to work. And Julius and Lottie took Beth to the city. To this Dr. Greenberg. They spoke to him and he said that it was important that he examine her. Although she was feeling much better this morning. Still, you have to be careful. With these things."

"Is Lottie mad at me?" I asked.

Dina shrugged. "She's very upset. When people are upset it's hard for them to figure out how they're feeling. I think she's disappointed."

"And you? Are you disappointed, Dina?" I asked sadly.

"Me? No. I'm proud of you, Sharon. You did what you could for your cousin. Beth shouldn't have asked you to keep such a secret. It was too much."

"I wanted to help her."

"Of course you did."

My grandmother lifted Anna to her shoulder, carried her into the kitchen. As she passed my chair, she placed her hand on my head.

"Breakfast," she said. "You'll have breakfast, Shaindel. Milk. Cereal. A piece of toast." I understood that she was telling me that there was sorrow and there was death but daily routines prevailed. Life could not be avoided.

"I'll be in to eat in a minute, Buba," I said.

"Sharon, Samuel and Dolly are planning to go up to Grossinger's for New Year's. They've had the reservations for a long time. And you know how Dolly is," Dina said.

"I don't want to go to Grossinger's."

"I know that. What I thought was — you could spend the day with Dolly and they'd drive you to Woodstock in the morning. You'd be there for the Bassens' New Year's party. I have to see a lawyer today and then Nachum will drive me and Anna home."

"Why can't I drive to Woodstock with you?" I asked petulantly.

"It would be better if you stayed at Samuel and Dolly's today. If you went over there after you eat," Dina said gently. "I don't know exactly when I'll be ready to leave and you don't want to hang around here all day. Dolly wants to take you shopping. She says she never gets the chance to spend any time with you."

"You mean Lottie doesn't want me here," I said. "That's what you're saying, isn't it?"

"It's better for this house to be quiet today. Better for Beth and better for Lottie. They need time, Sharon. Lottie has to sort out what happened."

"Beth made me promise not to tell Lottie and Julius," I said and my eyes filled with tears. It was unfair to be blamed for something that was not my fault.

"I know that, Sharon. And Lottie will realize it when she thinks things through."

"But what if she doesn't want me to live here anymore?" My voice broke. I had not realized until that moment how vulnerable I was, how dependent I was on Lottie's kindness, her hospitality.

"She'll want you to live here." There was no hesitation in

Dina's reply. "We all love you, Sharon. We all want you. Edna and Leon. Me. Dolly and Samuel."

"But I want my father," I whispered. "And my mother." I covered my face with my hands, concealing my grief, concealing my tears, but Dina put her arms around my quivering shoulders and held me close.

I made my way across Brooklyn to Linden Boulevard, where Dolly and Samuel lived. The journey entailed a ride on the Coney Island Avenue trolley and a series of transfers to various buses. I carried the plaid valise that had belonged to my mother. It smelled of her dusting powder, and when I opened it I pressed my face against the faded blue lining and inhaled the lilac scent. Because the clasp was broken my grandfather tied the valise shut with a length of rope and I felt like a refugee as I struggled to carry it down the steps of the trolley and onto the bus. Dina and Nachum had offered to drive me but I had insisted on going alone. It had seemed important that I establish my independence, my ability to take care of myself, to maneuver my way from place to place.

I was exhausted when I reached Samuel and Dolly's apartment. Dolly, her hair dyed a new shade of strawberry blond and sculpted into the high pompadour that Deanna Durbin had made popular, greeted me with an odd shyness, her kiss tentative. It occurred to me that we had never before spent time alone together.

"Your hair looks nice," I offered.

"Do you like it? Really?" She blushed with pleasure. She was one of those women who concentrate fiercely on clothing and accessories, hair and makeup, fearful that without them they are undefined and unrecognized.

We ate lunch in the dinette, which, like the rest of the apartment, resembled a room in an impeccably furnished dollhouse. The walls were painted pale blue, and the chairs were covered with taffeta tufting of a matching color. A blue cloth blooming with rosebuds covered the table, and the china closet was filled with the blue Wedgwood that Dolly collected. Dolly had prepared what she called a "light lunch." Like many childless women, she shopped prudently and measured out her food with great precision. I was careful to eat every bit of the single scoop of curried tuna fish salad, the two carrot wands, and the three cherry tomatoes artfully arranged on the blue-rimmed white plate.

"I think food should look pretty. But, of course, your family doesn't take that kind of trouble," she said.

I reflected on Lottie's stews and pot roast, Dina's casual meals of pasta and salad, Edna's swiftly prepared broiled meats. It seemed disloyal to allow Dolly to dismiss them with such disdain.

"Well, they're all pretty busy," I said. "Especially now."

"Oh, I know. It's terrible about Beth. But maybe it's for the best. That she lost the baby, I mean."

"How could it be for the best?" I stared at Dolly and she blushed, the color mounting beneath the layer of makeup that coated her Kewpie-doll face.

"The doctors do say that a miscarriage is nature's way — you know, of correcting a mistake. Of maybe preventing the birth of a child with a handicap. At least that's what I heard a doctor say — once."

"Did he say that to you, Aunt Dolly?" I asked daringly. I was spurred to cruelty.

"No. Not to me." She dropped her eyes, busied herself scraping crumbs from the cloth.

"Then to whom?" I persisted. I stared across the room at the family picture taken at Dolly and Samuel's wedding and placed in an ornate silver frame. My parents stood side by side, my mother's hand tucked beneath my father's arm. Everyone else in the picture turned to the bride and groom — Samuel in a tuxedo and Dolly in a beaded white dress — but my father looked down at my mother and she in turn smiled up at him.

Dolly followed my gaze.

"We had a nice wedding," she said. "Everyone said it was the nicest wedding in the family. Your mother and Edna were mad at me because I wouldn't let you and Heidi come. Beth was there, and Aaron. But you girls were too young. We couldn't have small children at the wedding."

"Because you don't like children?" I asked slyly.

"Why do you say that?" Her face sagged and I read the hurt in her eyes. "I know. You say it because you hear Edna say it. And probably Lottie and Dina. And maybe your mother, she should rest in peace, said it. But it's not true. I like children. It was because we couldn't afford it that we didn't invite you. It was a catered affair and we paid for it ourselves. Me and Samuel. My father gave us maybe a few hundred dollars. If we could have afforded it, we would have invited you."

"My mother never said anything about your not liking children," I said. "She just felt bad that you didn't have any."

"With Beth — last night — did she suffer a lot?" Dolly asked the question hesitantly, as though she feared I might take offense at it.

"It was all so quick," I replied. "I — I saw the blood, saw that she was in pain and I called Lottie and Julius. They got Dr. Kaplan to come over. He gave her a shot of something. And then it was over."

"She was lucky. A miscarriage is sometimes dangerous."

"But you can't die from a miscarriage." I said that to reassure myself because I had feared that Beth might die, and that fear had not yet left me.

"My mother" — Dolly spoke very slowly — "she had a miscarriage. She bled to death."

"I didn't know that," I said miserably.

"Why should you know such a thing? It was after my brother, Charlie, was born. She became pregnant and that baby she lost. And then again, she lost a baby. I was maybe ten years old and I stood outside her bedroom door crying. The doctor said to her, 'You can't keep on getting pregnant. You have to be careful. These miscarriages, they're nature's way of telling you that you're not strong enough to carry a healthy baby.' He wanted her to promise that she wouldn't try anymore but she began to cry. She said she wanted to have three children. She had to have three children." Dolly rested her elbows on the table, cupped her chin on her clasped hands. She smiled thinly as though recalling her mother's voice, remembering her insistence.

"But why? Why did she want three children?" I asked.

"Because she had had two sisters and a brother. She left them behind in Russia when she came to America. She told me how they pulled at her skirts when she got into the wagon that took her to the border. They sent her letters in America and signed them with all their names. Three names. Devora. Chaim. Fruma. And then there were no more letters until someone came from her town and told her they had been killed in a pogrom. My father said my mother couldn't stop crying. Three dead. Three lives gone. She dreamed about them and then she said that she would bring them back to life. She would have three children and name them for her sisters and brother. And so I was born. Dolly, named for Devora. And then my brother — Charlie for Chaim. And she wanted a name for Fruma, too. Fruma, she said, she had loved the best. When my mother left for America, this little girl, this Fruma, took her red ribbons off her braids and gave them to her. 'So you'll look pretty in America,' she said. My mother kept those ribbons and now I have them. So my mother didn't care what the doctor said. She wanted another baby — named for Fruma. So again she became pregnant and when the doctor came that last time, it was too late. Her bed was like a river of blood and she was dead. I was so young then, such a stupid girl. What did I know about how a woman's body worked? I thought she was dead because she'd drowned in that blood. Drowned." Dolly laughed bitterly but tears glinted in her eyes.

"Is that why you didn't have any children?" I asked. "Because you're afraid that you might die too?" My own temerity astounded me but I yearned to understand her secret terror. I wanted the knowledge of what had gone before to give me an insight into what was yet to come. I could not learn from my own parents; I had to scavenge for clues, boldly demand revelations.

"Partly. Yes. I was afraid. But I didn't deceive Samuel. I saw how much he loved his sisters' children. You. Your cousins. So I told him that I was frightened but if he wanted children I would fight that fear. But he surprised me. Yes, he said. He loved children. But what he really wanted was an orderly home. A quiet and beautiful home. Clean. A home like this." She lifted her hand in a wide sweep that embraced the apartment she had furnished with such care. "Nice things. He wanted nice things," Dolly continued. "He wanted me to take care of myself. To always look nice. To take good care of our things. He hates dirt, my Samuel. And stains. And smells. And children make dirt. They make stains. They make smells." She shrugged, as though her own words embarrassed her.

I remembered then that Samuel held Anna only when her diaper was newly changed, when she was fresh from her bath. When he left the table after our Sunday night dinners, he averted his eyes from the clots of mustard and the puddles of soda that littered the cloth. Often he had stomachaches because he was fastidious about using other people's bathrooms. Even my mother had joked about that with Dina and Edna, although Lottie had angrily reproved them.

"What do you know? You were born here. You didn't come over in the stinking steerage of a ship. You didn't have to share the toilet in a tenement with two other families. Sometimes I think I'll never get that stink out of my nose. Samuel and I used to stand outside the door and keep guard for each other when we went to that toilet."

She had laughed but Samuel never laughed. Nor did he ever speak of the distant days of his immigrant boyhood. He claimed not to think of them.

He was safe, he and Dolly, behind the door of their apartment, attentive to each other, shielded from the dangers of dirt and death. Their fears complemented each other.

It surprised me then that my aunts did not know that the decision not to have children rested with Samuel, the well-groomed brother whom they adored but whom they treated with the affectionate contempt strong women reserve for weaker men. I did not know that such truths are more easily revealed to the very young, to those who struggle for understanding and thus withhold judgment. And, I decided as I dried the dishes, I would not divulge Dolly's confidence. I aligned myself with my uncle's wife who, like myself, was an outsider, skating upon the periphery of my aunts' insular closeness. I replaced the milk white china bowl in which a red wax apple, a yellow wax banana, and a shimmering bunch of real purple grapes were arranged on the dining room table. The set was ready for the next performance.

Dolly and I went shopping that afternoon. At Abraham and

Straus Dolly bought me a long-sleeved white wool dress with a wide red leather belt that hugged my waist. At Martin's she used the last of her ration coupons to buy me a pair of red ballet slippers.

Samuel suggested that we go to the movies that night. We needed little persuasion. Movies were the national narcotic during the years of the war. We took refuge from our secret fears, from churning anxiety, in the calming darkness of the theaters, those gilded palaces of escape policed by matrons in white uniforms and ushers in gilt-buttoned jackets whose flashlights radiated beams of authority.

We arrived at the Brooklyn Paramount that night just as Movietone News began, and we watched Eleanor Roosevelt carry gift packages into a veterans' hospital. She paused to chat with a soldier in a wheelchair, to read a letter to a boy in a bathrobe whose eyes were covered with bandages. We listened to the strains of the Marseillaise as bodies were lowered into graves at a French military cemetery.

"Thus France salutes the victims of the brutal German massacre at Malmédy," the newscaster said in sonorous sorrow, and I covered my eyes with my hands. It was possible that I had just witnessed Alfred's burial.

Sadness swept over me and I fought it by sitting straighter in my seat as the news segued into a report on the flying-bomb attack over England on Christmas Eve. Some of the bombs contained letters from British prisoners of war which scattered like confetti on explosion. A girl in Finchley who spoke with a lisp smiled into the camera, toyed with her lank pale braid, and reported that she had found a letter from her own father on the sidewalk. "A miracle," she asserted. "A Christmas miracle." I wondered if her father had written that he loved her and was proud of her and that there was nothing to worry about because soon, very soon, the war would be over and he would be home. I had memorized my father's last letter and I heard his words as she spoke.

It has to be over soon, I thought and I applauded vigorously as the opening credits for *Hollywood Canteen* flashed across the screen.

18

It snowed as we drove north the next day. The large white flakes drifted across the windshield and jeweled the windows of the car with frosted stars. Samuel turned the heat up and I stretched out across the rear seat and imagined myself a small child, warmly swaddled and soothed by rhythmic movement. I felt oddly light. I had been released from the weight of Beth's secret, and the heavy sorrow of the previous day had receded.

Lottie had called me that morning. Her voice, drained of anger, was quietly sad. She was sorry not to have seen me before I left, she said. I told her that I was sorry too and before the silence between us could stretch to an uncomfortable tautness, I told her that I was sorry for everything.

"It wasn't your fault," she said. "Beth explained that it wasn't your fault." I heard the tears in her voice and I bit my lip. "It was no one's fault," she added.

"Will Beth be okay?" I asked anxiously.

"Here, you'll speak to her."

And so I had spoken to Beth, who sounded exhausted. Dr. Greenberg had assured her that she would be fine.

"He said that the miscarriage might have been caused by stress. A lot of servicemen's wives miscarry," she said and drifted into silence. She was no longer a serviceman's wife. She was a war widow. "Listen, Sharon. No one's mad at you."

"I hope not." I was fearful still. Lottie's forgiveness had followed too swiftly on her anger. "As long as you're okay, Beth."

"I'll be okay. I'll be fine. I think I might go back to Arizona for the spring semester."

I marveled that she could think of picking up her life again, of returning to where she had been when she had first seen Alfred and danced into his arms.

"Have a happy New Year, Sharon." Beth's voice faded.

"Oh Beth." My reply was strangulated. I wanted to wish her a year of healing, a year in which she would reclaim her youth, reclaim her life. But the words, of course, would not come. "It has to be a better year," I said instead and her acquiescence came in a small and trembling sigh.

And then Lottie spoke again.

"I bought a new lamp for you today. For the desk in your room. So you'll have more light when you study," she said and I knew that she was telling me that her home was still my home, that I must not think that I was not welcome there.

"So you spoke to Lottie and now everything is all right between you," Dolly said when I hung up. I nodded.

"Sharon, you should know — there is always a place for you in our home."

I turned and hugged her. It was the first time I had ever displayed any spontaneous affection for her. Like my aunts, I had always dismissed her as brash and superficial, but now, vulnerable myself, I understood her vulnerability and recognized her kindness.

Dolly had dozed off during the drive, but now she stirred into wakefulness as we neared Woodstock.

"What time is it?" she asked as she peered at herself in the mirror of her compact, tucked a stray lacquered tendril into place, and painted her mouth with a fresh layer of pinkness.

"Almost noon. We can get the news, I think," Samuel said and he turned on the radio and allowed the war to invade our car.

I leaned forward and listened to Eric Sevareid's wrap-up of 1944. The year, he insisted, was ending disastrously for Germany and Japan. In Europe all territory captured by Germany had been wrenched away. In the Pacific Japan's hostage empire was being eroded. Romania, Bulgaria, and Hungary were now part of the Allied constellation. And today, on this very last day of 1944, an exciting dispatch had just been placed before him. British bombers had leveled Gestapo headquarters in Oslo. "This time the Hun is definitely on the run," he said enthusiastically.

Samuel pounded happily on his horn. Dolly switched stations and found a big-band rendition of "Happy Days Are Here Again."

"You see," she said, twitching around to look at me. "The war will be over soon. A few months. A few weeks."

"Maybe a few days," Samuel bellowed cheerfully. "We got them on the run. They're geniuses, MacArthur, Eisenhower, Patton. FDR knew what he was doing. He knew how to win this war."

"And soon your father will be home, Sharon," Dolly chirped. "And I think I know just the right woman to introduce him to. Oh, I'm going to find you the most wonderful new mother."

I froze. I had not before imagined my father with another woman. I saw him still, in dream and fantasy, walking beside my mother, looking down at her with sweet affection, as he had in Dolly and Samuel's family wedding picture. I saw him placing his hand on her hair, his lips upon her cheek. His fingers traced their way across her neck, as long as my own. *My swan,* he called her in the love letter he wrote to her from Europe, the letter I had read to her again and again as she slipped into death.

"I don't want a new mother," I said fiercely. "I will never have a new mother. I had a mother."

"Sharon, Dolly didn't mean anything," Samuel remonstrated.

"Sharon, I'm sorry. I know how you feel. I spoke foolishly. Didn't I lose my mother too when I was a young girl?" She was repentant. She recognized her error and I nodded and forgave her, as Lottie had forgiven me. I was newly conscious on that last day of 1944 that time was precious and the harvesting of grudges and angers was wasteful and foolish.

Samuel and Dolly did not stay long at Dina's house. They did not even remove their coats. Samuel sat in his camel-hair overcoat, his tan fedora askew on his thick dark hair, with Anna on his lap. Dolly huddled into her fur coat and gazed at the clutter of Dina's life — books facedown on the coffee table, an unfinished report spread across the kitchen counter, Nachum's sketch pad on the couch, colorful pillows tossed carelessly about the room — as though she were a tourist in an alien atmosphere.

"So we'll go," Samuel said, surrendering Anna, his nose wrinkled. "She needs to be changed, Dina."

"Oh, does she?" Dina asked absently. She sniffed her daughter and laughed. "I suppose she does."

Dina sighed as she watched their car speed away.

"Poor Samuel," she said. "He really loves children. It's a pity that Dolly's so selfish."

I did not reply. I clutched my new knowledge to myself as though it were a secret treasure to be examined only in the privacy of my own mind and heart. A perquisite of solitude is the luxury of introspection. There was time, that year, to turn thoughts and feelings over and over in my mind, to polish insights and invent intricate fantasies. It pleased me that I knew things about Samuel and Dolly that my aunts had not even guessed. Secrets gave me strength, vested me with importance, and that gratified me because (as my therapist pointed out so many years later) I was haunted all that year by the feeling that I was not important enough to anyone. Except for my father, of course, and I schooled myself not to rely on him. The next three-starred telegram to arrive might be addressed to me.

"Are you going to the Bassens'?" I asked Dina because Peter had told me that his parents had invited friends to celebrate the New Year with them.

"A multigenerational Woodstock evening," Peter had said. "Adults upstairs, kids in the basement. We'll meet at midnight to sing 'Auld Lang Syne.'"

"No. I don't think so. Nachum doesn't feel like a New Year bash," Dina replied. "And I guess I don't either. Although we're both pretty glad to see 1944 disappear."

"Me too," I said, and we sat in silence for a moment and thought of the year gone by. Death had made its claims. My mother. Alfred. Nachum's wife, Manya. His daughter, Rachel. Their shadows drifted through our dreams, haunted our memories. But life had asserted itself during that year. Anna had been born. We had sung as we rode in a sleigh beneath the stars and laughed as we built a snowman; we had listened to the roar of the ocean against the esplanade and giggled as forbidden cigarette smoke drifted from our mouths. The years of war had taught us to seize our joys, to suck greedily at brief happiness.

Nachum Adler came in just then, set down the groceries he carried, and took Anna into his arms.

"I will change her," he said.

Even as Samuel shunned the stench of human odors, Nachum embraced them. A baby that defecated lived.

I went over to the Bassens' to help Peter and Karen with the decorations.

"No balloons," Karen said. "The rubber shortage is still on."

We made do with crepe paper streamers. I showed them how Beth had constructed the dove of peace out of oak tag and tissue paper.

Karen and I followed Beth's design and Peter suspended the doves from the beams of the basement ceiling so that they would sway gracefully above the guests. We draped the furniture with streamers and bagged the confetti and tinsel to be scattered at midnight.

I dressed carefully for the party. It pleased me that my skin had a tawny cast against the ivory whiteness of the soft wool dress. I twisted my thick dark hair into a loose French braid interwoven with red satin ribbon. I remembered the ribbons given to Dolly's mother so lovingly by her small sister Fruma. I imagined them tattered and faded, nestled at the bottom of one of Dolly's drawers, and indeed, decades later, when the task of closing Dolly's apartment after her death fell to me, that was where I found them, faded to a pink whiteness, almost moldering into dust.

I fastened the wide red leather belt and slipped on the red ballet slippers.

Dina studied me approvingly.

"A scarf," she said. "A red scarf." And deftly she knotted a scarlet swatch of chiffon around my neck. I put on my hooded red cape and kissed Dina and Nachum.

The Bassens' house was ablaze with light, and, shivering because my cape was little protection against the frigid night, I ran across the meadow and into its brightness and warmth.

"Sharon!" Sarah Bassen, in a black embroidered caftan, glided toward me, swept me into her embrace. "You look marvelous. Doesn't she look marvelous?" she demanded and at once I was surrounded by the faces of the summer. They beamed affectionate smiles at me, tweaked my braid, brushed their lips across my cheeks.

"I love your hair that way," Belle Langsam said and Edward nodded. He had been fitted with a prosthetic arm. I felt its metallic weight upon my shoulder and I thought him very brave to flex it with such casualness.

Marcie Klein, newly divorced and with her hair dyed a deeper shade of auburn, had a new man on her arm — a bearded journalist recently returned from the Pacific theater. She put her arm around me and invited me to her studio to see her new jewelry designs.

"How are you, Sharon?" Randy asked.

Franchesca stood beside him, her hand resting proprietorially on his shoulder. She wore a dark green silk sheath, and her black hair hugged her head, fringed her cheeks. As always, her face was a pale mask, expertly powdered; her eyebrows were etched with an ebony pencil, her lashes, heavy with mascara, brushed her high cheekbones like black spider legs.

"Hello, Sharon," she said.

I had not spoken to her since the night of Anna's birth, when I had called looking for Robert. The memory of that conversation made me blush but Franchesca looked at me with calm indifference.

Randy moved across the crowded room to speak to Teddy Bassen, and Franchesca leaned languidly against the wall.

"Randy and I are together again," she said. "But I thought you would know that."

I shook my head. I had not known, although I suspected that Dina might have been told — perhaps that was another reason for her absence.

"Hey, Sharon, where have you been?" Peter came forth to claim me, to drape my cape over his arm and lead me through the crowd of chattering adults down the stairs to the finished basement, where Karen had dimmed the lights, and their friends, who had come of age during the years of the war, danced beneath the swaying doves of peace.

I danced the slow dances with Peter, moving slowly to accommodate his limp, my chin on his shoulder, his arm firm about my waist. I did swift lindies with other boys and joined the line for the bunny hops and the conga, pulling a resistant Peter behind me. I helped Karen replenish the punch bowl, holding it steady while she poured a purloined bottle of champagne in the frothy mix of juices.

"My parents know I took it," she said, giggling giddily. "It's just another one of those things we don't talk about."

I nodded although I resolved that when my father came home we would talk about everything. I imagined the two of us walking down Commonwealth Avenue arm in arm, speaking softly, urgently. Surely, I thought, there would be a letter from him waiting for me when I returned to Brooklyn. A birthday letter; he could not have forgotten my sixteenth birthday, which had been marked only with small gifts because it had fallen on the third day of Beth's week of mourning. I took the champagne bottle from Karen and held it to my lips. It tickled my throat and filled me with a sudden warmth that I mistook for joy.

We passed around plates of sandwiches, bowls of potato chips. The phonograph blared out, "Rum and Coca-Cola," and Karen lifted imaginary glasses to her lips. We gathered in a circle and softly sang "How Deep Is the Ocean?"

Toward midnight we turned the radio on and listened to the broadcast from Times Square, where a huge crowd had gathered.

"What are we waiting for?" someone there shouted.

"For 1945!" the crowd yelled back in unison.

"What will happen in '45?"

"Peace! Peace! Peace!"

Their shouts thundered across the airwaves and we, too, in that Woodstock basement, took up their chant.

"Peace in '45! Stay alive in '45!"

Karen lit tall candles and switched off the overhead light. A hush came over the room. The flickering flames softened our faces. We linked hands and swayed slowly as the announcer in Times Square called out the seconds before midnight. "Ten — nine — eight — seven — six — " In the room above us the Bassens' guests repeated the numbers, and we joined their chorus, keeping our voices low. "Five — four — three — two — " The final words were uttered in a burst of joy.

"Happy New Year! Happy 1945!"

Faith sparked our joy as the candles were blown out and the confetti and silver icicles drifted down into the darkness. Peter's hand found mine; his lips brushed my eyes, my cheeks, settled gently on my mouth.

"Happy New Year, Sharon," he said softly. A strip of tinsel rested on the long fair cowlick that fell so gracefully across his high pale forehead.

"Happy New Year." I said the words as a prayer, my eyes closed.

Peter walked me back to Dina's house. We crossed the meadow, pausing to stare up at the sliver of a moon which was soon lost in a net of clouds. Even at that distance I could see the light in Dina's house and wondered if she and Nachum had fallen asleep in the living room. Lights flickered in other houses along the road and from the knoll the streetlamps sprayed the tarmac with golden cones of muted radiance. Suddenly a siren sounded, high-pitched and urgent.

"Damn it," Peter said. "An air-raid drill."

Within moments blackout curtains were drawn, the streetlights were extinguished, and we stood motionless in the thick,
impenetrable wartime darkness. I looked up at the sky, half expecting to see silver planes soar through that velvet blackness; my
mouth was dry and my heart beat rapidly.

"Don't be frightened," Peter said. "It's only a drill."

"I know." But inexplicably I began to cry. I could not bear
that terrible darkness, that terrible stillness.

"What is it?" he asked.

"I don't know. I'm so frightened. I'm so lonely." I did not
recognize my own voice. My words fell in fragmented whispers
upon the cushion of the night.

Peter took my hand and gently led me across the frozen
meadow. The siren continued to keen as we walked through the
inky darkness, down the sloping hill and into the glen, toward the
studio. Peter opened the door and we stepped into the cavernous
reconstructed barn.

"We'll wait for the all-clear." He understood my fright; he
sensed my need.

"All right."

Despite the darkness, I began to discern objects in the familiar room — Robert's easel against the wall, the high stool on
which I had perched as he painted my portrait. Only a few months
had passed since those sweltering summer days but I knew that I
was no longer the Sharon who had posed in rolled-up jeans and a
loose white shirt. So much had been compressed into that brief
period — so many experiences that had altered my perceptions,
altered my life. I felt a fleeting sadness for the girl I had been, naive
and flirtatious, indifferent to the danger of a teasing smile, a careless laugh.

Peter found a flashlight, and its beam directed us to the small
electric heater. I plugged it in and found the huge white drop cloths
used for draping canvases. I arranged them in a nest on the rough
floor.

"Now we can play house," Peter said.

"My favorite game. I'll be the mommy and you be the
daddy."

"No. You're Red Riding Hood and I'm the wolf." Peter slipped my hood off and touched my hair, plucking out the silver icicles which had settled on my braid. "You know, your eyes shine in the dark, Sharon."

"The better to see you with," I replied playfully.

I sank down onto the drop cloths, inhaling the scent of paint and turpentine that clung to them. I remembered how Robert and Franchesca had lain together upon them, their bodies writhing in unison, and I shivered.

"Cold?" Peter asked. He sprawled across the makeshift pallet, the flashlight balanced upright between us.

"No, actually I'm pretty warm. The heater's terrific."

"Then take off your cape, Red Riding Hood," he said and reached out to lift it from my shoulders. Peter removed his woolen coat and once again stretched out beside me, his hand touching mine.

Fingers entwined, we lay quietly in the darkness. Another siren shrieked and I tightened my grasp.

"The all-clear will sound in a minute," he said. "This is the civil air patrol's idea of how to start a new year. The jerks."

"I know. Welcome to the war, 1945."

"Hey, Sharon." He cupped my chin in his hands and kissed me, sliding his hands across the soft wool of my white dress. My hands stroked the back of his neck, plucking at the short silken hairs that grew there, as my lips trembled across the angular planes of his face and my tongue licked at the odd saltiness of skin. We came together then, seeking each other's touch and tenderness.

"Peter."

"Sharon."

Our names were secret passwords of joy. We smiled as we mouthed them, as they formed soft moist whispers against our ears. Like crippled children — for he was maimed by disease and I was hobbled by fear — we hugged and comforted each other, and when pleasure came, suffusing us with its wondrous gladness, we laughed and shouted in the darkness. Not until the all-clear signal sounded, minutes later, were we at last subdued into silence.

Afterward, we lay side by side in the darkness, daring in our nakedness, my white dress half blanketing us both, until at last he stirred and slowly began to dress, and I, without speaking, did the same. Wordlessly, we folded the drop cloths, on one of which a bullet of fresh blood glistened.

Peter knelt and slipped my red ballet slippers onto my feet, and when I stood he draped my cape about my shoulders.

"Red Riding Hood," he said.

"Friendly woodsman," I replied.

Hand in hand, we left the studio and emerged into the night once again illuminated by distant lights in frosted windows and the steady golden glow of streetlamps. At Dina's door he kissed me on the cheek, and I, in turn, reached up and touched the silken curves of his pale eyebrows.

Dina and Nachum were listening to the radio, to the first newscast of the year. Peter and I joined them and heard that at twelve minutes past midnight on that first day of January, a German flying bomb had fallen on Antwerp, killing thirty-seven civilians. And even as we listened, the skies of northern France, Belgium, and western Holland were crowded by a thousand German fighters whose lethal payloads were being emptied over Allied strongholds. I buried my head in my hands and Peter gently stroked my hair. My elegant braid had come undone, and confetti and silver icicles clung to the skirt of my white dress. I picked at them absently as I prayed to a God whom I regarded with fury and contempt.

19

The new reading lamp Lottie had bought for me formed a rose-colored cone of light, and in its glow I examined my face. I held a hand mirror close and studied each feature with great concentration. I frowned because I thought my forehead too high, my chin too pointed, my complexion too pale after its burnished tones of summer. I took up an eyebrow tweezer and plucked the tiny hairs that grew beneath and above my thick dark brows, sculpting them into smooth arches. I applied rouge and removed it almost immediately, rubbing so hard that I could not tell whether the brightness of my cheeks came from the residue of Max Factor's Peach Blush, the pressure of the Kleenex, or the heat that suffused my entire body and rose to my face when I thought about Woodstock, about the golden summer days and that last night of the year when a sliver of a moon sailed across the wintry sky.

Shame and terror fused, shadowing the remembered joy of Peter's touch upon my skin, his thrust into my deepest self. I knew that I had crossed a forbidden border, ventured into territory expressly prohibited to "good" girls of my age, of my generation. It was a given that we would not go "all the way." The term was well chosen. To go all the way precluded any possibility of return. It signified the abandonment of innocence, and for us the opposite of innocence was guilt, dark and unequivocal. I studied my reflection anew, surprised yet again that my face was unchanged. I smiled at myself and fondled the secret that at once thrilled and appalled me.

"Oh, you're bad," I murmured to my image, and a hard, familiar knot tightened within my abdomen. I wondered vaguely if I was still a "nice girl" or whether I could be lumped with the group Judy dismissed derisively as "tramps" — girls who wore tight angora sweaters, bright red lipstick, and thick coatings of makeup. They cut classes and sat at the counter of the Sweet Shoppe sipping cherry Cokes and smoking, flashing teasing smiles at the broad-shouldered athletes who wore blue-and-gray varsity jackets with their names embroidered on their pockets. I laughed aloud, wondering what I would say to them or they to me. We had, after all, only one thing in common, and perhaps not even that.

"Are you all right, Sharon?" Lottie called.

"Fine." I kept my voice light because I knew that my aunts were concerned about me. Lottie had talked worriedly to Dina about my lack of appetite, and Edna had commented on my new nervousness. It was true that my hands trembled and often I felt myself close to tears.

"She's upset because there hasn't been a letter from Richard for so long," Lottie told Edna. "And, of course, she misses Beth."

Their troubled voices traveled down the long hallway from the kitchen, where they sat together at the Formica-covered table, Lottie slicing vegetables and Edna righteously mending her thick flesh-colored lisle stockings. She had vowed not to buy any new hosiery "for the duration," a phrase so often heard that we used it automatically, grateful for its subdued optimism — it implied that the war was a temporary aberration of a limited time span. We would endure it, and it would be over. My father would walk up the steps of Lottie's house, his duffel bag on his shoulder. I tried to forget that it was now more than a month since I had heard from him.

"Not a long time, if you consider everything," the Red Cross volunteer who had visited our school advised me. She was a maternal woman who wore the blue-and-white-striped uniform of the volunteer and it was her job to travel from school to school to reassure students about their relatives serving overseas.

"No news is good news," she had added and she dutifully jotted down my father's APO number. It happened, she confided, that sacks of mail went astray or were jettisoned to make room for more important cargo. "You know how things are in wartime," she said and I nodded. It occurred to me that I could scarcely remember how things had been in peacetime. The wings of war had spanned the last years of my childhood and shadowed my adolescence.

And Lottie was right — I did miss Beth. Beth had left for Arizona in mid-January and our entire family had gone to Grand Central to see her off on the Twentieth Century Limited, its engine car festooned with American flags, a V for Victory banner fluttering from the black-paned window of the restaurant car. No enemy aircraft would spot that train as it crossed the continent. Servicemen lined up at every ticket booth and young women, many carrying infants and holding the hands of small children, hurried distractedly to departure gates. Urgent messages resonated over the public address system. "Lieutenant Cameron, please meet your wife at the information booth in the main terminal." "Mrs. Rogers. Mrs. George Rogers. Please check with Travelers' Aid for message from Corporal Rogers."

A group of WAVES, trim in their belted navy blue coats, their stylish hats resting smoothly on hair patriotically cut short (no iron curlers or bobby pins required) passed us, talking and laughing.

"I don't care what he says — I intend to get leave and meet him in Seattle," the tallest of the three asserted. She fished into her leather shoulder bag for a compact and powdered her nose as she walked briskly past us.

I wondered if she spoke of a husband or a lover and I envied her casual grace. How wonderful it would be to wear a uniform, to hang a leather bag over my shoulder and walk so rapidly, with such a sense of purpose.

Beth herself hurried, although we had arrived well before

train time. She was to disembark in Chicago, visit with Alfred's family for a few days, and then go on to Arizona.

"I'll see his room," she had said the previous evening as she and Heidi sat on my bed. "It's so strange. He was my husband and I never saw the house he grew up in. I don't know what he saw from his bedroom window."

"Walk more slowly, Beth."

Julius took his daughter's arm. He worried still that she was not strong enough, although there had been a second visit to Dr. Greenberg and assurances that Beth was entirely recovered, that the pregnancy and the miscarriage had had no impact on her health. The fetus had been cleanly expelled, Dr. Greenberg had said, a phrase which made a great impression on Lottie and which she repeated over and over. "It was cleanly expelled," she said. "There will be no complications because the fetus was cleanly expelled." She was a woman who took comfort from words.

"I'm fine, Dad," Beth said but she slowed her pace. She could not explain her impatience to be gone from her father. He would not understand that she hurried away from the scene of her loss; she wanted to distance herself from those who would comfort her. She had left behind her scrapbooks.

I understood that she did not want to take them with her. I too sought refuge from memory.

Lottie had given me my mother's jewelry — the delicate pins and brooches my father had given her for birthdays and anniversaries, her narrow gold wedding band, the pearls she had worn on her wedding day — but I had placed the violet-hued Louis Sherry tin candy box which contained them in the bottom drawer of my bureau, beneath sweaters that I seldom wore. I did not use the bright silk scarves that my mother had loved, although occasionally I would lift one or another and hold it to my cheek. The lilac scent of her perfume clung to them, and I wondered sadly when it would fade. There were nights when I turned the portrait of my parents that stood on my desk to the wall so that I would not see their faces before I went to sleep and yet again when I awakened. I needed a respite from sorrow. I needed not to think of them.

I knew that I had to bury the muted anger that shamed me, that I had to forgive them for deserting me — my mother by dying, my father by going off to war. I recognized that my anger and resentment were irrational but they could not be subdued. I wondered when Beth would subdue the anger she felt at Alfred.

"How could he have left me?" she had cried in desperation one night and she would not be comforted, just as I could not be comforted.

Beth was right to have left her parents' home and returned to Arizona; she was right to reconstruct her life. I thought of what I might do if my father did not come back. (I never said *if he dies* or *if he is killed* because to use those words might validate them and give credence to a possibility that I willed to be impossible.) I would, I suppose, finish high school at Lincoln — only one more year — and then, like Beth, I would start over. I would not go to college in New York, nor would I return to Boston. I would go to a distant city where no one would know about my parents or the lost home of my girlhood. Perhaps I would go to Palestine. Heidi, who now went to weekly meetings of a Zionist youth group and wore a royal blue shirt, had given me pamphlets to read and shown me magazines with illustrations of young people dancing horas in open fields, of students gathered in the amphitheater of the Hebrew university that overlooked the hills of Judaea. I could be such a student, such a dancing pioneer. As Beth had left her scrapbooks behind, so I would abandon my mother's box of jewelry, her silk scarves.

We had helped Beth board, arranged her things in the cozy roomette designed for one but shared by two because it was, after all, wartime. Her roommate was a WAC colonel. I wondered if Beth would place Alfred's portrait on her nightstand.

We waited for her weekly letter, the report cards of her recuperation. Her meeting with Alfred's family had gone as well as could be expected. She liked her classes. She had taken a part-time job in a Tempe dress shop. She was fine, or at least she would be fine, she assured us, and we repeated her assurances to each other.

"She needs time," my grandmother said. Unlike Bracha Liebe, my grandmother's cousin who had adhered to her parents' objections to her marriage, Beth was not petrified into eternal maidenhood. She had known happiness and she would know happiness again.

I missed my cousin. I wandered into her empty room at night, opened her drawer, and touched the blue sweater she had worn the day of Alfred's departure. Her pink dress, the one Alfred had favored, hung in her closet. I knew that she had not taken it with her because she did not want another young man to tell her how pretty she looked in it, to touch its soft wool. One night I tried the dress on. It was, of course, too small for me, and Lottie found me trying to button it as tears streaked my face. Very gently, she lifted it over my head.

"I know you miss Beth," she said. "I miss her too."

We clung together then in awkward embrace.

"You'll get a letter from your father soon," Lottie said in the singsong voice she had invoked to comfort small Aaron and smaller Beth. "And Beth will maybe come home for Passover. And who knows — by then the war may be over."

"I hope so." My voice was muffled because I did not believe my own words.

I knew that it was neither Beth's absence nor my father's long silence that caused my heart to beat too rapidly and an icy sweat to congeal beneath my arms and about my breasts as I stood on line in the cafeteria.

"I can't stand here — too many people," I muttered to Judy and shoved my tray at her.

It was not loneliness that caused a wave of nausea to wash over me during a biology lab so that I dropped my scalpel and tipped over a vial of formaldehyde which Letitia swiftly cleaned up.

I hurried to the girls' bathroom between classes and wakened in the night, my body tense and my head pounding. I bought a small pocket calendar and each evening I marked off another day, using a thick red grease pencil that bled its way across the bold black numerals.

Peter called me twice a week but our conversations were strained, threaded with a new awkwardness. We were wanderers, exercising caution in a foreign terrain, tongue-tied by a dialect that was still unfamiliar to us.

"Are you all right, Sharon?" Peter asked one night.

"Of course I'm all right," I replied curtly, irritated by the nervous urgency of his tone.

We found it easier to avoid talking about ourselves, and instead we discussed the progress of the war. As I think back, I realize that the war must have sustained thousands of relationships, bridged a myriad of uneasy silences. It was Judy Bergman who said, with her usual caustic honesty, "I wonder what my parents would talk about if it wasn't for the war."

And so Peter and I spoke of the fighting in the Ardennes, the landing on Luzon. A sailor from Woodstock was on the light cruiser *Columbia* which was disabled when the Japanese launched an attack, using explosive boats that they propelled close to American ships and then blew up.

We spoke of the new members 1945 had introduced to our pantheon of heroes. George Davis had been the commander of the destroyer *Walke*. When his ship was decimated by a Japanese attack, he was set on fire, but with his body aflame, he had continued to direct evacuation operations. Ted Chandler had demonstrated similar heroism in the same situation and had also died after directing the fire-fighting on the cruiser *Louisville*. At the Sweet Shoppe one snowy afternoon, the captain of the Lincoln football team wondered aloud if he would have had the guts to do what Ted Chandler had done.

"You'll never know, will you," teased his redheaded girlfriend, who wore his team jacket slung over her narrow shoulders.

He shook his head regretfully. The war was winding down too rapidly. It would not wait for him to demonstrate his manhood, his courage.

I repeated the exchange to Peter. "It's as though they can't wait to be martyred," I said derisively.

"Just like your Hannah Szenes."

"She's not *my* Hannah Szenes," I said, although it was true that I had spoken of her to Peter more than once. Heidi had taken me to a meeting of her Zionist youth group at which the story of the young woman who had left her kibbutz in Palestine to operate as a British intelligence agent in her native Hungary had been told. Because I had listened to the news of her execution on Election Day, I felt an odd intimacy with her.

He did not reply, and too quickly, I said that I had to hang up, that I was feeling very tired.

"But you're okay, Sharon?" he asked yet again and I knew exactly what he meant.

"Good night, Peter," I said, without answering him.

I did not want to tell him that I was not okay. January was almost over and my menstrual period was at least a week late. I smuggled Lottie's *Home Medical Adviser* into my room and by the rose-colored light of my new lamp I read the reasons for a delayed menses. It was with relief that I learned that pregnancy was not the only reason for such a delay. Malnutrition, inappropriate exercise, tension, even a virus could be imputed. I acknowledged that I was extremely tense, that I had not been eating well. How could I be relaxed when I didn't know if my father was alive? I might even have had a virus. Twice I had gone to the school nurse to obtain excuses from gym because I felt ill — exhausted and nauseated. Of course. I probably had a virus aggravated by tension. I was stupid to imagine the worst.

I went to Judy Bergman's house one Saturday afternoon, eager to escape the sabbath melancholy that permeated the house on Avenue Z, to evade the sound of Julius's gentle snores and Lottie's light and rhythmic breathing. They had both fallen asleep in the living room after lunch, and although such sabbath naps had long been their pattern, on that afternoon the sight of their heavy, sated bodies annoyed me. Julius's stomach was covered by the Friday copy of the *Jewish Daily Forward,* and Lottie's *Saturday Evening Post* was spread open at her feet. The war had aged my aunt and uncle, and I retreated from that recognition into a sullen anger, rejecting them for their slothful postures, resisting my own urge to waken them.

Judy's house too was silent. Marvin's furlough had ended and he had been stationed at an army base in Georgia.

"Have you heard from Marvin?" I asked dutifully.

Judy opened the window, even though the day was cold, because we were smoking our red-tipped Deb cigarettes.

"He sent a postcard. They wanted him to call but I don't think he could bear talking to my mother. He's an ordnance officer, whatever that means."

"That means he gets first crack at a lot of things other soldiers have to wait for. Linens. Candy. Cigarettes. Even condoms," I added daringly. "Ordnance officers are in charge of supplies. Very important men on base, according to Bernie, the great military authority."

"Gee, I wish Bernie was my cousin — then I'd know all sorts of crucial things like that."

We both laughed, as we always laughed when we spoke about Bernie.

"Your cousins have a thing for uniforms," Judy said, exhaling lazily. "First Bernie in his Junior Commando uniform and now Heidi in her blue shirt."

"She only wears it for meetings of her Zionist group," I protested.

"Then she's coming from a meeting whenever I see her," Judy said. "What do they do at those meetings?"

"They have discussions. And they dance — you know, circle dances — and they sing. They talk a lot about restructuring society, about the kind of collective community they want to build in Palestine. I went with Heidi last week and they talked about the different roles of men and women, about whether or not biology is destiny."

"Wow." Judy's tone was disparaging and I disliked her for it. "What did they decide, that men should have the babies?" She laughed harshly.

"They put that on next week's agenda." I joined in her laughter although I felt neither amusement nor merriment.

"Speaking of condoms and having babies, the rumor is that Rozzy Lang — you know, the redhead who always hangs out with Bert from the football team — anyway, the rumor is that she's pregnant," Judy said. "Try telling her that biology's not destiny."

"You're kidding." My stomach lurched and my hands felt clammy.

"I wouldn't joke about something like that." Judy was serious. She did not like Rozzy Lang but she was sorry for her.

"What will she do?" I asked.

Judy shrugged and lit another cigarette.

"There aren't a lot of choices," she replied and I wondered whether, in fact, there were any choices at all.

I did not go directly home when I left Judy's. Instead I walked to the esplanade, sat on the balustrade, and watched the gray-green waves crash violently against the rocks. The salt spray brushed my face.

I thought of Rozzy Lang and wondered if she and her Bert, like Peter and myself, had confused love and friendship. And then I scorned my own analogy, my own self-pity.

You're being crazy, I told myself harshly. What does Rozzy Lang have to do with you?

That night I crossed off yet another date on my calendar and considered how long I could wait before revealing my secret fear to someone else. Another two weeks, I decided. That would mark the absence of another menstrual period. I counted the days and circled February 14. Valentine's Day. I smiled bitterly at the irony.

I lay awake thinking of whom I might tell, who would be able to advise me. I thought of Heidi. My cousin would not be shocked. She flirted with dark fantasies and had somehow learned to control her own desperate fears. Heidi was possessed of a new vitality, a new certainty. She dressed with a unique flair and spoke with a quiet passion. She believed in Zionism and her new ideology energized her. She would share that energy with me, I knew, but I knew also that it would be unfair to turn to her. She was still so vulnerable.

I could not tell Peter. Peter had rights and I could not risk his determination to assert them.

I did not want to tell my aunts. They would be devastated.

A scrap of silver moonlight flittered across the framed portrait of my parents and I recognized the reality of my total aloneness. What would my mother have said, I wondered, and what would she have done? I imagined the gentleness of her touch, the softness of her voice. "Don't worry, Sharon, my Sharon." I spoke the words I assigned to her aloud into the darkness of the night.

At breakfast the next morning, Lottie looked across the table at me and said, "The strangest thing happened last night, Sharon. I thought I heard your mother's voice. I was certain that I heard Miriam speak."

Julius put his hand on her shoulder, a gesture of comfort, of commiseration. He was concerned about Lottie, who was restless and anxious.

I wrote my father, telling him of the churning agitation which now flavored every waking moment and invaded my light and fitful sleep.

"Dear Daddy — I am so frightened. What if I am pregnant? I don't want a baby. I'm not old enough to have a baby."

The childishness of my own words frightened me but I did not stop writing.

"Oh, Daddy, help me. Is there a way not to have this baby? Where can I go? What can I do? Please, Daddy, help me."

I did not, of course, mail the letter.

I knew the word *abortion* but I did not use it. Its very sound frightened me. Lola had told me of a classmate of hers at Cornell who had died in the back room of a small upstate pharmacy. Dina had spoken sadly of one of her cases — a teenager who had run away from home to follow her GI boyfriend and had been found half dead in a furnished room in Phonecia. "She tried to self-abort, using a clothes hanger," Dina had said sadly and Robert had muttered angrily about the corruption of the capitalist medical establishment.

"And does the wonderful Soviet revolution offer free abortions?" Dina had asked tauntingly.

Their remembered argument intruded on my own fear as I wrote, and I put my pen down because my hand was trembling.

"I'm all right," I told myself sternly. "I'm fine."

"I'm fine, Daddy," I whispered to my absent father.

"I'm fine, Mommy," I assured my dead mother.

But when Peter called that night I did not go to the phone.

"Tell him I'm not home," I whispered to Lottie.

I wondered if Peter knew that I stood within inches of the phone. I wondered if we would ever be comfortable with each other again. It was my first recognition of the fragility of friendship and the rigidity of its parameters. Peter and I had taken a risk, played a dangerous game; we stood alone in a no-man's-land of uncertain intimacy, fearful of proceeding further and knowing that we could not turn back.

I went to my room and crossed off the date with my red pencil. My menstrual period was now three weeks late. My breasts felt tender to my touch and when I stood naked in front of the long mirror it seemed to me that my waist had thickened.

"Shaindel."

My grandmother tapped lightly on the door and I swiftly shrugged into my bathrobe. I felt ashamed of my body, and for the first time, ashamed of myself.

"In a minute, Buba," I said but I did not open the door. I did not want my wise grandmother to read the terror that masked my face.

20

Aaron's letter arrived on a Thursday. By Saturday, the tissue-paper-thin stationery was frayed from being passed from hand to hand and the lead pencil scrawl seemed lighter, as though too many readings had caused it to fade. Julius read it aloud to the men who arrived on Saturday evening and gathered about the dining room table. His voice was hoarse and now and again he paused to translate a phrase into Yiddish, to look sadly at his friends, who bowed their heads and clenched their fists as they listened to Aaron's words.

Before Julius had finished reading, tears trickled down Meyer Liebowitz's cheeks. He was a large, florid-faced man, known for his strength. The owner of a small carting company, he had once lifted Lottie's living room couch by himself so that she might reposition it. But as he listened to Julius read, his strength seemed to ebb from his body and he sat slumped in his chair, his arms dangling, drained of all energy. He had left a large family behind in Poland, parents and younger brothers and sisters. His lips moved but no words came as he mouthed the names of his siblings, his nieces and nephews, his cousins. Moshe. Leah. Itzik. Yossi.

"*Nu?*" Meyer Liebowitz said when Julius had finished reading, when the letter was placed on the table and carefully refolded. "It's what we thought. No. It's worse than we thought."

"Worse. Much worse." Morris Birnbaum, a small man with avian features, hugged himself and swayed from side to side like a mourner at a funeral, unable to control his grief. "Oy. That we should hear such things. Oy. That such things could happen."

Lottie stood at the kitchen counter and sliced a coffee ring. Her eyes were red-rimmed, her face was chalk white. She had read Aaron's letter so often that surely she knew it by heart, but she would not repeat its words. They seared her memory. I filled the teapot and listened to the verse she recited in a voice too soft to be heard in the dining room, " 'In the aftermath of storm, the Milky Way is spun / God's sweet scent still rides around the sun.' "

"That's beautiful, Aunt Lottie," I said. Oh, how I longed for the storm of war to be over, for sweetness to replace the putrescence Aaron had described.

"A poem by Leivick. The Yiddish poet. He suffered. How he suffered. But still he saw the beauty. We have to remember the beauty, Sharon." She closed her eyes and I knew that Leivick's words had not been sufficiently powerful to negate Aaron's grim narrative.

I brought the teapot to the table.

"Here, Sharon." Julius handed me the letter. "This you'll put away. We have business to do."

On this night each man would write a check for double the amount anticipated. On this night everyone would undertake to find signers for the affidavits Julius distributed. The men drank the tea but they did not eat the coffee ring. On this night they could not tolerate any sweetness against their tongues. Meyer Liebowitz took the photograph of his family out of his wallet and passed it around the table. The men looked at the picture with the resigned sadness of visitors to a house of mourning who study the photographs of the newly dead.

I carried Aaron's letter into the living room and read it for the third time.

Dear Mama and Papa —

I hope you'll be able to read this letter. I'm writing with a stub of a pencil and my handwriting is a little shaky but it's only nerves. Nothing wrong with my fingers. All ten of them are still intact as is every other part of my body. Not even a shrapnel scratch. But I come honestly by the nerves even though they won't earn me a Purple Heart. I don't know how much news of what the Allied advance units are finding in Eastern Europe is getting reported in the States. Probably not much since the Russians are leading the sweep through Poland and they were the first to enter Auschwitz — that's the German name for the hell they built in the Polish city of Oswiecim, not too far from Papa's town of Radom. And, God help me, I was with them because I was part of a small group of American specialists attached to a Soviet unit. That Russian immersion course I took at Columbia helped me get the posting and when it came through I thought it was terrific. I was heading for drama and excitement. And maybe one day I'll think about the drama and excitement but right now all I can think about is the horror, the pain, the suffering. Oh God, Mama, Papa — the suffering . . .

That line ended abruptly, as though Aaron could not bring himself to complete it, and I thought of my cousin clutching his stub of a pencil, overwhelmed by sorrow. I remembered him as I had last seen him, almost four years ago — a tall, gangly young man, his Adam's apple curiously oversize, his dark hair thick and curly like his mother's, like my own. His face was long and narrow, his lips were too thin and his nose was too large, but his hazel eyes glinted with an electric humor, and his laughter was a generous roar of merriment. He distributed nicknames with whimsical irreverence. Bernie, a sloppy eater as a child, was dubbed Kid Shmutz, and my father was Poor Richard. When we arrived from Boston, Aaron would lope down the brick steps to help us with our suitcases, shouting up to his parents, "Uncle Poor Richard is here but he didn't bring his almanac," a joke at which everyone laughed without understanding the reference because Aaron's humor was contagious.

It was Aaron's job to make his parents laugh, to make them proud of him, to reward them for all the earnest effort of their immigrant lives. He was their American prince, born to all the opportunities that had been denied them. And he had not disappointed. He had sprinted from high school to Columbia, traveling the subway for almost two hours each day, his sketch pad on his lap, his science texts in his briefcase. He made dean's list and his cartoons appeared in the *Columbia Spectator*. Julius wanted him to go to medical school but Aaron spoke of astrophysics, a word which mystified and sobered his parents, who shrugged with proud acceptance. All right. He would get a Ph.D. He would still be Dr. Aaron Lieberman. They saw him in cap and gown, his diploma held as high as a scepter, the son of a man born in Radom, a Polish town which did not admit Jewish students to its secondary school.

And then the war had interrupted their dream. Aaron had not waited to be drafted. He had enlisted.

"This is our war," he had said. "And we have to win it. And naturally they can't win it without me. Captain Brooklyn to the rescue. When Hitler hears I joined up he'll wet his pants."

On the Monday after Pearl Harbor, Aaron was first on line at the selective service office on Coney Island Avenue.

Lottie and Julius did not protest. They knew that he spoke as a Jew, as an American, as a laughing young man who masked his deep seriousness and sense of duty with wry humor. They were proud of him and they were frightened for him but they learned to contain their pride (lest it tempt the evil eye) and to contain their fear. They feared to write him that Beth had been widowed, just as they had not wanted to write to him about my mother's death. They had schooled themselves to spare their children unhappiness.

The men in the living room argued mildly over their aims.

"We have to set up a fund at the Hebrew Immigrant Aid Society. They'll come here, those who survived the camps. We have to be ready to help them. Apartments, furniture, jobs," Julius said.

"More important, we should raise money to send to the Jews

in Palestine. That's where they'll want to go. That's where the future will be," Meyer Liebowitz objected. His voice boomed. His strength was returned. He had recovered from the shock of Aaron's words and was ready to press forward. I turned back to my cousin's letter.

Maybe I should have been more prepared for what we found at Auschwitz. We knew about the death marches. Once Budapest was liberated the Germans began evacuating the concentration camps, forcing the prisoners to march west into Silesia because they needed slave labor at their munitions factories there. It was cold. You can't imagine how cold. Our breath froze in the air. The snow formed into icicles as it fell and we shivered although we wore greatcoats over our winter uniforms and we had food in our bellies. The prisoners were starving. Some of them were barefoot and if they were lucky they covered their ragged uniforms with thin blankets. They say that hundreds died on the way and those who survived were packed into cattle cars and sent to the camps at Ravensbrück, Sachsenhausen, Buchenwald, Bergen-Belsen.

It snowed the night before we reached Auschwitz and when we got there everything was covered with gray snow. It was very quiet and we thought at first that the camp was deserted, that we had entered an uninhabited universe of destruction. And then we saw the eyes — not really eyes but huge sockets carved into skeletal faces with tears leaking from them, dripping onto cheekbones that shone through a thin snow-gray layer of skin — and we understood that we were looking at people. They came toward us, an army of moving cadavers, their bare feet silent upon the snow, their stick-thin arms outstretched, the ragged sleeves of their uniforms fluttering in the wind. I took off my coat and put it over the shoulders of an old man but then I saw that he wasn't an old man. He was a boy — probably Bernie's age. His name was Hershel, he said, and he came from Lodz. He took us to the building that he said was the infirmary. We went inside but I ran out and vomited onto the snow, onto my boots. The Germans had shot the patients before they left — shot and killed 150 men and 200 women. The bodies were on the floor, on the planks of wood they called beds, in piles against the wall. The floor was sticky with blood, slippery with guts. And even though it was so cold, they had begun to stink.

"We're smelling evil," a Russian soldier said to me and he was crying. I began to cry too but Hershel from Lodz — he didn't cry. I guess he didn't have any tears left. He'd been in Auschwitz for more than two years. He rubbed his face with the sleeve of my coat and his skin was so thin that he began to bleed. That is how I'll remember him — with teardrops of blood on his cheeks.

The air smelled of ashes and cinders. An intelligence officer told us that before they left, the Germans blew up the last of the camp's five gas chambers and crematoria. It took a while for that to sink in, for me to realize that I was in a place where people — most of them my own people — had been gassed to death and their bodies burned in a crematorium. The Russkie intelligence guy said that they blew up the installations to destroy the evidence but they could have saved themselves the trouble because the evidence was all around us — more than evidence. Witnesses. Hershel and the others with him were part of the 7,000 survivors still in Auschwitz — men, women, and children. I'm including here the girl with a kind of yellow fuzz growing on her bald head, blisters all over her body, and a smile frozen into place on her lips. She never said a word and she never stopped smiling, as though she had grinned her way into madness. But I'm not counting the boy one of the men in the camp held in his arms, carrying him from one Russian soldier to another, to me, to a British officer. He pointed to the boy and then to his heart so that we'd understand that the boy was his son and that he loved him. One of the Russians tried to take the boy from him because of course he was dead, his body rigid. But the man ran off. No one followed him. But sometimes I wake up in the middle of the night and I wonder if he ever laid his son's body to rest or if he's carrying him still.

The Russians did a statistical breakdown. We found 5,800 Jews at Auschwitz-Birkenau, 1,200 Poles at the Auschwitz main camp, and 650 slave laborers from different countries at Monowitz. The SS had burned most of the storehouses but they hadn't managed to get to a couple, and the Russians did an inventory. They contained 836,000 women's dresses, 348,000 men's suits, and 38,000 pairs of shoes. I don't know why those numbers seemed so important to me but I wrote them down in that little leather notebook Beth gave me just before I shipped out. I thought about the way you, Mama, and my aunts always shopped for Grandma and brought the dresses home and I wondered how many of those 836,000 dresses belonged to old ladies like my Buba and I began to cry.

Mama, Papa, I can't forget what I saw at Auschwitz. I can't forget Hershel or that little grinning girl who somehow made me think of Beth. And I know that I shouldn't forget them because if I don't remember them, who will?

I'm sorry that this letter has been so grim but I thought that it was important for you to know what happened here. In fact, I know that you would want to know.

Keep the home fires burning. Tell Kid Shmutz to make sure our blackout curtains are in good shape or I won't give him the German grenade I've been carrying around Europe just for him.

Hey, don't worry. I'm fine and I intend to stay that way.

Love,
Aaron

I thought of how hard Aaron must have strived to end that sad letter on a light note, to reclaim the humor that had sustained him always. I folded the letter and placed it in Julius's prayer book between the Eighteen Benedictions and the Kaddish. That was where Aaron himself found it so many years later, after Julius's death. My cousin, his hair graying and his shoulders rounded as his father's had been, read his own letter as though it had been written by a stranger and he wept for the young soldier he had been and for the world of darkness he had marched through in his heavy boots and his khaki uniform.

That night I remained in the living room listening to the murmuring voices of Julius and his friends, who had so swiftly translated their sorrow into plans for the future. They were businessmen and they understood how to cut their losses, how to diversify.

"We'll make petitions to the congressmen — they should change the quotas, maybe make special provisions for the survivors of the camps," Julius said and I envied him his energy, his ability to mourn and then to move on. I was paralyzed by my own worry and ashamed that in the wake of Aaron's revelations I remained fixated on my own anxiety. Across the world, boys and girls of my age had been cruelly enslaved, starved. Whole villages had been destroyed, families wiped out, and men wandered about cradling the bodies of their lifeless children. And yet I was consumed by fear for myself and for my future.

I dialed Peter's number but when he answered the phone I hung up. I could not bear to speak about Aaron's letter and there was little else I could say to him. I recognized that my dark trepidations were my own and I could not share them — not yet, perhaps not ever.

Again that night I drew a red slash through the date on my pocket calendar. I remembered suddenly how my mother had placed her fleshless fingers on the mound of Dina's pregnancy and I fell asleep thinking of the sweetness of Anna's breath against my cheek when I held her close. My lips twisted into a bitter smile, bemused, as I was and as I remain, by the odd dance of life and death.

Peter sent me roses on Valentine's Day. I stared at the bouquet and counted the burgundy-colored blossoms, wincing as a thorn jutted through the thick white paper and pierced my thumb. Sixteen. One flower for each year of my life, I thought dramatically, and I placed them in one of Lottie's tall vases, allowing the droplet of blood from my finger to float in a crimson speck on the water.

"Happy Valentine's Day," Peter's note read. "I'm thinking of you."

I carried the vase of flowers into my bedroom so that I would not have to explain them to Lottie and Julius, but I did not call Peter to thank him. Was he waiting for such a call? I wondered, and I imagined him listening for the phone, his pale face creased with anxiety as he nervously brushed his wayward fair hair back from his forehead. I felt a perverse, vengeful pleasure at the thought of his discomfort which was immediately replaced by a harsh anger at myself. I did not like the person I was becoming. I looked at the pocket calendar, at the circle I had drawn about the date, and my heart sank. I had reached my own deadline. The bargain I had made with myself was sealed. I called Heidi.

"I want to talk to you about something important," I said. "Can I come over tonight?"

"Actually, there's a meeting of the Young Pioneers tonight. I'm supposed to lead the discussion group and I want to talk about Aaron's letter. Why don't you come to the meeting — it's at that synagogue around the corner — and we can talk afterward. My father will drive you home." Heidi had inherited her mother's talent for organizing the lives of others, a talent that would serve her well in the years to come.

I agreed, and because I could not face my homework, I stretched out on the bed and turned the radio on.

The German city of Dresden was in flames. The previous evening hundreds of British bombers had struck at the heart of the city in an attempt to destroy the railway marshaling yard. A fire storm had resulted which burned through eleven square miles of the ancient city.

"And this morning," the announcer continued soberly, "four hundred and fifty American bombers attacked Dresden. The city is now in flames. We do not know how much damage has been done to the marshaling yards but residential and business areas, schools, universities, and hospitals have been destroyed, with an enormous loss of life." He spoke very slowly, as though uncertain whether the news he brought into American homes was good or bad.

I shut the radio off and took one of Peter's roses from the

vase and inhaled its scent. I pressed the velvety, wine-colored petals
against my cheek and I remembered that my parents owned a tea set
of Dresden china, delicate white cups and saucers trimmed with a
pattern of tiny pale pink roses, the cover of the teapot a full-blown
blossom. It was in storage now, with the other furnishings
of my vanished life. It seemed harsh that a city where such a beautiful tea set had been designed should now be in flames. I felt
confused, disoriented. Surely I should rejoice over an Allied victory,
but I felt only a heavy sorrow. I plucked the petals one by one from
the rose and then crushed the slender pistils that sprouted at the
flower's heart.

Nachum Adler, who came for dinner that night as he did once
or twice each week since we had become his surrogate family, drove
me to the meeting. A light rain fell but the heater kept the car warm,
and he played the radio, which he kept tuned always to a classical
music station. I leaned back and let the music wash over me in a
soothing, cleansing wave. He turned the volume up for the hourly
newscast. The Dresden raids dominated. There were no exact casualty figures but the estimates were high. Twenty thousand dead,
perhaps thirty thousand. Witnesses spoke of a red sky above the
city, a glow that could be seen for miles around. And fires burned in
London as well. Even as Dresden burned, fourteen V2 rockets fell
on the British capital.

I looked out the window at the quiet Flatbush streets and
shivered.

"I'm thinking about the people in Dresden. The women and
children. The old people. High school kids like me. Babies like
Anna."

"And small girls like my daughter, Rachel. And young women
like Manya, my wife," he said bitterly.

"Do you hate them?" I asked. "Do you hate the Germans?"

He did not answer immediately. The newscaster spoke about
American victories in central Burma, where the Japanese had been
beaten back. Nachum sighed, turned the radio off, and adjusted the
windshield wipers. The rain grew heavier, and ribbons of water
slithered across the glass, wafted across the golden reflections of
streetlights.

"I don't want to hate," he said at last. "I am afraid of what hatred will do to me, to my work. But I am only human. I had a wife, a child, a home, a homeland. All that, they took from me. How can I not hate those who destroyed my life?"

"What will you do?" I asked because I understood that he had a plan to rescue himself from that hatred.

"I think of returning to Europe. I have been recruited for the U.S. Army intelligence unit. My German is excellent. The liberating armies will need men like me — men who know the towns and cities, who understand the people. Perhaps if I can do something, anything, to make a difference, I will feel that there was some purpose in my survival." He spoke very softly but there was no uncertainty in his voice.

"What about Dina?" I asked. I did not want my aunt to hurt again. I did not want her to be abandoned.

He looked at me in surprise.

"Dina understands what I must do. And she also knows what she must do. We have been good friends. We have helped each other. We will always help each other. But we must each sort out our own life. There are things a person must do alone."

"Yes. I know." I pressed my cheek against the cold glass of the window and thought of all that I might yet have to do alone.

"Sharon, something is troubling you. Something that has nothing to do with the war."

"Yes."

"Do you want to talk about it?"

"Not yet."

"When you are ready I will listen. And if it is possible, I will help."

"I know."

He parked in front of the synagogue and I leaned over and kissed him on the cheek. For the first time in all those weeks, I did not feel myself totally alone.

I hurried into the building. The meeting of the Young Pioneers was already in progress. The members of the Zionist youth movement, most of them wearing their royal blue shirts, sat in a circle in the basement recreation room of the synagogue.

I took my seat and turned to Heidi, who was reading from Aaron's letter which she had copied out onto a sheet of looseleaf paper. She read slowly, allowing the word pictures he had drawn to come to life in her listeners' imagination.

"What happened at Auschwitz must change the way we think about ourselves and about the world," she said in conclusion. "It makes us realize that as Jews, we have only one alternative. There must be a Jewish homeland."

The young people nodded earnestly. They were an intense, dedicated group, some of whom had traveled from distant parts of the borough to be present at that meeting. Few of the girls wore makeup. They scorned vanity; their eyes were fixed on higher things. But their cheeks glowed and their eyes were bright. Their idealism birthed a fiery sensuality. They felt for the children Aaron had described, for the boy called Hershel, for the girl whose cracked lips parted in the leer of madness. And when they spoke, their voices throbbed with feeling.

"Of course. Something like this must never happen again. Never again. But there must be more than a homeland. We must demand more. There must be a sovereign Jewish state," a dark-haired girl said.

"A Jewish state. A nice dream. But meanwhile, the British are still enforcing the White Paper. The only way the Jews of Europe can get into Palestine is through illegal immigration," a tall youth named Jake said bitterly.

At a previous meeting I had heard him describe the rescue operations carried out in Palestine as ships dropped anchor outside the territorial waters and Jewish volunteers paddled out in longboats to transport the refugees to secret coves along the Mediterranean coast.

"They're doing something, the Jews in Palestine. They're not just dancing horas in a Brooklyn basement," he had said and I recognized — and shared — the jealousy in his voice. I too longed to do something, to translate anxiety into action, anger into effort. I wanted to test my own courage. Perhaps I too could be as brave as my father; as my cousin Aaron; as Manya, who had mocked the Nazis; and Nachum, who would return to confront them.

"But don't you see — what happened at Auschwitz will change all that." Rosalie, who spoke so emphatically, was older than most of us. She was an adviser to the group, sent from the national headquarters to direct and organize it. She was a thin girl, with a protean quality to her long, narrow face. Her eyes were a deep violet behind the thick-lensed glasses, and a wave of white rippled through her dark hair, as though she had worried her way into a premature graying. She was said to be very brilliant. She was still a student at Barnard but a poem of hers had already been published in the *Saturday Review of Literature.*

"When the world finds out what happened to the Jews of Europe, there will be a reaction, a feeling of guilt that no one did anything to prevent it," she continued. "And that guilt will translate itself into a kind of international atonement. There will be a recognition that something will have to be done for the survivors and the only thing that can be done will be to establish a Jewish state in Palestine."

Rosalie spoke with the same succinct clarity that would one day become familiar to public television viewers who listened to her lectures on foreign policy. It was on television screens over the years that I watched the white wave overtake the darkness of her luxuriant hair.

"I don't know. I read all the reports from Yalta. The Big Three never even mentioned the Jews in Europe. At least not in the published reports," Jake said.

"They didn't mention Dresden either, did they?" Rosalie asked. "But I would bet that they gave the green light on Dresden at Yalta."

"It's awful," I said. "A whole city in flames." I blushed deeply. I had not meant to speak. Everyone looked at me in surprise. I was not a member of the movement. I was Heidi's cousin who attended an occasional meeting and seldom participated.

"Yes. It is awful," Rosalie agreed. "But necessary," she added swiftly. "The Allies aren't firebombing a German city. They're firebombing German morale, forcing them to recognize that they will have to surrender."

"I don't think so. I think that Dresden is a punishment — our payback for the London blitz, for the V2 rockets they've been shooting into England and Belgium." The boy who spoke shifted his weight nervously from one foot to another and clutched a textbook covered with brown paper. He was a senior at Brooklyn Tech, his eyes on a scholarship to MIT. He had studied on his way to this meeting and would study on the subway ride home.

"But is that right? We say what they've done is horrible, inhuman. And then we go ahead and do the same thing. The Germans send a rocket over Hull and so we send bombers over Dresden. They kill ordinary people in movie theaters and supermarkets so we firebomb a whole city. It's a vicious cycle." Heidi's voice broke and her cheeks were ablaze. I was frightened for her. I did not want her to sink again into the desperate depression that had overtaken her just before Beth's wedding.

"It isn't moral to kill women and children, old people, patients in hospitals," I insisted stubbornly, looking at Heidi.

"But what if their deaths mean that the length of the war will be shortened — that hundreds of thousands of lives on both sides will be saved?" Rosalie asked. She turned to me. "Your father is overseas, isn't he, Sharon?"

I nodded, taken by surprise.

"Suppose you were told that the death of a German schoolboy in Dresden would mean that your father's life would be saved. Would you agree to it, even though the boy was innocent except for the fact that he happened to be born to German parents?"

"The children in Auschwitz were innocent," Jake shouted, "except that they happened to be born to Jewish parents. And their parents didn't start the war the way the Germans did."

"But what they did was wrong — and it's still wrong when we do it."

"Sometimes the end justifies the means."

"But if you have a corrupt means, the end itself will be corrupted."

"It's more dangerous to do nothing."

The arguments came thick and fast, insight and objection colliding, tremulous observations overpowered by passionate assertions.

"Sharon?" Rosalie had not forgotten me.

"I don't know," I said slowly. "No. That's not true. I do know. I would want my father to be saved. I would choose for my father." I sank back in my chair, honest but defeated.

"Sometimes there aren't a lot of choices," Rosalie said. "Sometimes the only choice is instinctive."

She did not look at me but I felt that she was speaking directly to me. I sensed her approval, and the tension that had held me in its grip for so long fell away, like a confining garment discarded with startling ease. Heidi reached over and took my hand, tightened her fingers around my own.

"One thing that we can be sure of — at least, I am sure of it — there will be a Jewish state," Rosalie said and her voice rose to a shout. "The nation of Israel lives! The nation of Israel will live!"

"*Am Yisrael chai!*" We all shouted the Hebrew response.

Jake took up his accordion, the chairs were pushed aside, and we linked arms and danced a hora. Invigorated by the music, we whirled about the room in rhythmic stamping frenzy.

The tempo changed. Heidi played the flute and we moved slowly, swaying from side to side, hands on one another's waists.

" 'He who makes peace in the firmament,' " we sang softly in Hebrew, " 'He will send peace unto us and unto all of Israel. And so we say Amen.' " The song was a prayer, familiar to all of us from the synagogue.

Our voices were soft. We sang of peace although we had grown up in the shadow of war, and war had darkened our earliest imaginings. We had learned to avert our eyes when we saw a gold-star banner hanging in a window. Death haunted us yet we whirled about the room in a dance of light.

The flute and accordion melded into a fast-paced dance, a celebration of water, water that would make the desert, our desert, bloom. We danced toward one another, danced out again.

"*Mayim, mayim, mayim* — water, water, water!" we shouted.

My voice grew hoarse and as I stamped in a pulsating beat — I felt a familiar cramp, a warm flow through my body. I eased my way out of the circle and found a bathroom. Locked in the narrow toilet stall, I saw the scarlet stains on my underpants and realized with an odd commingling of relief and regret that my long self-punishing vigil was over. My girlhood was restored to me.

"Are you all right?" Heidi asked when I returned.

I nodded.

"I just got the curse," I whispered and contained my inner hilarity at the thought that on this night the "curse" was a blessing.

The meeting ended. Chairs were stacked and the movement's literature distributed. There would be a rally on behalf of open Jewish immigration in Palestine in front of the British consulate. There would be a demonstration in Washington urging an easing of quota restrictions.

"Hey — what did you want to talk to me about?" Heidi asked as we waited outside the synagogue for Leon to pick us up.

"Oh, I was having a problem with an essay assignment but I figured it out," I lied blithely.

Dissimulation had become my skill that year, my cultivated defense against invasions of my privacy.

We huddled together in the synagogue doorway and looked up at the silvery beams of aerial searchlights that raked the ink black sky. Those searching rays reminded us that we were still at war, that the great cities of the world remained vulnerable, and that all our lives were at risk.

I called Peter that night and thanked him for the flowers.

"And I'm all right," I added, although he had refrained from asking. "Really all right."

"Swell."

I did not say good-bye but I replaced the receiver gently. I buried the pocket calendar at the bottom of my drawer and when I found it months later I stared at the red slashes with perplexity until at last I remembered the weeks of my terror and the night of my release.

Spring

21

Spring commingled with winter that year. Its sudden radiance startled us as we braced ourselves for the harsh winds and overcast skies of the dying season. Even in early March the wind that blew in from the sea was warm-breathed, and Judy and I unbuttoned our hooded plaid winter coats as we sat on the rock barriers at the esplanade and looked out at the cobalt-colored waves.

"My mother, in her infinite wisdom, has decided that there is a direct correlation between the weather and the war," Judy said. "And it is her considered opinion that an early spring means an early end to the war."

"Your mother has been known to be right before," I reminded her. Always I would think of Marvin's appearance at his parents' home on Thanksgiving Day as a minor miracle impelled by the sheer force of his mother's will.

"Ah, but she has also been known to be wrong," Judy replied unforgivingly. "Very wrong and very crazy." She stood up, shrugged out of her coat, and waved her red scarf into the wind.

"What are you doing?"

"I'm waving across the sea. To Europe. Do you think they can see me?"

"Oh, sure. They're all waving back. Can't you see my father?" I asked bitterly.

"Sharon. I'm sorry." She sat down beside me, put her arm on my shoulder. That was the closest she dared come in affectionate reassurance. We were of a generation of girls who danced with one another in finished basements and walked across broad Brooklyn avenues in matching club jackets with our arms about one another's waists, but in private moments we avoided touch or embrace. We were shy, wary of our own bodies.

"Your father will be all right."

"How do you know?" I challenged her harshly.

"I don't know. I just feel it." She removed her arm and looked out at the foaming waves.

"Yes. You're right, I'm sure you're right," I said, eager suddenly to believe her. Scavengers of hope clutch at the thinnest shred of optimism. ("Doesn't she look better today?" the daughter of a terminally ill mother will ask me. "I have the feeling the new chemo is working." I have learned to not loosen such talons of self-deception, to allow the families of my patients to believe whatever they like — although I myself do not deceive them — even as Judy allowed me my brief optimism that seaside afternoon when spring encroached upon winter.) "But since Aaron's letter, I worry about what would happen if my father was taken prisoner by the Germans. What if they find out that he's Jewish?"

"Sharon, stop being so morbid. Spring is almost here and I think this time my mother is right. The war is going to be over soon."

It was true that the war was being fought at an increased pace, that Allied forces everywhere had gathered momentum. We listened to the news with a fresh eagerness because the tide had turned, and each morning we anticipated a new victory, perhaps a final victory. Our hearts beat faster as we studied the news photo of the six GIs hoisting the American flag at Iwo Jima, and as February ended we celebrated the victory at Corregidor. American forces had crossed the Rhine and reached Dusseldorf. Germany itself was penetrated, and in Burma, British and Indian troops advanced along the Arakan coast, drove the Japanese from Tamandu and headed for Mandalay. The Allies were impatient. In his Fireside Chats, President Roosevelt was vibrant with a new urgency. Precision bombing was abandoned and Tokyo too was engulfed in a fire storm.

Julius spun his globe vigorously each evening as we listened to the news, his pencil darting from Europe to the South Seas to the heart of Japan.

"We'll show them — the *momzers*," he muttered. They were all *momzers* — bastards — the nations who had declared war on his beloved United States, who had killed his family. He, the gentlest and kindest of men, hissed epithets. "Nips. Damn Nazis." He never said Hitler's name aloud but referred to him in Hebrew as "He whose name should be totally erased from the annals of mankind."

Nachum Adler, handsome in his army uniform, came to say good-bye to us. Clean-shaven, he looked like the young man he must have been before the war aged him. He saw my worried expression and shook his finger at me warningly.

"I won't be gone long, Sharon. The war is almost over." He kissed me on the forehead. "Your father will be all right," he said. "I am sure of it."

I accepted his certainty as I had accepted Judy's. I grasped at the reassurances of others to balance my own ominous doubts.

"And you — will you be all right?" I whispered.

"Of course. I promise." We both laughed, at the absurdity of my question and of his guarantee.

I dreamed that night of my mother and father as I had seen them once in their airy Brookline bedroom, asleep in each other's arms. A siren sounded in the dream, a steady, threatening whistle piercing the silence. My mother remained motionless but my father jerked free of the linens and stood. He was tall and thin, his pale shoulders rounded by the long years spent at study tables and in laboratories, his gaze myopic and befuddled. His penis, swollen to a purple erectness, jutted forward like a huge accusing finger. The siren shrilled more loudly, insistently. My father groped desperately for a sheet. He covered his nakedness just as the window opened and one SS officer after another climbed over the sill and entered the room. The death's-head insignias on their caps glittered in the darkness and they marched toward him in booted feet that, wondrously, were as silent as moccasins on the polished floor. My father's mouth opened in a soundless shriek and he pulled the sheet tighter but the white linen disintegrated in his hand, became gossamer shreds that fell like spiderwebs about his ankles. His circumcised penis was revealed. The leading German officer pointed to it and blew a whistle, a silver whistle. I waited for its sharp shrill sound but heard instead a ringing — a telephone ringing again and again.

I jerked awake and sat up in bed, heard Lottie run barefoot down the hall to seize the black receiver, to shout a "hello" that vibrated with terror.

"Yes. Yes. This is the home of the family of Dr. Richard Grossberg. I am Lottie Lieberman, his sister-in-law."

I knotted the sheet about my fingers. I chewed my lip. An icy sweat coated my body but although I shivered with a sudden violence, I made no attempt to reach for a blanket or a bathrobe. I sat in the darkness, paralyzed with terror. The staircase door opened. My grandparents had heard the phone. They whispered anxious questions in Yiddish and Julius hushed them impatiently.

And then Lottie's voice was suddenly clear, as bell-like as when she recited Wordsworth.

"How wonderful of you to call, Lieutenant. We're so grateful to you. I'll tell Sharon. I can't tell you what this means to us. A safe journey. A speedy recovery." I heard the sound of Lottie hanging up the phone.

"He's all right!" Her joyous voice trilled through the house. "Richard. He's all right, Mama, Papa. That was a lieutenant from his unit. He was wounded and shipped home but he saw Richard only days ago. Richard gave him our number and asked him to call us. He called so late because he just arrived in New York and he leaves for the West Coast in an hour. Richard gave him letters for us and he'll mail those. Sharon! Sharon!"

She burst into my room, her face radiant beneath its mask of cold cream, and she embraced me, entangling me in the voluminous folds of her white flannel nightgown.

"That was a man who served with your father, who saw him less than a week ago. And he's all right. Richard is all right."

I rested my head against the soft cushion of her breasts and repeated her words.

"He's all right. He's all right." They became a mantra, a protective incantation, and I said them over and over because they would keep me safe from the dream; they gave lie to the phantasmagoria of my dark imaginings.

A new buoyancy sustained and energized me. I laughed aloud as I read the George Ade essays assigned by an earnest English teacher who announced that she wanted us to read something light to divert our attention from the war. Leatrice and Letitia looked up and rolled their eyes in disbelief. How could those of us with fathers and brothers in uniform forget the war even for a moment? They looked at me in amazement as my laughter exploded in the library, and chastened, I turned back to my book. But I did not begrudge myself those moments of merriment. Like the newly furled tender leaves on the trees, the overgrowth of yellow forsythia in the empty lots along Ocean Parkway, I was emerging from wintry dryness.

I went to the Sweet Shoppe with Judy and was relieved to see that redheaded Rozzy Lang, who did not acknowledge our presence, seemed both happy and reassuringly thin. Perhaps she, like myself, had worried needlessly, but had not been wise enough to remain silent. I congratulated myself on my luck and on my wisdom and paid for Judy's egg cream.

I volunteered to make posters for the Young Pioneers. JUSTICE FOR THE JEWS, I lettered extravagantly. FREE IMMIGRATION TO PALESTINE! Heidi and I went into Manhattan with Rosalie late at night and hung them on the wrought iron gates of the British consulate. We felt as daring as cinema heroines on clandestine espionage missions and we were disappointed that not a single newspaper mentioned the discovery of the posters.

I helped my grandfather prepare his victory garden, raking away the detritus of winter, filling bushel baskets with fallen leaves and branches, and pounding at the friable earth with a shovel to soften it. My grandfather, as always, wore his dark suit, a shirt and tie, his fedora, and an overcoat. Holding his scythe, he patrolled the small backyard, a white-haired and white-bearded gentleman farmer, cutting away at vines and overgrowth as he murmured softly to himself in Yiddish. Here he would plant tomatoes. Over there, carrots and radishes. He bought a lattice for the cucumber vines. He moved slowly, with great deliberation. My grandmother clucked angrily when he went inside after carefully removing clumps of earth from his high black shoes.

"Too much," she said reprovingly. She meant that he was an old man who had been warned about his health. Dr. Kaplan monitored his heart and prescribed gem-colored vitamins. Julius had purchased an ultraviolet lamp and urged my grandfather to sit beneath it. His wrinkled skin was milk white and paper thin. Blue veins bulged on the backs of his hands. He did not use the lamp, but occasionally as we worked together, he lifted his face toward the sun and stood immobile for a moment, his eyes closed. I did not know if he was simply reveling in the new warmth or praying.

"To make the garden helps me," he said.

It helped, I knew, to keep his mind off the news from Europe as each day more information about the concentration camps reached us, and doubts and fears became dread certainties. Nachum had told us of Terezin, and Aaron had described Auschwitz, but the map of Europe was dotted with places named Westerbork, Bergen-Belsen, Dachau, Treblinka — the list seemed endless to us and we knew that at each of these places, Jews had suffered and Jews had died. My grandfather's eyes teared when he read the Yiddish newspaper aloud to my grandmother, who twisted her apron in her hands and bit her lips. They wondered aloud about their relatives left behind in Europe — brothers and sisters, nieces and nephews, grandnieces and grandnephews — the cousins I would never know. There were the girls and women named Shaindel and Batya and Chaya, as I was called Shaindel and Beth was called Batya and Heidi was called Chaya. We were their secret sharers of a family past, but the European Batyas, Shaindels, and Chayas would almost certainly not share our future.

I tried not to think of them. I did not want them to interfere with my new happiness. My father was alive; at least, he had been alive only weeks ago. The letters mailed by the wounded lieutenant were full of his love and I read them over and over. He would come home and sweep me up in his arms. Oh, what a life we would build together.

In the rose-colored glow of my lamp, I wrote letters to my father, to Beth, to Nachum Adler. To each of them, I reiterated my newly discovered optimism. The war was speeding to an end and when victory was achieved the world would be changed forever. Already a blueprint was in place for a United Nations organization.

"The world will be a better place," I said to Peter during one of our long phone conversations. "There will never be a war again. We'll have learned too much."

"Oh, Sharon." I heard the warning in his voice but I cut him short. It had taken me too long to climb to this new height of hope; I would not risk being pulled back into the pessimism that had entrapped me for so long.

Samuel and Julius argued vigorously at a Sunday night delicatessen dinner about the imminent end of the war. They waved green wands of sour pickles for emphasis and drew golden diagrams of the European theater in mustard across their plates.

"By the first week of April the Krauts will surrender," Samuel said. "Already we've hit their bridges, their rail system, their cities. What do they have left? They tried to push the Reds back from the roads to Vienna and what happened? Their tanks got stuck in the mud. I say it's over by the beginning of April, maybe the middle of the month." He tossed a ten-dollar bill on the table. "I'll bet on it. Who'll match me?"

Lottie plucked up the money and returned it to her brother.

"No betting. You know I hate betting. Stop being such a know-it-all, Sammy."

"Don't speak to him like that. Have some respect. Samuel knows what he's talking about. All his customers — and some of them are very important people — ask for his opinion." Dolly's eyes glinted with anger. She tucked her white silk blouse into the waistband of her green skirt and glared at her husband's sister, who would never see Samuel as an adult, who thought of him still as the small boy who had whimpered in steerage and retched in the hallway toilet of their tenement apartment.

"Of course, Samuel has a right to his opinion." Leon, as always, was the peacemaker. Indifferent to power and recognition himself, he did not care who received it, but he could not bear harsh voices. "Who's saying he's wrong? But Hitler is unpredictable. He has a new submarine and they say it can reach our coast. And remember how he resisted at Budapest and now at Balaton. He's a maniac, and maniacs don't know from reality — they don't know when they're beaten. Even Churchill is worried that he'll go on fighting after he's already beaten."

"Churchill told you this himself?" Samuel asked. "Now it's not the Big Three but the Big Four. Churchill, Roosevelt, Stalin, and Leon Fenster."

"*Nu*. Enough." Julius glared at his brothers-in-law. "The war will be over when it's over. April. May. Soon. But meanwhile we have finally a letter from HIAS. They have lists, names from the International Red Cross. From the Russians."

"What sort of lists? What names?" Edna's voice was wary. She worked closely with Emanuel Weiner on rescue committees and she understood what such lists might reveal.

"Names of survivors. Names of the dead," Julius said flatly. "We've asked for such lists. We asked HIAS. They're not complete. It's a drop in the bucket, just a beginning. But it's something."

"They're probably full of errors," Edna persisted.

"Maybe. But Papa wants to see them." Julius turned to my grandfather, who nodded.

"If maybe someone is alive, someone from our family, we could do something," Julius continued. "Meyer Liebowitz went to the HIAS office. He found the name of his niece on the list. She survived Auschwitz. The Russians sent her to a displaced-persons camp and now he is getting papers to bring her here."

"So someone has to go to the HIAS office with Mama and Papa," Edna said. She had surrendered easily.

"Tomorrow," my grandfather said. "We want to go tomorrow." He looked around the table at his children and grandchildren.

"Tomorrow. Tomorrow I have to do the payroll," Lottie said worriedly.

"Monday is our busiest day." Edna closed her eyes, perhaps visualizing her desk in the Long Island City office piled high with invoices, requisitions, correspondence, and hearing Emanuel Weiner calling loudly for her.

"I have a shipment of records coming in the afternoon." Leon crumbled a slice of rye bread and swept the crumbs beneath a paper napkin. "Some hard-to-get seventy-eights. I have to check the shipment, sign for them."

"What about you, Dolly?" Samuel turned to his wife.

"Tomorrow's my day at the ration board. And then I have my hair appointment."

"Tomorrow's Monday," I said. "My last class is over at one-thirty. I can go to the HIAS office with Buba and Zeidey. And I want to." It was true. I wanted to shift the balance, to become the protector rather than the protected. I wanted to be recognized as a responsible young adult who could be relied on to guide my elderly grandparents through the maze of subways and the confusion of city streets.

"Sharon does know her way around the city," Lottie said.

"All right, then. That's settled." Julius looked at me gratefully and Lottie poured me a cup of tea.

My grandparents were ready and waiting for me when I arrived home from school the next day. They were dressed as they dressed for synagogue, as they had dressed on Election Day. My grandmother wore her fur-collared black coat and the black hat threaded with red cherries which was held in place on her white hair with an obsidian hat pin. My grandfather had brushed his overcoat and his homburg. Twice before we left the house he checked the pockets of his coat to make certain that his two large white handkerchiefs were in place and to count the change he would need for our journey, the three nickels for the bus to Sheepshead Bay station and the three nickels for the subway.

Julius had written the travel instructions out and I followed
them carefully, maneuvering my grandparents onto the Brighton
Express, finding them a seat together on a wicker bench, and selecting a seat for myself diagonally opposite so that I could smile at
them reassuringly as I turned the pages of *The Mill on the Floss*.

I looked up now and again as the train racketed its way
through Brooklyn and into Manhattan and watched them as they
sat side by side, dignified and silent, their hands clasped. If
they had been strangers to me, I would have admired them. But
they were my grandparents and my heart burst with love and pity.

We changed trains at Union Square and I stood between them
wearing my hooded red cape. Red Riding Hood guiding her grandparents through the threatening urban forest.

"Here, Buba," I said. "This way."

"Watch for the wide step," I told my grandfather as we exited the train because his eyes were weak and even the thick-lensed
glasses did not completely rectify his vision.

The HIAS office in lower Manhattan was overheated and
shabby. I motioned my grandparents to the folding chairs set
against the wall and I took my place on the line. They sat patiently
between a bald man who clutched a German-language newspaper
and an elderly woman who wore an unbuttoned gray raincoat
over her flowered housedress. Pink patches of scalp shone through
her thinning silver hair and her eyes were red, as though she had
been weeping for days. The line moved slowly. The woman at the
reception desk looked at her watch as each new applicant approached her. Wearily, she addressed their queries, studied the papers they held out to her, and motioned them to one office or
another, rising slightly to direct them.

"There you will find out about visas."

"In that office they will advise you about employment."

"Mr. Wallenstein will tell you about an apartment."

Everyone who entered that office was in search — in search
of relatives, of jobs, of housing, in search of reassurance.

The girl ahead of me spoke softly, pointing to her grandmother, the old woman in the flowered housedress. They had
heard that there were lists of names, the girl said almost in a whis-

per. From the camps. She choked on the word. Her grandmother was in search of her brothers who had not been heard from since their deportation from Krakow in 1940. Perhaps their names were on the list?

The receptionist pursed her lips.

"The lists are incomplete," she warned. "It's possible that they're filled with mistakes. I have to warn you. People go through the lists. They find a name. They get upset. Even hysterical. It's not always healthy."

"My grandmother won't get hysterical," the girl promised.

The old woman swayed from side to side, grimaced, clasped and unclasped her fingers. My grandmother inched away, pitying and disapproving.

"All right."

Reluctantly, the receptionist removed a cumbersome folder from the drawer, handed it to the girl, and directed her to a conference room. The girl guided her grandmother. I watched as she helped her out of the gray raincoat, as they sat side by side at a battered table.

I was more direct, more insistent.

"I want to see the lists of names the Russians compiled at Auschwitz. Mr. Weiner of Weiner Bakeries, who is a contributor to HIAS, suggested that we come. My grandparents are searching for news of their relatives — brothers and sisters. Mr. Weiner thought that the lists would be helpful. He is a close friend of our family's." I drew on the twin reins of connections and compassion, playing to both her snobbery and her sympathy. The war had initiated me into a manipulative sophistication that would serve me all my life. I had listened to Edna alternately cajole and threaten the secretaries of congressmen. ("It is a matter of great interest to Mr. Weiner. He will be very disappointed if his wishes are ignored. He will be extremely appreciative if you could accommodate him.")

"I have only two copies of the lists and I've just given one to the young lady who was ahead of you."

"Then you can give me the other list. Mr. Weiner assured me that there would be no difficulty." The lie fell smoothly from my lips. Emanuel Weiner was indeed a contributor to HIAS but he had no idea that we would be visiting that organization's office.

"Very well." She had taken the measure of my cherry red cape, my polished saddle oxfords, my grandparents' carefully brushed dark coats. She handed me the folder and directed us to the conference room where the girl and her grandmother sat huddled over the table.

We took our seats at the other table, carefully ignoring the old woman, who leaned forward tensely and listened to the names her granddaughter read out.

" 'Hoffmeyer, Rachmiel. Hoffmeyer, David.' "

"No. It has to be Hoffmeyer, Eli, and Hoffmeyer, Yosef. Look for those names. You didn't find them?"

"Not yet." The girl was very patient. She spoke to her grandmother with the forbearance I often detected in Judy Bergman's voice when she spoke to her mother. Those who love the half-mad are ever vigilant, ever wary.

My grandfather handed me a folded piece of paper. I stared at the names Lottie had copied out so carefully and I opened the folder.

The roster was separated into towns of origin, and the names were alphabetized. Occasionally there was a listing of the individual's age. Each name was marked with a symbol: an asterisk, a check, or a small circle. The code was explained. An asterisk signified death, a check meant survival, and a circle indicated the name had been included in a file with no reference to the inmate's fate. Beneath the explanation of the code was a note stating that HIAS had received the list in an unorthodox fashion and could not vouch for its accuracy. It was being made available to the public for humanitarian reasons.

The room was very warm and I removed my cape but my grandparents only unbuttoned their dark coats. I read aloud from the paper my grandfather had handed me.

" 'Grodno.' " Four names. My grandmother's sister and her husband. Her brother and his wife. Their children would be listed with them.

I ran my finger down the Grodno listing.

"No. Their names aren't here," I said. "Not even a name that sounds like them." (The girl, in despair, now read out the names of the Hoffmeyers, and as her voice rose and fell, her grandmother shook her head, pounded her cheeks with her fists, and moaned, "Lost. Forever lost.")

"What does it mean, that their names aren't there?" my grandmother asked.

"That they weren't at Auschwitz. That they were sent to another camp. Or maybe not to any camp. Maybe they went into hiding or maybe someone hid them." Already we were hearing stories of Polish Jews who had survived in forests, who had joined bands of partisans, who had been hidden on farms or in basements and attics.

"Now Radom," my grandfather said, and these names he read aloud. " 'Lieberman, Anshel and Menachem. Kossoffsky, Fanya and Chaim.' " They were Julius's brothers and his sister and her husband.

I flipped to Radom. The listing was long and there were many Liebermans. I concentrated hard, the small typewritten names dancing before my eyes, the asterisks and checks colliding as I struggled for focus.

The girl and her grandmother rose to leave. The girl searched in the pocket of the gray raincoat for a plaid wool kerchief which she tied about her grandmother's thin hair, knotting it loosely at the chin.

"You shouldn't catch cold, Buba," she said.

"Let me catch cold. Let me die." The old woman slumped like a rag doll, her head askew, her arms hanging loosely. Her voice was faint but the words were clear. They left the room, closing the door softly behind them.

"No Anshel Lieberman. No Menachem Lieberman," I said and turned to the Kossoffskys. There was no listing at all for that name.

"Bialystok," my grandfather said. He had saved his native town for last. The names of his brothers and sister, his nieces and nephews trembled on his tongue. "Usher and Zalman Schiff. Perele and Yehuda Meyerowitz. Levi Meyerowitz. Esther Hurwitz."

He had spoken to me often of his sister, Perele. She was the one he loved the best, whose picture he kept in his watchcase. A serious, dark-eyed woman, her expression serene, her full mouth curled into a half-smile. She was a clever woman who loved books. ("Like you, Shaindel. She hid in the doorway when the *melamed* came to teach me and my brothers. She learned to read and write.") A generous woman. She had emptied her purse and had given my grandparents the money they needed to buy steamship tickets for Lottie and Samuel. Yehuda, her husband, had not protested. She was a smart businesswoman and would earn it back. And she was beautiful, her curling hair thick and dark, her skin during the brief summer months like burnished gold. My grandfather had stared hard at me as I came dancing toward him at the craft fair in Woodstock; later, he told me that he had thought it was his sister, Perele, whom he had seen, that it was her laughter that he had heard.

Usher and Zalman Schiff were not listed. I found Esther Hurwitz's name, a check next to it. Perele's daughter had survived. Like Meyer Liebowitz's niece, she could be traced, visas and affidavits arranged. Levi Meyerowitz, Perele's son, had also survived.

"They're all right, Zeidey," I said. "Perele's children are all right."

"But my brothers?"

"Their names aren't here. That could mean anything." But we all knew that it meant they were dead. They were old men, both of them older than my grandfather.

"Perele's name? Look for it. She was younger than me. Ten years younger. And she never looked her age. When she married she looked like a small child. 'A baby has become a bride,' they said. So maybe she is all right. Read carefully."

"There are so many Meyerowitzes," I said.

I saw myself sitting in this barren room for endless hours, reading name after name, a litany of sufferers, letters and symbols blinding me, blurring my vision. There a few Yehuda Meyerowitzes, but there was a single listing on one line for both Perele and Yehuda Meyerowitz. I held my breath. The names were marked by a jet asterisk. Perele and Yehuda Meyerowitz were both dead and they had died in Auschwitz. The words of Aaron's letter echoed in memory: *The Germans blew up the last of the camp's five gas chambers and crematoria.* They had been gassed, their bodies burned. Nausea dizzied me. Perele, who as a girl had been enough like me to be my twin, had been asphyxiated by gas, her body incinerated. I stared at my own trembling fingers, imagined them aflame, tapering into cinders.

"What does it say, Shaindel?" my grandmother asked. She had seen my face and would not be deceived.

"Perele and Yehuda are dead." My tone was flat but tears spilled down my cheeks, and my grandfather moved toward me, closed the file, and encircled me in his arms. His white beard brushed my forehead and I thought that if I reached up and touched his face it would be awash with his sorrow. But when I stood and looked at him, I saw that his eyes were dry; sadness froze his features into the uncomprehending mask of agony peculiar to the newly bereaved.

Slowly, as if in a dream, we made our way back to the reception area. I returned the folder to the receptionist.

"Oh, did you find . . . ?" she began, but she saw our faces and she did not continue. Wordlessly, she returned the folder to the drawer. Julius would come another day to find out what would have to be done to redeem Perele's children from the kingdom of the damned.

We returned as we had come but it was rush hour now and we fought our way into the subway, onto the train. Two sailors gave their seats to my grandparents. My grandmother and I thanked them but my grandfather stared straight ahead, as though hypnotized by his grief. I grasped a strap and struggled for balance as I read the headlines of other people's newspapers. MONTY'S MOONLIGHT BLINDS KRAUTS, the *New York Post* shouted cryptically. I read over someone's shoulder and learned that "Monty's moonlight" was the tank-borne searchlights carried by Canadian and British forces when they crossed the Rhine. The light had blinded the defending Germans and ensured the Allies' victory.

But I took no joy in that victory. On that afternoon, it seemed that Germany had been victorious over my family. Alfred was dead. Perele was dead. Other relatives in Europe were still unaccounted for. My father was still in danger. My joy had been premature.

It was my grandmother who opened the door to their apartment and led my grandfather in, as though he had suddenly gone blind. She helped him off with his coat and loosened his tie. She put the kettle on to boil but he did not sit down. Instead he rummaged in a kitchen cabinet and found a Yahrzeit candle, the white wax squat in the square-shaped glass. He lit it and we stared at the small brave flame that flickered wildly against the glass. My grandmother's lips moved; her prayer was a mournful assurance. "Perele." Her dead sister-in-law's name was barely audible.

My grandfather took up a large kitchen knife and moved it toward his body.

"Zeidey!" My voice trembled with fear but he lifted the knife and cut a deep rent in his tie. Then he covered his face with his hand and recited the Kaddish, his voice steady but thick with sorrow.

"*Yisgadal v'yiskadash* — magnified and sanctified be Thy name . . ."

"Amen," my grandmother whispered, and my grandfather swayed slightly and fell heavily to the floor, his fingers curled about the newly rent tie as though that symbol of grief might yet support him. His eyes were closed and spittle foamed at his lips.

"Velvel!" My grandmother stooped beside him and shouted his name, and it was her avian shriek of terror and despair that greeted Lottie and Julius as they opened the door.

22

"Will he die?" Heidi asked.

We sat side by side on a wooden bench in the waiting room of Coney Island Hospital, a sleeping Anna propped between us. We waited for Dina, whose turn it was to sit beside her father's bed, her hand upon his, her fingers caressing the bulging blue veins, the callused fingers.

"No. He won't die," I said and I was surprised by the certainty of my own voice. "Dr. Kaplan says he's improving every day."

My grandfather had suffered a stroke, and I thought the word well chosen. He had indeed been struck down by grief. Supine on the high white hospital bed, he stared up at the ceiling, the left side of his face twisted downward, his lips contorted, his eyelid sagging. The left side of his body was weakened, although during the days that had passed since his collapse, movement had returned. He bent his ankle, squeezed our hands in reply to softly spoken commands. Most important of all, he talked, the words struggling through his lips in a jumble of muffled sounds that we learned to recognize.

"Malka." He spoke my grandmother's name clearly and we took this as a good sign, a validation of Dr. Kaplan's optimistic prediction.

"He will recover," Dr. Kaplan assured us. "It was a minor episode."

It did not seem minor to us. We saw it as massive, overwhelming. We wakened in the night, our throats dry, our bodies tense with terror. Lottie and I each glided downstairs in our nightgowns to check on my grandmother, to listen to the whistle of her night breath and watch the silver streak of moonlight move across her long white braid as she lay sleeping. Dina, who had driven like a madwoman from Woodstock the night of my grandfather's collapse, made tea for herself at three in the morning and wordlessly poured another cup for Julius when he shuffled into the kitchen in his pajamas. We spoke little during those nocturnal meetings; we hesitated to reveal our fears and we had no reassurances to offer one another.

It was agreed that Dina and Anna would stay until my grandfather was released from the hospital.

"What about your job?" Edna had asked worriedly. She carried her own work with her wherever she went. As she waited to consult with doctors, she shuffled through her files, scrawled answers to correspondence, worried her way through invoices and inventory lists. Work was her obsession, her barrier against anguish.

"They'll manage. Or they won't manage," Dina replied wearily. "This is where I belong."

I envied her that sense of belonging. I myself often felt awkward, in the way. I brushed away Lottie's questions about school, about the meetings of the Young Pioneers. It did not seem fair that she had to worry about me. I was not an integral part of the household. And then at once I chastised myself for my ingratitude, for my self-absorption, and wakened as dawn silvered the sky to cut oranges in half and squeeze them vigorously for our breakfast juice, a domestic penance of a kind.

"You're up too early, Shaindel."

How soundlessly my little grandmother had mounted the

stairs. We stood together at the front window and watched the milkman make his rounds, the glass bottles clinking musically in his metal holder.

"Did you know that in Bialystok your great-grandfather had a small dairy? Your grandfather worked there with Perele and his brothers. I used to tease him and tell him that his skin smelled of butter. Such a sweetness on his skin."

Her voice was dreamy, as though she were a young bride still and not a woman bent with age whose husband lay in a hospital bed.

"No," I replied. "I didn't know that." I thought of all the other things I did not know, the secrets of a vanished life in a vanished world. If my grandfather recovered — no, *when* he recovered, I swiftly corrected myself — I would ask him to tell me the stories of the life that had been his.

I went to the hospital every afternoon after school. I took comfort from the large building with its ambience of urgency, its aromas of disinfectant and medications, its busy white-clad staff hurrying down corridors. This was my father's world, the world that would be mine one day. I felt closer to him and to my own future as I listened to the cryptic messages that blared forth on the public address system and watched patients on gurneys being moved from one floor to another. My grandmother went home then to rest and I sat in the straight high-backed bedside chair and read the afternoon newspaper aloud to my grandfather. I placed my hand on his and read him the dispatch that described the American strike into the Ruhr valley, the overrunning of the jet airfields in Darmstadt and Frankfurt.

It seemed to me that my grandfather stirred slightly when I read from the *PM* about Churchill's flight across the Rhine, that he blinked as I repeated the prime minister's thrilling promise. Even the chattering tiny woman in black visiting her emaciated husband in the neighboring bed fell silent as I read.

" 'The goal is not long to be denied to those who have come so far and fought so well under proud and faithful leadership. Forward all, on wings of flame, to final victory!' "

My own voice had risen loud and clear, and I turned as a

scattering of applause came from the doorway, where a group of doctors and nurses had gathered to listen to me. I turned back to my grandfather and felt his weakened left hand grip my own with a new strength.

" 'Forward all, on wings of flame, to final victory!' " Lottie intoned the words that night as we did the dishes. Churchill's message was poetry to her and we were all invigorated with new hope.

"How was he?" I asked Dina when she joined Heidi and me in the hospital's waiting room.

"Better. His speech is clearer. The aphasia seems to be diminishing."

"That's wonderful." I was grateful to Dina for using technical language and speaking to me in the language of the adult world.

She shifted Anna, who slept peacefully, onto her lap and smoothed the baby's auburn ringlets.

"What did he say?" I asked.

"He asked if we had begun to prepare for Passover. At least, that's what I made out."

"Passover," I repeated dully. My mother had been alive last Passover. Julius had carried her to the seder table and she had sat propped up by snowy bed pillows, her eyes glinting feverishly and her skin parchment pale. She had been too weak to eat but she had sipped the wine and I had prayed that it would somehow, miraculously and mysteriously, redden her blood, do scarlet battle with the leukocytes that had invaded her system. I imagined her seat empty this year, awaiting her ghost, as the full cup of wine at the table's center awaited the prophet Elijah. I remembered how my mother had leaned perilously forward when the door was opened, according to tradition, to admit the prophet. "Will he come soon?" she had whispered and our hearts turned as we realized that it was my father for whom she waited, the husband who wrote her tender letters from unnamed battlefields and whom she would never see again.

"Maybe we ought to pass our Passover this year," I said and Dina smiled wryly.

"Sometimes I wish I could pass over everything." She pressed her cheek lightly against Anna's head.

"Do you miss him a lot?"

"I miss him. We were together for a long time," she replied.

I realized that she spoke of Robert while I had meant Nachum Adler, and I looked at her in surprise.

"I think we ought to invite Peter and Karen to come for the seder," she said, as though to intercept my next question, to divert me from her own mood, her own dilemma.

"Why?" I asked coolly, although my cheeks blazed. With the egocentricity of adolescence, I wondered how much Dina knew, how much she had guessed.

"Because they're your friends and we could do with some lightening up around here," she replied and I realized that she knew nothing, had not guessed at anything.

"Well, maybe," I agreed grudgingly. I wanted to see Peter and I was afraid to see him.

"I could drive them down," she offered. "Although usually the Bassens come to New York for the holiday."

"We'll see."

Passover came at the end of March and much could happen before then. My grandfather could get better or he could get worse. He might die. Telegrams and letters altering the course of all our lives might yet arrive.

"Maybe Zeidey will be home from the hospital for the seder," Heidi said hopefully.

I shrugged.

"Who knows? It's almost two weeks away. It could happen. It might happen."

"Anything can happen," Dina said and she lifted Anna, who woke just then and looked at us sleepily, rubbing her eyes. She was a child accustomed to waking in unfamiliar places and she smiled enchantingly at a young coastguardsman, who grinned back at her and went to the information desk yet again to inquire about the condition of his wife.

We prepared for Passover, energized by my grandfather's

edict. Every cabinet was emptied and cleaned. We washed the Passover dishes and cleaned the silver. Laverta, the black cleaning woman who came to help Lottie once a week, came every day and sang as she worked. " 'Praise the Lord and pass the ammunition.' " Her voice rang out as she washed the windows, and passersby looked up, took note of the blue-star banners, and smiled approvingly, sympathetically.

Beth called from Arizona. She would be coming home.

"I may have to sit up or even stand the whole way east," she said. "Servicemen and their wives and children are getting priority."

"Tell them you're a serviceman's widow," I said daringly.

"Sharon, really." She did not laugh but neither did she reprove me and I took that as a sign that she was inching toward recovery.

"How is Zeidey?" she asked.

"He grows stronger every day."

I did not tell Beth that sometimes when I sat beside him he wept without warning. I wiped the teardrops from the deeply carved runnels of his cheeks with my handkerchief. Now, after years of observing patients' reactions, I understand that he was fearful, overwhelmed by the surprise assault on his mortality.

"Will Perele's Esther come soon?" he asked and I understood that he feared that he would die without seeing his sister's daughter.

"They are working on it," I said. Julius had spoken to the immigration lawyers, to officials at HIAS. Emanuel Weiner had badgered congressmen, sent a special-delivery letter to Herbert Lehman, the director of the United Nations' Relief and Rehabilitation Agency.

"And Aaron?"

"We had another letter from Aaron. He thinks he'll be posted to London," I said. He would be safe there. The V2 bombings had ended and it was said that children were being returned to the city from evacuation areas in the English countryside.

"He should come home. They should send him home," the old man said plaintively.

"Soon, Zeidey, soon."

I was both hurt and relieved that he had not asked about my father. I did not want to tell him that there had been no letter from him since those that had been mailed from the States.

Dina returned to Woodstock the day after my grandfather came home from the hospital. The neighbors had stood outside and watched as we helped him into the house, just as they had watched Beth descend the stairs in her wedding dress. It was a sense of shared beneficence that drew them to their porches to watch my grandfather's slow progress, using the walker that he had learned to negotiate with a skill that surprised the physical therapist.

"He has such will," she had said admiringly.

"Yes," I agreed. He had willed himself to survive the war so he could welcome the daughter of the sister who had been lost to him, and see his grandson's smile once again.

Mrs. Calderazzo, wearing the black garments of her endless mourning, came to see my grandfather, carrying a bundle of forsythia.

"Get well, Mr. Schiff," she said. "You have to work on your garden."

"My garden," he repeated sadly and clenched and un-clenched a pink Spalding ball in his left hand as the therapist had instructed him.

"You think because a person gets sick a garden stops grow-ing." She shook her flowers at him. They had not ceased to blos-som although her Johnny, who had set the forsythia bushes into the friable Brooklyn earth, had died. Within two months she would observe the anniversary of his death and I would light my first Yahrzeit memorial candle for my mother. I felt strangely be-trayed. D Day was supposed to have heralded the end of the war but we were still aloft on Churchill's "wings of flame," flying and flying to that elusive "final victory."

When Peter called that night, I invited him to the seder.

"And Karen too," I added.

"Great," he said. "I'll tell her." I heard the commingling of disappointment and acceptance in his voice. We remained caring friends but we could not step back across the weeks and months and cancel out all that we had said, all that we had done. We acknowledged our own vulnerability, and miraculously, as I see it after all these years, we had the wisdom to be wary of our youthful tenderness.

We intensified our cleaning efforts, scouring and polishing, rolling up carpets and taking down draperies. We cleaned in celebration and anticipation. We celebrated the onset of spring and my grandfather's homecoming; we anticipated the peace and freedom that might coincide with the festival of peace and freedom.

Heidi and I helped my grandmother. We washed down the walls, emptied and cleaned every drawer, covered the counters with oilcloth. We scrubbed ourselves into a new season, and like Laverta, we sang and smiled at our reflections in the newly sparkling windows. The world was chaotic. We were powerless against the vagaries of war, but we could subdue dirt and grime, we could create order in those pleasant rooms where our grandparents would live out the last days of their lives.

Lottie and Edna shared the cooking, using both Lottie's kitchen and my grandmother's, all of us scurrying up and down the stairway with baskets of vegetables and covered pots. For days before the seder, the aroma of roasting chickens and fragrant sponge cakes filled the house, and the bright vegetables of spring covered the counter. My grandmother beat egg whites into foamy hillocks, and Lottie grated horseradish as tears ran down her cheeks and poetry streamed from her lips.

" 'Sweet spring, full of sweet days and roses,' " she cried out and segued swiftly from George Herbert into the Song of Songs. " 'The winter is past, the rain is over and gone. The flowers appear on the earth.' "

" 'And the time of the singing of birds is come.' " Beth stood in the doorway, a smiling golden-skinned Beth. We rushed toward her. She looked wonderful but I saw that her eyes were still shadowed by pain and loss.

And birds did sing the morning of the seder. They chirped in the branches of the red maple that stood in the front garden, caroled happily from the crown of the ailanthus tree. We took their songs for a sign and hummed as we set the table. Clearly, we were poised at the edge of a new beginning.

The silver and crystal sparkled on the snowy white cloth. We kept the radio on and listened to it above the clatter of cutlery, cheering softly as H. V. Kaltenborn announced that American troops had captured Frankfurt and that Soviet troops were only fifty miles from Vienna.

My grandmother filled the embroidered matzoh covers. The royal blue one had been made by Perele as a leave-taking gift for my grandparents, and the white one, decorated with doves and apples, was my mother's handiwork. My grandmother passed her fingers across the intricate satin stitching, mended a frayed fringe, then set them in place. The needlework of the dead women declared their presence at our table, their enduring lives in memory.

At sundown, the women blessed candles. Lottie's outstretched arms encircled the newly kindled flames. Like Edna and my grandmother, she covered her eyes with her hands as she murmured the blessings, but when her mother and her sister completed the benediction and turned to embrace each other, Lottie's eyes were still closed and her lips still moved in silent prayer. She prayed for Aaron, I knew.

I blessed candles for the first time that seder night, using the small brass candlesticks that had belonged to my mother. I prayed for my father and for Aaron, and because he had no one else to pray for him, for Nachum Adler. The flames kissed my fingers with their warmth as I whispered the final prayer of thanks to God for His sustenance and preservation. But the words were clumsy upon my tongue as I thought of all those who had not been sustained, whose lives had not been preserved.

Beth watched me, her hand resting on the strawberry-colored birthmark veiled by her soft golden hair. She did not bless candles nor did anyone ask her to. This was not her year to praise a compassionate God.

Our guests arrived, their hair dampened by the light rain that had begun at sunset, their voices determinedly gay. The war would not mute their celebration of the holiday.

Emanuel Weiner and his wife brought bottles of wine, a huge box of chocolates. He took my grandfather's weakened left hand into his own. "You will be all right," he boomed authoritatively, as though his wealth and power could will recovery and strength.

My grandfather nodded with acquiescent dignity.

The Bergmans, whom Lottie had invited when I told her that they would be spending the seder night alone, brought a floral arrangement of red, white, and blue carnations rimmed with small paper American and Jewish flags. Judy grinned when she handed it to me. We had walked past the florist shop on Brighton Beach Avenue and seen such arrangements displayed.

"Who would buy that?" I had asked.

"Now you know," Judy said and we giggled as I placed it at the center of the table, next to the tall silver cup of Elijah which Julius had brought from Europe. We were still laughing when Karen and Peter arrived, their faces rain-streaked because they had walked from Sheepshead Bay station.

"But why didn't you drive down with Dina?" I asked when I had taken their wet coats and given them towels, but before they could answer there was yet another knock on the door and I hurried to open it. Samuel and Dolly, then Leon and Bernie rushed in, puddling the vestibule with their furled umbrellas, apologetic about their lateness.

"We should start the seder." Lottie glanced nervously at the clock. "I don't want Papa to get too tired."

"We must wait for Dina."

But even as Julius spoke the front door opened and Dina came in, her copper-colored hair draping the shoulders of her kelly green raincoat, her face flushed above the huge spray of lilacs that always bloomed early in her Woodstock garden. Robert stood behind her, elegantly casual in his belted trench coat and plaid scarf, his handsome face wreathed in a defiant smile. He carried Anna, whose head rested on his shoulder, and he leaned forward slightly as though his daughter were a peace offering extended to our family so that we would forgive him and make him welcome. No one moved or spoke for a brief moment and then Leon moved forward, kissed Dina on the cheek, and shook Robert's hand.

"It's good to see you and your beautiful daughter," he said. "Give me those wet coats."

Dina and Robert looked at him gratefully and moved into the living room, toward a suddenly effusive wave of greetings.

"Look at the baby's dress. Where did you find it, Dina?" Edna and Lottie fingered Anna's gingham frock.

"Was there much traffic from Woodstock?" Samuel asked.

"Such a beautiful dress, Dina," Dolly gushed.

They covered the awkwardness of the moment with a flurry of small talk. Their hypocrisy astounded me. Edna took Anna from Robert and asked him about his current exhibit as though they had spoken only recently. I was enraged that both Edna and Dolly kissed him, that even my grandmother accepted his embrace, although she held her small body rigid beneath his touch.

"How can they?" I hissed to Beth.

She shrugged.

"Things change, Sharon. People start over. They make their peace with whatever happened and they move on." Sadness tinged her words and my heart turned. My cousin's quiet wisdom was hard-gained.

"Did you know?" I asked Karen and Peter. We stood in the hallway as Dina and Robert circled the living room.

"He came back about a week ago," Peter said. "He stopped by to see our folks and a couple of days later Karen saw him in the village. We didn't say anything because we didn't know how long he'd be staying, or if it meant anything. He'd come to the house before to spend time with Anna."

"But two nights ago we saw them walking through the apple orchard. They were holding hands and she was laughing. Robert could always make her laugh." Karen spoke very softly. "Then last night she called and said that she knew she had promised us a ride down but her car might be a little crowded, so of course we said we'd take the bus. And that was when we knew she would be bringing him to the seder. Look, Sharon, maybe this time things will work out for them. Randy and Franchesca sold their Woodstock house. They're moving to California."

I shook my head.

"That won't matter," I said and about that I was both right and wrong.

We took our seats at the extended table. The large armchair, its seat and back covered by high down pillows that had supported my mother the previous year, was given to Anna. Her flame-colored hair was bright against the white counterpane, her chubby arms and legs rosy, rubbed dry of the rain. I remembered my mother's stick-thin arms, the skin threaded with lapis needle pricks, against the white linen. She had turned the pages of the Hagaddah but her eyes were fixed feverishly on my face, as though she would memorize my every frown and smile. I know now that the dying harvest their memories with intense zeal, gobbling up moments of intimacy with the greedy desperation of those who know that soon, too soon, the feast will be over. But I was very young on that seder night and my mother's feverish gaze filled me with annoyance, and that annoyance, in turn, filled me with guilt.

Small Anna, still unborn on that night when I cut my mother's food into bite-size pieces and recoiled, oh so imperceptibly, from the touch of her bony fingers, cooed sweetly from her pillowed perch.

" 'Why is this night different from all other nights?' " Bernie bellowed out the four questions which introduce the Passover story and we waited for Julius to begin the reading of the Hagaddah. But Julius remained silent and it was my grandfather, his face bright with effort, who began reading.

" 'We were slaves unto Pharaoh in Egypt . . .' "

The words were muffled but they were recognizable and we listened with rapt attention as he chanted them: it was a hymn of victory that was being sung at our seder table. We took up the recitation then, as had been our custom, each of us reading a section or singing in unison. We read in Hebrew and in English, and Emanuel Weiner lifted his wineglass high and read his verse first in English and then in German.

" 'Not only has one man risen up against us to destroy us, but in every generation, men rise up against us to destroy us. But the Holy One, blessed be He, delivers us from their hands.' "

We were silent then, thinking of Adolf Hitler, who had risen up against our own generation and who had not yet been destroyed. Lottie gripped her book and bit her lips. Her eyes flew to the two blue-star banners that hung in our front window, one for Aaron and one for my father.

Julius placed his hand on his wife's shoulder. When his turn to read came, his voice was verberent.

" 'The Lord brought us out of Egypt with a mighty hand and with an outstretched arm and with great terror and with signs and with wonders.' "

He looked at Lottie gravely, begging her to believe that Aaron would be brought out of Europe. They had no need for signs and wonders. History was on our side. The war was almost over. But Lottie's eyes remained downcast and I understood that she had reached one of those moments of darkness familiar to all of us who had for so long been sustained by only the faintest glimmers of hope. I did not understand then, nor can I explain now, why the blackness of despair enveloped us at particular moments. But I sensed Lottie's mood as surely as if it had been my own. Leon recited the ten plagues, and Lottie's face was bleached of all color as he intoned the last of the punishments — the slaying of the first-born.

It was a relief, then, when the reading of the first section of the Hagaddah was concluded and we began to serve the meal. The food and the cacophonous table talk banished the melancholy.

"This is wonderful," Peter said.

He looked up and down the long table, watching the animated faces, listening to the rapid-fire conversations punctuated by the passing of platters, the clatter of silver and china. Julius circled the table, refilling the wineglasses.

Anna slept peacefully amid the noise and movement and I remembered that my mother had fallen asleep a year ago, halfway through the meal, and I had wept when Samuel lifted her in his arms and carried her back to her room.

Emanuel Weiner leaned across the table.

"Have you had any success in your inquiries about your cousin?" he asked Julius.

"Not yet." Julius kept his voice low. He did not want to upset my grandfather.

"All the relief agencies have their hands full now." Emanuel Weiner crumbled a piece of matzoh into his soup. "They're trying to monitor the commissions taking testimony in Poland about the camps."

"The Russians will document everything," Robert said. "Depend on it."

"Oh, sure. We can really rely on Uncle Joe Stalin," Leon retorted bitterly. "He certainly protected Chaim Hirszman."

The story of Chaim Hirszman was familiar to all of us. Edward R. Murrow had related it in one of his famous "Minutes in Time" and Lottie had wept as she listened. Chaim Hirszman had been one of only two survivors of the Belzec death camp. He had been called to give testimony in Lublin but as he left the commission of inquiry he was murdered by Polish anti-Semites.

"Polish Fascists killed Hirszman," Robert said. "The death squads always come from the right."

"And your Communist brothers didn't protect him. They're too busy rounding up Polish Jews and sending them to Siberia."

My uncles slipped easily back into their familiar ideological postures. They bickered as though there had been no interval of anger and silence, as though Dina and Robert had never been separated. I recognized then how fissures in families can be so easily and superficially mended. Much could be forgotten but very little would ever be forgiven.

Dina smiled as though the argument had somehow reassured her. She touched Anna's bright hair, brushed her fingers across Robert's hand. And he, in turn, trained his brilliant smile on her, put his arm around her shoulders and toyed with her pale blue chiffon scarf. I did not see his casual embrace as a gesture of affection but rather as a statement of claim, and I stared angrily at my aunt. At that moment I despised her for what I discerned as her weakness. It was not until many years later that I realized I should have admired her for her strength.

"Have you heard from your father, Sharon?" Robert asked as I leaned over to clear away the dishes.

"About three weeks ago. Someone from his unit brought some letters and mailed them stateside. But I'm sure he's fine." I kept my voice strong and steady. It would not do to have Robert recognize my weakness and uncertainty.

"I'm sure he is," Robert replied and touched his own small daughter's dimpled knee.

When the table was cleared we resumed the seder. We sang the grace after the meal, and Judy Bergman's father surprised us by leading the benedictions in his strong, authoritative tenor. The prayer had special meaning for us that night and we sang very loudly, as though we would force God to hear our words. " 'May the God of Mercy bless all who sit here — may He bless their households, their children, and all that is theirs. May He bless us and all that is ours.' "

Lottie and Julius looked at each other and then at the portrait of Aaron that stood on the china closet. It was for Aaron they prayed — he who was theirs.

Beth remained silent, her Hagaddah closed. She had not been blessed. No mercy had been shown to her or to Alfred, her tall young husband. She had willed herself to fortitude but a wave of sadness swept over her; she had learned not to struggle against its tide lest she drown in her own misery. Alfred had been dead for only three months. She had been a widow for exactly the length of time that she had been a wife.

Julius intoned the blessing over the wine and we drained our cups. Anna whimpered with weariness, and Robert lifted her into his arms and fed drops of wine to her from a teaspoon. We smiled as she grimaced and buried her face in her father's shoulder, her wine-reddened lips staining his white shirt. He kissed her lightly and I knew that we would forgive him everything if he would be a loving father to his daughter, and I understood that Dina herself had decided as much.

Perhaps that was what Nachum Adler had meant when he told me that Dina would have to sort out her own life. I realized that he must have known that she and Robert would be reconciled. He had accepted that knowledge with the resignation in which he had cloaked himself since the day he had cradled the bodies of his wife and daughter, kneeling on the bloodstained cobblestones of the quiet Prague street. Those who embrace such resignation, who believe that the very worst has already happened to them, are released from the anxiety of expectation, the uncertainty of anticipation. They approach life with a ghostly gentleness, unsurprised by evil, inured to terror. I thought that if my father was killed, I too would become such a wandering ghost.

Leon circled the table, filling the fourth and last cup of wine. Bernie went to the front door as we sang the traditional hymn urging Elijah the prophet, he who would herald the messianic kingdom of peace, to join us in our feast of remembrance.

" 'Elijah, Elijah . . . come speedily to us, in our generation — with the Messiah, the son of David.' "

Our voices soared in the plea of yearning; we had been so long at war that even now, as our armies won battle after battle, peace seemed as elusive to us as the advent of the Messiah. Churchill himself spoke of peace in biblical terms. It would come, he had said, on wings of flame; it was in a winged chariot of fire that the ancient prophet had been carried away after his death. We sang on, leaning forward, and the flickering candle flames, almost guttering now, bathed our faces with a soft radiance. Bernie opened the door. A cool breeze tinged with the sweetness that comes after a spring rain wafted toward us and we turned our faces to meet its brush and we peered into the darkness.

We had anticipated silence but heard instead slow footsteps mount the high brick steps. A tall figure appeared on the porch. He was silhouetted briefly against the ink dark night, slightly stooped beneath the weight he carried on his shoulder.

My throat was dry and my heart beat arrhythmically. I gripped Peter's hand, cut into the softness of his palm with my nails. A barely audible sigh bubbled from Lottie's lips. My grandfather half rose in his seat, gripping at the cloth for balance. His distorted lips struggled to shape the word but when he uttered it at last it was wonderfully clear.

"Aaron," he said and my tall, gangly cousin, his garrison cap askew, the jacket of his uniform unbuttoned, set down his duffel bag. His pale face was wreathed in a smile as he sprinted forward, his arms outstretched, to embrace his mother, who could not stop trembling, just as she could not control the tears of joy that streaked her cheeks.

23

Spring overtook the streets of Brooklyn, filling the air with the tender scent of newly cut grass and early blooming lilacs and primroses. Neat pyramids of shimmering green hedge clippings lined the curbs. Children set up lemonade stands on street corners: three cents for a paper cup, with all profits going to the Red Cross. Sunlight descended in a radiant sheath upon the quiet waters of the inlet at Plum Beach.

Judy and I rode our bicycles there on a Thursday afternoon in mid-April. We sprawled across the gritty sand, turned our faces to the sun, and removed our saddle shoes and anklets. We cuffed our pedal pushers and waved our legs in the air, wiggling our bare toes. We luxuriated in our own indolence, in our escape from chores and homework. We were glad to be away from the frenetic atmosphere of our homes, from the incessant blare of the radio and the urgent ringing of the telephone.

The nation anticipated Germany's surrender, and our families were seldom far from a radio. Judy's mother played the radios in the kitchen, the bedroom, the living room, and even the bathroom simultaneously so that as she wandered from room to room, pushing the carpet sweeper, cooking, distributing laundry, and simply stopping to sit quietly, the chorus of newscasters comforted her.

I too was glad to escape the endless dialogue of WEVD, the Yiddish station to which my grandparents kept the radio tuned from early morning until late at night. It was good to evade the telephone, which rang constantly when I was home. Aaron, who had been assigned to a base near Washington, D.C., after spending Passover week at home, called almost every day. He wanted to touch base, he said casually, to find out how my grandfather was. But I knew that he called because it was still a miracle to him that he could so easily hear our familiar and loving voices; it was important that he know that we were safe in the quiet home of his boyhood.

Aaron, Beth, and I had walked to the boardwalk on the last day of Passover. Sitting on a bench, alternately munching matzoh and scattering bits and pieces to the pigeons, Aaron had told us about a recurring nightmare.

"I first had the dream a few days after my experience at Auschwitz. I come back from the war and I take the brick steps two at a time because I'm in such a hurry to see everyone. I push the front door open and I'm staring into empty space, into nothingness. No rooms. No family. Nothing behind that door except swirling whorls of blue smoke. And I'm screaming, 'Mama. Papa. Beth. Sharon. Buba. Zeidey.' But no one answers and I wake up shaking, my throat hoarse. Sounds crazy, huh?" He looked at us in embarrassment and relief, smiling nervously.

"Not a hard dream to figure out after what you saw at Auschwitz," Beth said. "What will the survivors find when they go home?"

I wondered if Nachum Adler would go to his house in Prague, if he would push open a heavy oaken door and confront a void where once he had lived his life. I had received two letters from him, brief scrawls across V-letters, describing the beauty of the woodlands through which his unit traveled. "Nature does not know that we are at war," he wrote and drew a picture of a newly blooming tree, its tender leaves unfurling to form an umbrella of shade over two small sleeping children.

But there had been no mail from my father and again the Red Cross volunteer had attempted to reassure me.

"They tell us that things are really chaotic in Europe and that cargo of mail sacks is given very low priority. Besides, this is the mop-up stage. The army is always on the move, especially medical units. Your father may not have the time to write."

She had trained her benign smile on me but I was wary of her explanation. The fear that I had thrust so determinedly aside returned, and my mantra, silently repeated (*He's all right; the war will be over*) no longer consoled.

"Do you have dreams, Beth?" Aaron asked his sister now.

"Sometimes, like you, the same dream, again and again. I'm with Alfred in the desert. I'm wearing my wedding dress and he is wearing his dress uniform but we are both barefoot. We dance across the sands toward each other but it gets dark suddenly — a cloud passes across the sun. I continue to dance. I am moving very slowly, my head down. I watch the way my long white skirt sweeps across the ocher sands. I think my toes are too long and very ugly. I laugh out loud. 'Don't you think my toes are ugly?' I ask Alfred but he does not answer. The cloud lifts and I see that he has vanished."

I sat at a slight remove from them and felt myself an intruder on their intimacy. I envied Beth her brother's gentle concern. Who was there to ask me about my dreams?

Aaron put his arm around his sister's shoulder.

"I'm sorry," he said. "I'm sorry I never knew him. I'm sorry I never saw you as a bride."

Beth returned to Arizona and she, too, called often from Tempe, concerned about our grandfather.

My aunts and uncles also called the house on various pretexts throughout the afternoon. Lottie called to ask about the mail, Julius to tell me to check the gas jets, Edna to ask if I was going to the meeting of the Young Pioneers with Heidi. Samuel called to ask if Dolly had called, and uncannily, Dolly always called five minutes later to ask if Samuel had called. But I knew that all of them really wanted me to reassure them that my grandfather was fine, that he remained stable. And I always did exactly that, although since the night of the first seder, I thought that he did seem paler and often he dozed off without warning, succumbing to the deep fatigue that dulled his eyes and weighted the words that he uttered with such effort.

It was a relief then to escape to Plum Beach with Judy and to briefly forget the war and my family's anxiety.

"What are you going to do this summer, Sharon?" Judy asked.

"I don't know," I said. "It depends. You know — on my father."

"Oh. Of course," Judy replied and the unspoken words lay awkwardly between us.

"What are you going to do?"

"I'm going to go to summer school so I can graduate in January. I'll find an out-of-town college that will accept me midyear. I've got to get away from home, and from my mother." She spoke without embarrassment. "You could do the same thing. But I guess you'll want to go back to Woodstock. Because of Peter."

"No," I said. "Peter won't even be there. He's going to Wyoming to work on a ranch. The doctor told his parents that that sort of experience would build him up, maybe even strengthen his leg. And then he'll be off to Harvard. But that wouldn't make any difference. Peter and I are just friends now."

We had walked along the esplanades the day after the seder, Peter and I, speaking earnestly and honestly of our feelings for each other. We had set the parameters of friendship, with the naive confidence that those parameters, once defined, would not be breached.

"I like you, Sharon. I like you a lot," Peter had said as we leaned against the iron rail and listened to the crashing waves. "I think about you and I worry about you. But . . ."

His voice trailed off and I plucked up the unfinished sentence and softly completed it.

"But we're too young. We're much too young. We're just beginning."

"We'll be friends," he said.

"We'll always be friends."

"And more than friends."

He had kissed me lightly on the lips and I had brushed the soft wisp of his fair cowlick back from his high forehead. And so it was, with tender touch and gesture, that we sealed our new affection.

"And I don't want to go back to Woodstock in any case," I added to Judy now.

I did not want to stay with Dina and Robert, who were slowly and awkwardly rebuilding their lives together. It pained me to watch them as they walked and talked. His laughter was too loud and her voice was too soft. Anna was their buffer and they passed her from hand to hand, gifting her with the affection they could not yet offer to each other. I had been relieved when they left for Woodstock after the second seder.

"You could always go to the Young Pioneer camp with Heidi."

"No." I knew that I did not want to spend a summer caught up in the vortex of ideological intensity. "Maybe I'll just stay home. They need me to be with my grandfather. To help my grandmother take care of him, to work in the garden with him. And I owe it to them, after everything they've done for me."

"But he is much better, isn't he?" Judy asked.

"He's old and he's had a stroke."

My reply was harsher than I intended but I was weary of answering so many questions about my grandfather, tired of reassuring my cousins and my aunts and uncles.

We rode back in silence and at the Emmons Avenue causeway, we waved to each other and cycled off in opposite directions. I noticed as I pedaled down sun-dappled Sheepshead Bay Road that the pedestrians moved very slowly. Even the buses and cars seemed to have decelerated. A radio blared in the doorway of the large electrical appliance shop and a small crowd had gathered to listen. I did not pause. Probably there had been another major battle in the Pacific, I thought. An especially grim report of the fierceness of the fighting on Okinawa. Or perhaps the discovery of yet another Nazi atrocity in Europe.

I cycled more swiftly. I did not want to hear the news. I wanted to revel in the sunlight, in the sweet fragrance of spring. Still, I wondered at the lines that formed at telephone booths. Was it possible that peace had come and there was an urgent need to phone friends and relatives and share the good news? But there was no cheer on the faces of those who waited to use the phones. The busy thoroughfare was oddly quiet. Perhaps Allied forces in Europe had suffered a terrible defeat. Perhaps there had been a devastating Japanese attack in the Pacific.

Two women stood on the corner at Coney Island Avenue and embraced.

"Can you believe it?"

"Who could believe it?"

Their words, broken by sorrow, drifted toward me as I pedaled into the wind. Gripped by a new apprehension, I did not put my bicycle in the garage but allowed it to fall onto the lawn. I flew up the brick steps and burst into the house. Although it was only five o'clock and ordinarily they still would have been at work, the entire family was congregated in the living room. Lottie and Julius, Edna and Leon, Samuel and Dolly. My grandmother sat on the couch between Heidi and Bernie, each of them holding one of her hands, so that her tears fell upon their fingers. My aunts wept. Lottie's eyes brimmed, Edna's cheeks were streaked, and tears stood on Dolly's rouged cheeks like luminous punctuation marks. The eyes of the men were red-rimmed, and Bernie, the scarf of his uniform unknotted, bit his lip valiantly.

"He's dead?" My question was a scream. I imagined my grandfather lying pale and inert in the bedroom, his blue-veined, gnarled hands folded upon his chest, his white beard, as always, neatly groomed, his white hair, as always, neatly combed. I gripped the back of a chair for support.

As one, they turned to me and nodded.

"He's dead," Samuel said, his voice heavy with grief. I closed my eyes. My heart sank and my stomach turned.

Not my Zeidey, I thought. *Not my Zeidey.*

"You didn't hear, Sharon?" Lottie asked wonderingly. "It was on all the radios. Businesses closed. Government offices. It happened this afternoon. At Warm Springs."

I sank to the floor, my head in my hands, relief and regret commingling.

It was not my grandfather who had died on that sunlit April afternoon. It was Franklin Delano Roosevelt, who had been president for almost my entire life. He had suffered a cerebral hemorrhage as he sat for his portrait in his Georgia home. His death struck at our hearts, sucked all vibrancy from our souls. We mourned him as though we had lost one of our own, as though he was a member of our own family who been taken from us forever.

Julius lit a memorial candle and I placed it in the window. Small flames quivered that night in all the front windows on our street, and American flags hung at half-mast on every porch. Julius and Samuel went to the synagogue for the evening prayer service. They would say the Kaddish for the fallen president.

Lottie roamed the room, puffing up pillows, straightening lamp shades, and reciting a Robert Frost poem that she had memorized only a week earlier.

> Ah, when to the heart of a man
> Was it ever less than a treason
> To go with the drift of things,
> To yield with a grace to reason,
> And bow and accept the end
> Of a love or a season?

It was difficult for us to accept the end of the long season of Franklin Roosevelt's presidency and although we did not say it, it seemed a treason that he had died before his voice could triumphantly announce the victory in Europe.

"It's not fair that he should die now," Heidi said petulantly.

"Like Moses," my grandfather said and sighed. Even as Moses had guided the children of Israel through the wilderness and died before he could enter the Promised Land, so Franklin

Roosevelt, who had guided his nation through the war, had died before he could witness the advent of even a partial peace.

The men returned from synagogue, and my grandmother placed the photograph of Roosevelt which hung in her dining room on Lottie's coffee table. Julius produced a copy of the telegram that the president had sent to the last convention of the Zionist Organization of America, which had been duly reproduced and mailed to every member.

"Such a wonderful man he was. He cared about the Jewish people. Listen to what he said." He read aloud, his accented English somehow deepening the impact of the words. " 'I know how long and ardently the Jewish people have worked and prayed for the establishment of Palestine as a free and democratic commonwealth. If reelected, I shall hope to bring about its realization.' "

Leon, who had not gone to synagogue, whose expression was sober although his eyes remained clear, snorted.

"Words," he said. "The promises of an election year. He made promises to Ibn Saud, too, when he met him after Yalta. Yes, he was a good president, a great president. But what did he do for the Jews? Did he bomb the rail lines to the concentration camps? Did he issue emergency visas so that more Jewish refugees could come into his country? Did he argue with his friend Churchill against the White Paper so that there could be open immigration of Jews to Palestine? So a couple of weeks before Election Day, he sent a telegram. What did it cost to send a telegram? And all the big *machers* of the ZOA forget that he told Sumner Welles and Chaim Weizmann that his idea for a homeland for the survivors of the camps was land in the trans-Andean part of Colombia. Like the Jews from Minsk are going to go running to South America. I voted for him. Three times I voted for him. I'm sorry that he's dead. But a saint for our people he wasn't. Moses, he wasn't. The truth is he didn't give a damn about the Jews and even his Jewish friends knew it — Morgenthau, Bernard Baruch, Sam Rosenman, Rabbi Silver, Rabbi Wise."

Samuel, his face white with anger, slammed his fist down on the table and strode across the room. He seized the front of Leon's shirt, jerked him forward.

"You speak that way about our president! You should be ashamed, Mr. Know-it-all Who Knows Nothing. What are you, a Communist? Go live in Woodstock with Robert. Artists, musicians, ask them, they know everything."

"Samuel! Leon! Enough. Such fighting I don't need in my house."

Julius crossed the room, separated his brothers-in-law. He took Samuel by the arm and led him into the kitchen. Bernie guided his father out to the porch, and Lottie and Edna, without looking at each other, straightened the chairs.

Trembling, I went into my room and lay down on my bed. The argument had frightened me. I saw how swiftly the tight weave of my family's solidarity could unravel. Petty jealousies and ideological differences marred the intricate weft of their affection. It had been important to me since my mother's death to think of them as an intact unit. I had ignored their secret angers because I could not bear to acknowledge them. My mother's family had been the safety net that sustained me through her death and my father's absence, a net that would be in readiness should he be killed. *And he could yet be killed.* That too I admitted as I lay in the half darkness, filled with fear because my uncles' argument had revealed the fragility of their togetherness.

"Sharon, what are you doing alone?" Heidi stood in the doorway and stared down at me. Her cheeks were flushed and her eyes were dangerously bright. She too had been frightened by the argument.

"Nothing."

"My father and Julius went to Brighton for delicatessen. We're all going to have dinner here."

"Okay."

It was important that we repair the fabric of the family. A shared meal could restore the peace. My uncles were careful with each other during dinner although they did not meet each other's eyes.

Leon played his violin after dinner. The family dismissed him as a *luftmentsch,* an unrealistic dreamer, an unreliable interpreter, but I saw Leon as a realist. I understood that he withdrew from the daily fray and played his violin because he declined to participate in battles he knew he would lose.

I hugged Leon hard when he left that night. I loved him for his cynicism and for his honesty.

"Thank you, Sharon," he said gravely, as though he had read my thoughts.

Flags fluttered in the breeze throughout April as the pace of the war in Europe accelerated. A letter arrived at last from my father, a few lines scrawled lightly in pencil as though he had scarcely had the strength to press down. There had been no time to write, no time to think, he said. His medical unit had been with the first troops to enter Buchenwald and he had worked around the clock: "We were surrounded by the sick, the dying, and the dead. I could not write sooner. My hands tremble even now so I will be brief. I cannot describe what I have seen. Oh, my Sharon, know yourself to be very lucky. Our unit moves on. I will write when I can but everything is very uncertain. This is the strangest and most unpredictable phase of the war, but soon, very soon, it will be over."

My self-pity melted, my fear vanished. I was lucky and I had to make reparation for that luck. I joined other members of the Young Pioneers in the basement of the synagogue and we packed cartons of clothing for the survivors of the concentration camps who were being sent to displaced-persons centers. We carried petitions to the British consulate calling for free and open immigration into Palestine. We collected money for telegrams to be sent to President Truman. SAVE THE REMNANT OF THE JEWISH PEOPLE. URGE CHURCHILL TO OPEN THE GATES OF PALESTINE. KEEP YOUR PROMISE: A JEWISH HOMELAND NOW! I scurried about the borough, about the city. The harder I worked, the safer my father would be.

We danced wild horas to celebrate the liberation of Leipzig, the liberation of Nuremberg. And two weeks after President Roosevelt's death, we raucously boarded the Brighton Express for the ride to Times Square, where we joined the crowds who sang and danced in a frenzy of exultation because American and Soviet troops had met at the German village of Torgau. With such a united front, surely the war in Europe was almost over.

Emanuel Weiner called to tell us that Perele's daughter, Esther Hurwitz, had been located. For the first time since his stroke, my grandfather smiled. That afternoon he leaned heavily against me as we staked the young tomato plants in his victory garden. The earth was soft upon my fingers when my grandmother came outside to tell us that Mussolini was dead. He had been shot by Italian partisans.

"The end is beginning, Shaindel." My grandfather looked up at the sky as though he might read an announcement of peace in the fleecy drifting clouds.

On the last day of April a special assembly was convened in the Lincoln High auditorium. The principal looked at us gravely and announced that Berlin had fallen. The Russian banner flew over the Reichstag, and Adolf Hitler had committed suicide in a bunker beneath the city.

As she had almost a year ago on D Day, Miss Glenn, the blue-haired music teacher, played "God Bless America" on the piano and once again our voices soared in song. But there was no sadness in our voices that day, only lilting strength and pride of triumph. Leatrice and Letitia, who had wept as they sang all those months ago, smiled brilliantly now. Their father was safe. Hitler was dead. Victory was within our grasp. Joseph Guerera stood at attention as he sang. His father had been killed in France that winter, and he hurried home each day after school to sit beside his mother in the darkened bedroom where she nursed her grief. I put my hand in his and he nodded in acknowledgment of my sympathy, although we were not really friends.

We waited all that week for the war in Europe to run its course. The German surrender at Wageningen ended the war for Holland. The camps at Ebensee and Mauthausen were liberated and German forces at Breslau surrendered to the Russians. But fighting continued in Czechoslovakia, where resistance forces in Prague battled the Nazis.

"Do you think Nachum Adler is in Prague?" Dina asked me when she phoned. Her voice was very low. She did not want Robert to know that she was haunted by worry about the Czech artist who had shared our lives during that last year of our war.

"No. I'm sure he's not," I said, although it turned out later that I was wrong. Nachum had indeed been in the second of the three American army transports that arrived in Prague on May 7, the very last day of the war. He had driven down the narrow street where his wife and daughter had been killed but he had not dared look out the window of his vehicle lest he see again their crimson blood puddling the cobblestones.

That evening our family gathered together in front of the Stromberg Carlson radio and listened to Edward R. Murrow describe the surrender of the German garrison at Saint Nazaire to American troops. Julius spun the globe until he found that town on the Atlantic coast where at last our war had ended. We sat for a moment in silence and then Lottie phoned Beth in Arizona.

"It's over, Beth. It's really over," she said and we knew that Beth was weeping.

VE Day, Victory in Europe, dawned with a brilliant blaze of sunlight, and the white rosebush in our backyard burst unexpectedly into early bloom.

"Happy VE Day," Mrs. Calderazzo shouted from her porch and waved her arms, encased as always in the winged black sleeves of mourning.

"Happy VE Day," we shouted back, her joy sanctioning our own.

American flags and red, white, and blue bunting festooned houses and stores. Windows were flung open, and radios and phonographs blared music onto the streets. Drivers honked their car horns in tympanic rhythm, and men and women danced with each other on the crown of the road, laughing and crying.

"Isn't it wonderful? Isn't it marvelous?"

The bright spring sun brushed our faces, the joy of the great victory filled our hearts. Soon Japan too would capitulate and the war in the Pacific would be over. Peace would be restored to us.

Children danced in circles, tossed bags of red, white, and blue confetti at each other, draped parked cars with tricolored crepe paper streamers. We went to school but there were no classes. We danced in the gymnasium, snaked our way through the auditorium and out onto the football field. A group of laughing girls encircled the principal and danced about him, and he, in turn, red-faced and perspiring, did a rollicking polka with Miss Glenn.

An impromptu color guard marched up Ocean Parkway, Joseph Guerera in the lead carrying the flag. We sang "The Marines' Hymn" and "The Caissons Go Rolling Along" and "The Battle Hymn of the Republic." A passing soldier was lifted onto the shoulders of a group of students.

We dashed into the Sweet Shoppe, where open canisters of licorice twists and long pretzels stood on the counter, free for the taking that day, and we slaked our thirst with glasses of cherry Coke. The drivers of the Good Humor truck and the Eskimo Pie tricycle doled out ice cream pops and Dixie cups and drove away when their refrigerated cases were empty, ringing their bells in joyous tintinnabulation.

Avenue Z celebrated with a block party that night. Long tables lined the curb. Platters of kosher delicatessen, huge vats of spaghetti, mounds of lasagna, and enormous bowls of salad were set out. Frankfurters sizzled on grills, and trays were laden with glazed doughnuts and cakes frosted with icings of red, white, and blue.

"Eat! Eat!" the women urged. They ladled the food onto paper plates. Their faces were flushed and their feet twitched in time to the music.

The musicians gathered on an improvised bandstand at the corner. Leon played the violin, Dr. Kaplan played the accordion, the chubby boy who lived in the corner house played the clarinet, and Bernie blasted away on his trumpet. Their music competed with that of the merry-go-round hired for the younger children, but no one minded. Young couples lifted their children onto the painted horses and then danced their own way across the street.

Fireworks lit up the sky. Fuchsia rockets danced toward silver stars. Arrows of red, white, and blue streaked earthward, and Heidi and I hugged each other and gasped in wonder.

"It's over," Heidi said. "It's really over."

"Almost." It would not do to forget the fighting in the Pacific or the men in the European theater whose fates were still unknown. It would not do to forget my father.

The phone rang and I ran up the brick steps to answer it, my heart pounding. I lifted the receiver, irrationally expecting to hear my father's voice, wondering if I would remember its sound. But it was Peter, calling from Dina's house, and so I spoke to him and to Karen and to my aunt.

"Isn't it wonderful?" we asked each other and I told them about our block party and they told me that the village of Woodstock was a festival of joy. Belle Langsam had danced down Main Street playing her silver flute, and the proprietor of the Italian restaurant had set up a long table lined with Chianti bottles in the middle of the street.

"Hey, Happy VE Day," we shouted into the phone as Anna cooed softly.

Laughing, I went out to the porch to tell my grandparents, who sat side by side on the glider, their fingers interlinked, that Peter had called and Dina too was celebrating.

"Sharon." Heidi called my name, then slowly walked up the steps. Her expression was grave, almost frightened. Her skin was blanched. She held an envelope, a yellow envelope.

I clutched the iron banister. *No*, I thought. *This is not happening. This is not what I think it is. It cannot be.*

I did not move.

"The Western Union messenger came just as you went inside. I signed for it." She spoke almost in a whisper and held the envelope out to me but I could not take it. My hands trembled. My arms had lost their power. My breath came in stertorous rasps.

"You read it," I said hoarsely. "You read it and tell me what it says."

I closed my eyes. The music and the shouting from the street below were amplified into a cacophony of conflicting sounds that beat wildly against my ears and caused my head to ache. Heidi's voice floated gently above it. The thin yellow paper of the telegram fluttered in her hand. I strained to hear her and I did not want to hear her.

" 'Sharon. Am on a troopship somewhere in the middle of the Atlantic. On my way home to you. Happy VE Day, my darling daughter.' "

Heidi read it once and then again.

"It's a ship-to-shore message," she said.

"Ship-to-shore," I repeated and we burst into laughter, as though the alliteration rather than the message triggered the hysteria and relieved and released the tension of the long months, the very long year.

" 'It's a grand old flag, it's a high-flying flag . . .' " The singing from the street drifted up to us.

We added our voices to the chorus, and standing on the porch, our arms about each other's waists, we kicked our legs Rockette-style and danced our way into peace.